The Rebel Christian Publishing

Copyright © 2022 Valicity Elaine

ISBN: 9781957290164
Print: 9781957290171

This is a work of fiction. Any references to historical events, real people, or real places are used fictitiously. Names, characters, and places are products of the author's imagination. Inclusion of or reference to any Christian elements or themes are used in a fictitious manner and are not meant to be perceived or interpreted as an act of disrespect against such a wonderful and beautiful belief system.

Cover illustrated/designed by Valicity Elaine

The Rebel Christian Publishing LLC
350 Northern Blvd STE 324 – 1390
Albany, NY 12204

Visit us: http://www.therebelchristian.com/
Email us: rebel@therebelchristian.com

1 1

2 11

3 23

4 35

5 48

6 56

7 68

Part II 85

8 86

9 93

10 110

11 121

12 131

13 142

14 151

15 163

16 170

17 181

18 190

19 206

Part III 213

20 214

21 222

22 230

23 239

24 252

25 263

26 275

27.. 288

Part IV 295

28.. 296

29.. 310

30.. 321

31.. 328

32.. 337

33.. 347

34.. 361

35.. 372

36.. 380

37.. 391

38.. 400

Series Order:

Cross Academy

The Howler's Cry

The Nine Births of Carnage

The Testament Relics

Cross Academy: Book V

Other Books by Valicity Elaine:

Patches

The 'I' Word

I AM MAN series:

I AM MAN

I AM LOST

I AM BROKEN

I AM FREE

I AM COMPLETE

Withered Rose series:

Withered Rose

Clipping Thorns

Starting Over (coming Fall 2022)

For Jesus Christ
For God the Father
For the Holy Spirit

The Howler's Cry

Cross Academy: Book II

By Valicity Elaine

A Rebel Christian Publishing Book

His Word is in my heart like a fire, a fire shut up in my bones.

Jeremiah 20:9

Part I

1

Yadira

The boy is the vessel. I saw him with my own eyes. I *felt* his energy up close." Yadira stared into the flames burning in the center of the room, her silver hair glowed red from the blaze.

"Yet, you returned emptyhanded."

Her dark eyes swept from the fire to the slender man across the room. He wasn't smiling, but he didn't need to grin for her to know he was mocking her. Yadira bared her teeth, she hated him. He should be punished for disrespecting a higher Birth, but she knew his insolence would go unchecked. No one even seemed to care that his hood was down, revealing his bronze-colored skin and long, ebony hair. Technically, they were in their lair—the Womb—so they weren't required to keep their velvety red hoods pulled over their faces, hiding their identities. But the new guy was here and half of them still weren't sure they could trust him yet, so the hoods remained on. Except for his.

"I hadn't expected there to be a sundancer," Yadira explained. "I was told the village held no blessings." She eyed the man right beside her, her gaze full of anger. "Number Five?"

1

He stirred. Yadira could just make out the way his lips quivered beneath his low hanging hood as he took a shaky breath. *He's nervous. Good.* He just ought to be nervous; Five was the one who'd given her that lousy intel. If she had known there was a proficient sundancer in the village, she would have been better prepared. Now she was being ridiculed by a lower Birth in front of the other members.

Five cleared his throat. "All my research indicated Wi had no blessings behind their Walls."

"Well, your research was garbage." Yadira crossed her arms.

"Still," a rumbling voice interjected. Yadira glanced to the side, staring at the hooded figure next to Number Five. He was nothing but a cloaked ball of gas—like a puff of smoke had pulled on a giant red robe, its black toxins filling the sleeves and torso of the coat to make it human-shaped. Yadira had no idea where the voice was coming from, or if there was anything inside the cloak other than the dark fumes. Number Four had always been the creepiest of the Births.

"He was only one sundancer," Four went on. "You should have been able to handle him, Number Six."

She ground her teeth, avoiding the man's gaze from across the room. He was still staring, his hood lowered, his sharp eyes focused solely on her. She wanted to bark at him to gawk at someone else, but she knew she would be scolded. Her failure in Wi had tainted her reputation enough, acting out at their meeting would do her no good.

"Now that I know what I'm up against," she began, "I could try again."

A collection of grunts rose from the red cloaks standing around the fire. All eight figures shook with amusement—even the new guy. Yadira took a deep breath as she endured her shame.

"Try again?" said the Fourth Birth. "Not a chance. You've already proven yourself useless. We won't take a gamble on you again."

2

"You're still gambling with *him!*" She jabbed a finger at the new guy. His red mask glowed beneath his hood, flames dancing over polished leather. He wasn't even a real Birth, just a replacement for Number Nine, but the others had decided to send him in again—even though he'd come back emptyhanded just like her.

"The Red Face did not retrieve the boy as planned," a feminine voice joined the conversation. Yadira knew who it was even before glancing at the ladylike figure at the head of the circle. Number One, the Firstborn of Carnage. Her delicate, red-painted lips were the only thing Yadira could see as she shifted her gaze to the tall woman, the crimson hood hid all the rest of her face. "But," the Firstborn continued, "he did more than enough damage to the Cross to make up for his failure."

"*Literally,*" said the unhooded man. *Now,* he was smirking and the sight of it made Yadira want to summon her blades and decapitate him where he stood. His body would hit the ground before he even realized what'd happened.

"I am the Sixth Birth of Carnage," she declared. "I deserve a second chance before he does." Her dark eyes glared at the Red Face. "I don't care that he set fire to the Cross."

"You must remember, our goal is not simply to retrieve the boy, but to totally destroy the Cross. Not just the building. Not just the Walls of Jericho. We must crush their foundation—their *faith.*"

The room shifted, hoods turning to gaze at the man who'd spoken. He was normally a quiet Birth, only speaking when he absolutely had to. Despite the boredom in his whisper of a voice, Yadira could not deny the truth behind his compelling words.

Secretly, she had always admired Number Three. He had a quiet strength, reserved power exhibited with the utmost control. *He should be Number One,* she had always believed, but she kept that thought to herself. There wasn't any proof, but demons whispered of the power of

3

the Firstborn—that she could peer into the minds of others. If Number One ever saw such a traitorous thought in Yadira's head, she would have her *unborn*—removed from the Nine and thrown into the depths of Pitch Black.

It wasn't hell. But there were some who would claim it wasn't much better. The chaos where the Nine had been born, crafted by Black herself—a fallen angel whose power rivaled that of Beelzebub. Yadira hadn't been to Pitch since the Ninth Birth had been sealed away years ago. That was when the realm of chaos had begun to crumble into the void of despair it was now. Nothing but a realm of grey and sorrow and fear.

Number Nine's return couldn't wait a moment longer. Every day the child roamed free was another day Pitch Black tipped further into chaos. The only reason it hadn't crumbled into nothingness yet was because of the induction of the new guy. The Red Face had joined them three years ago, somewhat stabilizing the insanity threatening to implode their realm. But he was just a temporary replacement. His Dark energy was strong, but not nearly as powerful as the original Nine's had been.

The Rebirth Ritual had almost killed Red; they'd had to stop halfway through, leaving him in spiritual limbo. Not fully demon, but not fully human, either. Still, even as a mere half-demon, having Red fill Nine's shoes helped keep the madness at bay. If only somewhat. Pitch wasn't crumbling anymore, but the chaos still stirred. Growing stronger every day.

Their realm needed all nine of the Births. They were the pillars of darkness on which it'd been built. Without them, the imbalance of Dark energy would cause a storm of turmoil within the spiritual realm that even they could not contain. Their world would be destroyed. And that couldn't happen, no matter what. They needed Pitch Black. It was their haven; a realm created as a reprieve from the everlasting flames of

4

judgment waiting for them all. But once it crumbled, they would have no place else to go but hell. And they didn't want to go there. Not ever.

"Number Three is right," the Firstborn said. "Our goal is not merely to retrieve Number Nine, but to destroy the faith of the Cross altogether. When the Red Face set fire to the Academy, every demon of the Four Regions saw that burning cross as a symbol of hope." She raised a fist, her brown skin illuminated by the flames. "The destruction of Cross Academy *is* possible. Our day *is* coming."

Number Two nodded agreement, gaining everyone's attention—not that she wasn't already noticeable enough as she was the only one in the room levitating over the stone floors. Apparently, *standing* was beneath her.

She pointed at the Red Face and the figure beside him, another feminine-shaped cloak. "Red and Number Eight will return to Babel."

Yadira stepped forward. "I must argue—"

The flames of the firepit tripled in size, Yadira could feel the searing heat kissing both her cheeks before she jumped back with a yelp.

"No," the Firstborn said sternly, "you must *not* argue."

"It has already been decided," Number Two went on as if she'd never been interrupted. "We will not drift from our plans."

A chuckle went up from across the room, low and teasing. Yadira glared at the unhooded Birth. "What is so funny?" she growled.

"You got passed up for two lower Births." He laughed and the sound of it was like the cracking of ice. He'd always been a cold, crude Birth.

"I don't think you would do much better, Hosenké," said Number Three.

Those sharp eyes seemed to slice through the Thirdborn as he glared at him for using his real name in front of the Red Face. Hosenké had been the most vocal about not trusting the new guy, despite him proving his loyalty time and again over the last three years. Others around the fire still held on to their distrust, but that was because they had been working together as a family for centuries, three years of grunt work wasn't enough to change their minds. Hosenké's distrust, however, was based purely on the bitter fact that the Red Face was his best friend's replacement. He was just angry because he missed Number Nine. Like a lovesick puppy who'd lost its owner.

The whole thing was ridiculous, really. Because Hosenké wasn't an original Birth, either. He'd joined the family when the first demon holding the title of *Seventh Birth of Carnage* was defeated by a powerful Priestess of the Academy. Granted, that was over four hundred years ago, but still. The other Births hadn't shown him half as much distrust as he had toward Red.

Yadira almost felt sorry for Number Seven. Except, whenever the sympathy pooled into her black heart, it was quickly washed away by his chortling snorts or his unnecessary remarks, reminders of the fact that Number Nine had been sealed away because of his stupidity.

Seven, Eight, and Nine had always been troublemakers. Making dirty deals with the witches. Taking on jobs they weren't strong enough to handle. Their foolishness got Nine hurt so badly he'd had to be sealed away to heal himself. And then they screwed that up by losing track of the boy they'd chosen as his vessel.

Technically, this was all Hosenké's fault. But no one was going to call out any of his failures. Because he was Number Three's favorite. If Four's gossip held any truth, the Thirdborn knew Hosenké when he was still a human. He'd even looked after him like some sort of dark guardian angel. Then Hosenké was reborn as the Seventh Birth, but their relationship still held the air of brotherhood.

He had a real *brother before all this.* Yadira snuck a glance at Number Three while Hosenké spouted off some nonsense about the importance of keeping their identities a secret from the Red Face. Number Five pointed out the fact that he was the only one here without his hood up. Hosenké set loose a string of curses—*real* curses that turned the flames of the firepit a dazzling blue color and sent them streaking across the floor at the older Birth. The Fifthborn held up his hand and sucked the flames into the black hole sitting in his palm.

Yadira shivered. Void was one of the scariest curses of the Four Regions. Number Five had mastered it centuries ago, proving shadow-dancing could be controlled with time and patience.

"Enough!" Number One cut in to stop the little spat that'd broken out. Everyone fell silent at the sound of her voice. "We move on as planned. The Red Face and Number Eight will return to Babel and wait for their signal to move in." She turned to Hosenké. "You will go as well."

Raven eyebrows lowered on a smooth, brown forehead. "Why?"

"Because we will not fail again. I'm tired of playing these games. The Moon witches are moving, possibly making alliances with other covens. If that happens, we will almost certainly lose the boy."

No one could argue with her. The Moon Coven had been allied with the Nine for nearly the entire Demon War. Yadira couldn't remember any other witches ever performing their rituals except those of the Moon. But that longstanding alliance was violently broken three years ago when the Red Face lost control of his power during his Rebirth. He killed over half the witches in attendance. Of course, it had been an unforeseen accident, but the Moon Coven wasn't pleased, and they weren't willing to accept any apologies over the issue. They wanted blood. But the Nine was not an organization to be bossed around, certainly not by the likes of a mere witch.

Their demands for blood had been met with more blood*shed*. The Moon Coven was nearly decimated as punishment for daring to issue orders to the Nine Births of Carnage. While they slunk into the shadows

7

to lick their wounds, the Nine had moved on. Now, the Moon witches were back, going after the boy to both regain their strength and get vengeance on the Nine.

The Firstborn's worries over the witches were easy to understand but moving more than one Birth into the city could wind up causing more trouble than it was worth.

Number Three took a breath, his voice coming out as a soft murmur from beneath his heavy hood. "The Cross will notice us if too many Births show up. Our Dark energy is potent when we're together."

"Seven will only go in *after* the Red Face has begun his attack," Number One responded. "So it won't matter if he is noticed."

"But why *me*?" Hosenké demanded angrily.

"Because you can summon the howler," the Secondborn explained. "If the Red Face and Number Eight fail. Summon the creature and use it."

The lair fell to a hush. There hadn't been a howler summoned since the start of the Great Demon War. To have Hosenké call one from the depths of Pitch Black now would certainly help them get their hands on the elusive child, but it would also make it easier for other forces to grab him, too. As if it hadn't been hard enough to infiltrate Babel without getting caught by the Academy, keeping an eye on the boy with the Moon Coven and other demons coming after him would be a nightmare.

Still. They were desperate.

The Firstborn stepped forward. "You have your orders. This meeting is adjourned."

With a whoosh of black vapor, she disappeared into nothing. The other Births followed, dispersing to various locations, returning to whatever business they'd been taking care of before the Firstborn had summoned them back to their Womb.

Yadira remained, staring absently at the flames, wondering what she

8

could do to fix her tarnished reputation. She hadn't realized she wasn't alone until she heard the low, whispering voice behind her.

"Worry not. All will be well once we get Nine back."

She turned to blink up at Number Three, surprised when she saw that he'd removed his hood. Wild red hair tumbled over broad shoulders, taking no attention from his striking, calm face. Yadira was enamored, stunned into silence as she stared at him.

"You did the best you could in Wi," he went on, voice rich and warm like the velvet of his cloak.

He'd given her a compliment. The Third Birth of Carnage had just told her she'd done her best. "T-Thank you, Seganamé." She bit her lip, unsure if she should have used his name instead of his number.

He gave her a gentle smile.

She felt weak in the knees.

"You're welcome." He turned to leave, and she felt an ache in her chest.

Desperate for him to stay a moment longer, Yadira blurted without thinking, "Will you be able to face him? If it comes to that?"

She was talking about his brother. His *human* brother who had used his blessing of *Longevity* to stay alive all these centuries. Searching for him. Seeking to destroy him. They had come to blows throughout the Great Demon War. Neither man ever able to best the other. According to Number Eight's reports, he was somewhere in Babel now. Protecting the boy. Which meant if the Red Face failed again, and the Academy and the Nine went to war over the child, there was a chance Seganamé would have to face him. A man who'd become a demon battling his Christian brother.

She shivered again, despite standing beside a dying fire.

The look on the Thirdborn's face was enough to freeze over the glowing embers. The soft, delicate lines of his face creased into hardened

9

edges as he turned and glared down at the smoldering firepit. It was the most dramatic expression Yadira had ever seen on him. It made her heart leap with a skittish fear. But just as quickly as his visage had changed, it was suddenly back to normal. The storm of rage calmed into a quiet anger.

He turned away again, and a shadowy portal opened before him. "I'll deal with my baby brother just like I would anyone else. If it comes to that."

Without another word, Seganamé stepped through the portal and disappeared, leaving Yadira to her thoughts and failures.

2

Fox Fire

Fox Fire felt heat gather in her body, storming through every limb, every blood vessel, every cell. She called it to her core, directing the flow of this great energy. When enough of it had pooled in her chest, pressing at her ribcage, she charged it toward her closed fist.

Nothing happened.

Fox sighed and fell into the grass. She still couldn't sundance. Even after putting out the flames that'd burned down half the Academy, even after holding a flame in her own palm, she couldn't draw the power out of herself.

"What's wrong with me?" she muttered, staring up at the blazing sun.

"You suck. Simple."

She sat up on her elbows, glowering at Kohlannis. "No one asked you."

He shrugged, glancing up from his stretch to eye her. His hair was stuck to his sweaty forehead, gentle blonde waves whispering against his lashes. He blinked, making them shift like curtains moving away to reveal his striking blue eyes. Fox tried very hard not to notice the way his new haircut complimented his angular visage; how square his jaw looked now, how full his lips were, how his nose seemed perfectly sculpted for his face.

Kohl had gotten injured during the fire at the Academy when him and KI were trapped inside the burning building waiting for help. A healer had been able to clear his lungs of the smoke he'd inhaled, and patch up the minor burns he'd sustained, as well as repair his sprained ankle. But he'd had to cut his hair, trimming down the singed ends so he didn't look silly. Instead of his normal hair that'd once sat sloppily on his head like a blonde mop, he'd given himself an undercut, shaving the back and leaving the top just long enough to fall into his face whenever he dipped his head.

He sat up now and ran a hand through his hair, smoothing it back. His arm seemed to strain with that simple movement, cords of muscle twitching from soreness. His Academy t-shirt stuck to him like a second skin, sweaty and see-through after hours of training on the Grounds.

Fox looked away, not even listening to his snide remark about how she was probably going to die during the entrance exams. *Did those healers pump him full of muscles and testosterone, too?* she wondered with a sigh. It didn't help that KI had undergone a similar change. He'd already experienced a rapid growth in his strength and physique, due to the demon lurking inside him, but after the fire, he seemed to have grown even more.

She stole a glance at the quiet boy, sitting against the giant oak, sipping water from a skin. He hadn't done much training today. Or much talking. Or much of anything except resting in the shade and watching his two friends work hard. Fox hoped he hadn't noticed her looking over at him every few minutes. He'd gotten patched up by the healers after the fire, had even been re-sealed because the Academy was paranoid the stress of the attempted kidnapping might have done something to weaken his seal.

Fox could see the thick black lines of his seal crawling from beneath

12

the sleeves of his shirt now. The markings hadn't been so long before. So intricate. Now they wrapped around his biceps, trailing down to his elbows in a winding design that made Fox's heart hammer in anxiety.

The demon is getting stronger.

Shade suddenly appeared around her, darkening the area. Fox blinked and looked up to find Kohl standing right in front of her, a scowl on his face. "You aren't listening."

She frowned. "Why would I listen to you insult me?"

His scowl became a teasing grin. "If you had been listening, you would have realized I was actually giving you a compliment this time."

"You? Giving *me* a compliment?" She laughed. "That is grand."

"I said your fighting is good without your flames." He crossed his arms. "But if you still aren't confident, I can help you out."

She eyed him cautiously. "How?"

"Remember what Master Jo said about spiritual energy before our training was cancelled?"

She nodded. Master Jo had crammed an incredible amount of knowledge into their heads regarding spiritual warfare and faith and demonic oppression. Fox remembered that blessings, anointings, and gifts came from God to help humanity fight against the forces of evil. The power fueling these supernatural abilities was called Light energy, and it came from the Spirit dwelling within every single Christian on Earth. Those who used their powers for evil were of darkness; their tainted spiritual energy was called Dark energy and their powers were referred to as curses.

There were some Believers who strayed from the path of righteousness and used their gifts for their own gain, but with repentance and forgiveness, their Dark energy could be cleansed as the evil was purged from their lives. It was a complicated process, but Master Jo had said it was definitely possible.

13

During that particular lesson, Fox had asked if repentance would be enough to cleanse someone who was demon possessed. After calming down the snickers and hisses thrown at Fox, and especially at KI, Master Jo had replied that she couldn't answer that question—not because she didn't know the answer, but because that depth of knowledge wasn't allowed to be shared with trainees. Once Fox passed the entrance exams and became an official student of the Cross, Master Jo would be free to share much more information with her.

Fox had thought this wasn't fair. But then she remembered the Biblical verse, Matthew 7:6, *do not throw your pearls before pigs*. The trainees certainly weren't pigs, but they also weren't learned enough to fully grasp all the information Master Jo had to share. Not yet at least.

Kohl was speaking again, drawing Fox from her thoughts. "You know our spiritual energy can be used for more than just activating and manifesting our blessings, right?"

Fox thought a moment. Everyone contained spiritual energy, it was the source of that energy that determined whether it was Light or Dark. This energy was used for everything regarding blessings and curses and, like supernatural fuel, once the energy was depleted, the user was no longer able to manifest their blessing. Those with incredible amounts of spiritual energy had great reserves, stored up from meditation or prayer or even fasting. The best way to strengthen one's Light energy, or to expand their stores of energy, was to strengthen their *faith*. The closer you were to God, the stronger your Spirit was, which meant you could produce more Light energy to manifest a more powerful blessing.

"I don't think my problem with sundancing has anything to do with my faith," Fox said to Kohl. After all, Roaring was a powerful sundancer, and she was sure he didn't have nearly as much faith in God as she did. At least, that's what she'd always told herself.

Kohlannis shook his head. "I'm not talking about manifesting your

14

gift, I'm talking about using your spiritual energy for things other than your gift."

Fox squinted, totally confused now. She was sure Master Jo hadn't mentioned anything about this in their training before. "I'm listening."

Kohl took a fighting stance. "Give me a good shove."

She walked over and shoved him hard. Kohl tripped to the side, rolling his eyes as Fox laughed at him.

He took another fighting stance. "Now try it again."

Fox gave him another push. This time he didn't budge.

She brought a hand to her chin, examining her friend closely. "I don't get it. What did you do?"

"I directed my spiritual energy."

"Please explain." She sat in the grass and blinked up at him like he was her teacher. She wanted to laugh; Master Hunger didn't sound nearly as cool as Master Jo.

Kohl sat in front of her, cross-legged; he felt in the grass and found a small rock. "Spiritual energy flows throughout our entire bodies. But if we focus, we can direct our energy to specific parts of our bodies."

Fox nodded. "That's kind of like sundancing. I have to direct the flow of my inner flames to expel it from certain parts of me." She held up a fist. "My fire doesn't exist inside my *hand*; I just *direct* it to my hands and shoot it from my fists." She frowned. "Well, I try to do that, at least."

Kohl gave her a smile, half his mouth turning up slightly, his eyebrow raising—the perfect image of mischief. "This is even cooler than that."

"Cooler than shooting fire from my fist?" She crossed her arms. "I don't think so."

He held one of the rocks in his palm so she could see. "When I concentrate my spiritual energy in my hand, it makes that part of my body stronger." He closed his hand, squeezing the rock with little effort.

15

When he opened his hand again, the rock was cracked. "It allows me to do things I normally couldn't."

Fox reached for the rock, needing to touch it in order to believe what she'd just seen. Up close, she could see the fine lines and ridges etched into the stone from the great pressure it'd been under. To think this had been done in the palm of someone's hand...

She looked up at Kohl to find him grinning at her. "It's like having a second blessing."

"It is," she breathed. "How do I do it?"

"The same way you tap into your flames. Think of sundancing—of redirecting your inner fire. But instead of calling out to the heat, find the energy that fuels it. Call out to the Spirit within."

Fox stood, ignoring Kohl's queer look. "If it's anything like sundancing, I think it'll be easier to try it in a fighting stance." She spread her feet apart and held her fists up in front of her chest. She clutched the rock in her right hand and took a deep breath. Closed her eyes.

Heat flickered to life in her chest, crackling and spitting inside her, yearning to be set free. Fox ignored the blaze and dove past it, searching for the fuel wetting the wick of her flame. Underneath the fire, she found it. A radiant pearl of light resting peacefully within. Shyly, she called to it and gasped as it eagerly responded, almost as if it'd been waiting for her to do so.

Energy poured into her chest, invigorating and thrilling, as if she'd just come alive at that very moment. Trying not to let it overwhelm her, Fox quickly directed the energy to her hand as she squeezed the rock.

She heard the crack before she felt the stone crumble in her hand. And then she heard Kohl gasp and her eyes flew open to find nothing but a handful of dust in her palm. Dust that was charred black.

"Whoa..." Kohlannis breathed.

Fox sucked in air, staring wide-eyed at the black debris. "I crushed it."

"And burned it."

Almost sundancing.

"I don't understand." Fox exhaled, watching as the dust flew away in the breeze. "I've been calling to my flames for weeks and nothing ever happens. Now that I'm calling to my own energy, I end up scorching a rock?"

Kohl scratched the back of his head. "I don't know anything about sundancing, but maybe it's because you called to your Spirit instead of the flames? I mean, the Spirit is the source, after all."

Fox tilted her head sideways. She had never once tried to connect with the Spirit dwelling within her. She had always thought of her Spirit as nothing more than something inside her. Just a pool of Light energy for her to feed off when she needed to. But then she had seen the pearl of light, had called out to it, and had felt it respond.

Her Spirit wasn't a pool of energy waiting to be used at her beck and call. It wasn't an *it* at all. *He* was the Holy Spirit, alive and sentient and part of God—part of the Holy Trinity. All this time, Fox had believed her *flames* were alive. Had thought of them as living things. But she'd been wrong. Her fire *was* alive, but it had been given life by the Holy Spirit within.

Maybe I've been calling to the wrong thing, Fox thought. *Maybe I should try to connect to—*

"Stop zoning out," Kohl scolded, waving a hand in front of her face.

Fox took a step back. "Sorry," she mumbled.

He rolled his eyes and crossed his arms. "Now that you've clearly got the gist of this, you should consider practicing it more. Concentrated energy is convenient. You can focus it in your legs to run faster, or give yourself sure footing." He leaned closer. "Like how you couldn't push me over earlier."

17

Fox nodded. "Maybe I'll try some training at night. Find some rocks to crush."

He laughed. "If you don't die, you might actually be able to pass the entrance exams without your gift."

"If I don't die." She reached for her water skin and removed the cork to take a sip.

Kohl shrugged, one broad shoulder going up then down. "We all know there's a chance we might not make it through the exam. It's a risk we're willing to take for the Cross."

"It's a very high risk."

"True."

"Which is why I don't understand why the Academy moved up the exam date."

Before the fire had occurred, the trainees had nearly a month of training left before the entrance exams would take place. And then an assassin appeared and tried to kidnap KI, nearly burning down the Cross in the process.

For a time, the training grounds had been closed and the exams postponed. But once KI had been healed up, Master Jo made the announcement that training would resume, and the exams would take place in a week.

That was two days ago.

"Master Jo says we're ready," Kohl said, toeing the dirt with his white shoe. It was stained with streaks of green and brown from running through the forests and sparring in the rings. Fox stared at his shoe as he spoke, wondering what their new uniforms would look like once they passed the exams.

"If she thinks we can handle it, then there's nothing to worry about," Kohl added.

Fox glanced back at KI. "You really think we have nothing to worry about?"

Kohl hesitated, his sharp gaze sliding over Fox's shoulder to peer at his friend. It was no secret KI was the only trainee on campus the Hunger boy was fond of, though he had warmed up to Fox quite considerably after she'd rescued them both from the fire.

KI and Kohl had a lot in common. Both boys lived at the Academy, monitored by a team of Hunters and Priests. Considered dangerous for what was sealed inside of them. A dark creature growing within KI. A natural born power thought to be a curse dwelling inside Kohl.

The other students had treated them both with contempt when they'd first started training with Marlo Jo, after word spread that the man who'd burned down the Cross had been after KI, things had only gotten worse. Kohl, being used to such treatment, took it all in stride. But KI had grown distant. Receding into the shadows in a sullen silence that wasn't like his normal self. Fox couldn't get him to talk much, not even when they were first united after KI had been held at the Academy under suspicion of his involvement with the Red Face.

Kohl had told her he'd stood trial before Bishop Jericho himself, but KI hadn't given his blonde friend any more details than that. Fox could only wonder what'd happened. If they had accused him of working with the Red Face. If they still believed he was a threat to Babel. If they saw him as an innocent victim in all this.

Whatever had happened during his trial hadn't left him unscathed.

"This world is dangerous," Kohl's voice was raspy, grinding out a warning that sent a shiver down Fox's spine. "The battle never stops. You just learn how to fight."

She pulled her gaze from KI to stare at the friend before her. "I don't know if we can win this fight."

"He's our friend. We don't have a choice but to win."

"I just wish he'd fight with us. It's like he's given up."

19

Kohlannis gazed down at her. *He's standing too close*, Fox thought. She could smell his scent from there; an earthy smell, mixed with something dark and masculine. His voice seemed to fill the entire space around them, deep and smooth and oddly comforting. "He hasn't given up. Just give him time."

She nodded. "I hope you're right."

"Speaking of people quitting," Kohl finally stepped back, exiting her personal space, "where's your brother?"

Fox groaned. She'd known they would eventually ask. She just didn't want to explain. *Roaring should be here to tell them himself*, she thought in annoyance.

"Roaring quit the training program. He doesn't want to join the Academy anymore."

Kohl moved to grab his own water skin and supplies. "Huh. That's interesting."

"It's because he wants to go back home."

"Home?" He looked genuinely confused, which wasn't surprising for a guy who'd been born and raised in Babel. Kohl had never even left the city before—apparently, Hungers weren't allowed beyond the front gates of Babel. Most of them didn't even leave the Hunger sector; not that they needed to leave. Their district was like a small city itself. They even had their own council and representatives who took their concerns to the Council of Babel.

Fox had learned a lot about the accursed tribe during her time off from training at the Grounds. The Academy library didn't hold much detail on the powers of the Hungers, but they did include more than enough on the history of the Hungers and the role they played in shaping Babel as well as the Four Regions. Kohl's extended family ruled the entire Region of Shadows. One-quarter of the mapped world was united under the rule of a single household. All because of their cursed powers.

20

Because of the overwhelming strength it gave them.

For some reason … Kohl had vowed never to use this power. He hated his own gift.

"Home. Where sundancing originated." Fox met her friend's questioning eyes. He chose not to use his gift because of what others thought of it. What Fox wouldn't give for the luxury of being able to choose when she could use her gift. At this rate, she'd make almost any sacrifice to produce even the flicker of a candle.

"The Village of Wi," Kohl said.

She nodded. "Our village was destroyed a few months ago. That's why my family relocated here as refugees. We were rescued by members of the Academy."

"I know," he told her. "The attack had something to do with KI."

"Yes," she gripped her water skin, "it did." Though she knew it was mostly her own fault. *If I hadn't disobeyed the village rules,* she thought bitterly, *if I hadn't gone beyond the Walls of Wi. If I hadn't dragged KI with me.*

Fox let out a shaky breath, trying to clear her head. "The Academy promised my people they would help us rebuild our village once it was safe to begin construction."

Kohl nodded thoughtfully. "I guess you've been given the okay to begin rebuilding."

"We have. And Roaring wants to lead the project. Then he wants to move back home."

A moment of silence stretched between them.

"Do you want to go home, too?" Kohlannis asked in a quiet voice.

She frowned. "Of course not. I'm staying right here in Babel. At the Academy. With KI."

He pressed his lips together like he was offended. "Just KI?"

Her frown deepened. Who else would she stay for?

Then realization hit her, but it was a little too late. Kohl was shaking

21

his head and walking away, saying it was time to meet Master Moneek for their after-training briefing.

Fox watched him leave. She had been so obsessed with making sure she was ready for the exam, making sure she was strong enough to protect KI, to stand by his side, she never thought about how Kohl would fit into any of this.

If he passes the exams, we'll all be together.

3

Evelyn

First Lieutenant Evelyn Diaz stared at the Hunters before him. A team of hardened warriors, shoulder to shoulder, at attention. Weapons sheathed at their hips, blessings mastered and under their full control. Their faces void of emotion.

He was not impressed.

Evelyn paced before them, hands clasped behind his back, eyes glaring. He scrutinized everything about them, examining their uniforms, their posture, even the creases in their beige colored pants, the shine on their leather boots, the neatness of their ascot ties.

He stopped in front of a beefy man who stood head and shoulders over him. "I want to let you know," Diaz began slowly, "you owe your lives to Major Marshall."

The old man smiled behind him, giving a little wave to the Hunters who all shifted uncomfortably.

"I had absolutely no problem with kicking each one of you out of the Academy. But Major Marshall pleaded for you." Evelyn rolled his shoulders, trying to get rid of the ache in his back. "I've decided to be merciful."

There was an audible sigh in the room.

"Naman of the Heko Clan," Diaz said, glancing up at the beefy man before him.

He nodded, offering a smile speckled with dark gaps from his missing teeth. "Yes, sir."

"If you ever touch Lady Talon again, I will personally have your hands removed."

The smile withered on his suddenly dry lips. "Y-Yes, sir," he muttered.

Diaz turned to Mung who'd been cowering behind her grey bangs. "Mung, you have been demoted one rank."

She winced but nodded. "Yes, sir."

He looked at Hemiah. "You have been transferred to a new battalion. You will report immediately."

"Yes, sir," he whispered, unable to meet his sharp gaze.

Diaz nodded, pleased with the discipline he'd issued. "Dismissed."

The Hunters scurried from the room, quiet and shame. Once the door closed behind them, Major Marshall burst into laughter.

"When you asked me to join you in your office, I didn't know it was to be used as your scapegoat."

Lieutenant Diaz placed a hand on his desk and bent over to massage his own back. "Yeah, well, you wouldn't have agreed if I'd told you what I really wanted."

"That's true." The major chuckled. "A bunch of nameless low-rank Hunters." He shook his head. "They really believe I vouched for them. You're puffing their ego."

"It's better than the truth," Diaz grunted, rubbing his knuckles into his back.

The truth was that after pulling their outrageous stunt in Koh— taking Lady Talon hostage and accusing her of using witchcraft— Lieutenant Diaz had every intention to kick the group of incompetent

Hunters out of the Academy. Then the Red Face attacked, and Bishop Jericho declared they needed every hand available. The Hunters were saved by the skin of their teeth. But they didn't need to know that.

They didn't need to know how desperate the Academy was for soldiers; they didn't need to know how shorthanded they were. They didn't need to know the Academic Council was so strained they were willing to send in fresh graduates with no experience if it meant getting men on the battlefield.

Diaz had been forbidden from kicking those Hunters out, but it was easier to say he'd been merciful than admit his bosses were being stubborn.

The lieutenant grunted again, hunching his back to stretch out the muscles. "At least I got to discipline them somewhat."

Major Marshall studied him a moment, dark eyes watching in silence. "You okay?"

"I'm fine, old man."

"Doesn't look like it."

He stood upright, his back tingling, threatening to summon memories of the injuries that'd caused his current pain. When he closed his eyes, Evelyn could see the demon that'd taken his mother and chased him through the woods. Could still remember the feel of its branch-like hand whipping out to slash him across the back as he'd tried to run away. The scar it left behind throbbed under the lieutenant's shirt, pulsing against the thick black markings that covered it.

A seal. Just like the boy's.

Diaz sighed. "I'll be fine."

"Izzy could take a look—"

"I don't need Izzy to take a look." The words came out harsher than Evelyn intended.

Major Marshall raised an eyebrow at his tone but said nothing more.

25

"We have a meeting." Diaz took a step toward the door and Marshall took the hint, following him out into the hall. He sighed as he fell into step beside the young lieutenant.

"This meeting won't be half as entertaining as the last."

Diaz nodded, unable to form words. *Unwilling* to form words. He didn't want to think about the upcoming meeting—he still hadn't even processed the fact that the Academic Council had agreed to see him and hear his request. Then again, these were desperate times and he'd played an important role in uncovering the secrets hidden behind the Walls of Wi. Plus, his adoptive father had put in a good word with the higherups of the Academy military—something Major Marshall couldn't help but remind Diaz of whenever he got the chance.

Like right now as he walked beside him down the Academy corridor toward the conference room where the meeting would be held. "Don't embarrass me, son," the older man warned, dark skin wrinkling as he gave him a very cheery smile. There was no joy behind the grin on his face, his expression was more of a cold warning that sent a slight shiver shimmying down Evelyn's aching spine.

Major Marshall wasn't a very impatient or irritable man. He'd been kind to Evelyn growing up in Babel and had rarely lifted a hand to discipline him, but Lieutenant Diaz had distinct memories of each and every time he *did* raise his hand and the thought of it increased his anxiety tenfold. He was too old for spankings now, being twenty-four and just a few ranks below his own adoptive father, but something about the icy smile on the major's face let him know this was not the time to screw things up. Marshall had called in all his favors for this. More than just Diaz's reputation was on the line now.

He sighed. "I won't shame the Marshall name."

Major Marshall chuckled and gave him a wink. "I know you won't."

Inside the conference room sat a large table with a few members of

26

the Academic Council. Two generals from the Academy military sat at the end of the table, with two high-ranking Priests of the Cross on the other end. Master Marlo Jo sat beside the powerful Priests, looking very out of place, considering she was just a Master—nothing more than a glorified schoolteacher. But she was KI's instructor and since this whole mess centered on him, her presence was justified.

In the center of the table was a woman with stony eyes and a stiff smile. She wore a long white gown, attire Diaz had never seen before, and her hair was left hanging loose, gentle chocolate waves pouring over both her shoulders. As the lieutenant crossed the room to stand in the center of the floor, her eyes remained on him. The intensity of her gaze felt like needles raking over his skin. Evelyn tried not to crack under her scrutiny.

Major Marshall chose this time to abandon his adoptive son and take a seat at the table beside one of the Academy generals. He smiled at Diaz, gave him a reassuring nod that did nothing to calm his nerves.

Evelyn cleared his throat. "Good afternoon."

"This meeting was called as a favor," the woman said. "Do not waste this opportunity."

As if the chance to speak face to face with the Academic Council was lost on him. Evelyn Diaz was just a First Lieutenant. He was highly skilled and had earned himself a relatively fair reputation around the Academy—being the major's son certainly played a role in his status in Babel, but it didn't make him blind to how important this meeting was. The Academic Council made all the decisions for both Cross Academies. They were responsible for the very spread of the Gospel. Their word was as good as law and was even upheld by partnering villages across the Four Regions.

Diaz was grateful for the chance to speak to the Academic Council, but he couldn't help but notice a few key members were missing. There weren't any Cardinals present, for one, and Bishop Jericho was missing, too. He had no idea who the woman before him was, but the lieutenant doubted she had as much authority as she'd like him to believe.

Still … he was standing in the room with members of the Council. He wouldn't waste this chance, no matter how much or how little power this woman held. She had all the authority she needed to accept or reject his request.

"My name is Roma Donda," the woman said, inclining her head. "I am the overseer here at this meeting and I will be the one who decides the fate of your request."

Diaz nodded.

"My peers beside me will weigh in on the conversation, of course," she went on. "Their expertise as Hunters and Priests who work and live here in Babel cannot be ignored."

Live here… Evelyn squinted, realizing Roma wasn't from the city. *Did she travel here from the other Academy? No.* He inhaled quickly, taking in her white gown and her black crucifix and her long, flowing hair. He recognized her.

She's from Central.

The mapped world consisted of four distinct Regions, the Region of Ice in the North, the Region of the Lion in the East, the Region of Smoke and Ash in the South, and the Region of Shadows in the West. But in the center of the map, where all Four Regions crossed, was a fifth province called Central. It was a district of free land unclaimed by any of the other Regions. It remained neutral during times of war and focused on providing peace, knowledge, and the chance for growth to the world. Central was the home of the Academic Council and the place where the largest library of the Four Regions rested.

Evelyn had only been to Central twice. The first time was for sightseeing when he was just a kid and Major Marshall—only Second

Lieutenant Marshall at the time—had wanted to take something of a family vacation. The second time he'd gone to Central was to do research on the seal on his back. He had left the Academic Library with more questions than answers.

But Diaz remembered one thing he'd learned at the library. The people who ran Central were nothing like those at the Academy. They weren't focused on fighting or training their bodies. Their blessings centered on intellect, analytics, and anything that enhanced the mind.

It was impressive to master the flame or the wind or super strength, but mastery of one's mind—*wisdom*—was a far more dangerous weapon. Elegant strength. Controlled power so intense it left visitors in awe of the fortitude of the Academic Council. Cardinals were not the same as mere Priests, just as the woman before Diaz was not the same as Mung or Lady Shakira or even Bishop Jericho. She wasn't a Priest or a Cardinal or a Bishop. She was something greater, something elevated.

Lieutenant Diaz dipped his head in reverence. "Thank you for accepting my request and taking the time to travel here, Saint Roma."

The ghost of a smile danced across Roma's face, impressed with his recognition. "You know who I am?"

He nodded. "There is a statue of you in Central, just outside the Academic Library." He remembered staring up at it as a kid, absently listening while Marshall explained what it took to become a Saint.

The fact that Roma Donda had achieved such status while living summoned a storm of emotions within the lieutenant. He'd thought his request hadn't been taken seriously because there weren't any Cardinals present, not even an earthen statue in place of Bishop Jericho.

Instead, he'd been gifted with the opportunity to meet a living Saint in person. No wonder Major Marshall had been so serious. Messing up in front of Roma Donda could end his entire career—might even ruin the reputation of the entire Marshall bloodline.

29

Evelyn gulped. Shame summoned a dewy sweat onto his forehead. He couldn't believe he'd underestimated the power Saint Roma held just because she'd come alone. You don't need an entourage when you singlehandedly outrank every Hunter and Priest in an entire city.

"I didn't realize how seriously the Council had taken my request."

"We take all matters regarding the safety of our students seriously."

"Right."

Roma eyed him, tapping a fingernail on the table. He noticed how old her hands were, veins visible beneath her wrinkled cocoa brown skin. "The Academy of Babel has decided to proceed with the entrance exams despite the presence of an assassin in the city. This concerns you," she said.

He nodded. Cleared his throat. "I understand we are shorthanded at the moment, but we cannot put those recruits at risk—"

"I have been assured by Bishop Jericho and a master of the Academy that the students are ready for the exam."

"That may be true," he conceded.

"Then what is the issue?"

He took a breath. "Being ready for the exam is not the same as being ready to face a possible assassin. Or whatever other forces may also be waiting to strike. We are walking these children into the lions' den. It isn't right."

"You said it yourself, the Academy is shorthanded. Babel needs the extra manpower."

"Why can't Central arrange for the second Academy to send reinforcements?"

The room fell silent. Diaz mentally kicked himself because he'd already known the answer to that question before it'd slipped from his lips. The second Academy was located on the very edge of the Region of Smoke and Ash—right along the border of the Region of Shadows.

While the Academy here in Babel trained to fight demons, the one in the south trained to defend itself from the Shadows. They were the only force remaining between the power hungry Hungari of the West and the rest of the world. It was the broken Hungari treaty that inspired the Academic Council to place the second Academy in that location. They were the guardians of the southwest, standing sentinel in the face of darkness. They could not afford to spare any soldiers. Not now. Not ever.

"You care for these children," Saint Roma was speaking again.

Diaz found himself nodding without thinking, his head mechanically bobbing up and down like a puppet's.

"Do you have any relatives enrolled?" she questioned.

The suggestion shook him from his thoughts, and he wrinkled his brows at her. He didn't have any relatives at all. And he hardly saw how any family members in the training program would make a difference here.

"I'm not voicing my concerns because I have friends and family taking the exam," he said slowly, trying to keep his anger from rising. "I requested this hearing because I believe my superiors are making a grave mistake."

She bristled in her chair. "So you thought it wise to go over their heads and take your concerns directly to the Academic Council?"

Evelyn couldn't help himself. He shot a glance at Major Marshall, trying to read his emotions, trying to see if he'd gone too far. His father sat motionless and blank in his chair, as if he were watching the grass grow or the clouds drift across the sky. He almost looked bored.

Diaz supposed boredom was better than anger or embarrassment.

He swallowed. "I mean no disrespect to my superiors—"

"No," she quirked an eyebrow, steepled her fingers, "you simply mean to get your point across."

Slowly, the blinds were pulled back and the lieutenant realized what this was really all about. He wasn't being honored with Saint Roma's presence; he was being threatened. The decision over the entrance exams was final. Set in stone. All the way up to the Academic Council. It was official; the Academy prioritized catching the Red Face, securing KI, and dispelling any forces who might come for him. The young recruits would be collateral damage.

Saint Roma was not here to give Evelyn a fair hearing, she was here to deliver the Council's message in person, effectively silencing anyone else who might have risen up in protest against the Academy's decision later on.

The Lieutenant couldn't stop himself from looking down the table at Master Marlo Jo. She had called herself KI's instructor and was one of few people to speak up on behalf of the boy—boldly voicing her disagreement with Bishop Jericho's decision. A mere Master of the Academy was not important enough to be invited to this meeting. Saint Roma's message was for her, too.

Roma Donda rose from her chair and placed her hands on the table. The motion was so elegant that Evelyn blinked at her almost in admiration. Her white robes spilled around her, flowing over her chair, and piling onto the floor. Her dark hair created a chocolate mane that framed a deceptively angular face—small round nose, dimpled cheeks, sharp eyes that might have been motherly once. Now they only looked cold and serious.

"Cross Academy will be moving forward with the entrance exams. That is final." Saint Roma paused, waiting for him to argue. When he didn't speak, she narrowed her gaze. "Do you think this is a grave mistake, Lieutenant Diaz?"

He'd already done enough damage. Might as well be honest. "Yes, I do."

His boldness seemed to impress her, if only a little. She surrendered what looked like a smile on her flattened lips, pressed together tightly. "At the very least, I appreciate your dedication to the students here at the Academy."

He nodded.

"That's why we have decided you should lend aid to the masters at the Academy and help oversee the entrance exams." This time, she did smile. Full grin showing teeth. "Since you're so sure this is a mistake, you now have the opportunity to prevent further mistakes from happening."

He clenched his teeth, feeling the muscle in his jaw spasm. "I am a Hunter of the Academy." The mere suggestion of overseeing the exam was such an insult to his rank he almost couldn't put it into words. This wasn't an opportunity … it was punishment. *Mung* would be out on more serious missions than him, even after being demoted.

Lieutenant Diaz exhaled slowly. "I have far more pressing business to deal with—"

"More pressing than the safety of those precious recruits?"

She had cornered him.

Diaz took a breath just to keep himself from swearing at her. He couldn't imagine the sort of trouble he would get into for cursing a Saint to her face.

He took another breath just to make sure he was calm enough to speak. Stole a glance at Major Marshall. He looked worried now, the crease in his normally relaxed brow reminding Diaz that his reputation wasn't the only one at risk here.

The lieutenant's shoulders sagged in defeat. "I would be honored to help oversee the exams," he said through gritted teeth.

Saint Roma gave him another teeth-gleaming smile. "Good." She straightened and glanced down the table at the others. "Any other concerns?"

No one spoke.

"I think we're done here."

4

Roaring

Roaring stepped from the carriage and turned to thank the driver. The older woman gave him a grin, tipped her hat, and then snapped the reins of her horse. He glanced up at the giant cross-shaped building and clutched the slip of paper tighter in his hand. So much had happened since the last time he'd ridden to the Academy in a carriage. At that time, all he'd wanted was to go back home to Wi and rebuild what'd been lost. Rise again.

But now ...

Now, he had to go. There was no other option. Talon had finally returned from her trip to Wi with a positive report confirmed by the Academy. They could finally begin reconstruction. If everything went well, Wi could be fully repaired in less than two years—especially considering the Region of Smoke and Ash never experienced winter. They could work all year round, sweating in the blazing heat. But before any of that could go down, Roaring had to hand in that slip of paper.

He held it up and gave it one last read-through. It was a letter of resignation; an announcement to the world that he was leaving the Academy training program. He would have simply never showed up at the Grounds again, if it were up to him, but Fox had told him there was a process to getting out of the preliminary courses and Talon had insisted on him doing things right.

"I don't care if you quit," she said, though the look on her face seemed to hint the opposite, "but if you're dropping out, at least do it right!"

Talon had gotten considerably bolder since returning from her trip. Roaring made a mental note to ask her exactly what'd happened on her journey when he got home later. He would have asked much earlier, she'd been home for days now, but so much was going on with the Academy and Fox and KI and the Red Face. Roaring was tired.

Someone walked up to him and tapped his shoulder. He turned, noticing the old man step back to give him room to do it. The Prince of Fire frowned. He was a big man, bigger than most, but he never thought of himself as *that* big. Then he glanced down at the elderly man and realized his own body was providing shade for him. He let out a sigh.

"What is it?" Roaring grunted.

The older man tilted his head to the side. "I was going to ask you that. You've been staring between that paper in your hand and the building for a few minutes. Are you lost, son?"

He wanted to sigh again, but he felt like he did that a lot. So he pressed his lips into a thin smile and shook his head. "I was just heading inside."

The man opened his mouth to say more but Roaring turned to leave and ground out a quick 'Thanks for your concern,' before any words could leave his wrinkled lips.

Inside the Academy sat the lobby Roaring remembered from the first time he'd entered this building. Briefly, he wondered if the Priestess from before would be hanging around somewhere. Lady Shakira was her name. Tall—even taller than Roaring—with broad shoulders and big hands and brown skin and odd blondish hair. She was nice to look at, in

36

the same way that a strange, exotic animal was nice to look at.

But Roaring didn't find Lady Shakira anywhere in the lobby, all he found was a small man with an attitude sitting behind a desk. He looked him up and down when he approached, sunlight glinting off his spectacles.

"What do you need?" Then, as if just remembering, he added, "Sir."

"Just to turn this in." Roaring thrust the parchment at the young man who stared at it without taking it. He worked his mouth, chewing *something*, as he scanned the words. Then he pressed his lips together and gave the slightest shake of his head.

"It's always the tough-looking ones."

"Come again?" Roaring asked, leaning closer to the desk.

The man snatched the paper and stamped it, then he set it aside and glanced up at Roaring with a pleasant smile on his face as if he hadn't just insulted him. They stared at each other a moment, the rest of the lobby bustling around them, and then the man raised one of his eyebrows. It was a simple gesture, one which could have been done out of habit or awkward nerves. It could have meant nothing at all, but Roaring took it as, *Are you done?*

He turned around, grunted, "Thanks," and then marched back through the front doors, shockingly happy that Fox hadn't convinced him to stay in the program. He had an odd feeling he wouldn't have enjoyed the Academy as much as everyone thought he might.

"Roaring!" a voice called just as he went to hail a carriage.

He jerked back from the curb as recognition hit him. "Master Jo?"

She was right in front of him when he turned back around, wearing a long black gown with her hair down, flowing all around her. He'd never noticed just how long her dreadlocks were.

"I thought I caught a glimpse of you leaving the lobby. I ran all the way out here to make sure I wasn't just seeing things." She beamed at him, making his gut twist with guilt. Master Jo would be the only person he missed in this entire city, besides Fox who he knew couldn't be dragged away from Babel unless KI was dragged away, too.

"Shouldn't you be at the Grounds?" he asked.

She gave him a sly smile. "Shouldn't you?"

"I—uh—"

"I got called away for a meeting here," Marlo explained. "Moneek is holding things down until I get back, which should be soon." She smiled again and jerked her head at a carriage pulling up. "Wanna share one?"

"Actually." He rubbed the back of his neck. "I'm not going back to the Grounds, Master Jo."

She frowned. "What do you mean?"

"I dropped out of the program."

Understanding claimed her features, smoothing the wrinkles of her forehead. "That's what you were doing in the lobby. Turning in your letter of resignation."

He nodded, then crammed his hands into his pockets. "I should go," he said, stepping toward the parked carriage.

"Wait," Marlo grabbed his arm. Her grip was strong enough to yank him back from the carriage door. He almost stumbled backwards into her as he lost his footing and gasped.

She's so strong.

Marlo stabled him. "We should talk about this."

"My mind is made up—"

"Give me a chance to change it."

He shook his head. "This is about a lot more than just learning how to fight demons."

She squeezed his arm which made him look down at her. Her face was serious, forehead wrinkled again, eyes focused on his. "I know."

He almost sighed, but he caught himself and ended up just taking a deep breath instead. "Let's share a carriage, then. And talk."

He didn't know where else to go, so Roaring took Marlo Jo to his apartment. She spent the ride talking about the Red Face and her suspicions on his identity, how reckless she thought it was that the Academy would not only go forward with the entrance exams but move up the date.

Roaring had listened intently, mentally combining her information on the Red Face with his own, trying to put the pieces together. The situation had worried him, too. But there was nothing he could do about it. Fox would never leave the Academy as long as KI was there, and he couldn't stick around to find the Red Face himself. It was time to leave.

"This is serious," Marlo was saying as Roaring opened the front door. She cut herself off when she stepped into the apartment, glancing at the mismatched furniture and tribal wall hangings. Roaring didn't care to impress anyone with his temporary home, but he was suddenly *very* aware of how badly the place needed a fresh coat of paint.

He cleared his throat. "Cat's been bothering us to buy new decorations."

Marlo looked confused, walking in behind him and taking a seat on the sofa. "Cat?"

"My little sister."

"You have more sisters than Fox?"

He smirked. "I have three, actually."

Just then, Chava rounded the corner and pricked her ears, tilted her massive head to the side as she stared at Marlo. The young Priest smiled, glancing between Roaring and his loyal hunting hound.

"She won't attack, will she?"

Roaring chuckled. "Not unless I tell her to." He whistled and Chava bounded over, taking little sniffs at Marlo as he ruffled the silvery fur of her head. "Hold out your hand," he said to Master Jo.

She complied with a giggle that disarmed him. He'd never seen her so relaxed, so cheery.

Chava sniffed her hand and then gave it a lick. With another sweet giggle, Marlo ruffled her fur too. "Three little sisters." She said the words in awe, like she was jealous. Somehow, that made Roaring's heart swell with pride. He loved his sisters. "I bet you spoil them," Marlo said.

Not exactly. Cat ran the house, Talon ran the village, and the only thing Fox had learned about sundancing came from her standing in the middle of a burning building. He'd been a virtually useless instructor and brother so far.

Roaring shifted uncomfortably. "I want to spoil them," he admitted. Then he turned to the kitchen and asked, "Would you like something to drink? My sister makes good tea—sweet lemon tea."

She nodded. "Chilled, if you've got it."

Roaring brought over a pitcher and poured two glasses. Marlo smiled when she took a sip, wiping at the corners of her mouth. "It's good."

"I'll tell her you said so."

She looked serious again. "We need to talk, Roaring."

"I already told you I'm not going back. The Red Face isn't enough to keep me here, Master Jo. I've got an entire village to rebuild—two-thousand refugees waiting to go home."

"I respect that," she said with a nod. "But all of Babel will suffer if things go badly during the entrance exams. That's nearly one-hundred thousand civilians, including your refugees." She leaned forward, placing a hand on his arm. She did that a lot. Roaring sort of liked it. "You might leave to rebuild soon, but the refugees of Wi will remain here until the reconstruction is at least partially done, right?"

He nodded.

40

"That means they will also be impacted by whatever happens next week."

"Why are you so sure something is going to happen?" he asked, glancing up to watch Chava curl up in a corner of the room.

Marlo retracted her hand from his arm to clutch the glass of tea in her lap. The muscle she'd been holding suddenly felt cool without her touch. Roaring resisted the urge to stare at his arm, willing the gentle warmth to return.

He took a sip of tea just to do something in the awkward silence.

"I can't tell you all the details," Marlo said softly, "so please don't ask. But I'm not sure something is going to happen. I *know* it is. Because the Academy is planning for something to happen."

Roaring squinted at her. It was a cruel thing to ask him not to ask questions. He could think of a million different ones right now, but he was a leader, too. He knew how important it was to keep things on a need-to-know basis. In a way, he felt sorry for Master Jo. She was obviously suffering from whatever knowledge she had, and there was no one she could confide in. Roaring wouldn't allow himself to wonder what it meant that she was *sort of* confiding in him now. At least, as much as she could without giving away anything incriminating.

She looked at him, uncharacteristic tears filling her eyes. "My students are everything to me. Class G-Five." A little smile formed on her lips. That was the first time Roaring had heard her call the name given to her class. The sound of it filling his small living room made everything real. Class G-5 was going to take the entrance exams. The trainees would soon become official students. If they lived through the test.

Marlo sniffled. "I would give my life for any one of my pupils. But I won't be there during the exams. I won't be able to protect them when they might need me most."

41

He glanced down at the glass in his hand, his tea half gone. "But I can protect them," he muttered.

Her hand was back again. He closed his eyes for a moment, allowing himself to enjoy her nearness. "You are strong, Roaring," Marlo said. "Stronger than the rest of the trainees. I'm sure you would pass the exams with flying colors. But the rest of the students aren't like you."

"They're gifted," he said. "Some of them have better blessings than my own."

"It's not about their blessings," she told him. "It's about their experience. You've seen demons face to face. You've fought them. *Burned* them. The rest haven't. Training to fight is much different from actually standing on the battlefield."

He couldn't agree more. But he didn't think he was the answer to all Marlo's problems.

"I don't think one extra person at the exams will make that much of a difference."

She nodded. "Yes, you will. You'll make all the difference because you'll be the only one expecting something to happen. You'll be ready." She squeezed his arm, fingers desperately digging into hard muscle. "You'll be able to protect them—as many of them as possible. But especially the ones who need it."

He sucked in a breath. "Fox Fire and KI."

"KI is the one the Red Face is after. Since Fox is always by his side, it's inevitable that she will be in danger, too."

He stared at her, eyes going wide.

Marlo muttered something under her breath, pulling her hand away to clutch her tea again. "I shouldn't have said that."

"My God," Roaring whispered. "You think the Red Face is going to attack again. During the entrance exams." Her words came back to him.

The Academy is planning for something to happen.

42

"Cross Academy knows he'll attack again. And they're going to let him.""

Marlo lowered her head, too ashamed of her slipup to look him in the eye now. "Please don't say anything," she begged quietly.

He let the silence swell between them, unsure how to respond. Unsure how he even felt about the whole thing. No wonder Master Jo was so worked up. She believed a trained assassin was going to show up at her students' exams and no one was going to stop him.

But the Cross wasn't reckless like that. They were the force of good in this world. Fighting the darklings and the demons and everyone else in between. They wouldn't just sit back and let the Red Face enact his plans without good reason.

Roaring rubbed his chin, dark stubble bristling against his fingers. Cat had been bothering him to shave, but he was only a boy of nineteen. The thought of growing in a beard was as exciting to him as getting a new dress was to his spoiled little sister. She wouldn't understand, even if she was right when she said the shadow on his face made him look old. He preferred the word *mature*.

"The Academy wouldn't do this for no reason," Roaring muttered, still rubbing his chin.

Marlo took a breath. "They're trying to lure him out."

"Using the exams as bait."

She nodded. "You catch on quickly."

"It's like you said, I have experience." He shrugged one meaty shoulder. "Wi didn't have any assassins running loose, but I did my fair share of hunting dangerous creatures in the forests beyond the Walls. Sometimes ignoring a monster was the only way to trap it."

"They always come sniffing once they realize you've stopped chasing them."

He gazed at her. "If you understand why the Cross is doing this, then

43

why are you—"

"Because it is still reckless," she insisted. "Catching the Red Face is not worth the gamble they'll be taking with the lives of my students." She clutched her glass so tightly, Roaring feared it would crack right there in her hands. "My class is twenty strong," she glanced at him, "twenty-one, including you. But I'm not the only Master on the Grounds. There are hundreds of us with our own groups of trainees, doing our best to prepare the students for what's to come."

Roaring raised both eyebrows, truly shocked by just how many people wanted to get into the Academy. He shouldn't have been surprised. There were only two Academies in existence and enrollment came around only once every three years—even less often if the Academic Council felt they had all the manpower they needed in this spiritual war.

Still. Roaring remembered all the tents that'd lined the outskirts of the Grounds. He remembered passing other trainees with their Masters. He had come to enjoy Fox's class and had even thought of those kids as special. But the truth was that they were just another flock in the field. Thousands of trainees would be taking the entrance exams. Only a hundred or so would make it in.

Marlo Jo was right. Gambling the lives of thousands of fresh students was reckless. *But maybe*, Roaring mused…

"Maybe the Academy plans to intervene before the Red Face has the chance to hurt anyone else. He's only after KI. He might ignore the other students and go straight for him."

Marlo shook her head. "We shouldn't be willing to even take that chance."

Roaring sighed—he couldn't help himself—but before he could say anything, Marlo was talking again. "But since they are taking that chance, I'm going to do everything in my power to do what the Cross chose me to do."

"Which is?" He raised a single, dark eyebrow.

"Nurture the next generation of Hunters and Priests. I cannot lead my flock if I willingly throw them into the lions' den."

"So, what now? Am I your secret weapon?"

She gave him the saddest smile he'd ever seen. "You're my last hope."

Roaring's heart thudded in his chest as he blinked at Marlo Jo. He hadn't expected her to sound so sincere. To look so earnest as she pleaded with him.

"Please don't resign. Not yet, at least," she said softly. "I was born here in this city. I have no idea what it's like to lose your entire village and your parents, too. I can't ask you to put aside the reconstruction of Wi. But I can ask you to stay with us until the restoration has begun."

Roaring set his jaw, already knowing what he was going to say before she finished asking.

Marlo leaned forward again, taking his hand this time, instead of just squeezing his arm. "Just take the exam. One more week in Babel is all I'm asking for."

Before he could nod and agree to stick around a little longer, the front door swung open, letting Cat into the apartment. His little sister paused when she stepped inside and found the Priestess on their sofa, a glass of chilled tea in one hand, tears very close to spilling down her cheeks.

"Um," she said, eyes flicking back and forth between them.

Roaring immediately pulled away from Marlo, dropping her hand so he could stand and smile awkwardly at his sister. "Hey."

"Hey." She adjusted the hemp bag on her shoulder. "I didn't know we were having a guest for dinner. I think I've got enough, though. As long as Fox Fire doesn't eat like it's a competition again."

Marlo stood, head shaking and hands up as if in surrender. "Oh no, I didn't realize it'd gotten this late. I should actually be leaving now."

45

Cat blinked. "So, you're not staying for dinner? I'm making fried chicken."

"I've got a lot of work—"

"I could make goulash if you prefer." Cat laughed, turning to trot into the kitchen so she could drop her heavy bags on the countertop. Her heels clicked with every step she took; she didn't seem to mind the noise. "I'm craving cornbread, so we've got to eat something that goes with cornbread tonight."

"I should be leaving," Marlo said a little more firmly.

Cat sighed, offering a defeated smile. "My brother finally brings a woman home, and she can't wait to get out of here."

Roaring bit his tongue, fighting the urge to tell Cat that Marlo's visit was nothing like that. But he knew trying to explain would only deepen his sister's suspicions, so he turned to Master Jo with a nervous smile and said, "Let me walk you to the door."

Marlo's full lips pressed into a very thin line. "Thanks for the tea."

He wanted to say, *You're welcome*, but all he could manage was a low grunt. He figured Master Jo wasn't offended. She was used to his brooding by now.

When she turned to him at the door, her tightlipped smile was somewhat more relaxed. "Think about what I said," she told him. "One more week."

He nodded. "I'll try."

"Try what?" Cat asked once he'd closed the door.

He didn't feel like talking about it. "I'll help with dinner, if you want."

His sister gave him the side eye, more than aware that he was avoiding her question. "Fine. But don't think giving me a hand means you're out of the woods. I expect the full rundown on that pretty lady."

"She's just an instructor at the Academy."

Cat waggled her eyebrows. "You're dating your teacher. That's hot."

46

Roaring rolled his eyes. "I'm not dating anyone." Then he reached for the apron hanging on the wall of the kitchen. "Let's get dinner started."

5

Talon

Sparks flew into the air as Li hammered his sword. It was a project he'd taken up before Talon showed up outside his shop asking about the apprenticeship. She had surprised herself when she'd decided to go to the little wooden cabin. It didn't make sense for her to try to get a job in Babel; she wouldn't be here forever. Especially since the Academy had told her they would be moving forward with reparations within the next few weeks. She had less than a month left here in this great city.

But, she thought, staring at the sparks as they shimmered before her. *I don't have to leave Babel until reconstruction is complete.* It would be pointless to try to pitch a tent and live in the dilapidated village right now. It wasn't like she could offer much in regards to building houses and cabins and walls. Maybe she could stay in Babel until Wi was fully rebuilt—and who knew how long that would take? Months? Years?

By then, she would be a master at Imbue. And Fox would be training hard at the Academy and Cat would probably be married off to some bachelor right here in Babel. And Roaring … Talon chewed her lip. Roaring would be in Wi. There was no way he would sit here in Babel while other men laid bricks for his own home, built cabins for his storage, erected walls for his village. He'd likely oversee the entire project

48

if he could.

Talon swallowed. *Roaring would do what a Grand Chief should do.*

"You see that?" Li held up the sword. It was finely made, hammered into perfection and so hot it was glowing red. "She's gonna love this!"

"Who's the customer?" Talon asked, fiddling with her skirt as she sat on the stool.

Since she'd started her apprenticeship, Li hadn't taught her anything at all. Just told her to sit and watch while he hammered away and took care of orders for different customers. Yesterday, he made a small dagger and a dozen iron arrowheads. Talon had sat quietly as he'd whispered into the ore, making it glow an odd shade of purple she had never seen before. Imbued with his spiritual energy, the dagger would be able to extend to the length of a sword on command, and the arrowheads would be able to track their targets. Talon didn't know how Li got all that to work out—maybe in the words he'd whispered—but she loved watching, nonetheless.

Li was still smiling at his sword as he answered, "This one is for my granddaughter!"

"Lieutenant Kotaro?" Talon perked up, somewhat excited about watching the lieutenant's grandfather make a weapon for her, but Li shook his head, white hair swishing back and forth.

"I have more than one granddaughter."

"Oh?"

"Got thirteen, to be exact!"

Talon stared at him with her mouth open. "Thirteen granddaughters," she repeated. "Any grandsons?"

He nodded, his smile growing even wider. "Nine grandsons."

"Sounds like your family is quite large."

"Not incredibly large. But big enough to make me a proud grandpa."

Li hummed as he dipped the hot sword into a metal bin filled with

49

liquid. Steam erupted from the bin, clouding the room for a moment. Talon fanned the air and tried not to cough. When the steam cleared, Li was holding up the weapon, inspecting it closely.

"It's a beauty," he grumbled, rubbing his chin with his free hand.

"Which granddaughter is it for?" Talon asked.

Li sliced at the air, thick arms defying his age. "Himari, she's Tella's older sister."

Tella? Talon wondered.

"That's the Second Lieutenant."

"Oh!" She laughed. "I never knew her first name."

"She's not a lieutenant over here. Just little Tella."

Talon smiled warmly, watching the burly blacksmith take a few more practice swings at the air. Li Kotaro was a large man, thick shouldered and muscular from hammering all day. His tan face was always slick with sweat and smeared with oil, but Talon had never seen him frown. All he had was smiles and jokes and big, burly laughs. He was pleasant to be around in this sweltering shack with the fire blazing and sparks flying and the oven burning at all hours. Still, Talon wished she could do more than just sit and watch. She wished he would teach her something already.

"What blessing did you grant to the sword?" Talon prodded.

Li smiled at her and then held the sword straight up so she could see as he ran two fingers along the flat of the blade. Light trailed his fingers as they moved, crackling into flames that engulfed the entire sword from hilt to tip.

"I blessed it with fire!" Li roared over the crackling of the great blaze.

Talon had to cover her eyes for a moment. When the fire dimmed, she blinked at Li and exhaled. "That's amazing."

"I thought you'd like that," Li said. He reached for a sheath, burying the sword and its flames all at once. The room immediately felt cooler, much to Talon's relief.

"How did you imbue it?" she asked, gazing at the covered weapon.

Li laughed heartily. "You'll learn soon enough, little bird. Don't rush the process."

The nickname made Talon pause. She had only heard it a few times before, from someone she'd been trying to forget. Without warning, his face flashed in her mind, and she held her breath, suddenly remembering Kotaro's question.

When did you fall for him?

The inquiry had caught her off guard. For some reason, Talon hadn't been expecting Lieutenant Kotaro to pry into her heart and mind, even though she had pried into hers first. When the question rang into the air, tearing through the awkward silence that'd settled, the Grand Chief hadn't been able to come up with an answer. She wasn't even sure there *was* an answer to that question, and she refused to come up with one.

Since arriving back in Babel, Talon made a point to keep herself busy, holding Council meetings, spending time with her siblings, even sketching out blueprints for Wi's reconstruction. She did anything to keep her mind from wandering into places it didn't need to be, focused on thoughts it shouldn't ponder.

It was pointless to entertain any idea surrounding a certain someone—she refused to even speak his name, not even in her own thoughts. She would be gone once Wi was rebuilt. And he would be here in Babel. And that would be it.

For now, Talon simply wanted to focus on her apprenticeship and her chiefdom and her siblings. Cat needed help running the house, Roaring needed help running the village, and Fox needed help in her training. There wasn't much Talon could offer when it came to sundancing, but she could help with this. She wanted to design a weapon for her baby sister, one that was special. Imbued.

51

Fox had wanted to get a spear designed for herself when she'd earned her knot back in Wi. *Maybe I can finally give her that,* Talon mused, watching Li shine the metal sheath for his granddaughter's new sword. No matter what she wanted to give Fox, she would first have to learn from Li, but he seemed intent on making her wait.

"When will you start training me?" Talon asked. "Seriously training me."

Li raised his white eyebrows, his forehead wrinkling. "This *is* serious training."

She sighed. "You know what I mean. I want to make a weapon for my sister—she's entering the Academy, that means she'll need it soon."

"She will have it when she has it," Li said matter-of-factly.

Talon knew she should drop it, but she couldn't stop herself from rising from the stool and marching over to Li. "I've been doing nothing but watching you work—"

"You've only been here a few days. What's the rush?"

"The Academy's entrance exams are in less than a week!"

Li laughed one of his great, rumbly laughs. He sounded like a madman—looked like one, too, with his goggles sitting up on his stark white hair, and his face streaked with black grease and oil. His eyes seemed to shine, despite the gunk on his skin, but his smile was the brightest thing on his entire round face. "The first thing you need to learn about imbue…" he held up a finger. Talon leaned in closely. "Is patience!"

She wanted to scream, but she settled for a very deep, very heavy sigh that seemed to expel the grumbling she felt in her very soul. "Li, I don't have all the time in the world. I don't even have a week—"

He shook his head. "Imbue cannot be rushed. Do you know why there aren't thousands of Hunters and Priests running around with anointed weapons?"

52

Talon paused. She had never thought about it before.

"Imbue isn't a blessing unique to any particular tribe," Li explained. "Anyone can learn to imbue weapons or inanimate objects. But the Kotaros have mastered it over the centuries. But why us? Why doesn't everyone try to use it?"

Talon shrugged, resisting the urge to groan. She knew it didn't matter whether she had the answer or not, Li was going to make his point.

"It's because imbue requires an incredible amount of spiritual energy and grit. It isn't simply whispering into your butter knife to turn it into a razor blade. It's about connecting with your Spirit and with the Spirit of the customer. You have to go before the Throne of Grace and inquire of God when you use imbue. Because it is God who decides the blessing you have the honor of bestowing upon your weapon."

Talon slowly lowered her gaze, chewing her lip in thought. She wouldn't admit she had believed the process would be simple or easy. But she wasn't too proud to acknowledge how amazing it sounded. To be able to ask God for His personal input, to carry out His own request, was more than an honor. It was a precious responsibility she couldn't put into words.

"So," Talon thought aloud, "you didn't choose to give your granddaughter a sword of fire?"

Li smiled. "Now you're getting it. I asked God what *He* wanted to gift my granddaughter with, and fire was what He chose." He held up the sword. "Himari asked for this sword eight months ago. God just now gave me the inspiration for it."

Eight months...

Li's words opened a pit of dread in Talon's stomach. She didn't have eight months to wait for inspiration. She had to come up with a weapon right now. From what Fox had been telling her about training, she wasn't sure she would even survive the entrance exams. This weapon had to be

53

amazing. It had to be able to save Fox's life as well as others.

And it had to be done in less than eight months—less than eight days.

Li seemed to read her thoughts. "God knows what your sister needs, little bird. Trust in His timing as much as His gifts."

Talon let out a long breath. How could she argue against that?

"There's a reason for everything," Li said, wiping his hands on his smock. "Your village was destroyed for a reason. You relocated to Babel for a reason. Your sister enrolled in the Academy for a reason. Her powers awakened for a reason. And you discovered your incredible spiritual energy for a reason." He pulled his goggles from his head and smoothed his hair back. "You are meant to be my apprentice. Because you are meant to help your sister as well as others. So don't disregard any part of this training. Patience might be the toughest lesson to learn, but I promise it's the most important."

Talon nodded, hating how right he was, but thankful for his words, nonetheless. "Is there any way I can train while I'm away from the shop?"

Li rubbed his thick chin. "Using imbue is essentially praying. Work on cultivating your relationship with Christ. Spend time meditating on the Word of God. Take your designs and ideas for this weapon to Him."

That almost sounded too easy, but Talon didn't voice this. She simply smiled and nodded. Besides, it wasn't like she didn't *need* prayer; adding more meditation to her day would be beneficial. Maybe it would help keep her mind focused on the Lord instead of thinking about—

She shook her head, refusing to broach the subject. *There's no point,* Talon told herself yet again. *I don't have the time. And,* she hated to admit, *I'm not even sure if he feels the same.*

Li was in front of her now, holding up the sword and offering a smile. "Let's head home for the day?"

"Oh—uh, y-yes!" Talon stammered, hoping he couldn't see her

blushing in the evening haze.

"I've got to drop off this fancy new weapon to my granddaughter. Are you all right to walk home alone?"

Ever since the Cross went up in flames, Babel had been more than diligent in making its citizens feel safe. There were extra men on patrol, Hunters walking every street, Priests offering prayers day and night. Despite there being an assassin on the loose, Talon had never felt safer in the city.

She nodded at Li. "I'll be fine."

6

Fox Fire

"Gather 'round." Master Jo gripped her staff as she stood in the center of the encircling students. Moneek sat on a heavy rock beside her, watching them closely.

Fox hoped Moneek didn't see her shiver beneath her scrutinizing gaze. Moneek had always been tougher on the students compared to Master Jo, but she'd been particularly hard the last few days. Likely because of the upcoming exams, rushed as they were.

Some days Fox felt like her head was spinning. Between physical and spiritual training, she somehow had to find time for her family, her friends, and now this—actual school lessons from her instructors. They had been doing this lately, spending the last hour of their sessions scribbling notes on various topics. Yesterday had been biblical history, before that was basic mathematics. Fox wondered what today's topic would be as she unrolled her parchment and dipped her pen in the small pot of ink sitting between herself and her older brother.

That was one good thing about all this. Roaring had decided to stay enrolled in the training program. He'd announced his decision during dinner a few nights ago. Fox remembered gasping so loudly she'd nearly sucked a piece of fried chicken down her throat. She hadn't realized how much she'd missed having the Prince of Fire around until he was gone. Even Kohlannis had asked about him, and KI managed a small smile when he saw him step onto the Grounds again.

Speaking of KI...

He still wasn't his normal self, but he'd started opening up over the last few days. Kohl wouldn't give Fox any details on what was happening at the Academy, but he promised her best friend was fine. Well … Fine for a demon possessed kid considered one of the greatest threats to Babel in the last one-hundred years.

Fox sighed, forcing herself to focus on her notes. Master Jo was going on about their possible schedules after the entrance exams.

"Once you pass the exams, you will be an official student at the Academy," she said, tapping her staff into the soft earth. "Master Moneek and I will still be your instructors, but your schooling will include a range of subjects beyond teaching you how to use your blessings or fight demons."

The crowd shifted. No one was pleased to hear about getting homework and other boring assignments.

Master Jo smiled at their frowning faces. "Don't worry, it won't be as insufferable as you might think. You should be happy most of us will be sticking together."

"*Most* of us?" a girl questioned. Her name was Danté of the Shoren Clan, a small girl with a muscular build, like she could fist fight Master Jo and expect to win. She furrowed her brow as she asked, "I thought you just said we'd all be in the same class with you as our instructor if we passed."

Master Jo nodded. "I will remain as your instructor, and you will still be in Class G-Five. *If* you get placed into the Gamma Division."

Whispers of confusion rang through the students, even Kohl shifted, his butt squirming in the grass.

Moneek said, "There are three different divisions within the Academy. The lowest rank is the Gamma Division, then the Beta Division, and finally the Alpha Division. After that is graduation."

"You already know not everyone here is on the same level," Marlo added. "Not necessarily because of the power of their blessing, but because of their *mastery* of it." She paused, which Fox was thankful for because her hands were cramping from trying to jot down every word. She had never heard anything about the details of the structure of the Academy. Her only goal had been to pass the exams, what happened after hadn't been a thought until that very moment.

Master Jo went on, "Passing the exams is one thing. But your performance during the exams, as well as a few other factors, will be taken into consideration when determining which division you will be placed in when your first semester begins."

Fox stole a glance at KI beside her; his head was low, dark hair falling into his face as he scribbled notes in his sloppy handwriting. She wondered if they would be placed in the same division. KI and Kohl had outperformed her in almost every challenge their masters had given them during their time on the Grounds. Fox refused to believe she was the worst student in her class, but she also wasn't confident she would get the same score as her two friends.

What if KI and I are separated after the exams? she wondered silently.

"Don't worry," Master Jo seemed to be reading her thoughts, "nearly ninety percent of passing trainees are placed in the Gamma Division. Chances are, everyone here today will be together again once the exams are over."

"*If* you all pass," Moneek added with an impish grin.

"What other factors will be taken into consideration when judging our performance?" Syren asked. She was a healer from the Danis Tribe who had spent more hours on the Grounds patching up students instead of sparring with them.

"Everything Master Moneek and I have been teaching you these past two months. Your experience in fighting darklings, your knowledge of spiritual energy, and even your maturity as a Christian," Master Jo explained. "We consider how well you work with your fellow classmates, how you handle yourself during training, and even how you respond to criticism. These factors are important because they give everyone a fair chance. That way, trainees with flashier blessings aren't given a free pass just for being born into a more powerful bloodline."

Fox exhaled a breath. That certainly gave her a fighting chance. Someone like Roaring Fire didn't have to worry about the exams or which division he would be placed in. He was powerful; born with a flashy blessing and fortunate enough to have years of experience with it. Fox wasn't like her brother—at least not in terms of skill. But even if she didn't have mastery over her blessing, she knew she had handled herself well during her training, she got along with most of her classmates, and she had experience in fighting darklings. She had killed one all by herself back in Wi.

Amber eyes gazed at KI again. Fox chewed the inside of her cheek. *Even if I'm not the strongest here, there's still a chance we'll be together after all this is over.*

"If we're all placed in the Gamma Division," Syren continued, "how long will we have to wait until we graduate into the Beta Division?"

"Good question," Marlo replied. "Cross Academy is not a normal school by any standards. You won't move on to the next level just because the semester is up at the end of the year. Students graduate into the next division by passing another exam like the one you're about to take."

Fox's mouth fell open. *We'll have to go through all this again?*

"Yes," Master Jo nodded, making Fox gulp in surprise. She hadn't realized she'd spoken aloud. Her ears burned in embarrassment as her master chuckled.

"The Division Exams will be your next goal after making it into the Academy," Marlo said. "But there is a way around the exams."

The students all leaned forward.

"Sometimes students are bumped up a rank based on merit." Master Jo held up her hand, counting off the achievements on her fingers. "If you accomplish a great feat while at the Academy, if you complete an outstanding number of high-ranking missions, or if your master turns in a recommendation that gets approve by the Academic Board. Any of these things could get you an early graduation."

Fox relaxed a little, until a question tickled the back of her head, and she raised her hand. "What is a high-ranking mission?"

"Ahh," Master Moneek smiled. "This is the fun part."

Master Jo nodded. "No matter what division you're in, you will take on missions as members of the Academy student body. Each mission will be assigned a rank to determine its level of difficulty. D class is the lowest, all the way up to A, and then rank S. Our special class missions."

"Obviously off limits to you guys," Moneek teased.

"For your safety, you won't be allowed to take on certain assignments, but you will have no shortage of operations to choose from," Marlo said. "Perhaps the most rewarding part of going on missions is the *reward* itself," she said, earning another few raised hands. She chuckled and began to explain. "You'll all be getting paid for whatever mission you complete."

Fox raised her eyebrows, suddenly ten times more intrigued than she'd been a moment ago. Her family needed the extra coin.

"Taking on a mission isn't something you'll be doing for fun," Master Jo said. "You will be carrying out an assignment directly from the Cross—acting on behalf of the Academy itself. Yes, it is part of your training and education; it will help you master your skills and your spiritual energy. But missions are also a way for us to earn a living." Marlo shrugged. "How else will all the Hunters and Priests take care of themselves? It's not like we have time for a day job."

That's right, Fox remembered. Master Jo was a Priestess. She spent all her time there at the Grounds with her students instead of taking on assignments—or maybe *this* was her mission. Training and cultivating the next generation of great warriors.

"Just like the entrance exams," Marlo said. "There will be a lot of factors taken into consideration when missions are assigned to you. But don't think too deeply about all this just yet. We still have to pass the exams, right?"

The students groaned, earning a laugh from their master.

"Who's ready for tomorrow?" she asked in a more serious tone.

Fox stiffened. She could hardly believe the exams were happening in less than twenty-four hours.

"Don't worry, my pupils," Marlo assured them. "I know a lot has happened in the last week or so. Things we didn't see coming. Events we can't even explain. But we're here now and all we can do is move forward." She pounded her staff into the earth, the sound of it echoed through the Grounds. "You are ready. Each and every one of you. I have great faith you will all pass these exams. I can't give you details on what the exam will be like, but I can tell you that it won't be anything you cannot handle." She looked at them seriously, really looked at them—taking a moment to make eye contact with every single student. Fox shivered under her gaze, but the chill in her spine turned into a burning curiosity when she noticed Master Jo's gaze linger on her brother.

Fox glanced up at him, but he kept his vision forward.

The sound of Master Jo's staff hammering the earth snatched her back to attention. Marlo was standing ramrod straight, her muscular arms flexing as she clutched the handle of her weapon. Her dreadlocks were swept up in a heavy-looking ponytail, pouring over her shoulders and gently thumping against her back as the breeze picked them up. Her eyes seemed aglow in the sunlight.

"Remember your training," she said sternly. "You *can* make a difference in this world. It starts with this exam."

As Fox packed her things to leave, she felt a tap on her shoulder and turned to find Montell smirking at her. She hoped he didn't see her wince as she gazed at him. Montell hadn't been unkind to her, but he had been weird. He'd kept his blessing a secret—an ability to copy the gifts of anyone he touched. The secrecy itself wasn't what was so suspicious, it was that his gift seemed to be the perfect set of skills for pulling off a kidnapping. Just like the Red Face.

Fox wasn't fully convinced Montell was the man behind the mask, but she couldn't shake her suspicion.

"What's up, Monty?" she asked, tucking her parchment under her arm. KI and Kohl stood beside her as they listened in—Roaring stepped away to speak with Master Jo. If the Lin brothers weren't standing right in front of her, Fox would have followed her brother to tease him about whatever was going on between the two of them. But she was trapped.

Vinny raised his eyebrow as he scanned her from head to toe. The look on his face made her squirm. "Hey, pretty girl."

"What do you want?" Kohl clipped. Fox couldn't help but notice he kept a safe distance from Vin. The Lin Clan had the power to adjust the weight of whatever they touched. Last time Kohl and Vin were face to face, Vin added fifty pounds to his t-shirt and wouldn't remove it. Montell had come to the rescue instead.

Vinny held up his hands like he had no idea why Kohl was being so hostile. "We just came to talk."

"Then talk," Kohl grunted. His voice was so loud other students blinked over at them.

Vinny narrowed his eyes. "We came to invite you guys to hang out later this evening."

Fox stared at them. "You're kidding, right?"

"Why on Earth would we hang out with either of you?" Kohl spat. Even KI had folded his arms.

Vinny sighed. "I know we haven't been the closest of friends—"

"We aren't friends at all!"

At this point, Fox felt the need to step in just in case Kohl lost it and started swinging. Thankfully, Montell was thinking the same thing, but before either of them could utter a word, Terra ran over and draped an arm over Monty's shoulder. She grinned as she waved at the three friends. "Are you guys coming to the party?"

"Party?" Fox repeated dumbly, like she'd never heard of it before.

Terra nodded, red hair falling everywhere. "Wunda is throwing a party at her parents' lake house—"

"The Cyrusons are totally loaded." Montell grinned, gazing off at nothing, like he was fantasizing about being rich.

"Everyone is going," Terra said.

"Why would we want to party at a lake with you guys?" Kohl practically barked. He was loud enough for Wunda to hear; the large girl walked over with an amused grin on her face, round hips swaying as she marched.

"Because some of us want to celebrate each other before we take the exams," she explained. "No one is guaranteed to pass. This might be our last night together as classmates."

"Don't you want to enjoy yourself before I run circles around you

63

all?" Terra teased.

Wunda rolled her eyes. "Your super speed will only get you so far."

The redhead snorted, looking heavy Wunda up and down. "You could never catch up to me."

Fox pressed her lips together as an awkward silence rolled over them. Vinny snorted, like he was trying to hold back a laugh. His attempt to hush himself only made the situation worse. They all knew what Terra had truly meant by her comment. It was obvious just from looking at the girls that Wunda wasn't built for speed. She was heavyset and full-bodied. Thick arms, strong legs, full breasts, pudge in her belly. Terra was a skinny little thing who could run faster than the speed of light. They were totally unmatched.

As if to demonstrate this, Terra took off running, going in circles around the group—kicking up dust as she ran. Somehow, Wunda seemed unfazed by neither the remark nor the dust clouding around them. She very calmly folded her arms and pressed her bare foot into the earth.

Fox watched as the grass around them withered and the dirt turned into soft mud at her command. Just as Terra rounded them again, she slipped on the mud and went skidding across the field.

Everyone laughed.

Wunda marched over to her. "I don't have to get faster to catch up to you," she said confidently. She came to a stop right before the girl, hands on her heavy hips as she stared down at her. "I just have to slow you down."

For a second, Fox thought a fight would break out between them. But they surprised her by bursting into laughter as Wunda extended a hand and helped Terra to her feet.

"Good one," the redhead mumbled, adjusting her crooked goggles.

"I keep warning your skinny butt not to mess with me." Wunda

64

bumped her shoulder as they walked off.

"So, are you guys coming or what?" Vinny waved his hand in front of Fox's face. she blinked, realizing everyone was staring at her. Waiting for an answer. Even Kohl was quiet now, trying not to look at her for too long. Pretending he didn't care whether she went or stayed home.

"Think on it," Montell offered with a wink. "If you decide to come, bring a dish to share."

"A dish?" Kohl's anger was back. "If the Cyrusons are so loaded, why can't Wunda provide all the food for the party?"

Vinny cackled so hard he doubled over to hold his stomach.

"Because her parents don't know she's throwing this party, duh," Montell laughed lightly.

"Why am I surprised by your stupidity?" Vinny said.

Kohl took a step forward, which wasn't as intimidating as he thought it was because he was like six feet away, so he only moved a few inches closer. "Who are you calling stupid?" he dared.

Vinny was not afraid of him. "I'm calling you sheltered geeks stupid. Haven't any of you ever been to a party before?"

Montell patted his brother's shoulder, subtly trying to tell him to chill out. "KI and Kohl live at the Academy. And Fox isn't from here," he tried to explain.

Fox wanted to tell them that she'd been to plenty of parties before. She was a chiefana. She had to attend great ceremonies and celebrations on behalf of her Tribesmen all the time. There was always music and dancing and wild boar roasting on a spit. Sometimes the Hunting Regiment would perform a routine for the crowd—once, Fox had to dance before the entire village Council to present herself at her thirteenth birthday. It was a celebration of her womanhood, announcing to the rest of the village that her parents had now considered her eligible for courtship.

Somehow … the parties she'd attended in Wi didn't seem like the sort of party they were throwing by the lake. Wunda's parents didn't even know she was doing it.

It felt sort of wrong to sneak off to the woods and hang out—why couldn't they just hang out here? During the daytime? Better yet, why couldn't they just go home and get a good night of sleep?

There was no way Fox could voice any of her concerns. Vinny had already called her a geek. And said she was sheltered. She gazed at Kohl and KI, both of them were silent—queer looks on their faces like they had no idea how to respond to the Lin brothers' jeering. At least she wasn't alone in her sheltered geekiness.

"I'll be there," Fox told Montell.

A grin split his face, meanwhile, Vinny stared at her with his mouth open like he hadn't expected her to say that. "You're actually coming?" he asked.

She nodded. "Yeah. All three of us are coming."

Kohl glared down at her, but she refused to look at him, letting his sharp blue eyes burn holes into the side of her face. "And we'll bring a dish, too."

"I ain't bringing squat." Kohl crossed his arms.

"I'll bring enough to make up for their missing food," Fox quickly said before Vinny could sneer something nasty.

The Lin brothers both put their hands on their hips at the same time. It was almost weird to watch. Fox had to remind herself who was who as they gave her matching expressions. Both boys were laughably short, but Montell was slightly taller than Vinny, despite being the younger twin. And Vinny had a little beauty mark on his left cheek, right above the dimple that never seemed to go away. Because he was always smirking.

"Well," they said in unison. "See you guys tonight."

Montell stayed a moment longer as Vinny turned to leave, his eyes glued to Fox's. "We're meeting here right before sunset. Wunda's taking us all to the lake house together."

"Right before sunset," she repeated with a nod.

He winked and walked off.

"I cannot believe you agreed to go to that stupid party." Kohl's eyes seared into Montell's backside as he watched him leave.

"You don't have to go," Fox told him.

"And leave you alone with the Lin brothers?" He grunted something under his breath.

"They're not a threat."

"They won't beat you up. But they'll…" he paused, glancing down at her as his eyes roved her frame.

"They'll what?" Fox asked.

He couldn't speak properly anymore. "T-They'll try t-to…" His cheeks suddenly turned red. Blaringly red.

Fox frowned. "You okay?"

"I'm *fine*!" he nearly shouted. Then he turned on his heel and stormed off, literally stomping his feet as he marched away.

"I don't get it," Fox mumbled. She looked at KI. "You're coming, right?"

For the first time in what seemed like a really long time, he smiled at her. "I'll be there, Foxy."

7

Fox Fire

Fox stared at her clothes all set out on her bed. She had two uniforms for training, three skirts, four blouses, and a pair of Roaring's old trousers that were way too big for her. She'd been meaning to ask Cat to take them in and use the leftover material to make a nice headscarf for herself.

She chewed the inside of her cheek, glancing at her shoes. There were only two options; her white training shoes or a pair of horrible shoes Cat had picked out for her. They were pale pink with a low heel and a strap that buckled at the ankle. Fox hated those shoes. Not only were they noisy, but they hurt her feet and made her toes feel like they were on fire. But she couldn't go to the party in her *training* shoes.

A very exasperated sigh blew from Fox's lips as she reached for one of the skirts and grabbed a blouse. This would have to do.

She fought her kinky coils into something that looked *cute enough*— parted to the side and decorated with a butterfly pin she'd stolen from Cat's collection. Her sister had a million accessories; she wouldn't miss this one.

When she finished dressing, Fox stepped back and stared at her polished mirror, standing on her tiptoes to see her waistline.

"I should tuck in my blouse," she muttered, stuffing the yellow shirt into the hem of her scarlet skirt. It came down to just above her knees, leaving enough of her legs out for her to feel daring but hiding enough for Talon not to raise questions about her attire. *I'm sixteen*, she told herself, *I can wear a short skirt sometimes*. Fox rolled her eyes. She had never—not a single time—cared about the length of her skirt.

Tiptoeing, she walked through the apartment while holding her breath, somehow feeling like if she breathed too loudly her siblings would realize she was going to a party and forbid her from leaving. There was no point in all her precaution, really, she could hear Cat's voice in the kitchen before she even rounded the corner.

All three of her older siblings stood hovered over a pot of something on the stove. "It needs salt," Roaring was saying.

Cat shook her head. "It tastes fine as it is."

"I'm the one who made it, I know my dish better than any of you."

Talon giggled. "When did Roaring learn how to cook?"

"Cat's been teaching me"

"Sure has," she said proudly. "I don't care if you're the *man of the house*—you got a stomach, you should know how to fill it."

Talon nodded, then high-fived her little sister. "You tell him, girl."

Roaring groaned and turned away from the stove, eyes widening as he caught Fox tiptoeing across the kitchen. "Where are you going, little paws?"

She sighed, shoulders sagging. "I was, uh, heading out."

Now her sisters turned around, Talon with her hands on her hips, Cat with a big, wooden spoon grasped in her slender fingers. All three of them raised one eyebrow each.

"Heading where?" Talon said.

She didn't want to say *to a party at a lake house*, but she also didn't want to lie.

69

"I'm going to hang out with KI."

Roaring tilted his head to the side. "The Academy's letting him go out?"

"It's almost dark out," Talon said.

"And dinner is almost ready," Cat reminded her. "I made gumbo."

"I know." Fox palmed the back of her neck. "The class is having a get together before the exams. And I wanted to go."

Cat let out a cackle of a laugh, dropping her spoon onto the counter. "I cannot believe this."

"Believe what?" Roaring asked.

"A get together in the evening with all your classmates." Cat snorted. "Fox is going to a *party*."

Talon gasped so loudly Fox thought she'd hurt herself for a moment. She had her hand clasped over her mouth, eyes all big and bulgy. "A *party*," she repeated, horror mottling her face.

"Yes," Fox rolled her eyes, "a party—not a brothel. It's not a big deal. Sheesh."

"I think it is a big deal when a group of unsupervised teenagers get together at night," Talon argued.

Fox grunted. "*You're* a teenager, too!"

All of them were. Roaring was the oldest at nineteen and each sister was an additional year younger. Talon at eighteen, Cat at seventeen, and Fox Fire at sixteen.

"Yes," Talon admitted, "but we're different."

"Why wasn't *I* invited to this party?" Roaring folded his arms, a dejected look on his face.

"Because you're old," Cat teased.

"I'm *three* years older than Fox."

"There is a big difference between a sixteen-year-old and a nineteen-year-old," Cat said plainly.

70

Fox couldn't argue with that. A week ago, Roaring was the acting Grand Chief of Wi. Now he was whining about not being invited to a party with a bunch of fifteen and sixteen-year-olds.

Talon shook her head. "I'm still not comfortable with this."

"I have no idea what's going to happen after the exams," Fox pleaded. "This could be my last night *alive*. I want to spend it with my friends."

Cat frowned. "I'm going to choose to *not* be offended by the fact that you'd rather spend your last night alive with your friends instead of your family. Insults aside," she looked over at Talon, "I think we should let her go."

Fox smiled.

"As long as Roaring goes with her," her older sister added, wiping that smile away.

"*Roaring?*" she whined. "But he's—"

"I'm what?" His brows were knit together; the thick skin of his forehead wrinkled.

"Uncool," Cat snorted when Fox didn't answer.

He rolled his eyes and marched down the hall toward his room.

"Make sure you don't do anything irresponsible," Talon warned.

"I won't."

Cat walked over with a crooked grin on her face. "I bet those little murderers know how to party."

"They're trainees, not murderers."

"If they pass the exams, they'll be murdering darklings soon enough."

Murdering. Fox had never thought of it that way. And even if she had, there was nothing wrong with slaying demons. Killing them was the only way to stop the evil from spreading.

An image of KI popped into her head. Fox fought the sudden urge to cry.

He had a demon sealed inside of him. And the Academy wasn't equipped to remove it just yet. What if they *never* removed it? What if the demon inside him took over his mind and body? Would Fox have to slay him the same way she'd killed the demon bear in the forest? Or how Roaring had tried to kill the silver-haired warrior?

She shook her head, not wanting to think of such things right now.

Roaring came from his room wearing a pair of dark slacks and a shirt he didn't bother to button. Fox could see the tribal tattoos decorating his chest and shoulders as he walked to the door. "Ready?"

She nodded.

"Be back before sunrise," Talon said, voice high and panicky. "You're going to need a good night of sleep for the exams tomorrow!"

Fox grunted something in reply and walked out the apartment. Men in construction suits walked through the streets, stopping to light the tall lanterns dotting the neighborhood. Fox took a breath as she picked up her pace. They were supposed to meet just before sunset.

"Fox?" her brother called.

She glanced up at him. "Hmm?"

"I asked what's up."

"Oh, nothing. Why?"

He made a face that let her know he didn't believe her. "What's really happening at this party?"

"It's just some kids enjoying our last night together," she mumbled. Then she sighed. Roaring was going to the party with her, might as well be honest. "Wunda is throwing a party at her parents' lake house. Her folks don't know she's doing it, so we have to bring our own food."

He laughed. "Sounds like induction nights for the Regiment."

"I don't understand."

Roaring took a deep breath and when he exhaled, Fox caught the burning smell of smoke in the air. Her brother always smelled like smoke

72

or charcoal or ash.

"Whenever someone was inducted into the Hunting Regiment, we would throw a small celebration beyond the Walls." He smiled like he was recalling a fond memory, full lips stretching into a grin. Then he closed his eyes and let out a laugh, his deep voice filling the night.

"One night, we lit a bonfire so big, it actually attracted darklings. They were just small ones who smelled the roasted meat. Still," he laughed again, "we had to drop everything and start fighting to save our ribs. It was the most hilarious thing I'd ever witnessed."

Fox smiled. "I hope we can make memories like that with our classmates."

"Hopefully we aren't bombarded by demons at the lake house."

"Now," Fox said carefully, "what's really happening with you and the Academy?"

The joyful smile her brother had been wearing seemed to grow sour on his face.

"I thought you were adamant on going back to Wi," she said. "*Rise again.*"

He sighed at the words. "I still have every intention of getting back home—"

"Then why are you taking the exams?"

Becoming an official student at Cross Academy would keep him in Babel much longer than he'd ever wanted to be there.

Roaring bunched his broad shoulders. "Things are complicated, Fox. More than you know." After a few moments of tense silence, he added, "I'm taking the exams so I can be there for you."

Be there for me?

Roaring turned and walked to a cart with an old man selling biscuits and hushpuppies with different toppings. He bought a dozen of each and got gravy and sweet jam to spread on them. Fox watched, mouth

73

watering as the smell of sweet bread filled her nostrils.

Roaring smiled. "Couldn't let you show up to the party emptyhanded, right?"

"You say that as if you aren't going."

He pressed his lips together, staring down the road. "I'm going to walk around for a bit and then return home."

"You seemed so disappointed earlier. Now you're voluntarily staying home?"

He shrugged. "I'd honestly rather sleep tonight. But it would have been nice to be invited."

Fox smiled. "What will you tell our sisters?"

"That I got tired."

"So, this is it?"

Roaring passed her the sack of biscuits and hushpuppies. "Be back before sunrise."

She rolled her eyes as he lightly punched her shoulder, turning to watch him walk back toward their apartment. It took her another ten minutes of walking before the Academy Grounds came into view. Fox could see the crowd of students waiting beside one of the sparring rings. Anxiety swelled within her, churning into a swirl of excitement when she caught a glimpse of KI and Kohl. Montell appeared in the front of the crowd; he waved at her when his gaze landed on her figure.

"It's about time you showed up," he said once she'd gotten nearer. "We were just about to head out without you."

"No, they weren't." Kohl rolled his eyes. "Montell was just saying they should have the party here."

Fox laughed nervously, shoving the food at Monty. "I hope the snacks make up for it."

He took the bag and sniffed, his eyes twinkling with intrigue, then he opened it and pulled out a biscuit. "My favorite," he said, cramming half of it into his mouth.

Fox snorted out a laugh and then glanced over at her friends, her eyes scanning them from head to toe. She had grown up with KI, seeing him in tunics and pants and shorts all the time, but it was weird to see Kohl outside his Academy uniform. He had on a dark shirt and beige slacks, the colors made his pale skin seem warmer in the glow of the setting sun.

He quirked an eyebrow at her staring. "Need something?"

She blushed madly. "I was just wondering why you didn't bring any food to pass around."

Montell groaned beside them. "They said they couldn't bring anything."

"We were more focused on getting out of the Academy," Kohl insisted. "It was hard enough. Thank God Lieutenant Diaz was there to help us out."

Fox perked up at the sound of his name. He was the Hunter who'd united her with KI and had helped her enter the Academy in the first place. She wasn't surprised to learn he was still looking after her friend in some small way.

Montell elbowed Kohlannis. "You and KI are on cooking duty since you didn't bring any food."

Fox traced his gaze to the sacks of meat and other goodies being dragged away by her classmates. She fell in line with them, everyone following Wunda into the woods beyond the Grounds.

"I don't feel like cooking," Kohl said, annoyed.

"Then you should have brought a snack like Fox Fire." Montell tore into another biscuit and then held his fist out toward Fox. "These things are the best."

Fox fist-bumped him without even thinking. And then she swallowed, eyes going wide. He had touched her. Again. She couldn't figure out whether he'd done it on purpose; maybe it was a harmless, friendly gesture, or maybe it had been planned.

Images of the burning cross flashed in Fox's head. The Tower had been engulfed in flames—flames produced by someone with the power to manipulate fire. That fact had never been far from Fox's mind, though she had tried to avoid it as much as she could. Whenever she felt the heat of the truth, she couldn't stop the theories from crashing through her.

Montell Lin. It had to be him. There was no one else in Babel who could use the power of the flame besides Roaring and Fox. Montell wasn't a sundancer—he was something worse. Someone with a blessing he called *Mirror*. He'd touched Fox once before and had used her fire to scorch an entire nest of feeder demons.

Did he also use my fire to torch the Academy? Fox ground her teeth together, tripping over a small rock as she marched through the woods. A strong hand steadied her, and she glanced up to meet KI's hazel gaze. He was smiling at her, perfectly round eyes full of a warmth she had missed so much it made her heart ache.

Then, as quickly as his eyes had landed on her, they were suddenly shifting away. Montell had said something witty, stealing KI's attention. The fourteen-year-old surrendered another rare grin and said something back. The boys laughed together. Fox hadn't heard KI laugh since before the Tower burned. It seemed his joy and happiness had gone up in the blaze, too. He hadn't been the same since the assassin had showed up. And he likely wouldn't be the same until the assassin was apprehended and all this was behind them.

Who is the Red Face? Fox questioned, keeping pace with her classmates. They walked through a small strawberry patch and passed over a little bridge with a tiny creek flowing underneath. Wunda winked back at her peers as she pushed through the trees. A collective gasp rippled through the trainees when the Cyruson lake house appeared before them.

A giant cabin surrounded by lush greens and vibrant summer flowers waited for the students. The sun had finished setting, welcoming the fireflies and the glow bugs to usher in the night in all its glory. Fox could hear the singing of the silver doves and the gentle splashing of gulper frogs as they leapt from lily pad to lily pad.

The cabin was big enough to comfortably hold all the students, but they preferred to set up outside beside the lake. There was a firepit and thick slabs of wood surrounding it for the trainees to sit by. Wunda brought out a table and supplies from her family's kitchen. With a grand smile, she passed the tools to Kohl and KI to get started on cooking. The boys groaned as they got to work.

Terra, Andor, and Danté hung lanterns through the campsite as they chatted and exchanged jokes. Meanwhile, Vyanna Farron and her twin cousins used seadancing to retrieve fresh fish from the lake. Vy ignored Dart's flirtatious advances as he collected firewood in his strong arms. Slaine helped, silently carrying the wood, and dropping the logs into the firepit.

Dart wiped sweat from his brow. "You're up, Fox!"

She blinked, stunned to hear his request for her help. "I'm up?" she dumbly repeated.

He let out a hearty laugh, barrel chest swelling with joy. "Who else is going to light the fire for us, Miss Sundancer?"

Her blood ran cold. She still couldn't produce her own flames. She could feel the heat growing and churning inside her. Could hold and manipulate an existing flame. Could even produce sparks when she concentrated hard enough. Ever since she'd shifted her focus to nurturing her Spirit instead of her blessing, she had been able to produce little flickers of heat. Feeding her Spirit had changed everything. The stronger her faith, the stronger her blessing. Not the other way around.

But she still wasn't strong enough to light the firepit—maybe a candle, but certainly not the campfire Dart was expecting her to start. He was still watching her, a dark eyebrow raised, and his arms folded over his chest. Expectant.

"Well?"

"Well … uh—actually," Fox began, but Montell cut her off.

"I can start it!" he said excitedly. Before Dart could question him, he knelt and stuck his hand into the pit. Sparks crackled, followed by the acrid smell of burning wood and smoke, then the whole thing went up in a blaze so large, both boys stumbled back to avoid getting scorched.

The other trainees cried out in surprise, but their fear was quickly replaced with excitement and their cries turned to cheers. "Nice one!" Dart slapped Montell on the back, a huge grin on his face. He'd been in the cave back when Monty had first used his mirror ability, he shouldn't have been as impressed as he was, but the air was stirring with exhilaration. Even Fox was grinning.

"Come light the lanterns for us!" Danté called, waving Montell over.

With a sheepish smile, he shrugged at Fox and tipped an invisible hat at her. "Duty calls."

"They're going to work my brother to death," Vinny said, stepping beside her. He was eating the last of the hushpuppies she'd brought to share.

Fox frowned at him. "You should be helping."

"I don't have his blessing." His voice was as flat as his lowered eyebrows, almost forming a black line straight across his forehead. Fox couldn't tell if he was jealous or not.

His shoulders moved, lazily shifting up then down in a slow shrug. "I'm as useless as you are right now."

"I'm not useless," Fox grumbled.

He snorted, spraying hushpuppy crumbs into the air. "A sundancer

78

who can't dance. Sounds useless to me."

"Goodbye, Vinny," Fox said, marching away, but his hand was on her wrist, turning her back around.

"Wait," he said quickly. "Don't go. I didn't mean to—"

"To what?" she snapped, whirling back around. "To be a jerk?"

His face was somber, like he'd just now realized how insulting his words were. "Fox—"

She twisted her wrist away. "I don't care about your fake apology." Then she walked off without looking back.

Wunda and the rest of the girls were standing in a circle around KI and Kohl as they prepared dinner. KI was busy juicing fresh fruit to make into drinks that would be served in cups made of frozen water—courtesy of Vyanna and the Ool twins. Meanwhile, Kohl was descaling the fish and prepping the boar's ribs to grill over the open fire, along with skewers of vegetables to roast.

Kressa Lion's eyes danced with stars as she watched Kohl chop the veggies. Fox couldn't help but notice her eyes were mostly focused on his arms—his muscles flexing as he worked the knife.

"Wow," Kressa said, voice high and girly. "You're so good at cooking."

"My mother is a baker," he grunted. "But she taught me how to cook other things, too."

Kressa let out a dreamy sigh. "I can't believe how good you are."

"I can't believe how *bad* all of you are. How do you take care of yourselves?" His words seemed to criticize, but Fox caught the hint of a smile tugging at the corner of his mouth.

Kressa caught it too. She leaned forward and bit her lip, eyes locked with Kohl's. "Maybe I'm just looking for someone else to take care of me."

Time seemed to still as Fox realized what was happening right in front of her. Kressa was flirting with Kohl. And, from the way he smirked at her and let out a husky laugh, he was flirting right back. With effort, Fox stifled the annoyed groan that threatened to give away her jealousy.

Wait, she frowned, *I'm not jealous. I don't care who Kohl flirts with. Besides*, she glanced at KI who was busy squeezing lemons for lemonade. When he finished, he wiped his hands on his shirt, it clung to his form, sticky from fruit juice and sweat. Fox could just make out his figure beneath the thin fabric.

She gulped, trying to remember whatever point she had wanted to make.

"All right, love birds," Wunda said loudly. Her words seemed to jolt Kressa and Kohl from whatever shared dream they were having over the chopped vegetables. "Let's get this meat over the fire so we can start eating soon!"

Cheers of agreement went off through the classmates as Wunda and Kohl moved the meat to the flames. When they were done, KI passed out drinks, handing a 'special' iced glass of juice to Fox Fire.

"Sit with me?" he asked, his voice kind and almost pleading.

She nodded, following him to a small clearing beside a tree. She wasn't surprised when Kohl ambled over and plopped into the dirt, a cup of iced water in his hand.

"No juice for you?" KI said with a laugh.

He shook his head, wiped sweat from his brow. "Being near that fire dried me out."

Or maybe flirting with Kressa drained you, Fox thought. Disappointment flooded her as she realized what'd just poured into her mind. When did she start caring about who Kohl flirted with?

She stole a glance at him, gulping from his ice cup, head tilted back, throat bobbing. A drop of water dribbled from the cup, trailing down his chin and dripping onto his collarbone.

Fox's mouth went dry.

No, she shook her head. *It isn't that I care who he flirts with, it's that he's flirting at all.*

Kohl had been so distant and cold since the day she'd met him. He'd kept to himself, blocking out everyone except KI. Because everyone except KI had mistreated him for who he was. A member of the Hunger Tribe.

But now he was glancing back to wink at Kressa and watch her sway her hips to the beat of the drums Toad Ool was playing. At Terra's request, Wunda had brought out instruments for music—apparently, the redhead was quite good with a flute in her hands and the Ool twins weren't half bad at the drum and fiddle.

Kohl is getting along with everyone. Things were changing. Perhaps because this was their last night together as classmates, maybe even their last night alive, but things were different, nonetheless. Students had even been kind to KI, smiling as he'd passed them drinks, making jokes about him opening a shop if he didn't make it into the Academy.

For a moment, Fox had caught a glimpse of how different things might have been if their peers had set their differences aside months ago instead of just the night before their exam. How much easier would her training have been if she'd had more friends to support her? How much easier would things have been for KI and Kohl?

Fox's tense shoulders relaxed as she lifted her ice cup to her lips. The juice was sweet and fruity with a hint of mint underneath. A still sense of joy unfolded over her, smothering the dark jealousy that'd threatened to rise earlier. She wouldn't resent Kohl for enjoying this night. And she wouldn't allow any bitterness to swell over his flirtatious attitude. This was their last night together before the rest of their lives changed. She would do nothing but enjoy herself.

81

KI was looking at her, his eyes squinted as he watched her sip her drink. "You like it?" he asked shyly.

Fox nodded. "I love it, actually."

He smiled, then dropped his gaze to his own cup. "Um … I know I haven't been myself lately, guys."

Kohl seemed to pay attention now, finally able to pull his eyes from Kressa and her sensuous performance as she swayed and moved her body to the music played by Toad, Ren, and Terra. Danté and Syren had joined her, dancing by the fire while Montell shamelessly watched and turned the meat over the flames. Slaine grumbled in a corner with his arms folded over his chest. Dart, Vinny, and a boy named Wend joined the girls in their dancing—Fox had no clue what Wend's blessing was, but she had seen him on the Grounds plenty of times.

At the lake, Vyanna froze half the water and made literal ice skates for herself and three other students by dancing the water into sharp blades attached to the bottoms of their shoes. They skated over the ice together with smiles on their faces, meanwhile, Wunda used her earth-dancing to erect an earthen slide that climbed twenty feet into the air. She used mud to make the slide slippery and was the first one to go down, screaming as she cannonballed into the thawed portion of the lake. Andor was next, glowing like a light and illuminating the water so it looked like it was set aflame.

"Don't worry about it," Kohl said, lazily leaning back to sneak another glance at Kressa. "You've been through a lot."

KI shook his head and set his cup down in the dirt. "This is serious."

"What do you mean?" Fox asked.

"After the Tower burned, I was taken to a trial," KI explained. His voice was harried and higher than normal, his hazel eyes were wide and filled with fear. "I'm not supposed to say anything," he said. "So don't ask questions. But … at the trial, I learned something about the entrance exams. Something that could change everything."

Fox set her cup down now, Roaring's words ringing in her ears.

I'm taking the exams so I can be there for you.

The hairs on the back of her neck rose. She believed every word her friend had said. As if they had placed the pieces of a puzzle together, things seemed to click. Roaring's cryptic warning. KI's strange behavior. And now his odd word of caution.

A storm was brewing, and the Academy was now at the center of it.

"Something is going to happen tomorrow," KI said. "Something big. Something the Academy knows about. And they're going to let it happen." He took a shaky breath and then pulled a small knife from his pocket. Fox reared back, momentarily stunned, but her nerves calmed as he slit his finger and held it out. "Let's make a pact. Right here. Right now."

Kohl watched him, eyes half-lidded, blonde locks ruffling as the night breeze danced over his shoulders. Slowly, he reached for the blade. "What are we making this pact for?"

"Friendship," KI immediately answered. "We've always trained together. But the exam is designed to test us as individuals." He glared at his bleeding finger. "But no matter what happens. No matter how things turn out, let's make a pact that we will stick together and have each other's backs."

"Not just at the exams," Fox said, taking the knife from Kohl. He'd silently slit his finger and had been sucking the blood while he waited. "Let's stick together forever," Fox proposed. "Let's *always* be there for each other."

With matching grins, KI and Kohl extended their hands, the tips of their fingers smeared with blood. "It's a deal."

To finalize the pact, they painted a streak of blood across their palms and then shook hands, mixing the crimson liquid together. Binding them in blood.

Kohl wiped his hand on his pants and stood, a red smear going down his trousers. "Now, let's go have some fun."

Part II

8

Fox Fire

Towering trees stood up so high, Fox couldn't see the tops through the canopy of rich green leaves. The forest before her was massive—not just in how far it stretched—the trees, the branches reaching out from the trunks, the leaves that clung to the jagged bark, the bushes on the forest floor, even the bugs were huge. Fox was sure the tree branches were wide enough for her, Kohl, and KI to lie side by side on. She stared with her head tilted back and her mouth slightly parted until Kohlannis nudged her.

"You look like an outsider."

She wrinkled her brow. "Have you been here?"

The flicker in his eyes was the only sign the question bothered him. Of course he'd never been here before. They were outside the city now, in a forest owned by the Academy for training or examination, but that didn't matter. Kohl was a member of the Hunger Tribe, that meant he wasn't allowed beyond the gates of Babel—not even to a facility operated and monitored by them. The Academy had made an exception for him since he'd been allowed to join the training program. If he passed, they would be making many more exceptions. At least that's what Fox hoped.

Kohl looked away and then grunted, "No. But I've heard of it. It's called the Kanen Forest."

The name sounded familiar.

Fox gasped as she remembered where she'd heard it from. In the Book of Numbers, when God led the Israelites through the wilderness, He brought them to a land lush with green gardens and flowing with milk and honey, as promised. But there was already a population living there. Moses sent spies ahead to scout out the land; when they returned, they reported the inhabitants were *giants*. When the spies looked up and beheld the giants, they felt like grasshoppers.

The name of that land was Canaan.

Fox resisted the urge to tilt her head back and stare up at the massive trees of the Kanen Forest, but she didn't have to look up to feel so small. Even the bushes rustling in the breeze around her were enormous, like you could hide your horse and your cart inside it.

"That's where we're going to fight for our lives?" KI asked, stepping beside them both. He had been surprisingly talkative this morning, but Fox wasn't complaining. Ever since making their pact the previous night, he seemed to be in a better mood. Even when they had met before sunrise at the Academy Grounds to ride in wagons out to the forest. Most of the other students were silent and grumpy from the early hour, but KI had been pleasant and joyful, like they weren't about to look death in the face.

"That's where we're going to prove ourselves," Roaring corrected. He was standing beside KI, staring into the dense forest like the rest of them. "No matter what happens, make sure you all look after each other."

"Make sure we all *pass*," Kohl said with an attitude.

Fox swallowed her gut instinct to remind him that he'd made a pact to stick together just last night. Roaring hadn't been there for the pact;

87

he had no idea that she'd bound herself to her friends in blood. At the time, Fox hadn't thought much about it. Her sole focus was to keep KI safe and somehow keep up with Kohl. But now that she was standing beside her older brother, she wondered if she'd been hasty. And she wondered what Roaring would think of her promise to her friends.

"You think you won't need help out there?" her brother asked.

Kohl thought a moment and then casually shrugged one shoulder. "Don't know."

"It doesn't matter if he needs help," KI said. "We're sticking together no matter what."

That made Fox smile, but the look Kohl tossed over his shoulder wiped that smile away. He was staring at Kressa Lion, watching her saunter over to her friends who stood a few meters away. They were surrounded by students on all sides; with nearly a thousand trainees taking the exams, the Academy divided them into clusters of one-hundred, and then divided those clusters into classes of twenty. Each gate held one cluster, which left Fox and her classmates standing before Gate G with classes one through five.

Yet ... somehow—*somehow*—in a sea of a hundred different trainees, Kohlannis found Kressa.

He was staring so hard, Fox had to jab him in the ribs to get his attention. "*What?*" he snapped, cradling his side. "What was that for?"

"For being so desperate," KI teased.

Roaring crossed his large arms, a deep, hearty chuckle rumbling from his broad chest before he said, "Looks like my man has a crush."

Fox couldn't believe her eyes. Kohl was blushing—*blushing!* Turning red and glancing away from Kressa like he was a swooning little girl.

"I don't have a crush," he said.

"You have something worse," KI snorted.

Kohl glared at him, but Master Jo started speaking and whatever response he'd had died in his throat.

"Class G-Five, to me," Marlo said to her students. "Gather 'round."

As the trainees lined up in two rows, Moneek walked down the lines and passed them each a sack. Fox waited until she saw someone else open theirs before she dug into her own.

Two dried fish.

A skin of water.

A dagger.

And a small, silver bell—the kind Cat had purchased from the market and tied around Chava's collar. Fox held it up and listened to its high-pitched jingle. *What do we need this for?*

"Hold on to the items we have given you," Master Jo said. "They will help you along the way."

"The way to where?" Danté asked without raising her hand.

"Somewhere in the Kanen Forest is a placed called the Great Temple," Marlo began, "it is your duty to make it there."

"That's it?" Danté asked. "We just find the Great Temple and we pass the exam?"

"Not exactly," Marlo said. "The Great Temple is a three-day hike from where we are standing. You will have five days to make it there."

Fox would have rejoiced at the two extra days, but she knew better than to be fooled. The Academy wouldn't hand them extra days unless the trainees would absolutely need them.

"When you make it to the Temple, you will not be allowed to enter unless you pay a fee. But the fee is not a coin or a sacrifice or a prayer." Master Jo smiled at them, but it was Dart who spoke up, putting the pieces together before the rest of his classmates.

"It's our bells," he announced.

Marlo nodded. "Good job, Dart. To pass the exam, you must make it to the Great Temple in five days or less and present three bells to get

89

in."

Fox choked on her spit. *Three bells?*

"But you only gave us one," Terra said loudly.

Now Moneek chimed in. "That means you'll have to find two more if you hope to pass."

The temperature outside suddenly dropped fifty degrees.

Fox Fire glanced around at her classmates as reality set in. In the blink of an eye, they had gone from chummy friends who'd partied together all night, to vicious enemies standing in the way of survival and prosperity.

Of course the exams wouldn't be so easy as to simply require them to make it through the forest in five days. They would have to find the Great Temple, attack their own classmates to collect the required number of bells, defend the bell they already had, and somehow avoid encounters with whatever demons or creatures lived in the Kanen wilds.

And all they'd been given was a knife and some fish.

Vinny's hand shot into the air. "How are we supposed to find the Temple in five days with just these supplies?"

The other students began to grumble and complain but Master Jo slammed her heavy staff into the earth to silence them. "You might find supplies scattered throughout the forest. You might find your own classmates have been given different supplies from you." She paused, eyeing them closely. "If you hunt them down, you might even take what they have for yourselves."

The trainees all shifted uncomfortably.

Fox looked up at Kohl, he was standing in line in front of her. She wished she could glimpse his face to probe his reaction, but all she could see was his back. His shoulders seemed to tense, muscles going rigid as he straightened.

Is he worried? she wondered.

She definitely was. They had made a pact to stick together, but that was before they realized they would have to attack each other to pass. They'd known the exams would test them as individuals, but they never would have guessed it would pit them *against* each other.

The Academy required three bells from each student but had only passed out one to each of them. That meant there were only enough bells for one-third of all trainees to pass the exams. And even if you collected enough bells, you could still fail if you didn't make it to the Great Temple in time. Or if you died along the way.

Anything could happen once the gates opened.

Marlo Jo's face and voice softened as she addressed her class. "Listen to me, G-Five. In exactly three minutes, those gates will open, and I won't see you again unless you pass the exam. I know a lot has happened over the last few weeks. I know some of you might feel you didn't have enough time to prepare for this test, but you are my students. I know you're ready. All of you." She gripped her staff and gave it one last jab into the ground. "Remember your training."

Fox had expected her to say more, but Master Jo simply walked away and left them standing in line like prey waiting to be hunted down and killed. Silence rang through the trees, louder than the pounding of Fox's heart. No one had told them they couldn't speak or talk amongst themselves. No one had said they couldn't move. But no one uttered a word and no one made any movements as they counted down the minutes, staring at the gates with sharply focused eyes.

Lord Jesus, help me and my friends, Fox prayed inside. When she sensed movement behind her, she felt guilty and added, *Help Roaring, too. Even though he probably doesn't need it.*

Her brother shifted closer to her, whispering, "When the gates open, don't move. Tell the others."

She didn't ask why. Roaring was stronger, older, and more

91

experienced. Fox trusted her brother.

She poked Kohl in the back and whispered the message before he could get grumpy and ask why. "Tell KI," she instructed.

He said something back in an angry tone but faced forward and poked KI anyway.

Fox exhaled, cheeks puffing as she released every ounce of air from her lungs. If the counting she'd been doing in her head was correct, the gates should open in *three … two … one …*

9

Fox Fire

Chaos stormed through the waiting area as soon as the gates flew open. Students charged forward, some sprinting madly—desperately trying to get as far away from the other students as possible—others used their blessings to get a head start. Then there were the few who took advantage of the madness and launched a full-on attack at their nearest classmate.

Choking clouds of dust puffed around Fox Fire, forcing her to close her eyes as she remained rooted in place. She had followed Roaring's instructions not to move once the exams began, with screams and pleas for mercy echoing around her, she was glad she'd decided to trust his instincts.

When the dust began to settle, Fox realized her brother was not the only one with the wisdom to stay put. Nearly half of G-5 remained before the gates, staring into the storm of death and violence. In the distance, Fox could still hear someone screaming.

"All right," Kohl said, turning around and folding his arms. "We waited. Now we're behind."

"We're only racing against time," Roaring said.

Kohl shook his head. "We still have to hunt down other students.

We should have attacked right away."

"Attacked who?" Fox challenged.

His blue eyes landed on her; she was shocked to see them filled with hurt. "I'm not a traitor, Fox."

"Are we working together?" the voice came from Dart who was jogging over to them. He grinned at Roaring and gave him an approving nod. "I heard you tell your friends to stay put. I figured you had a plan." He winked and pointed to his ears. "I've got killer hearing."

Fox almost groaned. With Dart's blessing to shift into various animals, he also had enhanced senses. She should have known he would be eavesdropping, but she didn't blame him. Despite the Academy pitting them against each other, it seemed better for them to work as a team for as long as possible.

Roaring had the same idea. "Anyone who wants to stick together is welcome to join us," he said loudly. The other students who'd been too afraid to enter the forest slowly gathered around the Prince of Fire.

"He can't be serious," Kohl grumbled.

"We said we'd work together," KI reminded him.

"*We* said that. Not all of G-Five."

"It isn't all of G-Five," Fox told him, casting a glance around the circle of trainees. Dart, Andor, Danté, Wunda, and a student named Belinda had all stayed behind. "This is just about half the class."

"Well, half the class tromping through the forest together will draw a lot of attention," Kohl snapped.

"But there will be enough of us to stand together," Belinda said. She was a small girl with light brown hair and a voice that trembled when she spoke. Fox wasn't sure if it was because of the craziness of the exams or Kohl's overbearing attitude. Probably both. He had stepped closer to Belinda, towering over her with his height, and was glaring like he wanted to hit her.

"Chill out," KI said, shoving Kohl away from the girl. "I think we should all stick together."

"I think we should all get into the forest before we're automatically disqualified." Wunda pointed to the gates which were moving now, slowly closing.

Without even thinking, Fox and her classmates ran toward the metal doors, squeezing between them in a desperate clump of students.

"That was scary," Dart said, staring through the closed gates.

"No, being out there was fine," Danté corrected him. "Being in the forest is what's scary." She glanced around, wincing as something boomed somewhere in the woods. "We're locked inside."

"We can do this if we stick together," Roaring said firmly. He walked a few feet away from the rest of the trainees and dropped his sack on the ground. "Anyone who doesn't want to work together can leave now. Anyone who stays, empty your sack so we can see what sort of supplies we've got to work with. And get ready to share your blessing, we need to know if our team is better suited for offense or defense."

When no one moved, Roaring nodded. "Good. Looks like everyone is staying." He opened his sack and dumped everything out. "I'll go first."

A compass, two skins of water, and a small dagger similar to the one Fox received lay on the ground at Roaring's feet. He picked up each item and examined them as he explained his blessing to his new team. When he was finished, Fox went next, then KI who confessed that he didn't exactly have a blessing, but he was stronger and faster than normal. The students didn't question where his power came from.

Wunda explained her blessing, followed by Kohl who simply called it Void and refused to say anything further. Roaring let it slide since Kohl's sack contained nothing but food and everyone was already hungry. They munched on the strips of jerky he agreed to share with them while Dart shifted into a monkey to demonstrate his blessing. Andor glowed as she emptied her sack, shining even brighter when she realized she'd been given a map of the forest.

Next, Danté took the stage and emptied her sack, explaining that she was from the Shoren Clan.

"Aren't the Shorens supposed to be giants?" Dart asked, confused.

Fox Fire had met Lady Shakira Shoren once before. She was unnaturally tall, but the word *giant* seemed a bit extreme to her. In Danté's case, giant was more than extreme—it was a flat out lie.

Danté Shoren was taller than Fox Fire, but she still didn't reach 5'3 in height. She was thin and frail-looking, with round spectacles that she couldn't stop herself from adjusting every few minutes. There was simply no way she was a giant. It was hard enough to believe she came from the Shoren bloodline.

"Maybe the blessing skipped a generation," Dart joked.

Danté glared at him. "Our blessing is called *Titos*, and it didn't skip a generation."

Dart looked her up and down. "You sure?"

"Enough," Roaring cut in. "We still have one more."

Belinda stood and took a deep breath. "I don't have a blessing."

"*What?*" Kohl snapped. The air crackled with a sudden surge of spiritual energy as his anger flared.

Belinda winced like he'd hit her. "I—I don't have a blessing."

"You've got to be kidding me," Kohl grumbled.

Dart covered his mouth to hide his laugh. Wunda and Andor exchanged looks of both horror and shock.

"How did you make it this far without a blessing?" Danté asked.

"She worked hard," Fox said. She knew better than any of them how difficult it could be to make it through training without a blessing. Until recently, Fox couldn't use sundancing in any capacity; but she knew she had a blessing and the hope for strength and the dream of one day being able to use her gift had kept her going.

But Belinda had nothing. She knew no matter how hard she trained or fought, she would always be limited to her natural human strength. Nothing more.

"Just because she's stony doesn't mean she's deadweight," Fox said angrily.

Stony. It was a crude word used to describe students without blessings. In reference to the Parable of the Sower, when a farmer scattered seeds on stony soil. The seeds sprang up quickly but were eventually scorched and withered because they had no roots.

Trainees without a blessing weren't much different. They had spiritual energy, but without a blessing—or a *root*—to manifest that energy, they often fell behind and withered during training.

"I can hold my own," Belinda said confidently. "If anyone feels like I'm becoming a burden, I'll split ways and finish the exam alone."

"Brave girl." Wunda gave her a nod of respect. "If Belly leaves, I'm going with her."

"No one is going anywhere," Roaring said firmly. "We're going to stick together for as long as we can."

"Is that the plan?" Kohl asked. "Hold hands and hope we can find enough bells for everyone along the way?"

"Kohl," Fox sighed.

He pushed from the tree he'd been leaning against and threw his hands up. "There are nine of us—which means we need twenty-seven bells just to qualify. Not to mention enough food and water and weapons for all of us to survive—whether we qualify or not. A group this big is a liability."

"You're welcome to leave." Wunda placed a hand on her hip.

"Kohl has a point," Roaring conceded. "But we're up against a thousand other students. That's a thousand blessings we've never seen, plus our classmates who didn't stick around, and whatever creatures live out here in the forest." He paused as something howled in the distance, perfectly emphasizing his point. "The first day will be the most dangerous of all five. Everyone is eager—desperate to get this over with as quickly as possible. Students will ruthlessly hunt down and attack anyone they see. Even other kids from G-Five."

Fox couldn't help the shiver that tiptoed up her spine. She didn't want to think about fighting the Ool twins again, or Vyanna Farron. And what would happen if she bumped into someone like Slaine?

"You are right, Kohl," Roaring continued, "a group this large will be tough to feed and keep safe. But right now, sticking together is our best option. Our only goal for now is to survive the night. Once the sun comes up, we can consider going separate ways." He looked right at the blonde-haired boy. "Can you give me one night?"

All eyes shifted to Kohlannis as he mulled over his answer. Fox thought he might huff and say something he'd regret, but he surprised her by simply nodding.

Roaring let out a sigh of relief. "All right then. We've got decent supplies; this should work if we ration the food and pass out the weapons to whoever needs them most."

Between nine students, they had two daggers, one bow with a quiver of twelve arrows, one set of flint and steel, enough jerky and dried fish to fill an entire sack, seven skins of water, a map, a compass, and a cord of rope that measured seven feet.

KI picked up the bow. "Anyone know how to use this?"

"I'm great with a bow and arrow," Belinda volunteered.

KI raised his dark brows. "Are you?"

"I've mastered eight different weapons. My parents made sure I knew how to protect myself since I don't have a supernatural gift."

98

He whistled and passed her the bow and quiver. "I guess this is all yours."

"I'll take one of those daggers," Danté said, swiping it up before anyone could protest.

Roaring took the last dagger and passed it to Andor. When she frowned, he patted her shoulder. "I'm not calling you weak, but glowing isn't going to stop much out here. You need to be able to defend yourself."

With a reluctant nod, Andor took the weapon and tucked it into her waistband.

"I'll take the map and compass," Roaring said. He sat in the grass and unrolled the parchment. "I want to cover as much ground as we can before we hunker down for the night. We'll need a place that's secure and easy to defend."

Fox nodded. "I'll take the flint and steel, and the rope. While Roaring studies the map, let's divide up the food and water. We'll carry equal portions so if one of us gets taken—or sneaks away—they won't carry off all our food and water with them."

With the supplies finally distributed, the kids gathered around Roaring and watched him read the map.

"What about a cave?" Dart suggested.

Roaring shook his head. "If someone sneaks up on us, they could trap us inside or smoke us out to get our supplies."

"We could build a camp," Danté said with a shrug.

"With two daggers and a bow and arrow?" Kohl asked.

"We've also got rope."

"Danté's right." Roaring rolled up the map and tucked it into his pants as he stood. "We could cut down a few branches and set up a camp if we must. For now, we'll just focus on making it to Stone Ridge."

"Stone Ridge," Wunda repeated.

"It's a landmark on the map, about half-a-day of walking from here. If we can cover that much ground before nightfall, we'll be in good shape for tomorrow so we can head to Fells Lake."

"Fells Lake?" Belinda said.

"That's another landmark on the way to the Great Temple. It'll be our resting spot."

"What about collecting bells?" Andor asked.

"For now, we focus on surviving. We'll think about bells tomorrow."

"I'm sure we'll bump into other students along the way," KI said. "We can take theirs."

They walked for hours in peace. Every now and then, someone would scream in the distance, something would growl or howl—one time, they felt the earth quake beneath their feet, but they ignored the tremors and marched on. Roaring kept a difficult pace, only stopping once for water and even then, he only allowed them to empty *one* of the skins. The students complained, but no one put up a serious fight. They understood the importance of saving the food and water, especially since they hadn't spotted any sources of fresh water since they'd entered the forest.

The thought of making it to Fells Lake made Fox's mouth water. She hoped it wouldn't take long to get there. Roaring had made them all gather around and study the map during their break so they would have an idea where to go if they were ever separated. Fox tried to memorize her way to the lake more than any other landmark, imagining food and water and a stash of good weapons hidden somewhere on the property.

"How much further?" Belinda asked, tripping over a rock. Fox grabbed her arm to stable her. The area was rocky and uneven, traversing the side of a steep cliff. More than fifty meters below them, the forest stretched on in every direction, but Roaring thought it would be best to maintain the high ground, so they ascended the cliffside, tired and aching all the way.

"We've still got a few hours," Roaring answered.

Someone in the back groaned—probably Kohl, who'd been complaining most of the day.

"Can't we take another break? My feet are killing me," Danté whined.

"We need to cover as much—"

The earth rumbled beneath them, loud enough to interrupt Roaring's response. When it finally stopped, silence was all Fox could hear. Her eyes snapped to her brother, trying to gage his reaction but his face betrayed no emotion.

Roaring was still as stone, broad shoulders stiffened, the muscles in his back gone rigid. He was six and a half feet tall and every inch of him was perfectly controlled, perfectly in tune with what was happening around them. When the ground trembled again, he steadied himself so he wouldn't wobble to the side. When a flock of birds burst from the trees above, screeching as they flew overhead, he glanced up with a frown.

"Something's coming," he said calmly.

"Are you sure?" Andor asked, and as soon as the words left her mouth, the ground began to shake again—but this time, the trees shook with it.

Roaring's eyes never left the forestry as he gave a command. "Dart!"

With a nod, the young trainee shifted into a hawk and took to the sky at an incredible speed.

"Wunda, what do you feel?" Roaring snapped.

"Something big and heavy. Less than a mile out!" she shouted back, digging her toes into the earth.

"Everyone spread out, keep your bells tucked away and—"

Dart dropped beside him and shifted back into his human form. "It's

101

a troll."

"A what?" Andor cried. Genuine tears filled her eyes as she covered her mouth with a fist.

"A troll," Dart repeated.

"We should just run," Andor said, wiping at her eyes. "We can't fight a troll."

"We may not have a choice!" Wunda hollered, running into the tree line. "Incoming!"

A horrible roar resounded through the forest as a monster emerged from the trees. It was taller than the demonic beast that'd destroyed the Walls of Wi and looked more powerful. Thick green skin, bumpy and ridged like a lizard's, with claws on its hands and feet sharp enough to slice through the branches of the giant trees. It was built like a warrior and demonstrated its ferocity by tearing a massive branch from a tree and launching it at the group.

They scattered.

There was no time to wonder where the troll had come from. There was no time to form a plan. There wasn't even any time to feel fear. The monster roared again and raised its foot, intending to stomp on the trainees. It was shockingly fast for its size, but not quite fast enough.

Roaring and KI cleared the area before the troll's foot could squash them, but the backlash of the screaming dust and wind it kicked up sent them spiraling twenty feet away. Before Fox could worry about her friend and brother, the troll's foot was in the air again. This time, it was right above her.

She screamed. And then turned to run, trying to escape the foot-shaped shadow. It loomed over her like a magnet drawn to her pull, and with a panicked shriek of horror, Fox realized it was following her. *I'm not fast enough!* she cried inside, forcing her legs to pump harder. She could hear Kohl screaming for her to run, could hear Andor sobbing that she was going to die, could even hear Wunda bellow a choking sob as she wildly ran through the clearing.

And then Fox was grabbed violently by her shirt and dragged up onto something hairy. When she regained her senses, she realized she was on a horse.

Belinda was riding in the front, an arrow nocked, the bowstring pulled taut as she aimed for the troll's leg. "Are you all right?" she yelled, releasing the arrow.

Fox blinked. Dazed. "How?"

"It's Dart. I told him to shift and give me a ride," Belinda explained. She glanced over her shoulder and gave her a pretty grin. "Thanks for sticking up for me earlier. For saying I wouldn't be deadweight."

Right now, she was anything but. If it weren't for Belinda's quick thinking, Fox would have been dead, squashed beneath the foot of a troll.

She opened her mouth to thank her classmate, but the troll's roar silenced her.

"We're not done yet!" Belinda shouted, firing one more arrow at its calf. The arrow lodged into the thick muscle of the monster's leg, but it did little more than make it angry. The troll lifted its foot again, it's shadow looming over the three of them now.

Fox gasped. "You're drawing its attention!"

"I know!" Belinda yelled back, then she slung her bow over her shoulder and leaned forward, tangling her hands into Dart's mane. "Hold on to me!"

Fox did as she was told, wrapping her arms around Belinda's waist, and holding on for dear life. Dart picked up the pace, galloping at full speed to outrun the troll's foot. Everything inside told Fox to close her eyes or look away, but she kept her vision locked on the foot. If she was going to die, she wanted to see it coming. But Dart was faster than he looked. He swiftly outmaneuvered the beast and escaped the massive shadow into the trees.

"Wunda, now!" Belinda yelled.

The large girl ran forward and punched the earth just as the troll's foot made contact. Instead of crumbling beneath its foot, the ground turned to sticky mud and absorbed the impact. The troll roared as it squatted and tried to free itself, but all its struggling only made things worse. It sank deeper into the mud, almost as if the earth was swallowing it whole.

"I can make this mud pit twenty feet deep," Wunda taunted. "Keep struggling. You'll only sink."

As if it had understood her, the monster stopped its struggling and tore another branch from the nearest tree. It swung the branch like a massive bat, sweeping at the ground as it tried to kill Wunda. She immediately ducked and touched the earth, then pulled her hands back toward her body. The ground responded to her call, jutting upwards to form an earthen cocoon to protect her from the attack. The branch splintered but didn't break the hardened earth.

"Incredible," Belinda breathed.

"But we still need to defeat it," Fox said, watching the troll beat Wunda's cocoon with its branch. "We don't know how much more her shell can take."

"Take us over to Roaring, he'll have a plan." Belinda patted Dart's neck and he took off right away.

Sure enough, when Fox climbed down from Dart, she could already hear her brother giving orders to the other students.

"We should just run while it's trapped!" Andor was screaming.

Roaring leveled her with an icy look. "We are not leaving her behind."

"I can't stay! We're going to die! We have to run!" Andor grabbed at Roaring, digging her nails into his arm as she shrieked. "We're all going to die here!"

"Calm down!" he yelled, wrenching his arm free.

The troll roared again as it took another swing at Wunda's cocoon. This time, the rock cracked.

Andor ran.

Sprinting wildly through the clearing, she ran past Wunda's shell, trying to get as far away from the monster as possible.

Roaring chased her.

Horror gripped Fox as she watched him go after the mad girl. She went to chase after him, but KI's arms were around her waist, lifting her from the ground.

"Let me go!" she screamed, kicking at the air.

His grip tightened like she weighed nothing in his arms. "I can't do that," he breathed. "Roaring can handle himself."

"Please!" she sobbed.

Beside her, Dart sighed and shifted back into a horse, taking off after their teammates before anyone could stop him. The sight of the stallion galloping away sent hope through her heart, but Fox still struggled against KI.

"Put me down!" she ordered.

"Only if you promise to stay put," he said firmly.

"We need to fight!" Fox yelled. "Wunda won't last much longer, and now Roaring and Andor are in danger!"

"Fox is right," Belinda agreed, nocking an arrow.

"What's that going to do?" Kohl said.

"Distract it."

"You want to draw its attention to us?" he snapped.

"I want to draw its attention away from our friends."

"There is no need," Danté said, stepping forward.

"*What?*" Kohl frowned.

Across the clearing, Roaring had Andor in his arms and was dragging her toward the tree line. They were safe, but they couldn't hide there for long and with the edge of the cliff behind them, they had nowhere else to retreat. Dart was running circles around the clearing, trying to distract the troll from Wunda. For a moment, it worked. The monster stopped beating the stony shell to take a swing at the horse, but Dart galloped away just in time, running to join Roaring and Andor.

Danté pushed past her friends, removing her glasses, and dropping them to the ground. "This is my fight."

As she stepped into the open area, the air crackled with a sudden release of spiritual energy.

"Something's happening," Fox muttered.

"She's a Shoren," KI said quietly. "They have the power of Titos."

"What good is that for a shrimp like her?" Kohl asked.

"Some people in the Shoren Clan are born as giants—over ten feet tall, with big hands and even bigger muscles. But there are some like Danté, who are born 'normal' sized." KI swallowed. "Their strength is hidden until the sleeping giant awakens."

Light flashed in the clearing, and thunder clapped around them. It sounded as if an explosion had gone off. Fox slapped her hands over her ears, but she refused to close her eyes. She had to see what'd happened. Had to know if her friends were okay.

In the clearing stood another monster.

She was just a few feet shorter than the troll, a womanly figure with jet black skin and menacing grey eyes. Her clothes had been torn from her body, but where her breasts and groin should have been, there was instead a layer of iron—as if she had grown her own armor.

She had no mouth. And her head was completely bald. But she was still recognizable.

"That's Danté," Fox Fire whispered.

Kohl was not impressed. "Why didn't she do that earlier?"

"Who cares?" Belinda said. "Now that she has transformed, we have a chance to win this."

"What should we do?" KI asked.

"I'm going to circle around and litter its back with my remaining arrows. You three should try to regroup with Roaring and Andor. If you make it across the clearing, tell Dart to find me on the north side of the fight." Belinda ducked into the woods before they could think of a better plan.

"I'm going for my brother," Fox said.

KI nodded. "We'll all go."

"We have to wait for the right chance," Kohl said, his gaze focused on the two giants slugging each other.

Dante snatched the branch from the troll and gave it a good crack across its jaw. It stumbled backwards but with its foot still stuck in the mud, it went down with a roar. Arrows flew from the trees behind it, stabbing it in the top of its head.

Dante tried to stomp on the beast, but it kicked her with its free foot, and she went flying back—right towards Roaring and Andor's hiding spot.

Fox gasped, watching Dart run through the trees to escape Dante's giant body. She was clumsy on her feet, tripping through the massive woods, endangering her own friends. As horrible as it was to watch, no one was particularly surprised. Being that size was as much a help as it was a hindrance. She had likely only transformed a handful of times in her life, and she probably hadn't gotten to train much at this size. She would have destroyed half of Babel stomping around as a giant.

"We've got to do something!" Fox yelled, running forward, but she knew it was too late.

Dante went down on one knee, the impact sending tremors through the forest. With all the rumbling, the ground had finally endured enough. It began to crumble, breaking away right beneath Roaring's and Andor's feet. Dart tried to outrun the uneven ground, but he could only do so much. He shifted into a bird and tried to fly away, but a toppling tree whacked him and knocked him unconscious. The ground cracked and split, shattering half the cliffside.

Free of her cocoon, Wunda dodged the kicking troll and tried to stable the earth, but she was too weak from holding up her stony shell for so long. She sank to one knee and let out a wretched cough. "I can't…"

"No!" Fox shouted, reaching out.

It was a meaningless gesture. She was more than twenty meters away; her outstretched hand offered no help to her brother. But it did let him know that she had tried. As the earth slipped away and Roaring and Andor and Dart went over the cliff, his eyes locked on hers and her extended hand and the tears in her eyes, and she knew that he understood she had tried her best.

With her brother and her friends gone, Fox watched the utter chaos unfold. Danté was back on her feet, swinging at the troll who'd scrambled back up now. Its leg had been freed from the earth, thanks to all the cracking and splintering around the mud pit.

Now the real fighting had begun.

"We've got to go!" KI was beside Fox, yanking on her arm and tugging her away from the collapsed cliffside. Trees cracked and fell hundreds of feet to the forest floor. Wild animals ran past, trying to escape the madness, even a small cluster of little demons scurried from the tree line.

The troll let out a primal roar and tackled Danté to the ground, sending another shockwave of quakes through the earth. Fox felt the shaking in her very bones. She let KI pull her away as she tipped to the

108

side, stumbling over her feet. When he steadied her, she glanced around and realized Wunda wasn't with them.

"Where is she?" Fox hollered over all the noise.

"I don't know! We must have lost her in the madness!"

"We can't leave her!"

KI's grip on her arm tightened, almost painfully. He yanked her closer to him, dragging her deeper into the forest. "We can't stay here! The forest is falling apart!"

She hated to admit it, but Fox knew KI was right. She had watched Roaring and two other classmates fall over a cliff, she had lost sight of Wunda and Belinda, and now she would leave Danté to fight alone.

There is nothing more we can do, she told herself; and as she ran deeper into the forest, she almost believed it.

10

Fox Fire

Together, they ran for what seemed like hours. When Fox's legs couldn't take any more, she staggered to the side and fell into the soft soil. Much to her shock, Kohlannis didn't admonish her exhaustion, he didn't criticize her for resting, nor did he try to encourage her to get up and keep going. Instead, he slowed to a stop and placed a hand against the nearest tree. The other went to his hip as he heaved for air, blue eyes finding hers as he gazed across the small clearing.

They had run until the sounds of Danté and the troll were fading behind them, but even at this distance, Fox could feel gentle rumbles from the brutal fighting going on between the great warriors.

"Did we do the right thing?" Fox asked, panting.

KI didn't answer, sitting on the ground just a few feet away. He stared down at the grass and shook his head.

"We did the only thing we could," Kohl finally said.

Fox closed her eyes. "We left them. We left everyone."

"Roaring, Dart, and Andor fell over the cliff—there was nothing we could have done for them even if we'd stayed. Belinda was lost in the woods, Danté was fighting the troll, and we lost track of Wunda in all the chaos." He pushed from the tree and stood before her, his hands on her shoulders, his eyes staring right into hers, trying to get her to understand what he was saying. "We did the only thing we could." He squeezed her upper arms as he repeated himself, a gentle gesture that was meant to ease her rising nerves.

When she glanced down, Fox could see the way his hands tightened on her flesh, the way his long fingers curled around her arm, the veins in the tops of his hands, the few strands of blonde hair on his knuckles. It was strange, the things she noticed in the most random of moments. But she couldn't get herself to focus on what he was saying anymore. Her mind was gone, choosing to trace the line of Kohl's jaw rather than face the reality of her brother's possible death and her cowardly escape.

He shook her. "Fox! Are you listening?"

Yes, is what she would have said, but when she opened her mouth to respond, something over Kohl's shoulder caught her attention. The bush began to shimmy and rustle, parting to reveal a pair of eyes such an odd shade of blue, Fox would have argued they were lavender instead.

"Fox?" Kohl said again.

"We're in trouble," she whispered.

He sighed. "We're in a lot more than trouble. Roaring had the map and the compass. Danté, Belinda, and Andor had our only weapons, and Wunda and Dart had a good portion of the food and water. We're worse off than when the gates first opened."

"Do you still have your bells?" The voice did not belong to KI, Kohl, or Fox Fire. It had come from the bush over Kohl's shoulder. Kohl's body stiffened, and the look in his eyes went from concerned to alert in the fraction of a second.

The owner of the violet eyes stepped from the brush and into clear view. A young man with white hair and skin so pale, he was almost translucent.

He's albino, Fox realized.

111

The student smiled at them, though there was no warmth in it, but he wasn't carrying a weapon, so Fox allowed herself to hope he wasn't an enemy. At least for now.

"Do you still have your bells?" the boy repeated.

Kohl dropped his hands from Fox's arms and turned around very slowly. "Who's asking?"

The boy's smile widened. "My name is Crystal. I'm from Class B-Two."

"Your name is *Crystal*?" Kohl frowned.

He nodded. "Now, I've answered your question. How about you answer mine?"

"Our bells are none of your business." Kohl took a step forward, hands curling into fists.

Crystal studied him, purple eyes tracing his tall frame, then his eyes landed on Fox and slowly slid over to KI. He licked his lips. "You're Kohlannis Hunger. I've heard about you."

"Then you should know it's best you keep moving."

Crystal whistled and the bushes shimmied again, this time, Fox could hear the distinct ringing of bells as the bushes moved.

"I've heard you're strong," Crystal said, "but I think I'll stay."

"You really want to fight a Hunger?" Kohl challenged.

"You know what else I've heard about you?" Crystal asked, ignoring his question. "I've heard you don't use your powers. Is that true?"

Kohl hesitated.

In his silence, another figure emerged from the brush. And another. And another. And another. They kept coming until Fox and her friends were surrounded.

At least eight of them. Fox glanced around, shifting her stance so she could keep as many of them in her sights as possible. Without needing the order, KI had done the same, standing and angling his body so the

112

three of them held a triangle formation, keeping at least one eye on every enemy.

The students surrounding them didn't look impressive. Lanky kids with torn clothes and a collection of cuts and bruises. One even had a broken nose. They had obviously spent most of the first day fighting. But, despite their appearance, Fox couldn't ignore the confidence swelling from the group. Not just because they had the numbers, but because they had the bells.

The trainee beside Crystal had on the same white and red uniform as every other student in the forest, but his shirt was entirely covered in bells. Like they were ornaments on a Christmas tree. The bells jingled as he moved, taking slow, deliberate steps into the center of their circle until he was face to face with Kohl.

Up close, Fox could see how old the bell boy looked. A crease in his forehead, a patch of grey on the side of his head—right above his left ear—the beginnings of a scruffy beard on his thick chin. He looked older than Roaring. But he didn't look strong like him. Instead of hard muscles and a lean frame, the bell boy had flabby arms and a paunch belly so big it made him look pregnant as he leaned back and placed his thick hands on his heavy hips.

"Is it true you don't use your powers, boy?"

Kohl spat in the dirt. "Do I look like a *boy* to you?"

He laughed like Kohl had just told a joke. After a few seconds, the rest of his pack began to laugh too.

They're mimicking him, Fox noticed. *He's their leader*. She couldn't stop the next thought that invaded her head—*Why?*

The bell boy was older, but he was so out of shape it was laughable. Sweat stains soaked his underarms, his gut was so large his shirt didn't fit properly, inching upwards to reveal the soft hanging flesh right beneath his naval, and his legs were thick with fat that left his knees

113

swollen and red. Fox stared at them through the tears in his cutoff pants.

It was difficult to accept that he was the leader of all these students, but Fox couldn't ignore the fact that he was covered in bells. *Maybe it's his blessing.*

Fox shifted in her stance. "Kohl, be careful," she warned. "We don't know his blessing."

"That's right," the bell boy said, "but I know yours."

How?

"Crystal…" Bell boy ordered.

Crystal took a breath. "The chick is a sundancer. But she can't produce her own flames." He looked at Kohl. "The Hunger kid has the power of Void—"

"We get it," Kohl snapped. "You can tell someone's power just by looking at them."

"Some would say my vision is *crystal clear*," Crystal said with a snort.

Fox grimaced at his horrible joke.

"If you know our blessings, then you should be running for the hills," Kohl warned.

"We're fine right here," Crystal said, glancing at the bell boy. "Aren't we, Donner?"

Donner smirked. "Yes, we are." He took a step forward. "This is what's going to happen; you're gonna give us your bells and whatever supplies you've got. Then we're gonna walk away. You won't follow or attack us. Got it?"

Kohl's face wrinkled in anger. "You're delusional."

Crystal snickered. "No, you are."

"*Hush* up, Crys," Donner snapped. He took a breath and then repeated his exact words. "You're gonna give us your bells and whatever supplies you've got. Then we're gonna walk away. You won't follow or attack us. Got it?"

Again, Kohl's face wrinkled in anger—but before he could reply, KI started to walk forward. With his bell in his hand.

"KI!" Fox yelled, gripping his arm.

He gasped as she grabbed him, tripping to the side and blinking fast. "What... What just happened?"

"Oh, no," Fox whispered.

Donner grinned. "My blessing is called *Charm*. It gives me the power of influence. The more time I spend with someone, the stronger my influence." He shrugged, beady eyes landing on KI. "I'm also particularly effective against the weak-minded."

Now I get it, Fox ground her teeth together, *now I understand how this lazy slob got a troop of students to follow his every command.*

"How many bells have you taken?" Fox said slowly.

"Eighty-six." He smiled like he was proud. "Most of them I took without fighting. But some students are stubborn, and others have a strong will." He shrugged. "I've had to take down a couple kids, but it was necessary."

"Necessary?" Kohlannis hissed. "You don't *need* eighty-six bells to pass."

"What can I say?" Donner laughed heartily, fat belly jumping with his joy. "I want to see how many I can collect." He waved a hand at the students surrounding them. "Plus, my friends like to fight."

"They aren't your friends," Fox grated out. "They're your puppets. They wouldn't be fighting by your side if they had a choice."

"You're right. But they *don't* have a choice. And neither do you. Now, hand over your bells."

Neither Fox nor Kohl moved. KI tried to take a step again, but Fox grabbed his arm and held firmly. "Focus!" she hissed.

He nodded and wiped sweat from his brow. "I'm sorry."

Donner tsked like he was disappointed. "I guess we'll have to do this the hard way." At the flick of his wrist, the other students dropped into position, some of them brandished weapons, others held their hands out before them, ready to use their blessings.

Donner stepped back into the brush with Crystal following right behind. "Kill them. And bring me their bells."

The students rushed them without hesitation, all eight charging at the same time.

"Stick together!" Kohl shouted, holding up his fists.

Fox glanced at KI as he returned to her side. "You good?" she asked, but there was no time to answer. A student was right in front of her, swinging a blade in an upward arc. She jumped back to dodge, bumping into Kohl and knocking him off balance. Kohl spat out a curse as he stumbled to the side, falling right in front of a student with a bat. He swung the bat hard, but Kohl managed to pivot out of the way, shoving Fox as he shifted so she tripped away from the bat's swing.

Another student took a jab at her with his bare hand, like he was trying to stab her with just his fingers. As Fox sidestepped the attack, she realized his fingers had the appearance of sharpened glass. He swung his arm out in an arc, countering his first attack. Fox ducked, hoping KI and Kohl were out of his reach.

They were. But the boy's teammates weren't. His glass fingers ended up slicing across the chest of a boy who'd been going after KI with a hunting knife. Stunned, the boy stopped in his tracks and stared down at his bleeding torso. Fox took advantage of his surprise and grabbed him by the wrist, twisting until he screamed and dropped the hunting knife from his grip.

She tossed it to KI. "Here!"

"What about you?" he called back, snatching the weapon from the air, and quickly turning to cut down a girl who'd charged him head-on.

Fox untangled the sack still tied to her hip and dug out her flint and

116

steel. "I have a weapon," she muttered, striking the flint.

Crystal's vision had been clear. She couldn't produce her own flames. But with her tools, she didn't need to.

Sparks flew into the air. They were tiny, insignificant little bursts of heat. But they were more than enough for Fox. She took a breath and caught every spark in her mind, reaching out to the Holy Spirit within and asking for His power.

He gave it to her.

In the blink of an eye, the sparks exploded into a burst of roaring fire. The charging students scrambled over each other as they tried to back away from the flames, but it was too late. Fox forced the fire to go forward, following her enemies, sending tongues of fire to lick at their flesh. They screamed, dropping weapons and turning for the woods. She would not let them escape.

Fox held the sun in her hands. She commanded its power. And she told it to dance.

Her movements were fluid and smooth, an arm whipping out to direct the heat, fingers extended to give her pinpoint accuracy. Flames flew like punches of heat, screaming bullets of fire stabbing one boy in his backside as he tried to escape. His shirt went up in flames, leaving him writhing in the grass. Another went down with a shriek, taking a blast of heat in his face when he'd tried to go for Kohl. And one more was engulfed in a swirl of raging red when he aimed his bow and arrow at KI.

There was someone else screaming. In the thick fog of violence, in the haziness of all the smoke, Fox heard another strained voice crying for help.

To her horror, Fox recognized the voice and turned with a gasp to find KI on his hands and knees. His face and chest were burned and wrinkled; his arms were charred black.

The flames had grown around them, spread by the escaping students she'd set on fire, and latching on to KI. With one last whimper, he collapsed into the grass, his body smoking. Fox dropped to her knees beside him, mouth open in a silent cry. Tears replaced her words, racing down her reddened cheeks to drip onto his fleshy shoulder. She didn't dare touch him, but she wanted to hold him. She wanted to scream. She wanted to die.

Kohl was beside her, yelling, "Put the flames out! Fox! You have to extinguish the flames!"

She gasped as his strong hands shook her back to reality. Suddenly, the flames were gone—extinguished without her ever looking away from her companion. She wasn't even impressed with herself and her growing abilities. It was her lack of control that'd left KI in this condition. There was nothing to be proud of.

"He's dying," Fox whispered, watching him suck for breath.

Kohl knelt beside her, eyes glued to KI's chest as it rose and fell in short pants. "No, he's not."

Fox sniffled. "How do you know?"

He reached forward and tore away the scorched strips of KI's shirt.

Fox scooted backwards, stunned.

The black markings of his seal were glowing white, as if they had somehow been activated.

Kohl pointed to his burned flesh. "Look closely, the skin right beside the tattoos isn't damaged. He's healing, Fox. Slowly, but surely."

A fresh bucket of tears swelled in Fox's eyes. "How?"

Kohl shifted uncomfortably. "The demon inside. If KI dies, it dies too."

"It's saving him."

He shook his blonde head. "It's saving itself."

She didn't know what else to say, but she was grateful KI wasn't going to die so she mumbled, "Thank God."

Kohl made a face, glancing sideways at her. "Thank God there's a demon inside using its Dark energy to keep him alive and itself?"

She wiped at her nose. "Thank God he isn't going to die."

Kohl leaned forward and scooped KI into his arms. Her best friend had grown since arriving in Babel, but he seemed small in Kohl's embrace, suddenly weak, suddenly fragile. Much like the little boy she remembered him as.

"Where are we going?" Fox asked, walking beside Kohl.

"It's getting late. We need to find someplace to hunker down for the night."

She shivered, noticing the chill in the air and the laziness of the sunlight. The sunset would begin any minute now. "We can't go too far," she said. "I want to check the bodies for weapons and supplies."

He shook his head. "That Donner guy might be nearby. Waiting for his team to bring him the bells they didn't steal."

She patted the pocket where she kept her bell. "I've still got mine."

"So do I," Kohl said. "Which means we aren't safe. Not from Donner or anyone else."

"I know Roaring said caves are a bad idea, but if we find one, we need to use it."

Kohl nodded and let out a strained grunt. He paused for a breath and then adjusted KI before he kept walking. "We'll stop as soon as we see anything even remotely safe to stay in."

"I'll take first watch." Fox gazed at KI wrapped in his arms, his face tucked into the crook of Kohl's neck. "I want to look after him for a while."

"For now, just keep an eye out for shelter."

She agreed with a nod, eyes wide open, senses on alert. KI was badly injured. Their group had been divided. Her brother was lost or possibly

119

dead. They were low on supplies and had no weapons. They weren't safe yet, but they had done it.

They'd survived the first day of the exams.

11

Evelyn

Lieutenant Diaz shifted his weight from one foot to the other before retracting his hand from the woman's shoulder. He stood behind an older lady with a shaven head, sitting cross-legged on the floor. Her eyes were closed but her face was strained as she focused on whatever battle was raging in her mind's eye.

Evelyn had been assigned to the team of Hunters and Priests who overlooked the entrance exams. When he'd received the task, he'd been filled with anger but now, as he glanced around the room and silently analyzed everything he'd just observed, he was somewhat grateful for the opportunity.

The first day of the exams had gone the way they'd expected, but it was clear something was amiss. The air was charged with spiritual energy, swirling into a storm that ached to be set free. Diaz could only wonder who would strike the match that would light the Kanen Forest on fire.

"How's it looking?"

The lieutenant turned to find Master Jo approaching. She had no smile on her face, but she didn't look horrified and gloomy like the last few times he'd seen her. He supposed that was a good thing.

Marlo placed a hand on her hip and nodded at the bald woman sitting on the floor. She was in a circle of Priests and Hunters, all with shaven heads and closed eyes—faces pinched in concentration. "Did you see anything?" she asked.

Diaz took a breath. "I saw a lot, actually."

"Good. That means the Onté Clan is doing well."

The Onté family was a sister clan to the Ontellos, a bloodline whose blessing allowed them to shift into various animals. The lieutenant had seen a student named Dart use this blessing as he'd observed the exams, but this was his first time seeing the gift of the Onté Clan up close.

Like their cousins, the Onté family had an animal-related blessing, but instead of shifting into different creatures, they connected with an animal's spiritual energy. This allowed them to influence animals they connected with or even gave them the ability to see through the eyes of their captive animal.

In this case, the Ontés sitting in the circle around the small Academy office were each connected to a number of animals roaming the Kanen Forest, effectively giving them visuals of what was happening in the exams. When Lieutenant Diaz placed his hand on the shoulder of one of the Onté soldiers, they shared their sight with him so he could watch the fighting with his own eyes. He'd seen groups of students clash in battle and he'd watched a nest of wyrms devour thirteen trainees whole. But what had truly caught his attention was the appearance of the troll that'd destroyed part of the forest itself.

Diaz took a breath, trying not to let his temper get the best of him as he said, "I saw a troll in the forest. That's a level B demon. Why on earth is it in the exams?"

"There are a dozen level B demons roaming the forest," Master Jo replied. "But that's the highest rank we've permitted onto the premises. Every other creature will be level C or D."

"And what about the nest of wyrms?" He folded his arms. "They killed thirteen trainees in less than twenty minutes. We don't even have bodies to bring back to their families!" Diaz was panting, shocking himself and Master Jo with his zeal. He hadn't realized how much he'd cared. Or maybe it was difficult not to care when he'd watched the students suffer with his own eyes.

He stepped back and pinched the bridge of his nose, taking slow, deep breaths. The brutality of the exams shouldn't have been a surprise to him. He'd gone through the same training when he was a kid, side by side with Izzy and Kotaro. He had lost classmates, betrayed others, and had even taken the life of a few trainees whose faces he couldn't seem to escape when he closed his eyes at night. But this seemed different. This seemed wrong somehow.

"This has been the format of the exam for decades," Master Jo reminded him.

He nodded, still pinching his nose and taking deep breaths. "I know that."

"Then—"

"It's just that these kids weren't ready for this, Master Jo. Can't you see that?"

Marlo didn't respond right away, causing him to peel his lids back and spear her with his hazel gaze. The look on her face cooled his heated temper. Master Jo was just as upset as Diaz. He could see that in the hesitancy of her clenched jaw and the worry creasing her normally smooth brow.

"I trained those kids myself. I know they can survive this," she said quietly.

"Maybe they can survive the level B demons and maybe they can survive fights with students from other classes. But what happens when the Red Face shows up tomorrow or the next day—when they're all exhausted and too overworked to properly defend themselves?" Diaz stepped closer to her. "What happens then?"

Marlo met his glare, which wasn't difficult to do since she was two inches taller than the lieutenant and almost as muscular. "We have a plan in place," she assured him. "The Red Face will not take KI. No matter what."

Evelyn stepped back. "It isn't that I don't believe we will stop the Red Face, it's that I'm terrified of what we will lose in the process. The lives it will cost."

"If we spot him in time," Master Jo said, gazing down at the Onté woman again, "it won't cost a thing."

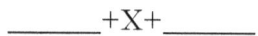

With the shadow of evening crawling over the Kanen Forest, Lieutenant Diaz decided it was time to return home. The observation center would be open 24/7 until the exams were over, but he'd seen enough for the day. Enough death. Enough violence. Enough fighting.

Somehow, he felt ashamed of the compassion blooming in his chest. He was a hardened Hunter of the Academy. He should have been used to this sort of gore, but he wasn't. And he never would be.

Slowly, Lieutenant Diaz flexed his burned hand open and close as he walked down the road. He should have been heading home, but he found himself turning corners and taking shortcuts so he could pass by a certain blacksmith's shop. It hadn't been long since Lieutenant Kotaro told him Lady Talon accepted the apprenticeship she'd been offered; Diaz wasn't expecting to find her sweating over a red-glowing sword, but he couldn't stop his nerves from firing off in every direction as he neared the little shack. He could hear Master Li roaring his hearty laugh before he reached the cloth hanging in the doorway.

He knocked on the doorpost.

"Coming!" Li called back. There was rummaging and the sound of clanging metal before the burly man appeared from the back of his shop. His face split into a grand smile when he saw Diaz waiting. "My boy!" he shouted. "Have you got an order?" Li's face scrunched in sudden confusion as he snatched a feather pen from behind his ear and licked the tip. He flipped through a few pages scattered over the countertop and then glanced up. "I don't see your name on my list—did you come to sharpen your swords? I've got time."

Diaz shook his head. He wasn't wearing his twin hook-swords, silently, he cursed himself for leaving them at home. Because now he was standing there trying to think of a believable reason for him to be at Li's shop without giving away his true intentions.

"Actually," he said slowly. "Well…"

"Everything all right, son?"

Just then, the curtain separating the workshop and the order counter parted to reveal a slender figure. "Master?" a feminine voice called. "I think I've finally finished the blueprints."

Lady Talon wore a safety vest to protect her from the sparks that sprayed the workshop while Li hammered out his weapons. Her hair was wrapped in a grease-stained scarf, and her hands were hidden inside oversized leather gloves. In her grip was a slip of parchment, which she promptly rolled up as she saw Diaz standing on the other side of the counter.

He smiled at her.

She looked like she was going to faint.

"What are you doing here?" Talon asked.

Diaz wished he had an answer. The truth was that he'd wanted to see

125

her, but now that he had, he couldn't get himself to admit it aloud or even understand why.

"Is this about Fox Fire?"

She was clutching the crucifix around her neck now, which made his heart break a little. He hadn't meant to worry or upset her, but now that she'd mentioned her little sister, he had a sudden reason for seeing her.

"Yes," Diaz nodded. "I've got a report about the entrance exams."

She covered her mouth and then dropped her gaze to the ground, the roll of parchment in her grasp crinkled as she gripped it tightly. "Please don't tell me…"

Sheesh. The lieutenant ground his teeth together. First, he'd made her upset, now, she was going to *cry*. This was not how he'd imagined his visit to the shop would play out.

Master Li patted Talon on the shoulder, his voice coming out in a surprisingly soothing tone. "Why don't you head home? I can close up the shop alone."

She nodded and passed him the parchment. "Goodnight, Master."

Li waited until Talon ducked into the back of the shop before he turned to Diaz and said, "What's going on? Really."

He sighed. Palmed the back of his neck. "Honestly, nothing."

"There are better ways to get a woman's attention than this, my boy."

"When I figure them out, I'll let you know."

Talon emerged from the back with a hemp bag hanging on her shoulder. She no longer wore the safety vest or the stained scarf, and her small hands were free of gloves. Lieutenant Diaz tried not to stare at her too much, reminding himself that she was upset and fragile right now. Because of him.

"I'll walk you home," he said, placing his hand on the small of her back to guide her out of the shop. He could not ignore the warmth that buzzed through him at the possessiveness of his touch. He smiled.

126

Once they were on the sidewalk, Talon turned to him with tears in her eyes. "Please tell me my sister isn't—"

"She's fine," Diaz said quickly. "I actually came to tell you she's doing well. She survived her first day. Along with KI and Kohl. They've been sticking together."

Talon smiled and wiped at her eyes. "Oh, thank God! I was so worried for a moment." She laughed. "I know Roaring can handle himself, but little paws isn't like him. She's small for her age, you know?"

He nodded, taking note of Talon's height and build. She was tall for a woman, almost eye to eye with him—but Fox was almost childlike. The sisters had only two years between them, but Talon seemed much older. She was eighteen, a woman by her culture's standards and Babel's as well. Diaz was twenty-four, six years older and far more experienced than the sheltered woman from the stone village. Her age gave him pause. But he didn't pause for long.

Talon carried an air of maturity that made him remember just how much of a woman she truly was. If that giant demon hadn't destroyed her village, she likely would have been married off by now, maybe even carrying a child. Now she was learning how to craft weapons at a blacksmith's shop and trying to lead her village in a foreign Region. She had grown up, seemingly aging ten years in a matter of months.

She even looked older now. When Lady Talon had woken in the hospital months ago, she had weighed less than 110 pounds, but she'd put on a little weight and had regained her strength since then. Even her hair was growing back in.

Diaz gazed at the tangle of dark coils that shined in the lazy sunlight. He liked her hair short, but he'd never seen her with it long. He supposed it didn't matter. He knew he would have liked her no matter how her hair looked.

Talon was going on about her brother and sister, absently walking

127

and chatting with a bit of joy in her tone now that she knew her family was safe. Diaz didn't want to ruin things by telling her he'd watched Roaring fall off a cliff and hadn't been able to find him since. Thankfully, Talon never asked for details on his wellbeing—she was sure he was strong enough to take care of himself.

"How is your apprenticeship going?" he asked.

She paused and then laughed girlishly. "*Wonderful!* I haven't gotten the chance to craft anything myself, but I've almost finished a design for something I plan to make for Fox."

"Really?"

She nodded enthusiastically. "At first I was disappointed because I'd wanted her to have the weapon to use during the entrance exams, but today I found out the trainees weren't allowed to take anything in with them unless it was required for their blessing." She shrugged. "God had it handled the entire time! I should have just trusted His timing instead of worrying."

"It happens," Diaz said quietly.

"Oh, yes, it does." Talon giggled. "But it all worked out in the end. I couldn't be happier. Especially since you came all this way just to tell me my siblings are doing well." Talon smiled at him as she stopped in front of her apartment door. "You don't know how much that means to me."

"I came for another reason, too," he admitted. He stood before her, his eyes drinking in her cocoa skin and amber gaze. She was beautiful, but there was no point in getting caught up in his emotions. Not when he was a Hunter who wouldn't be around for long periods of time, and she was a Grand Chief who would be leaving Babel in a matter of months.

He crammed his hands deep into his pockets just to keep himself from doing something stupid like stroking her cheek or brushing his thumb over her smooth, full lips. In the back of his head, Diaz could still hear Captain Payne mocking him for caring about Lady Talon. Caring so much that she had become a distraction to him. And then he could hear his mother's words echoing in the chambers of his empty heart.

Don't let it in, Eve.

He had stayed away from Talon since returning to Babel. Payne had been right; she was a distraction. But keeping his distance hadn't been enough. He had gone against his mother's advice—he'd let in all his emotions. And he didn't know what to do because every time he allowed himself to feel something, the only thing that was left when it was all said and done was pain. Horrible, gnawing pain that threatened to rip him asunder.

Warmth spread on his shoulder, and he jerked back, not realizing Talon had simply laid a hand on his upper arm.

She gasped and yanked her hand back, an apology spilling from her lips. "I'm sorry! You were lost in thought—"

He shook his head. "It's fine. I shouldn't have drifted. I'm sorry."

Talon took a slow breath. "Would you like to come inside, Lieutenant Diaz? It's just me and Cat until the exams are over. Dinner will be awfully quiet."

He took a step back. Going inside would be a bad idea. Walking her home had been a bad idea. Being around her was a bad idea.

Don't let it in…

Diaz squeezed his eyes shut, hushing the whispers of his nightmares. "It's getting late," he grunted. Then he turned and stalked away before Talon could say anything more.

He didn't look back.

If he had, he would have turned around and entered her home and she would have had to fight him off to get him to leave. She was more than a distraction; she had become an obsession. He needed to fix this.

Fast.

12

Fox Fire

An explosion went off somewhere in the distance, but even if it'd gone off right beside their hideout, Fox wouldn't have heard it. The only thing she could focus on right now was the sound of KI's breathing.

She stared at his chest, watching the rhythmic rise and fall as he breathed deeply. It was, perhaps, the most beautiful thing she had ever seen or heard in quite a long time. Kohl had pointed out that his accursed seal was healing him, the demon inside doing its very best to keep her childhood friend alive. But she refused to take her eyes off him until she knew for certain that he was all right.

After five hours of staring, she had disappointed herself and fallen asleep. Kohl placed his shirt over her shivering shoulders while she rested, instead of thanking him for it, she had woken in a rage and screamed at him for letting her sleep.

She didn't have time for sleep. She needed to be awake to watch KI. But with an annoyingly calm roll of his cool blue eyes, Kohl pointed at the young boy and Fox realized her worries had been in vain. What had once been bubbled, burned flesh had become smooth olive-toned skin overnight. KI looked as if he'd never been burned. His skin was glowing—no scars or bruises in sight.

Amber eyes narrowed on the black markings of his flesh, shyly tracing the bold lines, memorizing the swirling patterns. They were no longer confined to just his back but stretched over his strong shoulders and crawling down his arms and chest. It was scary up close, but Fox refused to look away.

So far, everyone in KI's life had looked away because of the demon living inside of him. Kifu Kato, his adoptive father, had abandoned him without hesitation or issue, the rest of the council followed, along with every other member of their village. The trainees at the Grounds had never accepted him to begin with, if not for the demon inside then for the simple fact that he was friends with Kohlannis Hunger. A child from a cursed bloodline.

Of course he's friends with someone like Kohl, Fox almost laughed to herself. KI was far too kind for his own good, too sympathetic to allow something like self-preservation to take root in his heart. He had no concerns for himself, and he didn't care what others thought of him, but he would die standing up for Kohl's reputation. He had even stood up to Fox when she'd tried to corner him with questions and rumors she'd heard about Kohl. Her very own best friend had taken his side, insisting he wasn't as bad as everyone seemed to think.

With a slight shiver, Fox adjusted herself, slinking further into the folds of Kohl's shirt. She'd put it on when she'd woken up, adding a layer of protection against the morning chills. Fox wondered if Kohl was freezing. He'd stalked out of their shelter after she'd screamed at him for letting her fall asleep, mumbling something about finding food to eat.

Who cares if he's freezing? Fox pulled the collar of his shirt over her nose and mouth. *It smells like him.* Like something dark and masculine and cold.

Just then, the blonde boy pulled aside the curtain of leaves he'd tied together to cover the entrance to their cave. Sunlight poured into the area, bathing everything in bright morning colors.

Fox squinted and held up her hand, barely making out the agitated scowl on Kohl's face as he stalked over and dropped an armful of fruit in front of her. He left the curtain hanging askew so there was enough light for her see the massive food. Clusters of berries, each one the size of her fist.

"How on earth—"

"Everything in the forest is giant," he grunted. "Thank God."

Her stomach growled as she bit into an apple-sized berry. Sweet juice burst into her mouth, nearly choking her. She swallowed and wiped her face with Kohl's shirt.

He frowned. "Give that back before you stain it."

She blushed, trying not to stare at his bare chest. "Sorry."

Kohl slipped into his clothes and leaned against the wall of the cave. "How's the kid?"

"Still sleeping."

"If he's not up in an hour, I'll carry him to the next shelter. We can't stay here forever."

Kohlannis was right. They had survived the first day of the exams but that meant there were only four left and they still had only one bell each, no map, and no idea where to find the Great Temple.

"I was thinking we should try to track Donner. He had plenty of bells and as long as we keep an eye on KI, we should be able to withstand his charm."

Kohl took a long breath and then tugged a berry from the cluster. "I was thinking the same thing. But that only works if KI is conscious. Until he comes back from the dead, we won't be able to do much except march from shelter to shelter."

As long as KI was knocked out, they would have to carry him

133

everywhere. Even Fox could haul him around if she channeled her spiritual energy into her arms to give her extra strength. But no matter who was carrying KI, the arrangement would leave one of them vulnerable while the other had to lead the way and keep watch.

"And we don't even know which way to go," Fox mumbled around her mouthful of fruit.

Kohl nodded agreement as if he had been reading her mind. "Roaring had said we were going toward Fells Lake when we were all together."

"But we ran off during the fight with the troll and didn't keep track of which direction we were going when we escaped Donner and his goons."

"I did some scouting while I was out. Even climbed a few dozen feet up a tree to get a good look around. I think we headed west last night, we need to adjust and start going northwest. It'll take us the rest of the day, but we can make it to Fells Lake if we get moving soon."

"Do you think Roaring would still go there?" Fox asked.

"I think so. If he's…" Kohl's voice trailed off, but Fox didn't need him to finish. She already knew what he was thinking.

If he's still alive.

He had fallen over a cliff, but that wasn't certain death. Roaring was strong. He would have found a way to survive that. He would have saved himself and done his best to save Andor and Dart, too. At least that's what Fox prayed.

Please let him be alive, Lord Jesus, she said inside. *Spare him like You've spared me and my friends.*

KI stirred, groaning as his eyes fluttered.

Fox gasped. "He's waking up!"

With a long moan, KI lifted his arms and pressed the heels of his hands into his eyes. His voice came out like a croak. "What happened?"

"You're okay!" Fox exclaimed, scooting to sit beside him. She helped

134

him sit up, watching for signs of pain or fatigue. "Does it hurt anywhere?"

KI glanced down at himself and patted down his bare chest. "I feel great."

"Not even hungry?" Kohl asked. He tossed a berry to him. "We've got fruit."

KI caught it and sniffed. "I hate grapes."

"You need food," Fox insisted.

"Actually," he rubbed the back of his head and let out a boyish laugh. "I'm not hungry. I really do feel great."

"You had both of us so worried," Fox said.

"What happened to me?"

"You don't remember?"

He shook his head. "I remember fighting Donner and his lackeys. Then everything went black."

Fox let out a small laugh, cutting her eyes at Kohl. "You ... almost drowned."

"Did I?"

Kohl rolled his eyes, not wanting to join in.

"Yeah," Fox said. "Kohl pulled you out of the water. You needed mouth to mouth."

KI's cheeks turned flaming red but he played it cool and leaned closer to Fox, a very sly grin on his face. "You gave me mouth to mouth?"

"Kohl did."

"**WHY!?**" KI screamed, sudden tears running down his cheeks. He wiped at his mouth so violently his lips turned red with fresh bruises.

"Why are you *crying*?" Kohl snapped.

"You put your nasty lips on me!"

Kohl threw his giant grape at him. "No, I didn't! Fox is lying!"

With a snort, Fox burst into laughter which quickly turned into a scream when KI shoved her sideways. "You're horrible," he grumbled, standing and stretching.

She sat up and watched him a moment, happy that he was alive and unscathed. Guilt gripped her and she fidgeted beside him. "The truth is that I burned you, KI. I was sundancing and I lost track of my flames. There were too many for me to control. You got burned and you passed out. Because of me."

He stopped stretching and stared at her. "I was burned?"

She nodded.

"Bad enough for me to pass out?"

She nodded again.

KI straightened and stared down at his chest again. "Burned where?"

"All over," she told him. "We thought you were going to die. But your markings started glowing white and your skin began to heal itself."

KI's eyes bulged just a little.

He isn't very surprised, Fox realized.

"Has this happened before?"

He nodded slowly, then his eyes shot over to Kohlannis who was watching him in his normal broody silence. "It's happened a few times at the Tower whenever Ana didn't pull his punches when we sparred."

Kohl let out a longsuffering sigh. "You can't toughen up if I always pull my punches."

"You hit below the belt when we train!" KI grabbed his crotch and shuddered like he was reliving a horrible memory. "Like, literally."

"Your enemy won't pull their punches. And they'll probably target your weak spots in a fight. You need to learn how to guard yourself better."

KI crossed his arms like a child but didn't argue with Kohl.

Fox ... didn't know what to say.

"Why didn't you ever tell me you could heal yourself?" she finally

136

managed.

KI hesitated. "I'm not really proud of it. It isn't even my own ability or blessing. It's the demon inside me just trying to preserve its vessel."

"Don't call yourself a vessel," Fox said quietly. "You're a human being."

"Human or vessel," Kohl cut in, "that doesn't matter. We've got to get out of this cave. Now that you're awake, KI, we can start heading toward Fells Lake. The plan is to get there and rest, then scout out a way to the Great Temple. The hope is that Roaring will be there with Andor and Dart."

"Maybe Belinda, Wunda, and Danté will even head that way."

"If they're still—" Kohl started, but Fox gave him a nasty look.

"Let's keep the speculation down and pack up. We need to get out of here."

Kohl stood and made his way toward the cave entrance. "I'll be out here when you guys are ready."

"Hopefully we'll bump into other students along the way," KI said, tucking two berries into a sack Fox passed him.

"You want to fight?"

"Well, we need to collect our bells and I also need a shirt." He laughed nervously when Fox glanced at him.

"It's warmer outside the cave."

"Hopefully."

"Guys," Kohl's voice drifted inside. "Get out here."

"We're coming." Fox let go of an annoyed sigh as she tucked her flint and steel into her sack and then secured it to her hip. She tossed a berry back and forth in her hands as she led the way out of the cave, but Kohl was speaking again before she could push the leaf-curtain aside.

"Get out here," he said again.

She shoved it aside. "I said we're *coming*—" Fox choked on her words as she emerged and found Kohl shoved against a tree with a knife to his throat.

"Come out and keep your hands in the air," the knife wielder ordered. She was a young girl, hardly more than a year older than Fox.

Fox couldn't see much of her face since she had her back to her and KI, but she recognized her voice. "Gloria?" Fox said.

The girl stiffened, pressing her knife deeper into Kohl's neck. A small trickle of blood ran down his neck and stained his collar.

Gloria was a student from Class G5. A quiet girl who only won a handful of her sparring matches and tended to keep to herself. But Fox remembered her well enough, mostly because her blessing was so cool— *Teleportation*—which allowed her to instantly travel to any location so long as she could envision it first.

Fox had seen her jump around the sparring ring, disappearing to dodge attacks and reappearing behind her enemy to knock them out of the ring. Her surprise attacks worked a few good times but after a little while, her patterns were easy to follow. Even Fox had beaten her once, predicting where she would appear and landing a horrible blow to her ribs that'd dropped her to her knees with a cry.

Now, Gloria was holding a knife to Kohl's neck. And it would only take her an instant to have that knife at Fox's throat. *No wonder she doesn't bother to turn around,* Fox thought, glaring at her backside. *She can dodge any of our attacks in the blink of an eye—and then we'd end up hitting Kohl.*

Still. . .

Fox took a step forward, but she was quickly shoved back by an invisible force. Shock froze her in place, but anger tore a shout from her lips, "Gloria, quit it! We're classmates!"

Gloria laughed, still clutching the knife to Kohl. "That wasn't me."

Fox blinked as a figure stepped from the shadows nearby, a scruffy looking boy with light hair and a dark smile. He waved. "Name's Eekay.

From Class A-Three."

"Huh?" KI scratched his head beside Fox. "Gloria, you teamed up with someone from a different class?"

She didn't reply for a moment, her grip on the knife was so tight Fox could see her hand trembling even from her stance a few feet away. "I don't care who I have to work with. I want to pass."

"Then why don't we all work together?" Fox suggested.

She shook her head. "Give me your bells and we'll leave without hurting you."

"There are three of us—" Fox cried out in shock as she was suddenly shoved ten feet backwards. Her body hit a tree with an audible thud, tearing another cry from her lips as she wheezed in pain. Through teary eyes, she looked up to see Eekay standing with his hands in his pockets.

"The Dundo Tribe has a blessing called *Tide*, we have the power to push things away from us." He took a breath and Fox screamed as she was jerked forward, her body flying through the air. She felt as if something had grabbed hold of her and was tossing her around like a ragdoll.

She stopped mere inches from Eekay, her feet hovering above the grass. He smiled at her. "We can also pull things closer."

"Tide," KI said with a snort. "Like the ocean tide. Push and pull. I get it."

Eekay rolled his eyes and suddenly KI was screaming and flying deeper into the woods.

"You should have taken his bell first," Gloria said.

Eekay slapped his forehead. "I forgot."

"You also forgot," Fox said angrily, "that pushing or pulling me around doesn't render me paralyzed."

With an angry shout, she thrust her leg up and kicked Eekay right in the face. His head snapped backwards as he stumbled away. With his

139

concentration broken, Fox dropped to the ground. She immediately rolled over, snatching her flint and steel from her pouch, and striking as quickly as she could.

Fire burst into the air, but she didn't get the chance to direct it. Eekay hurled her twenty feet away, into a prickly bush. With a groan, Fox climbed from the bush and clutched her tools. She half-expected Eekay to pull her back toward him, but then KI came flying past and she sighed.

She would have tried to save KI by shooting fire at Eekay but Gloria suddenly appeared in front of her and landed a punch to her jaw. Pain exploded in her face, and then ruptured in her gut, and bloomed on the other side of her face. Before she could focus enough to hit back or block, Gloria disappeared and then Eekay yanked her forward.

Fox screamed, clutching her flint and steel as she was dragged across the clearing. She managed to strike her tools and send a wave of fire at Eekay but he just pushed it right back at her. It didn't burn, but it did blind her long enough for Gloria to reappear and deliver three more horrible blows. Meanwhile, KI flew by in the other direction. Again.

This is ridiculous. Fox shook her head as she stumbled back and took a wild swing at the air, praying her fist would connect with Gloria's jaw. She missed and realized Gloria was long gone, exchanging blows with Kohl. At least he'd managed to twist her knife from her hand and was using it to keep her at bay.

Fox struck her flint and steel and fired at Gloria, she disappeared, forcing Kohl to jump to the side to avoid her flames. He yelled at her, but she ignored him and fired at the spot she expected Gloria to appear. The young girl cried out as she materialized before a blast of fire.

Fox smiled.

KI flew by again.

She huffed and shot a blast at Eekay just to distract him. It worked, and he lost his grip on KI, sending him skittering over the grass to tumble into a tree. Fox would have continued her attack, but when she glanced at her companion, a figure emerging from the shadows beyond the tree caught her attention.

Fox gasped, not believing what she was seeing.

He was not as tall as she had imagined. But everything else about him matched the stories she'd heard from KI and Kohl.

He really did wear dark colors and a red leather mask, like an assassin.

The Red Face stepped from behind the tree and reached for KI.

13

Kohlannis

Kohl could think of a lot of bad days he'd had. He was certain today would make the top five. He knew things were bad when he'd let his guard down and walked out his shelter to get ambushed by his own classmate. But things got *really* bad when the other kid showed up and started throwing Fox and KI around. And then things spiraled out of control when the Red Face showed up. Because it wouldn't make sense for Kohl's day to end on a good note. No. everything—*everything*—had to go up in flames or else the sun would fall out of the sky and the moon would crack open.

Kohl rolled his eyes as he watched the Red Face reach for KI. The kid sat there and screamed, which was worse than the first time they'd faced the assassin when KI flat out surrendered and agreed to go with him. That had given Kohl an instant migraine.

Fight back, he ground his teeth together as he watched the masked man grab KI by the hair.

KI screamed louder.

Kohl rolled his eyes again. Sometimes he felt like he was the only one in his group of friends with a brain.

He could use his gift, but he'd promised himself he would never do that. He didn't need his powers. He was good enough without them.

But KI was being dragged away by his *hair*, and Fox was still whirling around the woods thanks to Eekay. And Gloria—Kohl glanced around. Gloria was gone.

Well, that wasn't so bad. One less person to fight.

Kohl took a step forward, focusing his spiritual energy to his legs so he could chase down the Red Face. Mercifully, Fox set off an explosion right beside the tree where he was standing. It knocked him and KI off balance just long enough for Gloria to appear beside KI. She grabbed him by his arm and then disappeared.

"Thank God," Kohl grumbled, then he jumped in surprise when Gloria and KI were both suddenly standing beside him.

Gloria shoved KI toward him. "Here's your friend."

KI tripped into Kohl's chest, he shoved him aside. "Thanks."

"I'm out of here." Gloria said, but Kohl grabbed her sleeve.

"Wait, you're leaving?"

"Do you really expect me to stick around and fight the Red Face?" She shook her head. "That's the guy who burned down Cross Academy. I did enough by getting your friend back. Now, I'm out of here before he burns down the forest."

Before Kohl could stop her, Gloria teleported to Eekay, grabbed him by the shirt sleeve, and both of them disappeared.

"She saved me," KI said breathily.

"Shut *up*," Kohl snapped. He turned and stared into the forest where the Red Face had emerged. "We need to stay focused on this guy. We know he's strong and fast and can somehow use fire." He glared at the assassin. "I wish that Crystal kid was here so he could tell us what we're up against."

Without notice, Fox shot a fireball at the Red Face. The masked man turned and clapped his hands together, then he shoved them forward right into the flames. The fire split around him and dissipated in the air.

"Amazing," KI exhaled.

Kohl slapped the back of his head. "Do not compliment your own kidnapper."

"He hasn't kidnapped me yet."

"I have half a mind to *let* him kidnap you." *Then I wouldn't have to deal with this crap.*

The look of sadness that swept over KI's face made Kohl immediately regret his words.

Gosh, he's so sensitive.

Kohl sighed. "I'm not gonna let him take you. Sheesh."

His face brightened. "Okay, so, how do we do this?"

"Are you actually going to fight or just scream and surrender?"

KI shrugged and hummed, "Dunno."

Fox ran at the Red Face, shrieking like a madwoman. She was always crazy whenever it came to KI. Good. That gave Kohl a chance to formulate a plan while she kept the assassin distracted. Judging from all the blazing heat and explosions going off in the distance, he'd be busy for a while.

Plus, Fox is nearly unstoppable when KI's safety is involved.

Kohl held in his sigh. *He* should have run in screaming mad and left Fox behind on babysitting duty. That way he wouldn't be stuck here with the kid smiling and blinking up at him like they were making dinner plans instead of trying to save his life.

KI never knows when to take things seriously. Kohl tried to hold in another sigh, but it came out as a grunt that made KI frown.

"You all right, Ana?"

Ana. Kohl ground his teeth together. *That name…*

"Ana?" KI was poking his shoulder.

"I'm fine!" Kohl barked, then he cursed colorfully and shoved KI down into the grass. "Just stay here and don't get kidnapped." He tripped over a tree root and cursed again. "And don't die!" he shouted over his shoulder.

Kohl was always shouting. And snapping. And cursing at KI. It was a wonder he called himself a Christian.

It's not like I don't believe in God, he rolled his shoulders back as he stood in the clearing. *He's the One who cursed me.*

Power crackled in the air as Kohl charged his spiritual energy. The tree beside him splintered, bark shredding up its trunk. *I won't use my power*, Kohl concentrated, *I'll just release some of my energy to let him know I'm serious.*

He took a deep breath and released a surge of power on his exhale. The attack was concentrated, like a bullet of compacted spiritual energy firing right at the Red Face.

Just as he'd expected, Fox was still losing her mind, fighting the assassin like she was half crazed. The Red Face was too distracted to react to Kohl's attack. It hit him on his shoulder so hard he was knocked off his feet.

A ring of fire immediately surrounded him like a cage.

Fox stepped forward. "Surrender."

The Red Face ignored her; his dark eyes focused on Kohl. "That hurt."

Kohl shrugged one shoulder.

"I thought you vowed to never use your powers."

"I didn't use them."

"Who are you!" Fox yelled.

"No need to lose our tempers," Kohl said coolly. "We've got him, Fox. He'll talk eventually.

The Red Face laughed. "Do you really think this little trick will hold me?"

Kohl squinted. He'd heard that voice before, but he couldn't place it.

"How about this…" The Red Face reached into the pouch on his hip and dropped a small black ball onto the ground. Smoke billowed from it, clouding the area.

Kohl covered his face, squinting into the dark cloud to see the assassin backing away.

"Bring the boy to Fells Lake before sunset and I won't kill anyone."

When the smoke cleared, the Red Face was gone.

Fox screamed in anger. "How!?"

Good question, Kohl quirked an eyebrow, staring at the empty ring of fire. *Why did he even bother fighting with Fox if he could just vanish like that?*

"It's like he was toying with us." Fox sniffled and dropped to her knees. "We have to hunt him down."

"No, we have to pass this exam, Fox. Don't lose focus."

"Lose focus?" Her voice was dark. "Protecting KI is the only thing I'm focused on right now."

"KI is safe," Kohl said.

Speaking of the kid… He glanced over his shoulder to make sure KI was still where he'd left him. He was. Sitting in the grass, cross-legged, waving as he noticed Kohl watching him.

"Is it safe?" he called.

Kohl nodded and extended his hand to Fox. "Get up. He can't see you upset like this; it'll rub off on him."

Fox took his hand. "The Red Face said we have to bring him to Fells Lake—"

"I heard him," Kohl grunted. "We'll deal with it."

"How?"

*Jesus, I don't **know**.*

Kohl wanted to scream. What on earth gave Fox the impression that he knew how to handle this situation?

146

For the first time since he met the guy, Kohl wished Roaring was around. He didn't dislike the burly warrior, but he never missed him. Until now.

Okay, Kohl reluctantly admitted, he might have noticed when Roaring dropped out of the training program. But he hadn't *missed* him. Kohl had his own goals to chase after whether Roaring was there or not.

But we could seriously use his help right about now...

"Looks like you chased him off," KI said cheerily.

Kohl glared at him. It was like the weight of the situation had gone right over the kid's head. "Yeah," he grunted. "We chased him off. But he's going to be back."

"Then we'll chase him off again."

Kohl felt his blood begin to boil. "*We* aren't going to do anything. You're going to hide and stay back so you don't accidentally get kidnapped by a deadly, demon-powered assassin."

KI glowered. "I can fight."

"Could have fooled me," Kohl grumbled, stalking away.

"Where are we headed now?" KI jogged a few steps to catch up.

"Fells Lake."

"Seriously?" Fox was beside Kohl in an instant. "We are not going to Fells Lake."

"Why not?" KI asked.

"We are going," Kohl corrected.

"We are?"

"No," Fox snapped.

"*Yes*." Kohl stopped walking to glare at her.

She glared right back. "I am not handing KI over to the Red Face."

"Hand me over?" The color drained from KI's face.

Now *he realizes how serious this is.* Kohl let out a deep, heavy breath. "Just trust me on this, Fox."

147

She crossed her arms. "I don't trust anyone when it comes to KI's safety."

"We *all* took a pact at that bonfire," Kohl said, voice low and strained. "Not just you and KI. That means I get a say in how we watch each other's back."

"I'm not letting you hand him over." Fox set her jaw, the glare in her eyes letting him know she wasn't going to change her mind on this.

The tree beside them cracked as Kohl blew air through his nostrils, barely containing his anger. *Ugh, Fox is so stubborn sometimes.*

He lowered his voice in case anyone was nearby. "We were already headed to Fells Lake, Foxy. And so was Roaring. And everyone else on our team before we got separated. If we take KI there, the rest of our classmates might be there to help."

Understanding calmed her angry features. Fox let a pinched smile replace her frown. That was as much of an apology as Kohl would get. He didn't care for more, so long as she didn't fight him on this anymore.

With a grunt, Kohl turned and led the way deeper into the woods.

They walked in silence for the next few hours with KI's occasional complaint about being hungry the only thing to break the stony quiet. Fox wouldn't even look at Kohl, but he didn't try hard to catch her gaze. She was always stubborn and unreasonable when it came to KI, protecting him like he was her child instead of a six-foot-tall Hunter in training.

Kohl stole a glance at KI. The kid was almost as tall as him now, and he had come close to besting him in a handful of matches when they'd sparred at the Academy. Sometimes it was easy to forget that he was only fourteen years old. No matter what he looked like on the outside, KI was still young—three years younger than Kohl. *Maybe that's why Fox is so protective of him*, he thought, *she still sees him as the kid he was in Wi.*

Just fourteen… The same age Kohl's brother would be if he were still alive.

Maybe that's why I'm so protective of him.

KI didn't look anything like his little brother. But when he was smiling and batting his long lashes and looking at Kohl like he had all the answers in the world, their similarities were blaring. Wide-eyed kids too naïve for their own good.

"Ana?" KI said, dropping into the grass. He sighed and leaned against a tree. "I'm too hungry to go on."

"We need a break," Fox said.

Ana, Kohl repeated the nickname in his head. His brother had called him the same thing and he'd almost hated it back then. It was girly. But then, so was the name Karmen, so Kohl didn't mind him using the name. They both had girly names.

It had been three years since Kohl had heard 'Ana.' When KI had first used it, he'd thought Karmen had come back from the dead. Every time he heard it, he had to remind himself that Karmen was dead and KI wasn't his brother.

On good days, KI's presence was comforting. Like Karmen was still there following him around everywhere, exactly the way he used to. But on days like this, with death all around them, KI made Kohl want to punch something.

He hadn't been able to protect Karmen. For some sick reason, he'd fooled himself into believing he could protect KI—like that would make up for losing his brother.

He's not Karmen, Kohl told himself as he turned to face his friends.

"We shouldn't have left the rest of our fruit in the cave," KI whined.

Fox knelt and plucked a giant berry from a bush nearby. "Try this."

KI took it and bit into it without hesitation.

149

Volcanic anger erupted inside Kohl. He saw red as he marched over and snatched the fruit from KI's hands. "You don't even know what that is!" he shouted.

KI blinked at him; his mouth smeared with purple juice from the strange fruit. "Fox said it was fine."

"Fox is an idiot!" he barked, throwing the fruit as far away as he could. "That's not a berry, it's an egg from a poupo bug!"

KI burst into tears. "*WHY!?*" he cried. "Why did I just eat a bug's egg?"

Why ... why was I saddled with these two?

Kohl closed his eyes and took three deep breaths to calm himself, but the anger came back twice as violently when he opened his eyes and saw KI eating another poupo egg.

He snatched the egg away and smashed it on the ground. "What is *wrong* with you!" he hollered.

KI cowered. "It actually doesn't taste that bad."

"The poupo bug is *poisonous*!" He shook KI by the shoulders. "I ought to kill you and end this story right here."

"Am I going to die?" KI gulped and then, inexplicably, he fainted.

I can't make this stuff up... With a longsuffering sigh, Kohl channeled his spiritual energy into his arms and lifted KI from the ground. "Let's go," he muttered to Fox.

"Is he going to die?" Fox asked after they'd walked a mile in silence.

"No." *He'll just feel dizzy and nauseated for a while.* The demon inside had probably cleansed the poison from his systems already. Kohl didn't say any of this, he was too irritated to speak, and Fox seemed satisfied with his curt answer, so he didn't bother offering any more words than that.

14

Roaring

Roaring opened his eyes and immediately regretted it. Light punched holes through the leafy canopy overhead, glaring at him with the full force of the afternoon sun. He lifted a hand to shield his burning eyes and groaned as he realized how sore he was. Every part of his body ached; even places he didn't know could ache.

He tried to sit up and found he was as stiff as he was sore. A strained grunt tore from his lips, and he heard movement on the other side of the grassy curtain hanging before him. A few moments later, the curtain was swept aside and in walked a familiar figure; slender, with cocoa colored skin, and stark white dreadlocks that swayed around her as she ducked into the makeshift tent.

Vyanna's face was filled with sincere concern as she stared down at the Prince of Fire. He appreciated the way her lips pursed, and her brow wrinkled as she studied him, but he couldn't stop the embarrassing anger that swelled within him as he glanced down at his body and noticed the bruises.

"You're alive," Vy said in a whisper. She knelt beside him and placed a hand on his bare chest. He couldn't help it, his abs constricted at her touch—but not because of the softness of her hands, it was because of how cold they were. Like ice.

She caught him cringing and immediately pulled away. "Sorry. Seadancers are always cold."

He grunted and hoped it sounded like a chuckle. "Sundancers are always hot."

"I thought you were dead when I found you."

"Found me?"

She nodded. "At the bottom of a cliff, buried in rubble."

Now he remembered, and the jarring recollection of everything that'd happened sent him bolting upright faster than he would've liked. He gasped in pain and dug his hand into the earth, clawing up a fistful of dirt as his muscles cried out against the sudden movement.

Vyanna's cold hand was on his chest again, gently pushing him back down onto his pallet. "You need to rest."

"I need to find my team," he argued.

"They are safe."

"Andor—"

"And Dart are both fine."

Reluctantly, he let her guide him back down as he let out a shaky breath. "I take it they aren't as banged up as I am."

"You took the brunt of the fall. Andor was wrapped in your arms when I found you, totally unscathed. Dart was messed up, but Syren healed him."

He raised an eyebrow. "You have a team?"

"Syren Danis and my cousins."

Roaring didn't respond. He hated the Ool twins.

"I can go and get Syren; she'll heal you up."

"Why didn't she do that while I was out?"

"Healing takes a lot of spiritual energy. She didn't want to drain herself, so she rested last night and will heal you up now."

"How long have I been unconscious?"

He was afraid of what her answer might be, but his anxiety calmed when Vyanna replied, "Just one night. It's only day two of the exams." His relief must have been visible on his face because she smiled at him and said, "Don't worry, Prince of Fire, you still have plenty of time to show off."

He wrinkled his nose. He wasn't a showoff, was he?

No, he rolled his eyes, watching Vy leave. *She's just trying to flirt with me.*

"How do you feel?" The question came from Syren Danis, a girl Roaring had seen around the Training Grounds plenty of times. She was in Class G5, but she usually hung around Slaine and another girl named Kressa. *The one Kohl's been thirsting over*, Roaring smirked as he thought of the blonde-haired boy tripping over himself whenever Kressa was around.

"Looks like you feel great since you're smiling," Syren knelt beside him and studied his bruised torso.

He shook his head. "No. I was just lost in thought."

"I think you've got a broken rib," she murmured, then she clasped her hands together and closed her eyes, whispering something to herself.

Roaring stared in mystified surprise. He had no idea what she was doing or if he should interrupt. To anyone else, it might have looked like she was merely praying, but in the middle of the Kanen Forest, surrounded by hundreds of blessings he'd never seen before, Roaring figured she could be doing just about anything.

Syren opened her eyes and extended a hand to him. A tiny, golden crystal rested in her palm. If it weren't for the warm smile on her face, Roaring would have sat there and simply stared at the gem, refusing to touch it. But Syren looked so gentle and welcoming, he didn't even think before he reached over and took the little crystal in his large fingers.

He held it up. "What is it?"

153

"It's a physical manifestation of my spiritual energy." Syren smiled. "Eat it."

For a second, Roaring wasn't sure he'd heard her correctly. Then he realized her golden eyes were still on him, watching with such expectancy that he didn't bother tossing up any questions before he brought the crystal to his lips and ate it.

It burst with a crunch, like sugary glass shattering into a burst of sweet honey. Roaring's eyes went wide—first at the stunning taste, and then because of the instant relief that flooded his sore, aching body.

He sat up and rolled his shoulders back. "Amazing."

Syren laughed and clapped her dainty hands. "Are you feeling better?"

"I feel like I could run a hundred miles."

She laughed. "Thank God."

"That's some blessing."

"Being a healer has its benefits."

"I'm guessing you patched up Dart?" Roaring asked. He stood and put on the shirt Syren passed him.

She nodded. "He's been out scouting for us. You'll see him once he gets back."

"Scouting," Roaring repeated slowly. He pushed aside the tent cover and stepped into the afternoon sunlight. Outside rested a quaint little camp; one of the Ool twins sat stirring something in a clay pot over an open flame while Vyanna pulled water from the air and directed it into the open skins being held by Andor.

"Looks like you guys have a nice place set up," Roaring complimented as he approached Vy.

She wiped sweat from her brow and nodded. "My team is efficient. But the addition of your friends has not been a hindrance of any sort."

Roaring smirked internally, sometimes Vy spoke too formally for a teenage girl. He'd heard she was a princess of the Farron Tribe, but he wondered if she'd been born and raised in Babel. If he remembered correctly, the Farrons were originally from the Region of Ice, ruling the largest Region of the four from a place they called the Northern Fortress. But the Farrons in Babel had been in the great city for generations, according to records in the Academy library.

Maybe she traveled to Babel for the exams, Roaring decided as he took the water skin Vy had offered him. He drank it down in one go and then wiped his mouth with the back of his hand.

"Thanks."

Vy nodded. "Toad is making stew from some dried fish and herbs we found in the forest."

Roaring fought the urge to grimace. He hated the Ool twins, but he especially hated Toad. Ren was the better fighter between the two, but Toad was the most annoying. The Prince of Fire avoided looking at him as he sat down beside the little fire and looked at Vyanna. "What's the plan?"

"Every member of my team has the required number of bells. We plan to move toward the Great Temple today. You are welcome to join us, since we have our bells, we won't mind lending assistance in your search for bells."

Roaring patted his chest and then checked his pockets. His bell was missing.

Before he could ask, Vyanna said, "We took your bell when we found you. As well as Dart's and Andor's."

"Why?"

"Because we needed them."

"*Everyone* needs their bells." Roaring stood, but Vyanna was not intimidated. She waved off his comment like she was dismissing the complaints of a whiny child.

"We could have taken your bells and left you buried in that rubble. Consider them payment for saving your lives."

Anger crackled in Roaring's chest, threatening to spill out in the form of raging fire. He stared at the flames beneath Toad's cooking pot, ignoring the simpering look on the stupid boy's face. *The bells don't matter*, he told himself. He wasn't even here to pass the exam. He was supposed to be protecting KI from the Red Face. Obviously, things hadn't gone as planned, but that didn't make it okay for Vy and her cousins to take their bells.

Actually, it is *okay*, he realized. *This is how the exam goes. Every man for himself.*

Roaring let out a long sigh. "You're going to the Great Temple now."

"As I said, we will lend you aid in acquiring bells."

The last plan he'd had with his sister and the others was to head to Fells Lake. It was supposed to be their next stop before making a final push toward the Great Temple. Roaring had no idea what'd happened to Fox and her friends, but if she was well enough to walk, he knew she would definitely go to Fells Lake with the hopes of meeting up with him.

"I want to stop by Fells Lake," Roaring said.

"Are you serious?" He looked up to find Andor glaring at him with her hands on her hips. "We need to be searching for other trainees so we can collect our bells. This is our team now."

Roaring took a deep breath. The flames beneath Toad's pot grew and expanded when he exhaled, as if he'd breathed life into them. "We wouldn't be on a new team if it weren't for you, Andor. So if you think I'm going to abandon my little sister to stick with a spineless, glow-in-the-dark little girl, then you have lost your tiny mind."

Andor clamped her mouth shut.

Toad snickered beside them, still stirring his pot. When he glanced up and saw Roaring glaring at him, he cleared his throat and stood.

156

"Lunch is ready."

They ate in silence, sitting around the fire with bowls in their hands. Apparently, Vy, her cousins, and Syren had overtaken a small encampment of students and took their supplies on day one of the exam. Roaring was happy. He hadn't eaten much since he'd arrived at the exam gates. The soup wasn't even great, but he tilted his bowl back to gulp down the rest like it was the best thing he'd ever eaten. It tasted of roasted fish and earth, with bits of mushroom and a salty spice he couldn't place.

Just as Roaring turned to ask for another serving, a hawk screeched above him and caught everyone's attention.

"Dart's back," Syren said, staring up at the sky.

As if he'd heard his name, Dart dived toward the ground and shifted into a human just before landing. He smiled at Roaring. "Nice to see you up and walking around." He crossed his muscular arms. "You're just in time. I spotted trouble."

"What sort of trouble?" Andor asked, eyes bulging already.

Roaring suppressed a groan. If Andor freaked out this time, he was going to leave her.

"I heard explosions and saw smoke," Dart explained. "Went to check it out, and realized it was Fox Fire."

Roaring stood. "Is she with KI?"

"And Kohl." Dart nodded. "But you'll never believe who they were fighting."

"Who?" Andor pleaded.

"The Red Face."

Toad narrowed his eyes. Syren gasped. Andor fainted.

Vyanna calmly set her bowl down. "Where is Ren?"

"Right here." Ren pushed through the bushes, eyeing Dart. "You left me back there."

157

"I wanted to get the news back as soon as possible."

Ren stomped over and punched Dart on the shoulder, gently enough that he knew she wasn't trying to hurt him, but hard enough to make him wince once she turned away. Roaring watched him massage the thick muscle before he said, "I flew over just as they chased the Red Face away."

"You didn't stop to speak to them?" Roaring asked.

His eyes grew wide, like the thought hadn't crossed his mind until that moment. "I wanted to get the information back to you as quickly as possible."

"The Red Face is the assassin who was after KI, right?" Syren asked.

"Yes. And it seems he has somehow found his way into the examination arena." Vyanna glared at the ground, jaw clenching. "I don't understand how this is possible. The Kanen Forest is cloaked and protected by a spiritual barrier during the exams, that way administrators will be notified if an outside force breaches the area."

"Then our teachers have been notified. They'll come and take care of the Red Face," Syren said, but when no one responded she added, "Right?"

Roaring shook his head. "If Master Jo or anyone else was coming, they would have shown up the moment the Red Face crossed into the forest. But he had time to track down KI, attack him, and get away again. Without being interrupted."

"What does this mean?" Dart asked.

"It means the Red Face is a student here. He didn't breach the barrier because he entered with the rest of us."

"Basically," Toad said, staring into the small fire, "no one is coming to help us."

No, Roaring's hands curled into fists. *The Academy knew the Red Face would show up. Help must be coming.* "There may be other precautions set in

158

place," he told the group.

"But what if there aren't?" Syren was staring at him, tears wetting her lashes as she tried to blink them away. She was tougher than Andor, he would give her that, but the fact that the mere mention of the masked assassin could cause one student to faint, and another to cry left a cloud of darkness looming over Roaring. *How are these guys seriously going to make it out there in the real world?* he wondered.

"I'm going to find my sister," Roaring said, marching away.

"You don't even know where she is," Syren protested.

"If she managed to chase off the Red Face, she'll be heading to Fells Lake next. That's where we said we'd meet—"

Roaring cut himself off and pivoted to fire a blast of heat into the surrounding forest. Vyanna immediately turned, sending shards of ice shooting in the same direction he'd fired. Toad and Ren suddenly held daggers in their hands and Dart shifted into a gorilla.

"What did you sense?" Vy asked.

"You attacked without even knowing what was out there." Roaring chuckled. "You guys don't hesitate."

Syren stepped forward, crystalline wings sprouting from her backside as she moved. "We cannot afford to hesitate."

Roaring almost reminded her she'd had tears in her eyes a moment earlier, but he held his tongue and watched as she extended her right hand; her spiritual energy pooled in her palm; as it flowed between her fingers, it hardened to form a crystal sword before reaching the ground.

"What did you sense?" Vyanna asked again.

Roaring didn't have to answer. As he glared into the forest, darkness formed, overtaking the shadows, and crawling out into the sunlight. The grass withered and died right before their eyes, turning black as its life was sucked away. Trees bent and shriveled, toppling over, and turning to dust; bushes dried up, their leaves falling to the dead earth as a last

159

whisper of life.

"I sensed death," Roaring said.

There was a chuckle from deep within the black woods. "Death has a name."

"*Slaine.*" Ren spat his name like it was acid burning on her tongue.

"Slaine?" Syren stepped forward, lowering her sword.

Silence.

Then, very slowly, a figure emerged through the withered brush. Slaine stood with his hands casually stuffed into his pockets, like he hadn't just killed off a bunch of innocent plant life. Like he wasn't about to kill them the same way.

It was difficult to read his face with his skin rotting and almost falling off his skull. His cheeks were sewn together with crude stitches, jagged black lines of thread zigzagging over his face. There was a new set of stitching going right across his forehead, like his face had burst open and someone had tried to tie it all back together. His eyes were sunken into his burned flesh, bloody tears streaked his cheeks without eyelids to keep them at bay. It was a wonder he was alive and walking around. He looked like a walking dead man.

"What are you doing here, Sy?" Slaine asked, his voice suddenly much gentler than before—*when he was laughing like a villain and calling himself death*, Roaring thought. He stole a glance at Syren who had totally put away her weapon now, though her crystal wings remained. Without notice, she ran over and hugged Slaine.

Roaring cringed and swallowed a gag. How a pretty girl like Syren could hug a walking corpse, he hadn't a clue, but she was clinging to him like he'd come to rescue her.

"I can't believe you're all right!" Syren gasped. "Where's Kressa?"

Slaine shrugged one shoulder. "We got separated."

Impatient, Dart huffed and let out a low growl. Roaring didn't speak gorilla, so he could only guess what he'd said, but he assumed it was something along the lines of—"So what happens next?"

Syren looked back at him as he voiced Dart's concerns. "Slaine isn't here to hurt us. He would never do that."

His face was held together by a literal thread, but Roaring didn't miss the expression that flitted over Slaine's features. He looked agitated, like he wished Syren hadn't said that. *Or like he wished she wasn't here at all. So he could kill us all with his cursed gift.*

Toad spat in the dirt. "I don't trust him."

Irritation sputtered through Slaine's glare, but he didn't speak, just stood there as Syren took his gloved hand in hers and gave it a squeeze. "They're my teammates. You won't hurt them, right?"

A stony silence rolled over the little camp as Slaine eyed each one of them. He let out a breath and pulled his hand away from Syren. "Stay with them." Then he turned and walked back into the forest. The further away he got, the more Roaring felt like he could breathe.

He carries death wherever he goes.

Syren's shoulders sagged. "He left."

"Better than fighting us," Ren said.

Vyanna nodded. "But he knows where we are camped out. Our position has been compromised; we need to get moving now."

"He won't tell anyone," Syren argued.

"I was leaving anyway," Roaring announced.

"We can still travel with you to Fells Lake," Vyanna called. "It will be safer if we all go together."

He didn't want to travel with a large group again, but he knew Vy was right. With people like Slaine slithering through the forest, it was much safer to stick together.

"Just don't slow me down," Roaring grunted. "I've got to get there as soon as I can."

Vy issued orders behind him. "Dart, we need you scouting ahead. Toad, carry Andor. Ren cover our rear, Syren with me." She stepped beside him and patted his shoulder. "Don't worry, Prince of Fire, we'll get to your sister."

15

Kohlannis

Kohl could hear the soft whispers of his teammates as he pushed through the brush. He found them huddled together beside a small fire, courtesy of Fox, talking like they hadn't a care in the world. He wanted to roll his eyes and silently scold them for their nonchalance, but it was nice to see them relaxed rather than freaking out.

KI had awakened about an hour after passing out and was able to walk a few miles before he started complaining of hunger again. Soon after, they stumbled upon a destroyed camp. It looked like a terrible battle had taken place, leaving the bodies of three students behind. Mercifully, they didn't recognize any of the bodies as fellow classmates from G5, but the sight was still unnerving. Kohl decided to send Fox and KI ahead while he stayed back and searched the wreckage for any leftover food and supplies.

Fox looked up and spotted Kohl, a smile split her face as she waved him over. He dumped an armful of the supplies he'd scavenged onto the ground before them, and then sat.

"We need to talk."

"How far are we from Fells Lake?" KI asked.

"About a mile out." He eyed them closely, noticing how rigid Fox suddenly seemed. Her eyes were hard and sharply focused as she met his stare, but then KI was talking again, and her features were taken captive by a sudden flicker of joy. Kohl watched as she smiled brightly and turned to her friend, surrendering her full attention.

KI was the only one who could do that to her, change her mood with just the sound of his voice. He wasn't even talking about anything important, just complaining about how tired he was from all the walking they'd done—even though Kohl had carried him most of the way.

He ground his teeth together and resisted the urge to roll his eyes. KI was never serious when he needed to be. Never seemed to notice how dire their situations were. Not until his life was *this* close to ending. Normally, that wouldn't bother Kohl, since he was keenly aware of how childish the kid could be. But it irked him whenever Fox fed into his nonsense.

Like now. She was watching KI reenact their fight with Gloria and Eekay. KI started running back and forth like he was being thrown around by Eekay's blessing; Fox snorted in laughter and slapped her knee.

"We need to talk!" Kohl barked angrily.

KI immediately stopped running and returned to have a seat. "What's there to talk about?"

"What are we going to do once we get to Fells Lake? You know the Red Face will be expecting us."

"We're going to kill him," Fox said darkly.

Kohl sighed. "Suppose we don't kill him. Suppose we come to some sort of agreement."

Fox bared her teeth. "We are not handing over KI. I will die screaming before I let that happen."

"Did you find anything good out there, Ana?" KI asked, and then he started rummaging through the supplies he'd brought back—*probably to*

164

remove himself from the conversation, Kohl thought.

KI never liked when they argued, but Kohl wanted him to be part of the discussion. He watched him sort the food and water and weapons, clearly trying to distract himself from Fox's anger and Kohl's rising temper. *And the fact that we're discussing his fate right in front of him.*

Kohl leaned forward and grabbed a shirt from the pile of supplies. "Here, I brought back a couple shirts since Fox burned up your last one. Try them on and see which one fits."

"Thanks, Ana." KI grinned at him, cheeks bunching, big, hazel eyes squeezing shut.

Sheesh... Kohl looked away. *He's too cute for his own good.*

His heart began to ache as images of Karmen flooded his mind's eye. He had been just like KI in so many ways. Kind, naïve, and full of smiles. When he was still a toddler, he could get Kohl to do anything he wanted with a bat of his white-blonde lashes. Kohlannis had spoiled his little brother, giving him everything he'd ever asked for. Even when he'd asked to die.

Kohl heaved for breath, clutching his chest as crippling pain stabbed his heart. Fox and KI were staring at him now, a tense silence settling over them.

"Ana?" KI said slowly. "You okay?"

No. He wasn't okay. But he couldn't say that—he couldn't tell anyone what was really wrong.

He cleared his throat. Smoothed his sweat-soaked hair back. "I'm fine."

"This shirt fits," KI said, stretching out his arms so Kohl could see.

He nodded. "It does. You look good, kid."

Another grin that sent jolts of pain straight through his heart.

"We need to discuss what happens next," Kohl grated out.

"I already told you," Fox said, "we go to Fells Lake and kill the Red

165

Face."

"That's easier said than done."

"We are not negotiating with an assassin."

"We could at least try to talk—"

She stood. "I'll talk with my fire."

"I just want to find out who he is," Kohl said.

Fox hesitated. "I think I know who the Red Face is."

"How?" KI asked, gnawing on a piece of jerky.

"His power. Roaring and I are the only ones here who are sundancers, yet the Red Face set the Tower ablaze."

"You think it's Roaring?" Kohl asked.

She shook her head. "I think it's Montell."

Kohl raised a single eyebrow.

Fox said, "He touched me at the bonfire. He copied my sundancing the day before the exam so he would have the power available to use in capturing KI today."

Something didn't feel right about the accusation. Kohl placed an elbow on each knee and tented his fingers. "That makes sense. But—"

"But what?" Fox snapped.

"He didn't use fire back there."

She paused. Even KI glanced up from his jerky to stare between them. "Ana's right. The Red Face didn't use fire this time."

"Why would Montell make sure he copied your blessing but not use it when it mattered most?"

"Maybe..." Fox's voice trailed off, then she gasped. "Maybe Montell and Vinny are both the Red Face."

"Then he would have used his sturdy blessing," Kohl said. "I don't think the Red Face is Montell or his brother."

"But who else could he be?" Fox asked.

Good question. Kohl let out a heavy sigh that seemed to come from

166

deep within. He felt so tired. So drained. But he was expected to meet with an assassin soon and had no idea what to do or anticipate. They couldn't just hand over KI, but was it right to allow the Red Face to wreak havoc on the rest of the exams? This was the assassin who'd nearly burned down the Academy. Kohl had seen his skill up close; he knew just how much damage he could do. No one else should have to die for one person.

He swallowed. That was a noble thought, but difficult to enforce when the one person was your own friend.

"I don't have any guesses as to who the Red Face could be. But I think we should consider our options," he said slowly.

Fox's glare was dangerous. "What options? You mean all the different ways we can kill that monster?"

"Fox," Kohl sighed, but that was all he got to say. Fox abruptly stood and began marching away. "Where are you going?" he called.

She threw her hand into the air. "I just need a minute alone."

"She won't go far," KI said. "And she won't be gone for long."

No, Kohl agreed, gazing at him, *she won't.*

He cleared his throat. "What do you think we should do?"

KI looked nervous all of a sudden. "I ... I don't know."

"Think you can kill the Red Face?"

He smirked, trading some of his boyishness for a smidge of maturity. "If I have to."

"*Please.* You've never even beaten me in a sparring match, but you think you can kill a trained assassin?"

"You never fight fair," KI complained.

"There is no such thing as a fair fight when it's life or death."

"Our sparring matches are not life or death."

"But they're practice for times like this."

KI gave him a flat expression. "Times like what?"

167

Before the kid could register what was happening, Kohl snatched him by his collar and threw him to the ground. He settled on top of him and shoved his face into the grass. "Times like this."

KI groaned. "Not fair. I wasn't ready."

"You never are." Kohl chuckled, then he grabbed KI's arm and twisted it behind his back. "Yield."

He felt KI tense beneath him, but he didn't speak.

He twisted his arm further. "Yield, KI."

"No," he grunted.

"You're always so stubborn," Kohl muttered.

"Let me up," KI said. "This isn't a fair fight."

"What did I say about fair fights?" Kohl pulled his arm at a painful angle, earning a sharp hiss from KI. "Yield," he said calmly, pulling just a bit more.

KI's hiss turned into a yelp, and he writhed beneath him. "Kohl, come on!" he shouted.

He took a slow breath, and then he twisted his arm again, not letting go until he heard a sickening *pop!*

KI cried out, pressing his face into the dirt. "*Why?*"

"Sorry," Kohl said quietly. "I really am." Then he jerked the broken limb in the other direction. This time, KI didn't scream, he simply sucked in a little gasp and fell limp beneath him.

Kohl climbed off his friend and focused his spiritual energy into his arms so he could carry him away. He didn't have a long walk, but he wasn't about to pretend KI was an easy carry. The kid might only be 14 and childish, but he was still 6 feet tall and 180 pounds of lean muscle. Courtesy of the freakish demon lurking inside him.

Speaking of the demon... Kohl walked for ten minutes before he stopped to check KI's arm. The swelling was already down. *He's healing.* Kohl squinted at the injury, calculating how much time he had before the arm would be fully repaired.

He walked half a mile and then broke it again.

"I'm sorry," Kohl said, snapping KI's arm at the elbow. There was really no point in apologizing, KI was still passed out and couldn't hear him. But that's exactly what Kohl needed. It would be much easier to hand him over if he wasn't awake to get upset and start asking questions or trying to fight. He lifted KI and marched deeper into the forest, enjoying the silence for just a little while longer.

16

Kohlannis

Just before Kohl reached Fells Lake, he heard the bushes beside him rustle. Instantly, he pivoted and stared into the forestry. It took him a moment of blinking dumbly at the trees before he noticed a figure standing in the brush.

He gasped and took a sudden step back.

The Red Face stood right before him, staring down through dark eyes partially hidden by his bloody mask. "You came."

"I thought you said to meet at Fells Lake."

"There's a group of trainees camped out there. We're fine here."

Involuntarily, Kohl tightened his grip on KI's limp form. *Cool it*, he told himself, *this was your idea.*

"Where's the girl?"

"Not coming," Kohl said.

"Did you betray her?"

"That doesn't matter."

The Red Face stepped into the clearing. "Set him on the ground and walk away."

"Take off your mask first."

He paused. "No."

This was as far as Kohl's plan had gone. He mentally cursed himself, just now realizing how ill-prepared he truly was. *Did I really think he'd take it off just because I asked?*

Something in his peripheral shifted, Kohl turned, but there was no time to dodge—not with KI in his arms. All he could do was take a step back, but that wasn't enough. The Red Face was right in front of him now, his mask so close he could hear him breathing behind it. His eyes were dead beneath the covering, staring blankly at him the same way you would stare at a pile of rocks or an empty field.

The Red Face punched him. His jaw burned with the impact as his head snapped back, and he went sprawling to the ground. KI landed on top of him with a thud, and he shoved his limp frame aside so he could regain his footing, but the assassin wouldn't let him. He grabbed him by his blonde hair and dragged him backwards, landing two horrible blows to his chest. Each thud of his fist summoned a strained wheeze from Kohl as he tried to suck for breath that wouldn't come. His ribcage rattled in his chest with the next punch, on the fourth, he cried out, though it was more from fear of his heart stopping and his lungs collapsing than from actual pain.

He's trying to kill me! Kohl gasped, hands flailing, swinging at the air. The Red Face caught one of his arms and twisted it so badly Kohl thought he'd snapped it from his torso. He screamed. The sound of it rang through the trees, but it was quickly cut off as the masked man punched him in the throat.

Now he was choking and clutching at his neck. He suddenly felt weightless and realized he'd been hurled through the air. By the time he understood what was happening, he'd already hit the ground, feeling his ribs bend inwards on impact. His throat hurt too much to scream, and the Red Face was back again, marching over to him to finish his beating.

No ... Kohl crawled backwards. Fear prickled all the way down his spine, leaving a trail of raw panic behind. *I'm going to die.*

Kohl's back hit a tree and he glanced over his shoulder—bad idea.

When he looked back again, the Red Face was right before him, hand extended. He grabbed him by the collar and slapped him hard across the face, then he closed his hands around this throat.

"You … have the boy," Kohl said in a strained whisper.

The Red Face let out a scoff. "I know. But I'm not done with you yet."

When his fist met his stomach, Kohl heaved forward and vomited, despite the choking grip still holding his neck. The Red Face dropped him to his knees to avoid his puke and watched him retch.

"I thought the Hungers were supposed to be strong. Legendary." He squatted beside him. "Isn't your family motto, ***Fear us?***"

It was. And there was a reason behind it. A reason to fear the Hunger name. But Kohl refused to use the dark powers that haunted his very existence. It was his curse that'd gotten him into too many fights as a kid, and the Hunger curse that forced him to live in the gated sector of the city, like criminals. Worst of all, it was his curse that got his father killed and left his brother a cripple wishing for death.

Eventually, death came for Karmen, too, but that was a thought for another time.

Kohl wiped spit from his mouth as he looked up at the Red Face. "I will not use my curse to fight you."

The Red Face raised his booted foot. "Then you will die."

Kohl closed his eyes, anticipating the impact. He even felt the air whoosh against his cheeks as the assassin kicked at him, but the blow never came. Before his boot could make contact, the Red Face was suddenly blasted with a storm of raging fire.

The attack was accompanied by a shrieking cry of madness that Kohl could only associate with Fox Fire. He smiled as he glanced up and saw her hurling balls of fire at the masked man. She pushed him relentlessly, backing him into the woods until he was more than a few feet away from Kohl. Only then, did she let up and look over at him.

"What took you so long?" Kohl asked.

She huffed. "The plan was for us to take him together and then split up along the way."

That had been the plan… To have Kohl hand over KI while Fox prepared for an ambush. They had discussed it while KI was still unconscious after eating the poupo egg. But Kohl had no way of telling if anyone was listening, so he initiated the argument with Fox later on and took KI without her knowledge. It was more believable that way.

"You were supposed to wait for me to come back before you carried him off!" Fox snapped.

She hadn't wanted to be there when Kohl overpowered KI. He didn't blame her. He hadn't wanted to do it at all, and he'd almost changed his mind when he saw the pained look of betrayal cross KI's face just before he lost consciousness.

When he wakes up, I'll explain everything, Kohl decided. But first he had to deal with this assassin.

"Sorry about the change in plans," he told Fox. "But that still doesn't explain what took you so long."

She smirked down at him. "I didn't get the memo the meeting spot had been changed. But that's a good thing because I bumped into some friends."

Suddenly, the Red Face came tripping back into the clearing with yet another shrieking mad woman hot on his tail. Kohl's face lit up as recognition set in.

Kressa Lion.

Except she wasn't her usual self, small and thin with a pretty smile. Kressa's skin now glowed silver, like she was covered in a layer of sheet

173

metal.

She lunged forward and punched at the assassin, but he sidestepped, and she ended up punching a tree instead. Her fist blasted a hole into the trunk.

"She's strong," Kohl breathed.

"Having metal muscles will do that to you," Fox said.

Kohl opened his mouth to reply, but another figure stepped into view and his words were replaced by a shocked gasp. Both Vinny and Montell walked into the clearing with another boy trailing behind. Kohl recognized him as a trainee from Class G5, but he was too distracted by the Lin brothers to acknowledge the extra kid.

He glanced back at the Red Face, still fighting Kressa, and then back at the Lins again. "They're not the Red Face," he whispered.

Fox grinned. "Nope. You were right."

"Then who?"

"I don't know, but I'm glad I bumped into them and learned the truth. They were camped out at Fells Lake when I arrived. Once I explained things, they agreed to lend a hand."

Vinny glanced over and then nudged his brother who nudged the other boy. Together, the three of them made their way to Fox and Kohl while Kressa exchanged blows with the mystery assassin.

"I can't believe he showed up here," Montell said.

Vinny crossed his arms. "I can. As long as that demonic kid—"

Montell elbowed him hard. "We'll help however we can," he said before Fox could fly off.

"We need to get KI back." Kohl grunted as he struggled to his feet. "He's on the other side of the clearing. I left him when I—" he cut himself off. He'd almost said, *when I got beaten up*, but he glanced at the Lin brothers and changed his mind. "When I started fighting with the Red Face."

174

"I can go get him," said the new guy.

Kohl glanced over at him, he was average height with auburn hair and green eyes. A fresh tan stained his normally pale skin. "How?" he asked.

"You haven't seen Wend's blessing yet," Monty snorted, then he patted Wend on the back and said, "Go get him."

Wend leapt into the air, his legs clearing their heads and still climbing higher. It was an incredible jump, higher than any of the other trainees could achieve. But he was still climbing even *higher* and drifting further away from the group.

Kohl sucked in a gasp. "He can fly."

"Pretty cool, right?" Montell crossed his arms.

Vinny rolled his eyes. "He can't fight worth a lick."

"Why would he fight when he could just fly off?" his brother countered.

Vinny sighed. "Exactly."

"Good thing we don't need him to fight right now, then," Fox said. "He just needs to grab KI and fly back over to us." She glanced at the Lin brothers. "You two can take him to safety while Kohl, Kressa, and I finish off the Red Face."

Kohl nodded, barely paying attention as he watched Wend land swiftly and scoop KI into his arms. Once he was secured, he leapt into the air again and flew over the raging fight still going on below. Relief swelled in Kohl's chest, *this is amazing*, he told himself. And then his relief nearly choked him as he saw the Red Face shove Kressa and pivot.

Almost in slow motion, he punched at the air—and fire shot from his fist.

Kohl heard nothing but silence screaming through the forest as he watched Wend's shirt go up in flames. The young trainee's face pinched at the sudden pain, and he lost his grip on KI. Both boys tumbled from

175

the air, racing toward the ground.

The sound came back with a sudden clap. Kohl heard Wend shrieking as he spiraled toward them, flames eating up his back.

Vinny punched his brother's shoulder. "I've got KI!" he said, running forward.

Montell matched his pace, moving in sync with Vinny without a word. Together, they held up their arms and braced themselves, jaws clenched, eyebrows furrowed.

"Activate your power at the moment of impact," Vinny instructed. "Same time, okay?"

Montell grunted his reply.

"Now!" Vinny shouted.

For a moment, Kohl expected the brothers to be crushed by the falling students, but they had better control over their blessing than he thought. Vinny exhaled a breath as he caught KI, taking him into his arms like he weighed nothing more than a feather. Montell did the same, using his gift to lighten Wend's weight just as he caught him, but he still fell to the ground, trying to avoid the flames engulfing him.

"Fox!" Kohl snapped, staring at the raging blaze.

She ran over and held out her hands, her concentration locked on the swirling heat. In the back of his mind, Kohl remembered when Fox put out the flames in the Academy. At the time, he hadn't said anything, but he thought it was one of the coolest things he'd ever seen. Shooting fire from your fists was one thing, but controlling that fire, putting it out when it mattered most—that was extraordinary.

Fox stepped back once the flames on Wend's back were out. No one said anything, but they didn't need to. He'd stopped screaming before Montell had caught him. Kohl knew what that meant.

"He's…" Monty choked on the rest of his sentence, unable to speak the word.

176

Vinny had no problem saying it. "Dead."

"Shut up, Vinny!" Fox snapped.

"Don't be upset just because I said what everyone was thinking," he told her calmly. "If you want to be angry at someone, be angry at the Red Face."

Fox seemed to see the wisdom in his words, stepping into the clearing without wasting any time. Kohl felt the air charge with heat and energy as she moved, taking out her flint and steel. When she struck it, raw power charged forth. The flames were so hot, they glowed blue before blasting the masked assailant in his backside.

He shouted in pain and stumbled forward as Kressa danced out of the way, trying to avoid him as much as the heat. Exhausted, she was glad to trade places with the furious sundancer.

Kohl stood and offered his arms as she ran over to them. "You're okay," he said, hugging her.

"I held him off as long as I could." She pulled away as her skin shifted from metal to normal flesh again, revealing the pretty smile he missed.

"We need to help Fox," Montell said.

"There isn't much help we can offer," Vinny replied.

Kohl frowned, watching Fox and the Red Face exchange blows. He was using fire just like her, blasting her with scorching flames, but Fox was unfazed. She met him with equal force, her attacks clapping like thunder, screaming through the trees as her fire stormed around them.

"We'll just end up burned alive, like Wend," Vinny said casually.

Just then, Kressa glanced down and noticed the boy's smoking remains for the first time. Before she could scream, Kohl took her into his arms again, turning her away from the gruesome sight.

"Don't look," he whispered into her hair.

Kressa took a few deep breaths before untangling herself from him. She kept her eyes focused on his as she spoke. "I've seen death before.

You don't have to shield me from it."

Kohl only nodded.

"But thank you. That was still sweet."

"Can we talk about the assassin's powers, now?" Vinny asked over Kohl's shoulder. "We can't even join the fight because there are two sundancers going at it. Anyone else thinking what I'm thinking?"

Montell pressed his lips into a thin line like he didn't want to say anything.

Kohl sighed. "He's not Roaring."

"There are only two sundancers in Babel," Vinny insisted.

"It *isn't* him," Kohl snapped.

"What makes you so sure?" Montell asked.

Kohl looked at him, a small smile forming on his lips as he peered over Monty's shoulder into the forestry. "Because Roaring Fire is right behind you."

Kohlannis would never forget the look of pure terror that took over both faces of the Lin brothers. But, even more memorable, was the frightening sound of thunder that swelled around them when Roaring marched forward.

His amber eyes were filled with rage, his body rigid with tension— pinned up energy begging to be released. The air burned with the bitter smell of smoke as he passed them by. Roaring paid them no mind, not interested in the apologies muttered by the twins, or the gaping look from Kressa. His vision was forward, focused solely on his little sister and the masked assassin.

As he stepped into the clearing, electricity crackled around him, shredding the air as his uncontrollable energy rolled off him in waves. Lightning struck right where he stood, and Kohl cried out in shock. When his nerves settled, he realized Roaring hadn't been hit by the lightning—he had summoned it.

A cloak of pure light glowed all around him, shimmering and flickering with his power. He was surrounded by raw spiritual energy, a sundancer at his finest.

Roaring held out his hand and lightning struck again, this time, it didn't cloak him in a veil of energy, it yielded to its master and calmed in the palm of his hand. The sundancer held a bolt of lightning like it was a rod or a stick, like this was something he did every other weekend.

Kohl blinked, astonished by both his power and his composure.

I don't believe what I'm seeing, he thought, and, glancing at his gaping companions, neither did anyone else.

"Amazing," said a voice behind him.

Kohl turned to find Vyanna Farron and a small group of students standing with her. She glanced at him. "We were travelling together but Roaring suddenly charged ahead when we heard the fighting."

"Welcome to the show," Vinny said sarcastically.

"I'm glad he's on our side." Dart stepped forward and fist bumped Kohl. "Glad to see you made it out all right."

He nodded. "Yeah. Same."

"Should we help?" Vyanna asked.

"How can we?" Vinny said. "The man is calling down bolts of lightning like it's nothing. I'm not getting mixed up in that."

Kohl silently agreed as he returned his vision to the battle.

Roaring lifted the rod of lightning and hurled it at the Red Face, still locked in battle with Fox Fire.

Kohl felt the crackle of power split the air before the bolt hit its mark. He only had a split second to react, panic arrowing his heart as he realized the amount of power Roaring had just released.

"Get down!" he shouted.

Thunder roared around him, shaking the very earth as the lightning struck. Heat exploded against Kohl's backside, throwing him and the

179

rest of his classmates forward. They all screamed, hurtling through the woods, reaching for each other and clinging to the nearby trees as they tried not to get blown away.

Their struggling was futile.

Kohl tumbled over the ground and rammed into something hard, immediately knocking him unconscious.

17

Evelyn

A dozen members of the Taber Tribe stood in a circle mumbling prayers. Lieutenant Diaz glared at them as he waited for Marlo Jo to return. He wasn't angry with *them*; it wasn't their fault the training master hadn't taken his advice and sent in her team earlier—when they'd first spotted the Red Face.

Secretly, Diaz didn't entirely blame Master Jo, either.

When the Red Face had first appeared, his interaction with the other students had been so brief, Marlo's argument to further observe his behavior had met little resistance. The meeting at Fells Lake had intrigued everyone in the room and Diaz had to admit Master Jo's observations were critical.

Just as the students themselves had noticed, the Red Face didn't use fire the first time he'd tried to capture KI. Was it because he was trying to keep his blessing a secret? Or was it because he couldn't use fire before? Because, perhaps, the first Red Face wasn't the original one— the one who'd burned the Tower.

Master Jo thought so.

"We may be looking at multiple Red Faces. At least two people working together to throw us off. Which means, the assassin has allies.

There is more than one threat roaming through the exams," Marlo had said.

At the time, it had been an excellent argument and sound reason for allowing the masked man to roam freely for a few more hours. But now there was a student dead and possibly more to follow. This was the entrance exams, it was not uncommon for trainees to perish during these difficult trials, but their lives were never meant to be taken by a dark assassin.

Lieutenant Diaz closed his eyes, seeing the look on Wend's face as the fire first kissed his skin, hearing his screams all over again.

We have failed them, he ground his teeth together, *every student in the Kanen Forest.*

Across the room, the double doors to the observatory opened and Master Jo walked in with Moneek, Lord Izzy, and Second Lieutenant Kotaro hot on her heels.

"Is this it?" Diaz asked.

Marlo nodded. "I will place walls between the Red Face and the students while Moneek and Lieutenant Kotaro help them escape. Lord Izzy will take down the Red Face, you will be his backup."

"Are you sure we don't need any more manpower?" he asked.

Master Jo nodded at the cluster of Taber tribesmen and woman. "They will be on standby, ready to teleport others to our location if necessary."

Diaz had witnessed the power of the Taber Tribe while observing the exams. The student, Gloria Taber, had been there when the Red Face first appeared. It was her ability to teleport that'd saved KI. Now, skilled members of Gloria's tribe were there to teleport Master Jo and her team into the Kanen Forest to rescue the handful of students stuck in battle with the dangerous assassin. Diaz hoped they wouldn't be too late.

"How long will the process take?" Lord Izzy asked.

Diaz turned to look at the circle of praying Tabers when his breath froze in his throat. The shadows of the Tabers slowly came together to form one large blanket of darkness. The lieutenant's eyes widened in terror as he watched the Hunters and Priests sink into the black pool. Their eyes flew open as they fell into the abyss, but it was too late.

One of the Tabers cried out in fear, "I can't teleport! I can't—" her voice was cut off as she was dragged into the shadows.

"What is happening?" Master Jo muttered, stepping forward.

"We're being attacked," Diaz replied, unsheathing his hook-swords. "Stand ready!" he ordered loudly, though he hadn't needed to. Lord Izzy was already in a fighting stance, even Kotaro had drawn her daggers—one in each hand. Moneek was beside Master Jo now, passing her staff to her and aiming her sword at the lingering pool of darkness.

"This place is protected by a spiritual barrier," Marlo said.

"That means whoever's coming is powerful enough to break it," Diaz told her.

"Indeed." The remark hadn't come from the training master—or anyone else in the room. The deep voice that'd replied to Lieutenant Diaz had spoken from inside the floor of shadows. It was followed by a dark chuckle that echoed through the room, sending talons of fear scraping down Evelyn's spine.

He swallowed the lump in his throat as he gripped his weapons. "Stand ready!" he ordered again.

The laughing returned, this time, it grew louder as a figure emerged from the black pool. First a head, then a face, then the rest of his body. He stood before them in a red cloak with the hood pulled up to hide his face. Diaz could just make out the smile claiming his lips as the mysterious man tilted his head up. When he did so, his hood fell back to reveal bronze-colored skin and ebony hair so thick and long it fell almost to his waist. There was a smile on his face and an eerie sense of laughter that danced in his dark eyes.

"One of the Nine," Diaz growled, tightening his grip on his hook-swords.

The man nodded and then swept his arm out dramatically as he bowed. "The name's Hosenké. The Seventh Birth of Carnage." He lifted his head to smirk at them. "Don't forget it."

"What did you do with the Tabers?" Master Jo demanded, fearlessly pointing her staff at him.

He looked at her like she was stupid. "I killed them."

When Marlo took a step, he lifted his hands in mock surrender. "I had to do it. Can't have you swooping in to save the day."

Understanding stormed through Lieutenant Diaz. "You're stalling for the Red Face."

"You're as smart as you look," Hosenké said, grin stretching further.

"We don't have time for this," came Kotaro's voice. She stepped beside Diaz and gave him a sideways glance. He knew what the look meant. They were going to fight for Izzy to get an opening. It would take him a little longer than teleportation to get there, but the young Priest was the only one in the room with the ability to make it to the students before the Red Face overwhelmed them.

"We don't have to fight," Hosenké said calmly. "I'm just here to make sure none of you intervene with the Red Face. If you just stay put, I won't bother you. I'll leave once I'm certain my companion has achieved his goal and you'll never see me again."

Diaz pointed his hook-sword. "We don't make deals with demons."

Hosenké's face darkened. "Very well."

His arm shot out as he pointed at Diaz, a streak of black electricity shooting from the tips of his fingers. The lieutenant dodged the blast, but as he heard the horrible cry beside him, he realized the demon had anticipated that.

184

Kotaro's daggers clattered to the floor as she dropped. Evelyn felt his heart hammer in his chest as he turned and let out a strangled scream, but Hosenké was still attacking. Another streak of black lightning cast a shadow over the room as it whipped like a snake at the distraught lieutenant. He had only a second to lift his sword in defense, but he knew the gesture was futile.

Thankfully, Master Jo was there. She erected a transparent wall in front of him just in time. The black energy screamed over her barrier, rippling across the clear surface in a web of darkness.

Evelyn didn't care about the barrier or the lightning. He was beside Kotaro now, cradling her head in his shaking hands as he stared down at her. Blood trickled from her nose; her breaths came out in weak, labored pants.

"T—Tella," he whispered her first name which earned him a weak smile. Her eyes seemed to widen at the sound of it, papery lids peeling back to reveal bloodshot orbs.

Battle raged around them, Moneek and Master Jo exchanging gruesome blows with Hosenké. Small black pools of Dark energy appeared around the room, allowing dozens of demons to crawl from the depths of the hellish darkness. The darklings kept Izzy busy while the lieutenant sat lifeless and numb, staring down at his companion—his childhood friend.

Tella Kotaro, who had stood beside him at his entrance ceremony and had accepted her blade before him at their graduation ceremony. She had been there when Izzy had placed the black seal over his body, and she was supposed to be there when it was removed. But as Diaz gazed down at her through his bitter tears, he realized that wasn't going to happen.

Kotaro had always been the gentlest of the three friends; she had no blessing and had never ranked high in their combat courses during their

185

time at the Academy. Her focus was mainly analytical, which had made her seem weak, but Diaz couldn't think of anyone else he'd rather have by his side.

Panic tore through the lieutenant as the thought of replacing her hit him like a storm. There was no one else he wanted to fight beside, no one else he wanted to finish this journey with. But that decision was out of his hands.

Again, he thought bitterly, clutching Kotaro to his chest. *I'm losing someone again.*

Like the black pools swirling around him, Diaz felt a pit of darkness open deep inside. He felt despair and sorrow claw its way from the place in his heart he'd kept sealed off. Horrible sadness, grief, and bitter hatred—all the things he had tried so hard to never feel again.

A strangled gasp tore from his lips as his eyes blurred with tears. Kotaro stared up at him, but her gaze was lifeless and empty. The blood that'd poured from her nose stained her cheeks and chin as it dripped down to the floor. Evelyn's tears washed the carmine liquid away.

In the back of his head, he could hear his mother's last words. *Don't let it in, Eve.*

But it was too late, the pain was already there, breaking through the dam caging his heart and rushing in like an uncontrollable flood. Riding on the waves of this black storm was the bitter hatred he'd so carefully kept hidden in the dark corners of his soul.

Diaz set Kotaro's limp body on the floor before he rose to his feet. He didn't bother collecting his hook-swords—he didn't want to fight with them. They were battling darkness in its rawest form; he would face this evil with a darkness of his own.

Energy churned in his core, pouring into every limb and muscle. His skin began to burn as the power begged for release, winding through the maze of the seal inked onto his flesh. He was so hot he tore his shirt

186

from his chest, revealing the glowing black markings weaving over his body. They stretched over his muscles, riding the sculpted curves of his abs and shoulders, wrapping around his toned arms, and peeling over his scarred back. Power surged through the lines, making them glow white as Diaz channeled the energy. He felt it call out to him, whispering curses into his soul as it promised to overcome his enemies.

Use me, the darkness begged in a quiet, childlike voice. It followed the lines of his seal right to his chest—to his heart—brushing against the last remnants of his humanity. *Let me in.*

Diaz felt the power poke and prod at him, felt the barrier around his heart begin to crumble. He let out a strangled sob as the last of his will petered out; and like a light being smothered, he was suddenly shrouded in darkness.

But the veil was torn away as he felt a horrible pain charge through his abdomen. Suddenly, the darkness that'd gathered in his body and clouded his mind vanished, as if it'd been chased away by the sharp ache in his stomach.

Diaz's eyes snapped open, and he gasped for air as he realized he'd been stabbed. A dagger protruded from his abdomen, and the one holding it was his own companion.

Izzy.

The lieutenant felt faint. His knees buckled and he collapsed into Izzy's arms as the Priest still clutched the dagger. "I've got you," Izzy said in an oddly calm voice.

To anyone else, it might have looked like his own friend had tried to end his life, but Diaz knew better. Izzy had placed the now torn seal on his body. He had helped him lock away the foreign power threatening to take over his mind and body. And when that power had nearly been set free, Izzy was the one to send it running back to the dark corners from which it had emerged.

Diaz took deep breaths as Izzy laid him on the floor, just a few feet away from Kotaro's lifeless body. His head rolled to the side, and he blinked, trying to make out the figures ahead.

Master Jo and Moneek.

He had expected them to still be locked in battle but, to his surprise, everything had come to a standstill. Hosenké was just standing there, one woman on each side. Marlo stood with her staff extended, ready to attack or defend at a moment's notice. Moneek kept her dark eyes locked on the shifty demon.

It was then that Lieutenant Diaz noticed Hosenké's eyes. They were glazed over, as if he had drifted away. When they came back into focus, he gave the onlooking group a pleasant smile. "It seems I am needed elsewhere." He bowed again, like this was all fun and games for him. "It's been a joy." Then he vanished in a puff of black smoke; the pools of Dark energy slowly began to recede and return to normal floor and carpeting.

The members of the Taber Tribe didn't reappear.

Something touched Diaz's face; *a hand*, he realized, blinking up at Master Jo as she knelt beside him and brushed his hair from his damp forehead. "He's been stabbed," she said.

"I did it," Izzy admitted. He stood and turned toward the door. "Take him and Kotaro's body to an infirmary. Do not remove the dagger."

Master Jo nodded.

"If he begins to lose consciousness, twist the blade to wake him up."

Marlo swallowed but nodded again anyway. "Where are you going?"

"To stop Hosenké and the Red Face." Izzy opened the door.

"Wait," Master Jo called. She held out her staff. "Take this with you."

"Why?" Izzy asked.

"You'll see very soon."

Though it was clear he didn't understand what she meant, the Priest gave her a nod and then shifted his gaze down to Diaz for a moment. Evelyn tried to maintain eye contact, but shame and guilt and pain tore his vision away. He squeezed his eyes shut and breathed deeply, concentrating hard on not passing out. If he lost consciousness, he wouldn't be able to fight the darkness that still lurked inside of him, waiting for its moment to strike and take over.

Normally, he didn't have to fight so hard. His seal did all the work until his anger or hatred threatened to tear it. But the death of Kotaro had been too much for him to bear and he'd given in to the whispers without a second thought, seeking comfort in darkness when the light became too much.

With his seal torn, he was left to fight the influence of the darkness all by himself. He cringed, muscles spasming around the dagger as he tried to breathe and focus. Pain was all he could feel. All he could register in the mad storm swirling in his mind. But it was better to focus on the pain than the whispers.

Without thinking, Diaz reached out and grabbed someone's arm. He was surprised to see Moneek blinking down at him, concern and fear taking over her pretty features. "Pray for me," he rasped, then he bit down hard on his tongue, trying not to lose himself to the shredding pain. His heart, his mind, and his body ached. He wasn't sure which felt the worst.

Moneek nodded and began to mutter a scripture as she effortlessly lifted him in her strong arms. *"The Lord is faithful, and He will strengthen you and protect you from the evil one..."*

18

Fox Fire

Fox Fire watched as Roaring battled the Red Face. The only thing that'd kept her from losing consciousness after his lightning attack was the fact that she was also a sundancer. She couldn't be burned, but there were other perks to her blessing, too. Like the fact that her reflexes were as quick as the lightning Roaring seemed to wield like a blade, slicing at the assassin and tearing down trees in his ferocious attacks. She desperately wanted to join the fight, but something told her she would only get in the way. So Fox focused on helping Syren heal their friends— apparently, she was the only other student who hadn't fainted after Roaring's blast of energy.

Crystal wings sprouted from Syren's back, shimmering in the sunlight. She had flown away when the explosion happened, but she hadn't been able to take anyone with her in the madness. The rest of the students lay in the clearing, alive but unconscious.

"Are you hurt at all?" Syren asked, dragging Kohl's body over. They had lined up all their friends a safe distance away from the fight.

Fox watched as she cupped her hands together and said a short prayer. When she opened her hands, a dozen crystals lay in her palms. She turned and fed one to Kohl, he immediately regained consciousness and groaned.

Syren's eyes were on Fox, blinking at her expectantly. "Are you hurt?" she repeated, holding up a golden crystal.

Fox shook her head but accepted the gem anyway. "I'll give it to KI."

He'd been the first student Fox had taken the time to find and drag to safety. Guilt worked its way through her as she brushed his hair from his face and pressed the crystal to his lips. He had trusted her. He had believed he was safe with her. And she'd plotted behind his back with Kohl to use him as bait to lure out the Red Face.

Their plan had worked, but looking down at him now, Fox couldn't get herself to say it was worth it. "I'm so sorry," she muttered as the crystal turned to honey on his lips.

His brow crinkled as he closed his mouth and peeled his lids back. "What are you sorry for, Foxy?" he asked in a tired voice.

"I'll tell you later," she whispered.

He sat up, his eyes never leaving hers except to slowly trail his gaze down her cheek. He reached for her, and she would have turned away, but his nearness surprised her and froze her in place.

"You're crying," he murmured, brushing away a single tear. And then, suddenly, he leaned in and kissed her cheek. "Don't cry, Foxy." The words were whispered against her skin, making goosebumps pebble over her neck and chest.

When he leaned back, he was smiling. "See?" he said with a light laugh. "Better already."

With a start, Fox realized she wasn't crying anymore. "KI," she muttered, not really sure what else to say. Her brother was throwing fire at an assassin behind her, the rest of her friends were unconscious around her, and KI was busy kissing her cheek and whispering to her like he wasn't the goofy kid she remembered from Wi. Hours ago, Kohl had yelled at him for eating a poisonous bug's egg, now he was putting down the charm so hard she couldn't catch her breath.

Sometimes … it's like he's someone else. Fox stared at him as he brushed his hair back and stood, all serious and ready for battle. Kohl joined him, bumping his fist, and exchanging a very casual laugh, despite their circumstances. Then their eyes landed on her and she jumped.

"You just gonna sit there or come help?" Kohl asked, cramming a hand into his pocket.

KI winked at her. "Let's go help your brother, Foxy."

"How are we supposed to help?" Andor asked behind them. She looked panicked, exactly the way she'd been the last time Fox had seen her.

She couldn't stop herself from rolling her eyes. Fox hadn't missed Andor in the least. "Syren and Dart can provide an aerial assault to distract the Red Face, that should create an opening for myself and Montell to attack," Fox said.

Montell nodded. "I'm ready when you are."

"Why Monty?" Andor asked.

"Because he can use fire, just like me."

"And the rest of us?" Vinny asked, hand on his hip.

"Not all of us needs to go charging in," Kressa said. "I fought the Red Face. We shouldn't underestimate him."

Silence fell over them as she looked down at Wend's body, burned and stiff from death.

"Is there something you can do for him?" Vy asked Syren.

Reluctantly, the healer shook her head. "I can heal most injuries, but I can't bring someone back from the dead."

There was more silence, so dark and gloomy it threatened to break them before the fight had even begun.

Fox stood and wiped her hands on her dirty pants. "Guys, we have to stay focused. Wend's death is tragic, but more of us will die if we don't do something."

"Fox is right," Kressa said. "Those who don't want to fight, take a hike."

Vyanna's brows lowered very slowly; a reproachful gaze locked on Kressa. "My cousins and I will gladly escort others to a more secure location."

Toad stooped and slowly picked up Wend's body. "We'll be at Fells Lake, warning anyone who shows up to steer clear of this area."

"If you still hear us fighting in twenty minutes, come back to give us a hand," Fox said.

Vy nodded and led her cousins away. Andor was the only one to follow.

"Bro, you should go with them," Montell said quietly.

Vinny snapped his glare to his brother. "Excuse me?"

"This fight will be tough. It might be best—"

"I have an *outstanding* blessing," Vinny interrupted. "I can help you fight him."

Kressa snorted. "What are you gonna do? Run over and make him weigh five-hundred pounds?"

"That's not a bad plan," Vinny retorted. "He won't be able to move very well if he weighs that much."

Kressa's eyes narrowed, but it was Montell who spoke next. "You'd have to get close to the Red Face to be effective. So far, the only ones who've been face-to-face with him are Fox and Kressa. Fox is a sundancer and Kressa can turn her skin to metal."

"Are you kidding me?" Vinny spat. He jabbed a finger at Kohl and then KI. "Why are *they* staying? They don't even have blessings!"

Kohl's gaze narrowed. "I do have a blessing. You idiot."

"Well, you never use it."

"Vinny has a point," Kressa folded her arms and then winced as an

193

explosion went off nearby. Fox turned to see what was happening; Roaring had launched more lightning at the Red Face, but the assassin seemed to be holding his own, dodging and then countering with fire.

Kressa took a calming breath. "KI is the one he's after; he should run while he can." She looked at Kohl. "If you aren't going to use your blessing, you should go, too. You're just deadweight out here without powers."

"I fought the Red Face by myself, *without* my blessing, before any of you showed up," he said. His voice was calm, but Fox didn't miss the dark edge in it.

"You're a liability right now," Kressa said plainly.

He stepped forward. "Say that again, little girl."

Kressa stepped forward too, but Syren interrupted. "Guys, we should not be fighting each other."

"We don't have time for this," Dart grumbled. "If they want to stay, fine. Just don't get in the way."

Vinny grinned. "Sounds good to me."

"The plan is to attack from above and below," Fox explained quickly. "Dart and Syren will fly over; when I see an opening, I'll give the cue for us to charge in. Got it?"

They nodded.

"Let's move closer to get a better look."

She turned and carefully led them through the woods. Rocks, dirt, and debris lay scattered in every direction. Roaring and the Red Face had torn down massive trees and shredded bushes, casting no regard for the forest around them. As she neared the fight, Fox could feel the heat of their fire even from a dozen meters away. She glanced back at her friends, wondering if they could feel it too. Wondering if they felt any pain from it. Kressa had already turned her skin to metal, but Vinny seemed to have a grimace on his face. Kohl looked fine, but his forehead was sweaty, and his shirt was sticking to his chest.

"I'm not sure how much closer we can safely get," Fox whispered. "Kressa and I may have to continue alone from here."

"We can keep going," Kohl grunted.

"Syren and I will be flying overhead anyway," Dart reminded her.

She nodded. It wasn't like she could make them turn around or stay put.

She dared to cross a few more meters, by then the heat was hot even by her standards, but her friends were resilient—if not at least stubborn. They carried on without worry or complaint and when she stopped to give them orders, they nodded eagerly, ready to take down the Red Face.

"On my cue," Fox whispered, returning her gaze to the battle.

Roaring had stopped using his lightning now, and he'd lost his glowing cloak from before. *He's getting tired*, Fox noted, watching him take heavy breaths as he walked the circle of the clearing, no longer attacking but merely eyeing his enemy.

"No more lightning?" the Red Face taunted.

Roaring shifted and punched at the air. Fire tore through the clearing, right at the masked man, but he dodged it by pivoting and shuffling to the side.

Fox threw her hand into the air—cueing Syren and Dart. She heard the cry of an eagle before she saw it dive from the treetops, going straight for the enemy. Syren came from the opposite direction, launching sharpened crystal rods at him like they were short spears.

The Red Face adjusted in time to dodge the crystals, but he was hit head-on by Dart who crashed into his chest and knocked him off balance before quickly flying away.

Fox closed her hand into a fist, signaling Montell who was hiding in a bush across the clearing. Together, they shot fireballs at the assassin from two different directions. Roaring, ever the skilled warrior, took advantage of the great opening and added his own blaze to the mix.

A horrible cry ripped through the trees. Dark, and guttural, and almost inhuman. Dust and smoke cloaked the area, but there was an eerie stillness that followed. The fighting had stopped, but the darkness remained.

"Is it over?" Kohl asked beside Fox.

"I hope so," Kressa said softly. "I didn't even have to join."

"Deadweight," Kohl muttered.

Kressa gave him a sideways glance, but there was a playful smirk on her face. She bumped him with her shoulder.

"Guys," Fox whispered. "Look at the grass."

Instead of green grass and weeds, the ground was covered in a black field.

Kohl frowned. "It looks scorched. From all the fire."

"No," Fox shook her head. "It looks dead. Withered."

Slowly, she lifted her gaze from the dead grass to the figure standing in the cloud of smoke. The Red Face remained still, not moving a muscle, not making a sound. Beside him, the giant bush began to dry up and wilt. There was a sudden cry as Dart ran from the bushes to take shelter under a nearby tree. To everyone's horror, the tree began to wither—bark turning black and crumbling right before their eyes.

Fox gasped. She had only seen this sort of power from one other person.

"It can't be," she whispered, stepping forward, but something jerked her backwards.

"Don't get any closer!" Kohl shouted. He pointed to the grass around them, the decay was getting closer, claiming nearby bushes and trees, even tainting the very soil they stood on.

They ran. Scrambling away, desperately trying to keep the withering plants from touching them.

196

"He's killing everything!" Vinny squealed, shoving past Fox Fire.

When they had cleared a few meters, Fox stopped to catch her breath. "The Red Face," she said slowly. "Is Slaine."

Kressa glared at her. "Don't say that."

"Look around you!" Fox shouted. "Everything is dying—withering away. Only one person at the Academy can do that and you know it."

"Fox is right," Roaring said calmly. "I saw him up close before we all ran. His face is…" he shuddered. "It's got to be Slaine."

Fox looked over her shoulder, squinting through the dissipating smoke and dust. The Red Face stood in the exact same spot they'd left him. Perfectly still and quiet. But his mask was gone now, its straps burned away. Even from her distance, Fox could see the horror of his face.

"It's Slaine," she said confidently and then she gasped as a figure dropped from the sky before him.

"Syren!" Kressa screamed, running forward.

Kohl grabbed her by the waist, scooping her up like she weighed nothing. "Don't go over there!" he said quickly. "You shouldn't touch the dead grass."

"Let go of me!" she screamed. "He'll kill Syren!"

But Syren looked fine. Fox could tell from her bunched shoulders and wide, blinking eyes, that she was afraid and confused. But she seemed unaffected by the wave of death slowly claiming the forest around her.

"She's a healer," Fox said quietly. "His blessing won't hurt her."

Syren took a step closer to Slaine. "S-Slaine? It's not true…" She clasped her hands together as a sob escaped her. "It can't be you."

For the first time, Slaine moved. He leaned forward and reached for Syren, hand extended, the tips of his fingers grey and black with death.

"Don't let him touch you!" Kressa screamed, writhing in Kohl's grasp. She swung her elbow and caught him viciously in the ear. Kohl let her go as he grunted in pain, but he managed to grab her wrist.

Kressa turned on him. "If you don't want me to go out there then you do it!" She punched him in the chest, but it was a gentle blow that hurt her more than him. "You have to do something!"

"I …" Kohl glanced around. "I can't."

"With your blessing, you can," she insisted.

"It's not a blessing. It's a curse. And it's just as devastating as Slaine's." He shook his head. "I won't use a curse to get ahead."

"It's not a curse!" Kressa shouted, landing another punch to his broad chest. "*You* decide, Kohl. No one else gets to label your gift but you. The way you use it, and what you accomplish with it. *That's* what makes it a curse or a blessing." She punched him again, tears streaming down her cheeks. "You decide."

There was silence. A heavy, lingering silence that sent a chill whispering over Fox's skin. She felt the hairs on the back of her neck rise at attention, but that didn't compare to the breath of fear that filled her lungs as she felt the crackle of power splitting the air before her.

Kohl released Kressa and issued a single command as he walked away. "Stay back. No matter what."

Fox watched him go, saw the shadows beneath his feet begin to shimmy and grow as they slid along the ground, following him, forming shapes and patterns that she recognized as the image of people. As if an army of shadows had formed beneath him.

Kohl stopped walking when he was just a few feet away from Slaine, and all at once, the shadows stood up. Black beings ready to fight, crawling to their feet to defend their master.

"What on earth…" Vinny breathed.

"What exactly is his power?" Roaring asked.

KI answered, "It's called Void."

198

"That's not what I would expect from something called Void," Montell said. "It looks more like—"

"Shadow-dancing," Fox whispered. "Kohl is a shadow-dancer."

As if he'd heard them, Kohl pointed at Slaine, silently sending his shadows into battle. They ran forward with jerky, animalistic movements, like they'd never truly learned to walk or run. When they reached Syren, they engulfed her whole and then vanished.

Kressa screamed and tried to run forward but Fox grabbed her.

"He was supposed to save—"

Before she could finish her sentence, Syren appeared in the shadow of the tree beside them. She blinked in shock before coming to her senses. "What just happened?"

"That's what we're all wondering," Vinny muttered.

Montell nudged him. "Bet you wish you hadn't been rude to him all those times."

Vinny glowered but said nothing—even if he had, Fox wasn't listening anymore, she had returned her attention to Kohl, mystified by his power. She couldn't help but remember all the times Kohl had insisted he would never use his gift. Because it was cursed. She had never believed him. Had never thought in her heart that he was truly cursed. Until now.

Fear rippled down Fox's back as she watched the shadowmen run forward and leap at Slaine. They grabbed him by his arms and legs and held him in place, sending a jolt of relief through Fox's heart. *He got him. That easily.*

Two more trees behind Slaine withered and crumbled into black dust. That's when Fox felt the change in the air, the eerie charge that slithered through the forest as Slaine regained himself.

Despite being restrained, he managed to move a little, twisting his arm free from the black hands that held him, and blasting Kohl's

199

shadowmen with his fire. They shrieked as they faded away, but just as quickly as they were destroyed, there were more to come. Crawling from the shadows around them, standing up from the earth and marching toward him. Slaine was surrounded by darkness on all sides.

"I don't understand," Fox muttered, watching him blast the shadowmen with more searing heat. "How can Slaine use sundancing if his blessing is death?"

"His blessing isn't *death*!" Syren said passionately.

Fox tore her eyes from the traitor to look at her. She was glaring, like it was somehow wrong to insinuate his blessing was so dark.

Syren folded her arms. "Slaine's blessing is actually *Life*."

"You're nuts," Vinny muttered.

Syren glared at him, too. "I'm telling the truth. I knew Slaine before coming to Babel. I grew up with him."

Fox raised an eyebrow. "Really?"

She nodded. "He wasn't always like this."

"Evil?" Dart said.

"Dead," Syren corrected. "Slaine used to look normal." She shook her head. "I should start at the beginning. Slaine comes from a clan of healers, like me. Our villages are sister clans. My bloodline allows me to share my spiritual energy with others to heal them. But Slaine's bloodline has a power called *Life*; it drains energy from living creatures to heal its host."

Fox took a shaky breath. *What a dark way of healing. Something must die for the user to live.*

"So, whenever things start dying around Slaine, it's because he's healing himself?" Dart asked.

Syren nodded.

"Why doesn't he heal all his decaying skin?"

"He can't."

200

"*Please* elaborate." Vinny shook his head.

"A few years ago, Slaine's mother passed away. I don't know if it was demons or …" she dropped her gaze to the ground. "Or his father. Or maybe demons *in* his father. Whatever the case, Slaine changed after that. Started saying he wanted to be strong—strong enough to defend himself. I didn't live in his village, so I didn't see him all the time. But once he got power hungry, I saw him even less." Syren hugged herself. "Next thing I knew, he left his village. Ran off in search of a witch he'd heard could give him power. Like …" she swallowed, "she could give you a blessing."

"And the blessing she gave him was fire," Fox finished.

"When Slaine returned, he looked like this." Syren wiped at a tear running down her dark brown cheek. "I guess the witch was successful, but it's obvious the blessing came at a price."

"He was burned alive," Roaring said plainly.

It explained why he was so ugly and brutally scarred. Why his flesh was barely clinging to his own bones. But it also made sense because … "Sundancers cannot be burned." Fox looked at Syren. "Those who are born with this blessing cannot be burned by nature's fire or the flames of our gift. But Slaine wasn't born with this power. It was given to him through darkness and the price he paid was a life of never-ending pain." She couldn't stop the shiver that danced over her shoulders. "Every time Slaine uses his power, it burns him. Damaging his internal organs, searing his own flesh all over again."

"He uses Life to keep himself alive," Syren whispered shakily.

"Killing everything around him just to take his next breath." Vinny looked disgusted. "He shouldn't be allowed to live—"

"You don't know what you're talking about!" Syren screamed.

Fox pitied her. She understood what it was like to know and love someone who was seen as a monster.

201

"I knew Slaine before all this. Before he … changed."

"Did you know he was the Red Face?" Kressa asked, voice low and stern. Her hand was clenched into a metal fist, like she was ready to strike Syren depending on her answer.

Syren shook her head. "I had no idea. I didn't even know Slaine was in Babel until I arrived for the exams. I thought God had brought us together, but he was here as an assassin all along."

Kressa's metal hand returned to normal flesh and bone as she nodded slowly. "I see."

"So what now?" KI asked.

"All we can do is watch," Roaring said. "And be ready in case Kohl needs us."

"I am not stepping foot onto that dead grass." Vinny shook his head.

"Syren was right in front of Slaine and she's fine," Dart pointed out.

Vinny let go of a sigh. "She's a healer. Of course she's fine."

"The grass is just dead, it shouldn't hurt us," Roaring insisted.

Fox tuned them all out, glancing back at Kohl and his shadowmen. They were still charging Slaine, only to be blasted away by his violent flames. Fox remembered the fire that'd burned the Academy, how dark it had seemed. How Roaring hadn't been able to put it out. She had let that fire inside, had felt it whisper against her soul. It'd been dark. Evil. And it had scared her. But now that she'd connected with the Holy Spirit dwelling within her, she didn't fear Slaine's fire anymore. He couldn't hurt her; she was certain of that.

But he could hurt Kohl.

Fire raged in a storm around the Hunger boy, but his shadows leapt to protect him, crying out in agony as they were scorched into nothing. Kohl gritted his teeth, seemingly fed up with this show. He took a step forward, his own shadow stretching out before him, and then he fell face-first into the earth.

Fox gasped. She had expected him to hit the ground with a thud, but his body kept going, diving into his own shadow, and disappearing into the darkness. A moment of stillness swam over the woods, and then darkness descended, as if the night itself had been summoned.

A hand emerged from Kohl's shadow, inky black and glowing. *It's him*, Fox realized as a figure emerged, *it's Kohl*. He wrapped himself in darkness as he crawled from the earth, moving toward Slaine like a living phantom.

It was the strangest thing ... Fox had expected him to roar or scream or let out a cry of anger, but Kohl did none of that. As he charged toward Slaine, his figure gliding over the dead grass, he let out an icy *hiss* that seemed to chill Fox Fire down to her very bones.

He wields darkness itself.

Fox squeezed her eyes shut, trying to comprehend what she'd just seen, trying to block out the gasping cry tearing from Slaine's withered lips.

When she opened her eyes again, she saw the Phantom-Kohl holding Slaine by his throat. "Do you know what I love about shadows so much?" he asked the traitor in a voice Fox didn't recognize. "Shadows never hunger or thirst or rest. But best of all, they never *rot*." His hands tightened around Slaine's neck. "I am your worst enemy."

Fox took a step forward. "He's going to kill him."

"Good," Vinny scoffed. "Let him."

"He can't—"

"Why not?"

"Because the Red Face isn't working alone. We won't know exactly who sent him until we interrogate him. He must be captured, not killed."

"I could've sworn you were fine with killing him a few hours ago," KI muttered.

Fox stared at him. "You're okay with Kohl killing someone?"

203

"This is the exam, Fox. We're expected to battle to the death."

He was right. But ...

Fox looked back at Kohl, at the boy covered in darkness. That wasn't Kohlannis Hunger. That wasn't her friend anymore. And if he killed while he was in this state of mind, he would never be her friend again.

Fox took off running, not caring about the dead grass or about her friends reaching out to grab her. She sprinted toward Phantom-Kohl and Slaine, screaming at the top of her lungs. "KOHL! STOP! DON'T DO IT!"

He ignored her, choking the life out of Slaine like she wasn't even there.

She stopped running and took a deep breath. "ANA!"

The sound of his nickname seemed to snap him back to himself, if only for a moment. He whipped his head toward Fox, his piercing blue gaze landing on her like a dark kiss. And then his attention was back on Slaine and his grip was tightening all over again, but before he could finish him off, a pool of Dark energy opened beside him—as if a black door had appeared in the air.

Out of the darkness, stepped a beautiful creature.

A *creature*, because he was clearly not human with his ethereal gaze, his absolutely perfect glowing bronze skin, and his smile that almost seemed lethal.

For all his beauty, it was the inverted cross on his forehead that Fox couldn't stop staring at. *Of course he's beautiful*, she thought, *the devil comes as an angel of light.*

The beautiful creature smiled at her and Kohl who was so stunned, his shadows had completely disappeared. He was back to his normal form, and since his hands weren't covered in shadows anymore, he had to let go of Slaine or risk his fingers decaying.

Kohl jumped back a few steps, standing almost right beside Fox Fire.

"Who on earth—"

The creature swept his arm out dramatically and bowed. "The name's—"

"HOSENKÉ!" screamed a terrible voice.

Fox startled as she jerked her head to the side, searching for the madman who'd just screamed. Even the beautiful creature had fallen silent, his smirk slowly fading as he peered into the woods over Slaine's shoulder.

He frowned. "Not this guy."

A blur whooshed past Fox so fast, she screamed as her hair whipped around her. Dust flew into the air, kicked up by the sudden gust of wind. When it settled, she peeled her eyes open to find Lord Izzy standing between her and the man he'd called, Hosenké.

19

Izzy, The Guillotine

It'd taken more Light energy than he would have liked, but Izzy managed to make it to the Kanen Forest just in time. He'd had to exert himself, channeling his spiritual energy into his arms and legs to run faster and cover more ground, but he'd made it. And he didn't even feel winded, if he was being honest.

It took a glance to get the scope of the battle. Hosenké was there, with what looked like the unmasked Red Face. Fox Fire, Kohlannis Hunger, and all their friends just a short distance behind them. There were only two enemies, but both of them were part of the Nine—even the Red Face, if only by association. Izzy had faced worse odds, but he would have to separate the kids from the demons before any serious fighting could begin.

Vehenort, his apprentice, pushed through the brush behind him, panting. "Master…"

"You made it," he said, keeping his vision forward.

She responded by passing him Master Jo's staff. Izzy still wasn't sure why she had insisted that he take it with him, but as he hefted the weapon, he felt the slight hum of spiritual energy running through it.

I see, he stared down at the metal rod, *it's imbued.*

Before he could change his mind, Izzy launched the staff at Hosenké who easily dodged it by simply stepping to the side, but the Priest had expected that. The rod lodged into the bark of a tree a few meters away, quivering from the force of impact.

A moment later, it glowed bright white, its imbuement activating, and Master Jo appeared beside it.

So that's it, Izzy observed, *she can teleport herself to her weapon's location.*

There was no time for greetings, Master Jo immediately erected a wall between the students and the demons, effectively blocking them from harm's way. She even formed walls around Fox and Kohl, caging them in together.

Hosenké scoffed. "Those walls won't stop anything."

"They're impenetrable." Marlo's voice held an air of pride. "You're not getting through."

"Will they disappear if I kill you?" Hosenké asked.

Marlo responded by opening her barrier and stepping through to the safe side.

Hosenké laughed. "I don't need to get through your walls. I can just go around them."

Just like in the observation room, black pools of Dark energy opened throughout the forest, allowing demons to crawl forth—except all of these pools were located on the other side of Marlo's walls. With the students.

Shouts rang up through the trees as the trainees began to fight for their lives. Panic tore through Izzy but he kept himself calm by focusing on Master Jo. She grabbed her staff and immediately charged at her enemies, joined by Roaring Fire and a number of her brave students.

They can handle this, Izzy told himself.

"We only want the boy," Hosenké said. "We don't have to fight, but we will if we must."

Izzy shook his head. "We're not handing over KI."

"Then you will die."

Slaine stepped between Izzy and Hosenké, his eyes remained on the Priest, but his words were meant for the Birth of Carnage. "I'll keep them busy. You stay focused on the howler."

Howler?

Hosenké nodded and stepped back into the shadow of the trees. His eyes glazed over, and his lips moved, quietly muttering incantations to himself, but before Izzy could figure out what the demon was doing, Slaine was charging at him.

He gasped and jumped back, throwing up his arms in defense. He had heard about the Red Face, and had watched his encounters at the observatory, so when Izzy saw Slaine's hand coming toward him, he had expected fire. Instead, Slaine grabbed him by the wrist and held on, but that was fine with Izzy. It took only a moment for him to use his blessing—sharp blades jutted from his forearm, slicing right through Slaine's fingers.

With a yelp, the assassin pulled back and stumbled to the side. His dark eyes glared at Izzy's face before focusing on his arms where the blades protruded. They tore holes into the sleeves of his cassock, but Izzy was used to shredding up his clothes during a fight. That was what happened when your blessing turned you into a living weapon.

Today's form: The Guillotine.

"I've heard about you," Slaine said very calmly. He cradled his injured hand, but Izzy couldn't help but notice there was no blood. "I should have known better than to underestimate *Lord Izzy*."

His tone was mocking, but Izzy was unfazed. He couldn't afford to get distracted right now, not with Hosenké muttering curses in the woods and Marlo and her students fighting demons behind her barrier. Not to mention Fox and Kohl who were both going nuts, banging on the walls of their cage as a futile attempt to get free. Izzy was glad Master Jo hadn't let them out, they were safe—which meant two less people to worry about.

Slaine charged him again, this time he didn't try to grab hold of the young Priest, he threw jabs and punches that were so swift, Izzy felt the air brush past his face as he dodged his moves. *He's fast.* Izzy ducked and countered, swinging his arm in an arc that caused his blade to tear through Slaine's shirt. It didn't connect with his flesh, but it was enough to get him to back off. Slaine was quick on his feet, dancing to the side and punching at the air—this time, fire stormed right at him, but Izzy didn't bother dodging. He didn't need to.

The flames surrounded him like a vortex, licking at his flesh, but dealing no damage. When they dissipated, Slaine's eyes grew wide with shock.

"That's the second time you've survived an attack that should have killed you," he said coldly. "You have two blessings, don't you? A living weapon, and healing."

Izzy laughed. "Do you honestly think I'll tell you?"

In truth, he had thirteen different blessings—and none of them had anything to do with healing—but that was none of Slaine's business.

The assassin let out a growl before he shot fire at Izzy again, but the flames dealt no damage, so he rushed him and exchanged brutal blows up close. They danced together until Slaine was panting; Izzy could feel his agitation and fatigue getting the better of him. It showed when he lunged forward and grabbed Izzy by the throat.

A twisted laugh slithered from his disfigured mouth. "I've got you now," he said.

But nothing happened.

His eyes filled with rage. "WHY?" he shouted at the Priest. "Why won't you wither and die?"

209

Behind them, Vehenort stumbled to the side and sagged against a tree. The action caught Slaine's attention, and his gaze widened with understanding.

"You're as heartless as I am," he muttered.

Izzy swung at him, forcing Slaine to let go and jump back. He spared a glance at Vehenort; she had burns bubbling up her arms, peeking from the collar of her cassock. And one of her arms and her neck were completely black—decayed, like Izzy's should have been.

"She takes your injuries onto her own body, so you feel nothing," Slaine explained like he was almost humored by it. There was an odd sense of joy tangled up in his voice that sent a wave of anger over Izzy.

It was no secret the skilled Priest had taken Vehenort under his wing for her unique blessing. She had the power to bring herself and others back to life, but she also possessed extraordinary gifts of healing, like her ability to take whatever pain Izzy felt and place it on herself so he could continue fighting without injury. She had the power to heal herself up, but often in the swiftness of battle, there was no time to concentrate on her own pain. She remained focused on her master, quietly suffering in his stead.

Izzy bit his lip until he tasted blood. He had faced overwhelming scrutiny from the Cross for the dynamic he'd established with Vehenort. But each complaint was silenced by the incredible work he and Vehenort accomplished together.

Still … He didn't like that she suffered for him. He didn't like that his inability to feel pain made him reckless and uncaring at times. But there were some enemies so ruthless, they could only be bested by equal brutality. Vehenort made that possible for him.

Izzy watched her in silence, dragging his bright eyes over her scarred skin and rotting flesh. As she panted for breath, her wounds began to slowly heal. She gave him a nod. It was all he needed.

210

"You are more valuable alive than dead," Izzy said to Slaine.

The assassin's crooked smirk shriveled into a menacing scowl as he listened.

"I would rather apprehend you for interrogation, but if you insist on fighting then I will be forced to kill you. Take your pick."

Slaine spat in the dirt. "You're mighty arrogant for a member of the Cross. Isn't pride a sin?"

"I take pride in serving a God who never fails. There is nothing sinful about that."

Slaine ran at him, but he didn't make it more than two steps before a low growl stopped him in his tracks. Even Izzy stopped as he squinted into the darkness of the forest where the sound had come from.

Slowly, a white beast stepped into view, fleshy and ugly and reeking of evil. Steam rose from its body, like it had just crawled from the pits of hell, and its claws dug into the earth as it prowled the area on all fours. Eyeless, it sniffed at the air to gain a sense of direction, and when it was satisfied, it opened its massive jowls and let out a piercing cry—*No*, Izzy realized, *not a cry*.

A howl.

Slaine clapped his hands over his ears at the sound of the beast's howl, shoulders bunching in pain. Over Izzy's shoulder, Vehenort collapsed to her knees, covering her ears as well. The pain didn't hit Izzy for a few moments, when Vehenort had reached her limits and was too overwhelmed to cloak his injuries. The sound was thunderous, like someone had released a hurricane inside his very ears. And it seemed to pierce right through his head and dig into his mind, echoing in the chambers of his thoughts and secrets.

He couldn't focus on anything but the howler's cry. Mercifully, neither could anyone else. Slaine was just as incapacitated as he was, doubled over and vomiting from the excruciating pain. Even Fox and

Kohl were on their hands and knees behind their protective walls.

But there was one figure still standing.

Hosenké: The Seventh Birth of Carnage.

He walked through the field of downed bodies, his crimson cloak dragging behind him, his long raven hair flowing with his smooth movements. There was no malice or anger on his face as he regarded Izzy, just a very bored and very blank expression, like he was thoroughly unimpressed with the skilled young Priest.

"I'll be going now," he said in his deep timbre. And with a nod, he pulled his vision from Izzy and stooped to take Slaine into his arms, then he stepped back into the shadows of the woods with the howler following behind.

Part III

213

20

Evelyn

It was dark inside his room, despite the afternoon sun. All the curtains were drawn, leaving Diaz swimming in a tide of shadows and gloom. He didn't feel like pulling the curtains, didn't feel like letting in the light. For more reasons than one.

If he concentrated, he could hear the funeral procession even from his apartment on the other side of town. Most of the city had come out for the mournful event. He wasn't surprised. They had lost hundreds of people, but not just to the Red Face and Hosenké. Trainees had died, too.

Just part of the exam, Diaz reminded himself. If it weren't for the masked assassin, Babel would be celebrating the completion of the exams today, not mourning everyone who'd died because of it.

They had cancelled the last three days of the brutal test due to the disruption. Officials wanted to comb the Kanen Forest for other possible intruders and to collect evidence. They needed to treat the wounded and injured and conduct interviews on the kids who had fought the Red Face and the Birth of Carnage. Not to mention notifying families of their losses and arranging the mass funeral going on just a few blocks away now.

A dozen members of the Taber Tribe, Wend Knockel, *and Tella Kotaro*. Evelyn ground his teeth together, hands making fists as he sat on the edge of his bed. *Why did she have to die?*

He would have understood if it had been himself, he was cursed and full of hatred. But Kotaro had been good. Had been kind. Hadn't deserved to perish at the hands of a demon.

Evelyn's abdomen ached at the memory, and he clutched his midsection, gasping as the pain intensified. Izzy had stabbed him after Kotaro died, trying to keep him from giving in to the darkness lurking inside. In his anguish, Diaz had caused a tear in the seal on his body, allowing the cursed power to flow freely through him. He had bathed in the waters of darkness, letting evil feed on his festering pain and hatred.

Lord Izzy had stopped him, sinking one of Kotaro's own blades into his flesh to jar him from his pain. The ache of the attack still felt new, but it was the despair of his memories that seemed to open a fresh wound in his heart. He was bleeding from the inside out. And there were no bandages to ease the pain.

A strangled gasp tore from his lips, and he collapsed back onto his bed, staring up at the blank ceiling, blinking away his bitter tears. Thick black lines covered the full length of both his arms now, he could no longer hide them the way he used to beneath his military uniform. They curved around his wrists and even twisted over his hands, decorating each finger with a dark swirl. Evelyn held his hand up and stared at it through his tears. The seal was stronger now. It had to be.

Izzy's words haunted him. "I warned you not to slip up."

He had. Back when Diaz had travelled to Wi with Lady Talon in tow. His old friend had gone into his tent and told him to be careful of his power, to make sure he could keep it under control. But his warning had fallen on deaf ears.

At the hospital, where anxious nurses had treated Diaz's stab wound,

215

Izzy appeared again, smiling at the healers, and nodding his thanks. Evelyn hadn't missed the controlled rage swirling in his bright eyes.

That time, Izzy didn't warn him. He just shoved him into his hospital mattress and whispered the prayers of sealing before Diaz could protest. It had burned him. Searing pain running over his skin as ink appeared on his flesh. It ran down his chest and back like acid, scorching him as it formed his new seal. When it was over, he lay there panting, struggling for every breath.

"I warned you before. Now I'm done being gentle with you. Next time it gets out of control, I'll kill you," Izzy had said. The ice in his stare had sent fangs of fear biting into Diaz's heart.

He could only nod in response.

Evelyn hadn't seen Izzy since that day in the hospital. He didn't miss him.

The two had grown up together, but 'friends' was a word Diaz rarely used to describe their connection. Kotaro had been the warm glue holding their little group together. Without her, Evelyn didn't know what sort of relationship he would have had with Izzy. They had fought together and got along while on missions or doing research, but Izzy never got friendly with Diaz and Diaz never opened his heart enough to be offended by his distance. They trusted each other on good days— tolerated each other on most days. It seemed to be a dynamic that worked for them. But now, with Kotaro gone, Evelyn suspected Izzy would only be the cold man he'd been in the hospital. Threatening, dangerous. Almost mean.

Diaz shivered.

That was a side of Izzy he had seen before. The cold man from the battlefield, the one who had faced death more times than he cared to remember—and had even fallen to it more than once.

Diaz could recall the first time Izzy had died on a mission, he'd only graduated from the Academy a month before and then he was suddenly dead. There had been no tears, no particular reaction at all, really. But there had been utter shock and awe when Izzy's apprentice stunned the Region and brought him back to life. They'd been an item ever since.

Noise dragged Evelyn from his memories, and he turned his head to find Major Marshall standing in his doorway. He leaned against the wall and folded his arms over his chest, a very somber smile on his face.

"The funeral is over, son."

Evelyn frowned. He had locked his apartment door.

Marshall's somberness seemed to ebb away as he held up a set of keys. "You gave them to me when you first moved in."

Marshall had insisted. He'd called Evelyn his 'depressing child' and was paranoid he would slip away and recede from society if Marshall didn't barge into his apartment and drag him out to do normal things outside of missions. Things like socialize and go on dates with pretty women.

Diaz's frown deepened. He'd had women before. Fleeting, meaningless encounters that were more carnal than loving. But *socializing* was something he still hadn't gotten used to. He didn't think he ever would.

"I came to check on you," Major Marshall said.

Evelyn blinked at him. "Were her parents there?"

The old man nodded.

"Were there Psalms?" Evelyn loved the Psalms.

"The thirty-ninth," Marshall said.

He thought a moment and then muttered quietly, "Everyone is but a breath, even those who seem secure."

His adoptive father said his next favorite verse, "But now, Lord, what do I look for? My hope is in you."

After a long moment of painful silence, Diaz admitted, "I blamed

217

God. Because I didn't understand why Kotaro died but I was kept alive. She was good."

"Those who are good often face the most persecution." Marshall shrugged. "Why would demons waste time going after people who are already filled with darkness?"

"Why didn't God protect her?" Diaz asked.

Marshall shrugged again, like the question had never crossed his mind. "Does it matter? Will you stop believing if you ever find out? Or if you don't?"

Of course not. Evelyn's nose wrinkled in annoyance, but he understood what the old man was saying. There were things he would simply never understand about God, just as a mere speck of bacteria cannot possibly comprehend the massively epic universe around it. A human could not ever hope to fully understand God. But even if Diaz *could* understand, he wouldn't let it make a difference in his faith. It was his job to believe and follow, not to ask and debate. Paul said it best in Romans, *But who are you, a human being, to talk back to God?*

Still ... the pain hurt all the same. And Diaz wasn't sure he could cope. He knew that was why his father had shown up, to somehow slap some grit back into him. He braced himself, waiting for the emotional blow he knew was coming. Waiting for Marshall to tell him to get it together.

The old man just watched him from across the room, gentle eyes full of heartbreak and pity, but also wisdom and something stern. Something that made Diaz heave a sigh and push from his bed. He pressed the heels of his hands into his eyes and then marched to the water basin at his desk. Marshall didn't speak as he stripped naked and splashed himself with the chilly water.

"I know you have more to say than that, old man."

Marshall chuckled from across the room. "I figured you would be

218

hiding in your dark and gloomy room. That's understandable, considering the circumstances. But I took the liberty of recommending you for a mission, just to keep you busy."

Diaz glanced over at him, running his soapy hands through his dark hair. "I don't want to go on a mission."

"That's why I recommended you."

He grunted but didn't say anything more.

"It's about the boy."

That got his attention. Diaz flicked his gaze to his father as he rinsed his hair, dripping water onto his wooden floor. Marshall wasn't smiling but there was a glint in his eye that told him he would be interested in this job.

"His Excellency Bishop Jericho has seen the error of his ways. The council now admits it was a bad idea to continue with the Academy exams."

"No kidding," Evelyn grumbled, rinsing his chest and all the parts of him he should've been covering, but Marshall was his father and—truly—Diaz didn't care. This was his home, he would wash when he felt like it, no matter who was looking.

"After lengthy discussions and interviews with the kids, the council has decided it's best to send KI to the north."

Diaz raised an eyebrow. There was only one place up north to take a kid like KI, someone who was dangerous enough to draw the attention of the Nine.

"The Northern Fortress, in the Region of Ice," Evelyn said, reaching for a towel. From his peripheral, he saw Major Marshall nod.

"I don't think it's a bad choice," the old man said.

Neither did the lieutenant. The north was a barren ice land; few tribes and even fewer animals lurked the frozen Region. The Farrons and the Ools lived in the Region of Ice, regularly sending aid and soldiers to

Babel as some of the Academy's oldest allies. If KI was heading north, there was no doubt he would be guarded by formidable men and women from such families.

Briefly, Diaz remembered one of the students who'd been questioned about the Red Face. Vyanna Farron, heiress to the Northern Tribe. Her uncle was the one who was king of the north, but he was old and childless, which meant the crown would pass to Vyanna's mother when he perished. But Vy's mother had made it clear that her place was in Babel, fighting for the Academy. Whenever her brother passed away, she would both take the throne and abdicate it in the same day, effectively passing the Ice Crown to Vyanna.

That meant the Farron princess would have to return to the Region of Ice the moment they received news of her uncle's passing. The north couldn't be left without its king—or queen.

In the back of his head, Evelyn wondered if Vy Farron would join the mission. She was only a student at the Academy, nowhere near experienced enough to join the escort team, but being a Farron would certainly give her an advantage. The old tribe was said to be acutely in tune with the land of the north. As if God enhanced their blessings and abilities while in their native land. They had to be blessed if they managed to carve out a flourishing kingdom from what was nothing more than a frozen land of ice and sleet and snow.

But it was this barrenness that made the Region of Ice the perfect place to take KI. If something happened with the kid, there wouldn't be much collateral damage. Taking KI up there was a good idea, but the north was far from Babel and relatively isolated. The travel would be long and exhausting.

"When is this mission going to take place?"

"Couple weeks," Marshall replied. "I'm handling certain details, along with Captain Payne. For now, you've been assigned the task of

220

putting together the team."

Diaz slowly looked up at the old man. "The council wants me to put together the team that will be travelling north." It wasn't a question, so Marshall didn't offer an answer. He simply smiled at him which drew a sigh from Diaz's lips. "All I want to know is, why me?"

"Isn't it obvious?"

"If it were, I wouldn't be asking."

"I recommended you because I know keeping busy will help you cope with Tella's death."

Evelyn's jaw clenched at the sound of her first name. He'd never heard it much when she was alive, but since her passing it was all anyone wanted to call her.

"The council accepted my recommendation," Marshall went on, "because you were one of few who spoke out against their decision to proceed with the entrance exams." The major laughed, and the sound bounced around Evelyn's empty, dark room. "Basically, they want you to go because you are an exemplary and dedicated Hunter."

Diaz slipped into a shirt and then stared at him, knowing that wasn't the end of things.

Marshall smiled. "And also, you have a unique ability to call BS when you see it."

For the first time in a long time, Evelyn laughed.

"I take it that little snort means you'll accept the mission?"

He didn't want to. There was nothing appealing about the north at all. The mission would be cold and long and dreary. But no matter what he faced out there, there was no question it would be better than facing the dreariness of his own mind.

Lieutenant Diaz nodded. "I accept this mission."

21

Roaring

Roaring thanked God the Fire Tribe hadn't lost anyone in the chaos of the exams. The funeral had been a dark reminder of the death and grief his people had suffered not long ago. It'd awakened feelings of guilt and remorse within him; guilt that he had been trying so hard, fighting for a people and a city that was not his own, and remorse for not fighting for his own people with as much dedication and effort.

Talon shared these feelings. She saw the massive funeral as a personal wakeup call to get it together and be the Grand Chief her village needed her to be. That was why she'd called a Council meeting just days after the gloomy event. They were all squeezed into the living room now, Kifa Modon sat on the sofa, calmly petting Chava's big head while Ryko and Thunder chatted casually and munched on the snacks Cat had set out for them to eat—sliced fruit and raw vegetables and little dried fish that went well with avocado. Kifu Kato stood brooding in the corner, not interested in taking a seat or having a snack. His dark eyes were glued to Roaring like he'd somehow done something wrong.

The Prince of Fire remembered the last Council meeting he'd suffered through. It had almost been a nightmare, mostly because his uncle had tried to embarrass him and usurp as much power from the acting Grand Chief as he could. He had pointed out his nonchalance and disregard for the tribe, as well as his attire for the meeting. A dress shirt and slacks with the leather shoes that pinched his big feet. His toes felt sore just thinking about the shoes.

Today, he made sure his clothing was appropriate. He stood bare-chested in a loincloth and a beaded necklace Cat had made for him. She'd also retied his knot and wove it into the thick braids that trailed over his shoulders and down his back. His tattoos stretched taut over his crossed arms, the muscles in his chest and back straining against his smooth brown skin. A rahkai was strapped to his hip, the weapon of choice for members of Wi's Hunting Regiment. His feet were bare. His ears were freshly pierced, a ring dangling from his right lobe and a red bead studding the left one.

When he looked down, you could see the kohl Cat had painted over his lids, she'd even drawn streaks across both his cheeks. It was a common design for Hunters of the Regiment, Thunder's face-paint was similar, whereas Kifa Ina had worn something simpler, shadow over her eyes and a cross in the middle of her forehead.

Roaring had caught Ina staring at him more than once as they waited for Talon to appear. He was used to being stared at, for his great height or his stature, but right now her gaze made him squirm. It was an effort just to keep still as he leaned against the wall. It had been so long since he'd dressed as a warrior, the Prince of Fire had forgotten how little clothing they'd worn in the scorching dirt roads of Wi. He almost felt naked in his loincloth. He *was* naked in his loincloth. He could feel the breeze from the window flow right under his skirt and hit all the places he'd rather not feel right now. When another breeze danced in, he shifted away from the window for fear of his cloth whipping up and showing Ina what it meant to be a prince.

Finally, the bedroom door down the hall opened and the ladies

223

entered the living room. The Chiefana walked in first, Fox Fire as the youngest, in a buckskin dress and bare feet. Her hair was in box braids that brushed over her shoulders and collarbone. She wore warrior-style face-paint just like Roaring's.

Cat entered next in a handstitched kataa that covered her feet so Roaring couldn't tell if she wore sandals or not. Her hair was twisted into an elegant updo, tendrils of thick curls hanging loose to kiss her light brown shoulders, and she held a wooden box in her hands.

Last was Grand Chief Talon. There was an audible gasp as she entered and Roaring immediately understood why. She was wearing a simple blouse and a skirt she'd bought in Babel. The Flaming Veil was atop her head, covering her face so they couldn't see her expression, but that didn't make up for her utter lack of respect for the event.

Roaring felt anxiety and frustration uncoil in his chest. It seeped into his bones, making his back ache as he pushed from the wall. "Talon—"

"What is the meaning of this?" Kifu Kato demanded angrily.

"Grand Chief," Ryko said, his eyes wide. It was no secret the Hunter was in love with Talon, but he was obviously torn by her appearance, unsure if he should support her or chastise her like everyone else.

Talon removed the veil, earning another gasp from the crowd. "I am relinquishing my right to the Veil," she announced calmly.

Roaring had expected another gasp, but this time the room fell silent.

"Tell me you are joking," their uncle said in a desperate, quiet voice.

Talon shook her head. "I have thought about it. My mind is made up."

"You can't just walk away from the Veil," Kato insisted. "You can't just abandon hundreds of years of tradition!"

"I don't serve tradition," Talon replied calmly.

"You serve the Veil!" Kato snapped.

She bristled. "I serve God, Nuncle. And no one else.'"

224

"Did the Lord speak to you?" Kifa Ina asked gently. "Is this a commandment from God?"

Talon bit her lip. "In a way." When she saw the doubtful looks on everyone's faces, she quickly added, "I prayed about it. And I believe this is what God wants."

"God wants you to abandon the village?" Ina asked.

"God wants me to follow Him. And He's not going back to the village." She looked at Roaring and walked over to him. "But you are." She held out the Veil.

Roaring stared down at it as he realized what she meant. This wasn't just breaking tradition, it was blasphemous.

"A—A man cannot wear the Veil," he muttered. "A man cannot lead—"

"You can and you will," Talon cut him off. She shoved the Veil into his chest and then whirled to face the rest of the Council. "Let this be my last order as Grand Chief. I, Grand Chief Talon, hereby denounce the matriarchy and introduce a monarchy ruled by a Grand Chief who has the freedom to choose her or *his* heir of their own accord."

The room was stunned.

Ina found her voice first. "May I ask why you are doing this?"

"I have never been a good leader," Talon admitted. "I was born to be the Grand Chief but I was never truly accepted as one." Again, her gaze returned to Roaring who was still staring dumbly at the Veil gripped in his large hands. He was too shocked to find words. The Veil had been his dream since childhood, but he'd always known it was unachievable. He'd been born the wrong gender. Had all the right attributes, but all the wrong parts—according to the outdated matriarchal tradition. Now the crown was quite literally being handed to him. Hundreds of years of tradition wiped away with a single flick of Talon's slender wrist.

"My brother has always been an excellent leader. You all know that.

225

Most of you followed his leadership in the Hunting Regiment. I don't have to say anything to prove my point on that."

Despite his shock and dismay, Kifu Kato nodded agreement with Talon. "Why don't you choose one of the Chiefana?" he asked.

"Fox is staying here to continue her training at the Academy. Cat has chosen to return to Wi with Roaring, but when I offered her the Veil, she declined."

Wide eyes slid over to the young Chiefana, but Cat wasn't bothered by the staring. She shrugged when the silence went on for too long. "I've never wanted it in the first place."

"I thought you also never wanted to return to Wi?" Roaring said.

She smiled at him. "Who else is going to keep you in check?"

"I don't understand," Ryko muttered angrily. "How can you just walk away like this? We have so much in Wi."

Roaring got the sense he was talking about something else with Talon, but she kept her face measured and her response professional. "There is much in Wi. The recent events have made it more than clear that it is time for us to return home and God has made a way for that to happen. But He has also made it known to me that my place is here in Babel. With Fox Fire. With the Academy. With Master Li."

"Master Li?" Kato scoffed. "Who is Master Li?"

"He is the man who encouraged me to get closer to God. If it weren't for him, I would be packing up to leave for Wi once the reconstruction began." She turned to Cat and took the wooden box from her hands. "While staying here in Babel, I have learned that God has blessed me with a sensitivity to spiritual energy. Master Li taught me how to use that sensitivity." She opened the wooden box to reveal two plain metal rods. They weren't long at all, no bigger than two small branches, and totally insignificant in appearance.

Talon held up one of the rods and it transformed into a rahkai, and

226

then a battle axe, and then a sword. In the shocked silence, she returned the rod to the box and then handed the box to Fox Fire. "Master Li taught me how to use a skill called *Imbue*—it means pouring your spiritual energy into an object to make it more powerful. Under his tutelage, God blessed me with this design for Fox Fire. To help in her training."

Fox stared at the box in awe, exhaling the soft words, "Thank you."

"Thank God," Talon said. "He gave me the inspiration."

"Thank You, God," Fox said quietly.

"In Wi, I was not confident in myself. I felt I could not live up to the standards that'd been placed on my shoulders. But here in Babel I can make a difference. I can do something to help Christians fight this spiritual war that has gone on for far too long."

Thunder, who had been quiet the entire time, stepped forward. Her rahkai and her sword clacked against her hips as she walked, she was a formidable looking woman; tall and muscular and fearless, but when she stopped before Lady Talon, she wore a smile that immediately drained the intimidation from her.

"I am happy for you, Grand Chief." She pressed her lips together. "*Former* Grand Chief."

"How can you say that?" Kato hissed.

"Because Lady Talon failed as a Grand Chief. She did not live up to our expectations or make very impactful decisions. But she admits that." Thunder let her words sink in. "It takes great courage to admit defeat and failure. And it takes incredible resolve to try something new after facing failure. Yet, our Grand Chief has done both." She looked back at Kifu Kato. "While you have done nothing."

"Excuse me?" His voice was threatening, words slicing through the air to cut at Thunder, but she was not bothered by him.

She faced him head-on, eyes blazing. "You abandoned the boy you

227

raised as soon as he became an inconvenience to you. I have not forgotten that fact, Kifu Kato. And I never will."

"I support the Grand Chief's decision to stay," Ina Modon said, before an argument could break out. "God has blessed Babel to help us rebuild Wi, but who says we have to rebuild the village exactly as it was? Everything changes. Wi suffered because it had refused to change for centuries. Let's not make that same mistake again."

Ryko crossed his arms. Kato let out a low growl and then glared at everyone in the room—even Fox and Cat who were innocent in this.

"She is abandoning us all and everyone is okay with that," he said darkly.

Talon sighed. "I have never liked you and you have never liked me, Nuncle. The way I see it, this is a win-win situation."

Kifu Kato sputtered angry nonsense.

"Was it not you who tried to wrest the crown from my brow while the Walls of Wi remained?" Talon asked. "You're finally getting what you want. Be happy for once." She looked at Roaring again. "Do you accept this position as the new Grand Chief?"

He lifted the Veil and placed it on his head, smiling behind the hanging strips of material that hid his face. "I do."

Talon nodded. "You will be expected to meet with members of the Academy to make plans for the reconstruction of Wi. I will go with you if you'd like."

He almost thanked her, but he stopped himself in time. He was the Grand Chief now. That meant he didn't just inherit all of Talon's power and authority, he'd also inherited all the expectations and doubts she'd had to live with. The Council was looking to him now—with even more worry in their eyes than before. If he couldn't handle going to a simple meeting without his sister by his side, they would never trust him to do anything else on his own.

228

"I'll go alone," Roaring said firmly. "I'll make the arrangements, and then I'll rally a team and return to Wi for the first phase of restoration." He looked at his sisters and then dragged his gaze over each member of the Council. This would be his first time using his authority, he wanted to make sure his voice was stern and left no room for argument. So he puffed his nineteen-year-old chest and took a deep breath. "This meeting is adjourned."

22

Evelyn

There was a lot to consider for this mission. The Nine hadn't succeeded in capturing KI, but the Red Face and Hosenké had both gotten away, and the testimonies of the students clearly indicated the masked assailant hadn't been operating alone.

There were two Red Faces.

At first, it'd only been speculation, but when Diaz compared the reports from the kids, there wasn't a doubt left in his mind.

The report from Fox Fire and her brother had been the nail in the coffin. While Fox, Kohlannis, and KI were fighting the Red Face—along with Gloria and Eekay—Slaine was having a standoff with Roaring Fire. Lieutenant Diaz had compared their information and then cross-referenced it with detailed reports written by members of the Onté Clan who had participated in the observation of the exam.

If Slaine was standing in plain clothing with no disguise right before Roaring and a number of other trainees, then the man behind the mask who'd first tried to capture KI had to be a different person.

Which person, was the question.

It could have been anyone. Could have been a demon who'd breached the spiritual barrier around the Kanen Forest just like Hosenké had breached the observatory. It could have been Hosenké himself masking his immense Dark energy to remain anonymous for as long as possible.

Or, Diaz thought, *it could have been another student.*

The thought made his stomach churn as he left his office at the Academy that morning, but he had to check all his boxes before making any concrete decisions on his team composition for the upcoming mission. He didn't want to risk taking the spy along with them.

"If you don't want to accidentally take the spy, then don't take any students along," Major Marshall had told him when he'd laid out his concerns to his father over breakfast.

Diaz had shaken his head in disagreement. Since the exams had been disrupted, the council decided to allow the surviving students to graduate into the Academy. That meant every trainee who was alive and healthy would be welcomed into the Gamma Division once the semester started. The Lieutenant was quietly proud of the kids, especially those of Class G5—they had faced the Red Face and had witnessed the power of a Birth of Carnage up close. He wouldn't have opposed them being promoted into the Beta Division, but he was willing to settle on Gamma. That meant the students would be cleared to take on missions, maybe even one that involved escorting a boyish teen to the Northern Fortress.

Diaz wanted the students more than he wanted S-ranked Priests or Shadows of the Cross. It wasn't about power or skill, it was about experience.

"Those kids saw one of the Nine up close and they were ready to fight," he'd told his father.

"Because they were too foolish to be afraid and run."

"I need that foolishness. I need that brave naivety for this mission. And—" more than anything, "I need their willingness to protect KI."

It was no secret Fox Fire and Kohlannis Hunger would fight to the death for the kid, but that crazy battle in the forest had done something to the rest of G5. It had united them in a way they hadn't been united before. Turning a class into an army, friends into family. They were dedicated to keeping KI safe, more than the hardened Hunters of the Academy would ever be.

For anyone else, this mission would simply be a job and when things got tough, the mission would be abandoned. Worst came to worst, KI would likely be killed by a Hunter from the Academy just to keep the Nine from getting him. Diaz wouldn't even be surprised if the kid's throat was slit during the night while he slept right there in the facility.

The attack in the Kanen Forest had done nothing but draw more hatred and fear of him. Bishop Jericho wanted him out of the city as soon as possible, if not for the safety of Babel, then at least for his own security. The Bishop feared his own people might attempt to harm the boy just as much as the second Red Face.

Diaz shared his worries, which was why he'd made it his personal task to check on the boy every day until the mission began. He rounded the corner to his wing at the Academy and found his door, not bothering to knock before he entered.

KI and Kohl both looked up at him in surprise. KI was sitting on a bench in nothing but his underwear while Kohl was stark naked and hunched over a small table. Izzy was behind him, a palm flattened against his back, a hard look in his eye.

Kohl's gaze was colder than ice. "What?" he said so casually, Diaz was momentarily lost for words.

Then it clicked.

"You're getting sealed again."

The boy opened his mouth to reply but his words turned into a hiss as he squeezed his eyes shut and gripped the edge of the table. Webs of electricity scattered over his body, making his muscles seize and cramp.

He jerked his body forward, black lines appearing down his toned arms and crawling over his elbows. The patterns on his back stretched over his buttocks and wrapped around his thighs.

Diaz shivered, thinking of his own sealing and how horrible it had been.

The boys were unfortunate to have Izzy as their spiritual guardian. He was never gentle with his treatments or his lessons. The Lieutenant had learned that the hard way.

Kohl ground his teeth together as he breathed through the pain, taking slow breaths that filled his lungs and seemed to suck all the air right out of the room. Diaz's gaze dropped to KI who was watching with eyes so big it was a wonder they stayed in his skull.

The lieutenant sat on the bench beside him. "You get used to the pain," he muttered.

Kohl gasped and jerked forward again, making the table scrape against the stone floor.

"I know," KI said quietly. "I remember the first time I was sealed by Lord Izzy."

So did Diaz—he'd been there—but he didn't think the kid wanted to go back over the details, so he didn't carry the conversation any further than that. Instead, he leaned over and said quietly, "Why's he naked?"

KI snorted, cracking his usual goofy smile. "Lord Izzy came in while he was washing himself and didn't give him time to grab his underclothes."

Of course he didn't, Diaz rolled his eyes, thinking of how he'd barged into his hospital room and ruthlessly held him down in his own bed. Izzy hadn't cared about his thin hospital gown or his stab wound—he was wholly concerned with his mission. Nothing more, nothing less. In a way, Diaz respected him for it, but it did make their encounters awkward at times.

"Finished," Izzy said, retracting his hand from Kohl's back. He sagged onto the table, all his strength leaving him as he breathed deeply, tiredly. When he gathered himself and limped away to his room, Diaz saw the black image of Izzy's hand inked into the center of his back—the focal point of his seal.

"It looks bigger," KI said.

Izzy nodded. "It's stronger than the last one."

"Is that why it hurts?"

He shook his head. "Applying a seal only hurts because the markings are purifying you as they appear."

"Burning out the darkness," Diaz muttered.

"Will mine burn out the demon inside me?" KI asked.

"No. But it will burn away as much of the demon's Dark energy as possible, leaving your mind free of its influence."

"Until it comes right back," KI said in a defeated tone.

That was the difference between Diaz and KI; the boy's Dark energy was constant—flowing into his mind and body without his permission or control. But the lieutenant's Dark energy could only pour into his mind with his permission. His acceptance. His rejection of the Light.

That was how it worked, how the curse had been designed. *Give me your mind and your body and I will give you power*, the witch had promised. And after watching his mother die and his father burn, Evelyn had accepted her terms without hesitation.

And now he was cursed. Just like the Red Face—given a blessing he could barely control, at the cost of his own free will. He had given in to his curse whenever he felt himself overwhelmed in training or in battle while on missions. But each time he'd used it, he found it harder to regain control of himself. That was when he'd gone to Izzy for help, afraid that he would one day lose his mind and body for good, enslaved to the darkness lurking inside.

234

Izzy had helped lock the shadows away, but he still hadn't found a way to break the curse. If he could locate the witch who'd placed it on him, he could kill her, and the curse would be broken by the spilling of her blood. Unfortunately, Diaz had few memories of the blackhearted woman and none of them contained information on her identity. But Evelyn knew he would recognize her if he ever saw her again.

He didn't know her name. Or the name of her coven. But he knew her face. That was something he would never forget.

Movement beside him caught his attention, and Diaz realized KI was standing now, stiffly walking over to the table and leaning over to grip the edges with both hands.

"Will it be stronger?" he asked in a strained voice, anticipating pain.

Izzy's face was stony as he said, "Much."

KI gulped. "Will it hurt?"

"Likely."

He nodded slowly.

"I will purge as much of the Dark energy as I can. This seal will clear your mind and fortify your defenses against the howler's cry."

The howler. Diaz's nostrils flared as he exhaled hard. He'd read the reports about the fleshy beast that'd been summoned just to screech and then leave with Hosenké. At first, Diaz couldn't understand the significance of the event, and then Izzy had explained.

The howler was a creature from Pitch Black, a demon specializing in tracking spiritual energy. The howler's song had activated the Dark energy inside KI, speeding up the process of his transformation. But one of the beast's unique abilities was to call its prey to itself, like a siren luring sailors to their deaths. Once you heard the howler's cry, you were under its spell and once the spell was activated, you were drawn to its location. Mindlessly seeking out the beast so it could devour you.

Obviously, the howler's cry was loud. It was difficult not to hear it if you were within a five-mile radius. But their songs were direct, only enchanting their intended target. That meant Izzy and everyone else who'd been present would be unaffected once the spell was activated. Only KI would lose all sense and seek out the howler like a mindless puppet. That was why his new seal was so important. It would help him fight the howler's cry and ignore its beckoning.

Diaz prayed KI would have the strength to resist when the time came. All the more reason to hurry the mission along, but the lieutenant refused to rush this. He needed to be careful about putting his team together, gather as much information as he could so he wouldn't take the spy along. And, admittedly, he wanted KI to get a little more training in before they took off.

"The graduation ceremony is this afternoon, right?" he asked.

Izzy had already begun the sealing process, leaving KI gritting his teeth in pain, but Kohl walked back into the room, wearing loose pants with a towel slung over his neck. He nodded silently and then stood in the corner to brood.

Diaz had not warmed up to Kohl yet. But his prickliness didn't annoy him as much as it used to. Especially not after witnessing his painful sealing—while naked. In Kohl's defense, he was a tough kid. Not blinking at the fact that three people had just seen him nude and reduced to a writhing mess too weak to even stand.

Then again, two of the three of them had witnessed his incredible power during the exams. It didn't matter if he could stand or not, no one would ever forget the image of him skirting through the forest as a phantom and nearly killing the Red Face singlehandedly.

He would be a great addition to the team, Diaz thought, coolly regarding him with a single, aversive blink. *And it would do KI some good to have his friends around. Their presence might help him resist the howler's cry.* Which meant, of course, recruiting Fox Fire as well. Even if their presence had no effect on KI, Diaz knew he had to invite her along or else risk her sneaking out anyway and getting herself expelled.

She was a talented sundancer. The Academy could not afford to lose a student like her right now. It was best to just take her along and deal with the complaints about a Gamma student on an S-ranked mission later. *Besides,* Diaz resisted the urge to roll his eyes, if the council wanted him to take certain people and certain ranks, they shouldn't have given him complete control over putting together the team. He knew there would be protests. He knew the council would likely give him their own list of names to recruit. But he would fight them tooth and nail to take the team he truly wanted.

So far, Diaz knew he would have to take Izzy, the Priest had made it clear the lieutenant wasn't going anywhere without him for a long while. Which meant, of course, Vehenort would be coming, too. He wanted to take Vyanna Farron since she would make a good guide while navigating the North; naturally, the Ool twins would follow. Fox Fire had to come. Now, he wanted Kohlannis. *But who else?* he wondered and then pain shredded through his abdomen where he'd been stabbed by Izzy.

The only person missing was Kotaro.

He gripped his healed wound where only a dark scar remained. The spot throbbed, like a sudden reminder of everything he'd suffered that day. And every misery he'd relived every day since.

He stood abruptly, earning a glance from Izzy. Even KI managed to look up, blinking through his pain. Kohl kept his stony gaze on the floor, fascinated by the black carpet.

"I've got to go," Diaz announced in a strained voice. "I'll see you boys at the graduation ceremony. Congratulations on becoming students of the Gamma Division."

KI managed a painful smile. Kohl continued to glare at the floor.

With an exasperated sigh, Diaz turned and left. He just wanted to be alone now, hiding in the darkness of his room where the light was locked out by his drawn curtains and the pain was locked in by his closed heart.

23

Kohlannis

The graduation ceremony dragged on. Kohl watched as students walked across the stage and waved cheerily to their families, as if they'd actually earned this day. The only reason most of the graduates were here was because of the Red Face. Since he had caused so much trouble, every trainee who'd survived the exams was allowed to graduate and enter the Academy. Kohl was happy to be one step closer to achieving his goals, but he didn't feel like he deserved to be here. He hadn't earned his walk across the stage. And even if he had, he wouldn't have enjoyed it.

Sharp blue eyes watched as Terra Mochett's name was called. She walked confidently—one of just a handful of students who'd actually collected three bells before the exams fell apart. Kohl wasn't surprised, she was faster than the speed of light, she'd likely snagged three bells and ran straight to the Great Temple in less than an hour.

Next was Fox Fire. She walked across the stage and then stopped to hug her siblings—Roaring was in the audience; he'd turned down his chance to graduate so he could return home to Wi like he'd originally planned. For now, he was playing the role of 'big brother,' lifting Fox into his meaty arms as she laughed wildly.

Kohl watched quietly from his stance across the stage. His name was only a few students down the list. Then he would have to suffer the shame of walking across the stage to the sound of silence, because no one would cheer for a Hunger kid, just as no one had come out to celebrate with him. He only had a mother waiting at home. No father. No little brother. No one. Just Kohlannis and the cold woman he barely recognized. Literally. He wasn't even sure he'd be able to pick his mother out in the crowd if she had decided to show up.

Yes, I could, he corrected. *She'd be the most deranged looking woman in the audience.*

His jaw clenched as he thought of his mother, of how pretty she used to be and how grotesque she had become. *She looks more like someone who'd be Slaine's mother than my own.*

"Kohlannis Hunger," said the announcer.

As expected, the crowd of squealing parents hushed immediately and Kohl swallowed, his gaze turning stony as he lifted his chin and began a slow walk across the stage. He'd thought the screaming families were annoying, but the silence was even worse. A thousand people shouting was chaotic, but a thousand people *watching* made his heart hammer.

Let them watch, he told himself as he crossed the middle of the stage. *Let them see me succeed, despite their disproval, despite their anger, despite their hopes of me failing.*

He glanced out at the crowd and almost tripped over his feet. Every single eye was on him. Hard frowns and wrinkled brows. Ever since he'd fought the Red Face and used his shadow-dancing, he'd been getting those looks. Everyone had hated him before the exams, when they didn't know exactly what his powers were. Now that the mystery had been revealed, they feared him.

He wasn't sure which was worse.

Syren had nearly fainted when it was all over, Vinny and Montell had avoided him like he was a demon, and Dart couldn't hold his gaze. Only

Fox Fire and KI had approached him when the dust had settled. His only friends.

And, Kohl thought, sliding his gaze through the crowd to find a familiar face. Kressa Lion. *She still accepted me.* Kressa was standing to the side because she had no family. Kohl had no idea she was an orphan until her name had been called and only a Magus from the orphanage had come to watch. It was Kressa who'd gotten him to use his gift in the first place. Kressa who had told him his powers weren't a curse. And Kressa who still believed that notion even after witnessing his dark abilities.

Kohl reached the end of the stage and wanted to collapse from the pressure, but he kept his composure and made his way through the crowd. As he walked, hands crammed into his pockets, an old man stepped from the crowd and spat on the ground right in front of him. Kohl paused, but quickly recovered and stepped around the glob of phlegm.

"*Cursed,*" the old man hissed behind him.

The word seemed to echo around Kohl, slithering through the crowd as others repeated it.

"Cursed … Cursed … Cursed."

Like a dark song, the word rolled over the audience until it was all Kohlannis could hear. He kept his gaze focused on a tree in the distance and forced his legs to move, getting away the only goal in his head.

Something grabbed his arm and he turned so fast he almost threw the person to the ground. The stunned look on Fox's face made his heart split in two.

"I'm sorry—" he choked on the words, sudden tears stinging the backs of his eyes.

Fox reached for him again. "Come over for dinner."

He didn't want dinner. But he didn't really want to go home, either.

Facing his mother was something he would need the entire day to prepare for, especially since he hadn't seen her for the last few months. He'd been living at the Academy with KI and hadn't taken any time to visit her. Not even when Lieutenant Diaz had offered to give him the weekends off to go home. But since he'd graduated into the Gamma Division, the Academy reported that he would be allowed to return to his personal dwellings.

I guess they trust me now. He internally rolled his eyes.

"Coming?" the voice belonged to KI, walking over with a smile on his face. He gave him a hug. "Congrats."

"You graduated, too," Kohl grunted, then he punched KI hard in the gut. "And don't hug me again."

KI rubbed his belly in pain. "Sorry."

"Let's go," Fox said, grabbing both of them by the hand. "Cat is making oxtails."

She led both boys away, chatting like everything was fine. Like everything was right again. Like they hadn't fought for their lives in the exam and wouldn't have to do it every day once classes began. KI had caused yet another attack on Babel, and Kohl had used his dark powers in front of half his class. Things would only get worse for them from this point on.

But for now, Kohl thought, watching Fox and KI snort in laughter, *things aren't so bad.* He squeezed Fox's hand as he walked, and she looked up at him expectantly. When he didn't speak, she smiled and then mouthed something that nearly made his heart stop.

You're okay.

Am I? he wondered.

Cat was an amazing cook. Kohl had decided that when he'd first taken

242

a look at the pot of oxtails smothered in gravy. And then he'd tasted the oxtails and wanted to give her a kiss. She had made rice and cornbread and string beans simmered in a broth so spicy he was sweating by the time he'd cleared his second serving. Then Cat served dessert, a pudding she made from bananas and bread with a crumble on top. It was the most delightful thing he'd ever eaten, but the company of the Fire siblings was just as enjoyable.

Kohl didn't speak much during the meal, but he enjoyed listening to the conversation. He thought Cat was funny and Talon was pretty and Chava, the massive hunting hound, was incredibly gentle for a dog the size of a lioness. The family-friendly atmosphere took Kohl by surprise, though he shouldn't have expected anything less. Fox was obsessed with KI, but when she wasn't distracted by him, she was kind—to the point of being pushy.

Kohl remembered all the times she had forced her kindness onto him, always trying to include him in her training with Roaring, always trying to make sure he knew she was there for him, even sticking up for him against Vinny and Montell. It had been embarrassing and had even made him angry, but Kohl had never forgotten what she'd done. Had never let himself overlook the fact that she'd cared.

It was strange, being around people who didn't seem to mind who he was or what he could do. But Kohl liked the awkward strangeness, even welcomed it. At least it was better than the hissing from the crowd earlier. And it would certainly be better than the haunting silence of his home.

He glanced over at the window. The sun was setting. Which meant he'd have to go home soon. Kohl suppressed a groan.

"Want me to walk you guys back to the Academy?" Roaring offered.

Kohl stared at his plate. He hadn't told anyone except KI that he was moving back home. Since KI didn't have a home, he was still permitted

243

to stay at the Academy. He'd gotten upset when Kohl said he would be leaving, but it wasn't like they wouldn't see each other during class every day now.

KI stood and exchanged goodbyes with the ladies before tapping Kohl on the shoulder. He startled and then stood, too. "See you in class tomorrow, Fox," he mumbled, and then he walked to the door and waited outside for KI to appear.

"Walk me halfway?" He raised a brow.

"Where's Roaring?"

"I told him we would walk alone."

Kohl grunted and started a march down the road. It was muggy out, which made him sweat, but he didn't slow his pace until he was at the crossroads where the path to the Academy split from the path to the Hunger sector.

KI punched his shoulder lightly. "See you in class tomorrow."

He nodded and watched him walk until he was just a shadow in the distance, then he sighed and started his walk home. Kohlannis hated his home. Not because his father and brother weren't there, he hated it because his mother was. She wasn't unkind or cruel, in fact, she hardly left her quarters, but she wasn't herself anymore. And that haunted Kohl because it was his fault. His father's death had changed her, but Karmen's death had disturbed her. Driven her to the point of no return. Kohl didn't blame her. His father's passing had been an accident, but Karmen's had been nothing short of murder. And his blood was on Kohl's hands.

He curled his hands into fists as memories of that day played in his mind, unbidden and unwanted, but stained on his scarred heart like a cruel punishment. He couldn't forget no matter how hard he tried.

The official word was that Kendall Hunger died in a work-related accident. But the truth was that he'd been assaulted on his way home from work. He'd just picked up Karmen from an appointment and both of them had been headed home. They were outside the Hunger sector, since Karmen had been getting sealed at the Academy, which meant they'd had to travel through the streets with people hissing at them just as they'd done to Kohl at his graduation.

The hisses turned to shouts which turned to bricks being thrown and soon a fight broke out. The thing is … neither Kendall nor Karmen were beaten too badly, but since they were outside the Hunger sector, no hospitals would treat them. By the time Kohl's father and brother made it to the Hunger Hospital and Clinic, things had gotten bad. Very bad.

Kendall died in the hospital. Karmen was left crippled.

Kissenya, Kohl's mother, was devastated. The bakery she ran almost went out of business; extended family took over and decided to simply send her a check from the sales every month. That had been a terrible idea, Kohl realized later. The best thing for his mother would have been to keep working. To stay busy. Then she wouldn't have had time to obsess over Karmen. Constantly taking him from doctor to doctor to get him 'fixed.' She had only wanted him to get better, to be able to walk again, but her obsession with his injuries only made him realize how broken he really was.

When he'd told Kohl he wanted to die, he hadn't been surprised. And he hadn't stopped him when he took the razor to his wrists. The only thing Kohl regretted was not joining Karmen. Because now he had to live with the guilt and shame of doing nothing to stop him or help him.

He had watched his little brother die. And when his mother had barged into the bathroom, he'd said nothing to explain himself.

She blamed him.

She hated him.

He was a curse in her eyes. He was *her* curse. Because he'd let her son—her baby boy—take his own life.

245

"It should have been *you*," she had whispered as she'd watched the men lower Karmen's casket into the small grave. **"I'm stuck with you."**

She had tried to give him up for adoption after that, but the system didn't accept Hungers. Then she'd tried to kick him out, but he'd come right back because, where else could he go? His extended family didn't want the boy who'd let his own brother die. With no other option, Kissenya tried to leave him instead. The same way Karmen had left.

Kohl had found her. This time, he did help. Healers had arrived in time to stop the bleeding, but she'd been left with scars. *Horrible* scars on her face as she'd tried to carve a smile into her flesh, wicked lines on her neck as she'd tried to slice through it. She was as gruesome to look at as Slaine—and she knew this. So she stayed away, hiding in her room, avoiding Kohl and avoiding the outside world.

She had called him her curse only to become his in turn.

Kohlannis swallowed as he stood before his house. It wasn't a huge place, but it had been more than comfortable for his family of four, so it was extra spacious now that half of them were gone.

Kohl opened the front door—it was never locked—and walked into the ghostly home. Inside was deathly quiet and dark. No oil lamps or lanterns lit. His mother was either asleep or in her room staring at the wall. There was no way to tell. He sighed and moved to where he knew there would be a lantern hanging on the wall. Nothing about his house had changed since Karmen had passed. Not the decorations or the mess. His mother never cleaned anything, and Kohl tried to stay away as often as he could which meant the dust would pile up until he cleaned it himself.

Kohlannis could always tell when his mother decided to leave her quarters because she would leave a trail of junk and half-eaten food around. There were plates sitting on the sofa and stacked to Kohl's waist from the floor. Papers and scrolls and piles of dirty clothes thrown everywhere. Unopened checks from the bakery, ripped up letters from family members, a pool of some sticky, unidentified liquid in the corner of the room. The rest of the house was like this, so messy there was a foul stench drifting through the halls. Like death had come but couldn't quite find its way through the trash to claim his dear mother.

Kohl's skin pebbled with goosebumps. He hated his home. But he had nowhere else to go, so he rolled up his sleeves, brushed his hair back, and started cleaning. The house was at least bearable when it was clean, so he didn't mind sweeping up the dust or taking out the trash or washing the dirty clothes. So long as he didn't have to face his mother, he could deal with the mess.

Kohl cleaned as quietly as possible for the first hour but when it became evident his mother was either asleep or uninterested in finding out who was in her home, he made all the noise he wanted. He was sure it was past midnight when he finished. At least his body felt like it was past midnight. He ached all over from tiredness and dreariness, so when he opened the door to his room, he didn't bother lighting the oil lamp on his bedside table. He simply climbed into bed fully clothed and drifted into a restless sleep.

Something woke him less than an hour later. A light tapping on his door that soon became a thumping knock.

Bang! Bang! Bang!

"Who's there?" he called, sitting up.

No one answered, which was all the answer he needed.

Kohlannis stared at the door, eyes narrowing. In the silence, he could hear her breathing. Deep, heavy breaths that sounded more like painful wheezing than the gentle pants of a tired woman.

The knob on his door began to shake as she twisted it on the other side, trying to force her way in.

"What do you want?" Kohl snapped and the doorknob stopped moving.

Silence rolled through the room and just when Kohl thought she'd left, he heard her croaking voice. "Kohhhhhl," she called.

A horrible chill spider-walked down his spine.

His mother's voice was disturbing. It had changed since she'd taken the blade to her throat, slicing through flesh and muscle. When she'd left the hospital, she sounded like she'd been smoking for the last thirty years, even though she'd never even held a cigarette before.

Now, that dark, hoarse voice was crowing on the other side of his door. Calling his name and sending shivers up his back and nightmares into his head.

"Kohhhhhl," she called again.

He couldn't take it.

Kohl threw his covers back and hopped out his window, jogging into the night.

He hadn't planned on showing up outside Fox's place, but he didn't really know where else to go. Now that he was here, he had no idea what to do. It was the middle of the night, so he couldn't just knock on her door. He decided to walk around the side of the building and thanked God when he saw the flicker of a candle in one of the windows. A small girl sat by the candle; her concentration locked on the little flame. *It could only be Fox.* He channeled his power and felt the shadows around him come alive, ready to bend to his will. Then he sank into the darkness, travelling through the shadows until he emerged inside Fox's room.

She nearly screamed when he stepped from the darkness by her closet. But the joy of seeing him beat out the shock and she ended up smiling at him instead of yelling. "Shadow-dancing is so cool," she said quietly.

He crammed his hands into his pockets.

"What's wrong?"

"Nothing."

"You just showed up in my bedroom in the middle of the night. Something's going on."

He sighed. Palmed the back of his neck. "Can I stay here for the night? I can't sleep at my place."

"Your place?"

That's right. She had no idea he'd moved back home. Had no idea how much he hated it.

"I thought you'd be staying on dorm during the semester."

He snapped his gaze over to her. "On dorm?"

"Yeah." Fox rummaged through some papers on her desk and produced the packet they'd gotten at the graduation ceremony. It contained info about the Academy and their new schedules as Gamma Division students. Kohl hadn't read any of it.

"Since we're officially enrolled, we have the option to stay on dorm. I think it sounds exciting."

He stared at the paper. "Are you staying on dorm?"

"No." Fox sounded slightly disappointed. "Cat and Roaring are returning to Wi soon. I don't want to leave Talon in an apartment all alone."

"Mmm," he hummed.

"KI is staying on dorm. Maybe you could room together."

He didn't want to admit it, but that sounded nice. He'd much rather share a room with the kid than stay home with his mother jimmying his doorknob every night and croaking curses outside his door.

"Are you hungry?" Fox asked. She was standing now, and he realized she was wearing a nightshirt with her hair piled on top of her head.

249

He shook his head. "You should sleep. I didn't mean to disturb you."

"You didn't disturb me. I was just trying to practice sundancing a little. I'm glad you interrupted so I can finally get in bed now."

He glanced around. The room was simple, a bed in the corner, a desk, a small table with a water basin and a mirror. A closet. Fox's clothes lay strewn on the floor as if she'd started undressing by the door and threw her garments down as she walked around the room.

"I can sleep on the floor," Kohl said quietly.

Fox looked at him like he was crazy. "You can get on the couch. My siblings won't be upset if they wake up and find you."

"That would be kind of awkward, though," he said, but that wasn't the reason he didn't want to sleep on the couch. The truth was that he didn't want to be alone, so before Fox could argue, he kicked his shoes off and got down on the floor beside her desk.

Fox slipped into the bed and almost immediately began to snore. He would have laughed if he weren't in such a gloomy mood. He wasn't surprised at all by her snoring. She had never come off as the most delicate of girls. But as he listened to her snores turn to soft, rhythmic breathing, he realized she wasn't as coarse as he'd first thought, either. There was a gentleness to her features that softened his heart to her. The same way KI's big, kiddish eyes had softened him.

They're just alike, he thought, his eyes feeling heavy. As if the thought had never occurred before, Kohl realized he didn't want to lose Fox any more than he wanted to lose KI. The Red Face hadn't been after her, but he would have fought just as fiercely if the roles had been switched. They'd all taken a pact together. Not just to protect KI, but to stick together. All of them.

Kohl silently stood and approached Fox's bed, *she might wake and kill me*, but he was willing to risk her anger if it meant being close to her for a little while. He leaned down and kissed her forehead, holding his

250

breath as she grunted and rolled over, whacking him in the face with her mop of curls. Then he lifted her covers and climbed into bed beside her.

For a while, Kohl didn't move, lying stiffly next to Fox as she started snoring again. And then her snores ceased, and she shifted beneath the blankets. Her head was on his shoulder, and he felt her breath on his neck.

"You're okay," she muttered.

Any other time, he would have convinced himself that she was only talking in her sleep. He might have even thought he was just hearing things. But he let himself believe he wasn't going insane—if only for tonight. He enjoyed the sound of Fox's whispered words echoing through his mind.

You're okay.

Kohl kissed her forehead again. "I will be."

24

Fox Fire

Being in the Gamma Division was much different from being a trainee. First of all, Fox and her classmates were allowed inside the cross-shaped building for their learning, instead of kept out in the scorched fields. Their day started at eight in the morning with a ten-minute prayer for the entire student body. Then, students went to their respective classrooms. Fox was still in G5, along with KI and Kohl and everyone else from before—except Wend, Slaine, and Roaring. Crystal Leer and Eekay Dundo were added to the class, making G5 a class of twenty students again.

Fox hadn't been happy to see neither Crystal nor Eekay, but she had congratulated them on graduating, nonetheless. Crystal had even apologized for starting a fight with her, claiming he'd been under Donner's charm. She'd only shaken her head and laughed. No hard feelings.

There wasn't any time for hard feelings anyway. The semester had begun, and classes were in full swing from the moment Fox walked into the building. Master Jo and Master Moneek were still her instructors, but two new Masters had been added to the rotation. They taught subjects like history and mathematics while Marlo and Moneek handled their spiritual courses and physical training.

Master Jo also had a thirty-minute one-on-one session with each student from G5. It was meant to be used for spiritual and psychological counseling, considering everything the students had been through—and not just with the Red Face. The entrance exams had pitted them against each other and had permitted them to fight to the death. Killing wasn't necessary for them to succeed but the exam was meant to be a realistic example of the world beyond the Walls of Jericho.

Fox had killed students. She had almost killed KI. So when her half-hour session rolled around, she was eager to spill her thoughts and concerns to her teacher. Master Jo had listened quietly, never interrupting and never issuing any judgment or ridicule. When the room fell quiet and Fox found tears blurring her eyes as she talked about fighting Crystal and Donner and the kids who'd followed them, Marlo had only leaned forward and offered her a handkerchief.

When the session was over, the two of them prayed together and Master Jo left her with a list of scriptures to lead Fox to repentance for her actions in the exam and to help comfort her in her remorse and grief.

"It wouldn't hurt to fast during this time," Marlo said with a smile. "You're in a spiritually fragile state right now. Fasting will help fortify yourself and strengthen your dependence on God."

Fox nodded. She didn't mind fasting, but it just so happened to be time for lunch. Maybe she'd start a fast afterwards. Cat had packed her a grilled chicken leg and an apple to eat, but Fox refused to pass up the chance to get a good look at the Academy's cafeteria.

The main eatery had suffered damage during the Red Face's firestorm, but the temporary café wasn't half bad. Students from each of the three Divisions milled about the large open space, carrying trays of food, and finding seats to convene with friends. It smelled of roasted meat and garlic and plenty of olive oil. Fox's mouth watered as she

253

glanced at the different stations; a man serving steaming bowls of stew from his massive pot, another rolling wraps stuffed with juicy meat and fresh vegetables. There was even a woman who offered nothing but beans—Fox wasn't too excited about that stand, but she thought it was cool anyway.

Someone poked her shoulder. "Hungry, Foxy?"

She grinned up at KI. For some reason, he looked taller today. Stronger. More formidable than his usual goofy demeanor. The sparkle in his eyes wasn't because of his boyish charm anymore, it was because of something bolder. Something mischievous and darkly flirtatious. Fox didn't stop herself from looking him up and down, at his toned chest and his muscled arms. He didn't even bother to hide his tattoos anymore. With the Red Face's second kidnapping attempt, everyone knew about his seal. There was no point in covering them up now.

Fox walked beside KI, her eyes lingering on his biceps. "How was, um…"

"I had a session with Lord Izzy," he said plainly.

She knew his 'session' was nothing like the one she'd had with Master Jo, but she didn't want to ask for details, so she just nodded. "Where's Kohl?"

KI rolled his eyes. "He's with Kressa. They've been glued to each other all day."

That was definitely true. Kohl had developed a crush on Kressa since the bonfire, but after Kressa had boldly gotten him to use his blessing during the exams, his crush had nearly become an obsession. *Which makes no sense*, Fox simmered, walking with KI to find a table. Just last night he'd shown up in her bedroom unannounced—timid and upset and so unlike himself. He'd been vulnerable, which was something Fox had never seen in him before, but she'd welcomed him without question because he'd clearly needed someone, and she had certainly cared.

He'd even slept beside me, Fox remembered, unable to stop the blushing heat from rushing to her cheeks. She took a chair next to KI while he pointed at all the stations he wanted to eat at. Dart had come over to join them, claiming the chair Vinny had been reaching for. An argument broke out, but Fox tuned them out. There was no way she could focus on the Lin brothers while she watched Kohl and Kressa walk into the café holding hands.

Her heart shriveled at the sight, but anger chased away any embarrassment she might have felt swelling inside. *Kressa can have him*, she told herself, glancing up at KI who was animatedly talking with Montell about how badly he wanted to try the beans. When he caught her staring, he winked at her, never stopping his conversation with Monty.

Fox could have melted in her chair. Despite being a sundancer, she suddenly felt overheated. *I shouldn't be reacting this way*, she scolded herself. *Just yesterday we held hands while we walked home*. After the graduation ceremony, she had grabbed his hand and Kohl's hand without thinking, and they'd all walked to her house for dinner without breaking contact. It had been such a natural gesture, none of them had blushed or grinned or thought anything of it. Somehow, overnight, everything had changed.

Kohl was with Kressa, sitting across from her now and avoiding eye contact, and KI was winking and making her feel all crazy inside. Just like he'd done during the exams, when he'd kissed her on the cheek.

Fox realized KI was right in front of her now, his hazel eyes blinking like bright orbs in his face. "You there, Foxy?" He brushed a curl behind her ear and muttered something about how pale she looked. "Well, pale for a Black girl."

Fox frowned. "Shut up, KI," she said, swatting his hand away.

Dart, who was bronze skinned with black wavy hair, let out a low chuckle. "Tell him, Fox."

"Sorry." KI grinned like a kid. "Let's grab something to eat, yeah? I'm starved."

"We're gonna need energy for training with Master Jo next," Montell said. "I'm down for the beans."

Dart made a face. "Beans are horrible."

"But high in protein," Vinny countered.

Dart nodded thoughtfully. "I've been thinking since the exams ended, I want to get buff."

"You already are buff," KI told him.

He was right, Dart was thin and lean. But each of his muscles was painfully defined and always bulging. He looked strong enough to take on everyone at the table at once. But he shook his head. "I want to be buff like Roaring."

Suddenly, everyone was looking at Fox and she blinked like she hadn't a clue why. "What?" she said slowly.

"Does your brother have a special diet?" Dart asked.

A special diet. She wanted to laugh. Roaring ate whatever Cat cooked—or whatever she made him cook since she'd been giving him lessons in the kitchen. Not that his diet mattered much. Roaring had always been big and tall; Fox just hadn't paid it much attention before. At just over five feet tall, *everyone* was big and tall to her—even the Lin brothers, who were only 5'4. But she could see why her friends admired her big brother. He was abnormally large. At least 6'6 now, and he was only nineteen. *He's probably got an inch or two left in him before he stops growing completely*, Fox mused.

She looked at her friends who were still waiting for details about Roaring's diet. Somehow, she got the feeling they'd be disappointed to hear he was just naturally big and muscular because God had made him that way. She shrugged and glanced over at the bean station. "I think he likes the lentil soup here."

256

Vinny snapped his fingers. "Told ya. It's all the protein."

Dart conceded with a nod. "Honestly, I want a wrap, but Terra and Wunda are over there. So beans might be my choice—protein or not."

"What's wrong with Terra and Wunda?" Vinny asked.

"I think Terra has a crush on me," Dart said with a shiver. "She's cute and all, but I don't know."

Vinny stood. "I should call them over to our table."

"*Don't*," Dart groaned. "Both of them already cornered me this morning and made me promise to hang out after classes today."

"Seriously?" KI laughed.

He nodded morosely. "I'm just helping them move into their dorms. But I know it'll be a giggling torture."

"You're staying on dorm?" Vinny asked.

Dart nodded, his gaze flicking around the table. "I thought everyone was staying on dorm."

"I'm not," Fox admitted.

"Why am I not surprised?" Vinny said with a teasing grin. "You will always be sheltered."

She frowned at him but said nothing.

"Why don't we all unpack our stuff together tonight, so I won't be alone with Terra and Wunda," Dart suggested with pleading eyes.

Vinny placed a hand on his hip and shook his head like it wounded him to say no. "I'm not sure I feel like it, buddy."

Montell nudged him. "I think it'll be fun."

"Me too," KI said, then he glanced at Fox. "You can still come hang out, at least."

"I don't know," she mumbled.

"Come, it'll be nice to have more girls around," Kressa said.

Fox resisted the urge to roll her eyes. Before she could say anything nasty, Dart was talking again. "Actually, there are more girls in Class G-

Five than guys."

"Really?" Vinny squinted.

Dart nodded and held up a finger as he named his classmates. "Fox Fire, Kressa Lion, Vyanna Farron, Ren Ool, Terra Mochett, Wunda Cyruson, Andor Alonis, Danté Shoren, Gloria Taber, Belinda Jones, Syren Danis, and Hope Votoman."

"Hope Votoman?" Montell frowned.

Fox remembered the name and the face of the small girl. She had been quiet while on the Training Grounds and no one had bumped into her during the exams. But she'd apparently graduated with the rest of them. Fox shrugged; she would eventually see her. For now, her thoughts swirled around Syren who had been sullen and detached since everything that'd happened in the Kanen Forest.

No one was surprised; she had been close to Slaine and now he was marked as a traitor to the Cross. She had even been under suspicion of working with him, but after being interviewed by Major Marshall, his gift of *Discernment* determined she truly knew nothing of his betrayal.

Fox glanced at Kressa. The three of them had been a tightknit group; Slaine, Kressa, and Syren—just like Fox and her two best friends. But Syren was having lunch alone while Kressa snuggled up beside Kohl.

Fox stood abruptly, earning stares from her friends. "I'm going to get food," she mumbled before marching off. No one tried to stop her, they were all too engrossed in an argument over beans. Fox was thankful, she wasn't sure how much of her *bros* she could take. She wasn't the most feminine of girls in the class—not like Vyanna or Syren. But she wasn't *one of the guys*, either.

Thick curls brushed her shoulders as Fox shook her head and stepped in line behind a student at a salad bar. She didn't want salad, but this was the shortest line and fresh veggies would go well with her chicken leg.

The chef was a woman named Tay of the Odobo Clan; she had the power to manipulate plant life—an ability Fox had learned about from Talon's travels back to Wi. When Fox asked for a salad, Tay whispered into the pot of soil beside her and watched with a smile as a head of lettuce sprouted before their very eyes. She picked it up, rinsed the dirt off in the bowl of water beside her and began to chop while a vine of tomatoes grew up next. Fox had a fresh salad in a matter of minutes.

Just when she asked for some freshly squeezed lemonade, she heard a voice beside her. "I guess Babel will never experience a famine, right?"

She gritted her teeth and kept her vision straight, watching Chef Tay sing into the soil as a small lemon tree grew up. "What do you want, Kohl?"

He sighed. "Listen, Fox … About last night."

She shook her head. *This isn't fair.* He didn't get to come crawling into her room, asking for a place to stay, and cuddle up to her all night just to show up holding hands with another girl the next day. And then pull her aside to explain things—as if there was anything to explain.

Nothing happened. He's not my boyfriend or anything. And I already knew about his feelings for Kressa. I shouldn't be upset.

But she was.

"I don't care about last night," Fox clipped. When she glanced up at Kohl, she was shocked to see the stunned expression on his face. He regained his composure quickly, hardening his features into the cold look she knew so well. He was himself again, and that somehow made her relax.

"Alright then," he said icily, then he turned and left her standing there.

Fox couldn't go back and face her friends, so she grabbed her food from Chef Tay and went out to eat at the Training Grounds. Her conversation with Kohl had soured her mood which remained sullen

259

throughout her training with Master Jo and Master Moneek. She didn't even care when Dart beat her in a sparring match, and she wasn't interested when Marlo gathered the students to wrap up their classes with a prayer.

When she finished, she gave them all a pleasant smile. "Congratulations on finishing your first day as Gamma Division students." She slammed her staff into the earth two quick times. "As you know, being a student here means you will have the opportunity to take on missions on behalf of the Cross. It might seem a little crazy, but some of you have already been assigned your first mission."

There were gasps throughout the crowd, *now* Fox's interest was piqued.

Master Jo held a handful of scrolls. "You can always reject any mission you receive, so don't feel pressured to take this one on just because you've been invited," she said, handing the scrolls to a few of the students. Andor looked dejected when Master Jo passed her by, but Vyanna flashed a rare grin as Marlo stopped before her. The Ool twins got scrolls, as did Wunda, and Kohl, and KI. Fox watched as Master Jo made her way through the class, nearly fainting when she stopped and passed her a little scroll.

"Congrats," her teacher said.

Fox could only nod vigorously. She'd gotten her first mission.

"Open those and read them over when you have time. Most assignments have a forty-eight-hour response time, but it depends on how urgent the mission is." She folded her arms. "Don't feel upset if you didn't get a scroll. It doesn't mean you aren't good enough; it just means you'll have to check the open bulletin to find a job. If you don't receive requests from the Cross, there are always missions posted on the board for you to volunteer for—so long as you meet the qualifications."

When Fox arrived at the Academy that evening, the dorm master almost didn't let her in. Thankfully, Dart was downstairs arguing with Wunda about carrying all her boxes, he stopped and vouched for her to get in.

KI's room was at the end of the hall, he opened his door on the second knock. "You came," he said smoothly.

She nodded and held up the scroll. "Tell me you haven't opened yours."

"I have."

She dropped her shoulders. "I wanted to open them together!"

"I already knew what the mission was before I opened it."

"You did?"

He nodded and flopped down onto his bed, his dark hair falling into his face. "It's an escort mission."

"How did you know already?"

"Because I'm the one being escorted."

Fox worked her jaw, trying to find the words to say. She blinked around his room just to keep herself from panicking. KI's room was plain; a small rug in the center of the floor, a desk, a bench, two oil lamps. His bed was in the corner. It wasn't the most exciting room, but it was neat and tidy.

"Where are they taking you?" she managed.

KI shrugged. "We'll get that info when we accept the mission."

"Do you actually have a choice in accepting?"

He laughed, eyes growing dark. "No."

"Kohl got a scroll, too."

"He could be on the escort team, or he could have been assigned to another mission. Lieutenant Diaz didn't tell me all that much."

"When did you find all this out?"

"This morning during my session with Lord Izzy."

She took a deep breath and exhaled her nerves. "I guess there's no point in opening the scroll since you just told me everything."

"You'll have to turn in the scroll with your acceptance or rejection by tomorrow afternoon."

She nodded. "Do you know if Kressa got a scroll?"

KI made a face. "What?"

"I'm just saying, her and Kohl have gotten close and—"

"Why do you care if Kohl's gotten close to Kressa?"

"I *don't*," Fox insisted, crossing her arms.

KI peeled his head from his pillows, sitting up a little. "Good."

His eyes were on her, gazing intently in the growing silence. It was all Fox could do not to squirm as he regarded her. There was something in his eyes she hadn't seen there before, a shy confidence that suddenly made him seem years older.

He's doing it again, she thought, biting her lip and looking away. *He's acting different.*

Fox gasped when she looked up again. KI was *right* in front of her— she had no idea he could move so quickly or quietly. He leaned down and touched his nose to hers. "I'm glad you don't care." And then he pulled away and walked back over to lazily flop onto his bed like that whole scene was just another casual afternoon.

Fox took a shaky breath. "I'm going to, um, talk to my family about the mission."

He shrugged one shoulder and leaned back into his blankets, eyes closing as he hummed a song she didn't recognize. "Catch ya later, Foxy."

25

Talon

The workshop was quiet without Master Li. Talon used to find his rowdiness a little grating, but now she missed his big smiles and belly-shaking laughs. He'd entrusted the shop to her while he was away, mourning the loss of his granddaughter. Second Lieutenant Tella Kotaro.

Talon had attended the funeral, mostly because it was a mass event to honor all who had perished during the exams and especially during the Nine's twofold attack. It had been one of the worst services the Grand Chief had ever witnessed, only rivaled by the mass funeral she'd had to officiate for her own people just months before.

She sighed, leaning on the counter as she thought of both funerals. It seemed like a lifetime had passed since she'd left Wi—*and now I'm not even going back.* Secretly, the decision had been swift and easy. Talon just *knew* her purpose was here, especially after presenting her newly forged weapon to her sister.

Passing the Flaming Veil to Roaring had been the most liberating thing she'd ever done. All her life, Talon had felt useless. She had felt pathetic. She'd known she wasn't a great Grand Chief—she had never been a good Grand *Chiefana*. But she had tried, and she'd allowed herself

263

a small bit of comfort in at least knowing that she'd given it her all. But she couldn't hide from the truth. She was not a good leader. She had never been. And, perhaps, that was the only thing about her that seemed to have leadership quality. She knew when to throw in the towel.

Roaring will make an excellent Grand Chief, she smiled sadly. It was what he'd always wanted. What he seemed to thrive in—taking command, taking charge, issuing orders rather than obeying them. He was leader of the Hunting Regiment, he was Chava's chosen master, he was the Prince of Fire, and now he would be king.

Roaring Fire, First of His Name, Child of God, Dancer of Flames, Kifu of the Regiment, Knight of the Flaming Veil, Master of the White Hound, Protector of the Children of the Sun, Grand Chief of Wi.

Talon could not stop her cheeks from bunching. *Yes, he will make a wonderful Grand Chief.* And even though it was God's will for her to remain in Babel, Talon promised to visit home again. Wi would always hold her heart, as it'd held the hearts of her parents and so many others who'd fought bravely to protect it.

In a long-forgotten tongue, Wi meant 'Sun.' As the power of the flame faded, so did the memories of the very foundation of the great and proud village. Wi became just another settlement, lost in time. Seemingly insignificant. Until Lady Reign of Fire had been born. The first sundancer in centuries, with Roaring as the second. It was only fitting that he would eventually inherit the Veil, despite it traditionally going to the firstborn daughter.

I hope he's ready, Talon smiled, using a cloth to wipe down the counter. Roaring had done all he could for Babel and the students of the Academy. Fox wouldn't shut up about him glowing and throwing bolts of lightning. It all sounded so insane to Talon, but after moving to Babel, nothing surprised her anymore. Wi needed a leader as strong and experienced as her brother. All she could do was try to keep the council

264

in check, and she'd barely managed that.

But, Talon looked down at the ledger left by Master Li, his tiny handwriting scribbled all over the pages. *I can certainly manage this.*

Master Li had wept when he'd returned to work the day after the funeral. She'd never seen him express any emotion except joy before that moment. Even at the funeral, he had been the one to stand on stage and sing a ballad in worship to Christ, rather than say a tearful goodbye. But after it was over and he was behind closed doors, he couldn't stop the tears from flowing.

Talon had tried her best to offer him comfort, but he was inconsolable. And then customers started showing up and he was wailing loudly in the back—all she could do was tighten her smock and get down to business. She wasn't very good at crafting weapons just yet, but she did her best to write down orders, sell some of the finished projects on display, and had even used her lunch break to deliver some of the weapons marked as 'Ready.'

When she'd returned to the workshop, Master Li had gotten himself together. Wiping his watery eyes, he'd passed her the keys and said he knew God had sent her for such a time as this. She didn't feel she'd deserved such praise, but when Li confessed that he hadn't closed the shop in over thirteen years, her chest swelled with pride in being able to help him keep his doors open.

"They aren't going to close today, Master," she had said confidently. And she'd been right.

A full week had passed since then and Talon had been running the shop all on her own. She had taken six more orders, delivered three, and had even crafted a simple dagger for a student at the Academy. It certainly wasn't the same quality as Li's craftsmanship, but it wasn't bad. The student had even given her a tip.

Still, Talon pressed her lips into a thin line as she checked off orders

265

in Li's ledger. *If he doesn't return soon, we'll fall behind.* There was only so much she could do without him there. Her dagger had been impressive, but she wasn't ready to make some of the orders she'd taken.

Lord … what am I going to do? she wondered, untying her smock. She took the work apron to the back of the shop and hung it on a peg, grabbing her bag and yanking off her headwrap. Her hair was longer now, little coils springing in every direction. The wrap helped keep the sparks from catching fire on her head, but it made her hot and itchy. Taking off her headwrap at the end of her shift was the highlight of her day.

She heard the bell at the front desk ring, and she sighed. "We're closed!" she called. And then the curtain separating the front desk from the back area shifted to reveal a massive man.

Talon gasped. "Master Li!"

He smiled sheepishly. "Hello, lovely. Heading home?"

"I was just closing up." She looked him over, eyes roving his meaty frame. His lips were smiling but his gaze was dull. Still, it was a miracle he was even here. "How are you holding up?"

He rubbed his white beard. "I'm okay. Figured I had to get back to work eventually. Why not today?"

"Well, it's evening—"

"That's all right. I wanted to craft today, instead of dealing with customers."

She nodded. *Baby steps.*

"I can stay—"

He shook his head. "No way. You've got a date, don't you?"

Talon frowned. "A what?"

Now Master Li frowned. "What's Evelyn doing out front, then?"

All the air went out of Talon's lungs as she sighed. She hadn't seen the lieutenant since the start of the exams. And then everything had gone

266

wrong, and Kotaro had passed away. She wasn't surprised by his absence—she'd honestly expected it—but she *hadn't* expected a visit from him.

What am I supposed to say? she wondered silently.

It wasn't weird because she had a crush on him. She could be honest with herself and admit that much. But she didn't know how to deal with Kotaro and her lost feelings.

He doesn't know, Talon reminded herself.

Lieutenant Kotaro had been in love with him. She'd told Talon as much back in Wi when they'd travelled together. But she had never confessed this to Diaz, and now it was too late.

What am I supposed to say? Talon asked again.

Would it be right for her to go on as if Kotaro's feelings had never existed? Even though Diaz never knew, she *did* know. And she couldn't decide what to do with the information. If Kotaro hadn't told him, then maybe it was right for Talon not to say anything. They were her feelings. She chose to keep them to herself for a reason. And maybe she never planned to tell him. But would the lieutenant want to know? Would he hate her for not telling if he ever found out on his own?

"Lovely?" Master Li touched Talon's shoulder, making her jump.

"Sorry, Master. I'll get out of your hair."

Stiffly, Talon walked out to the front of the shop to find Evelyn standing by the door. He was staring at the floor, the lazy setting sun casting a glow over his frame. Illuminated by the light, Talon noticed he was dressed in civilian clothes, a plain tunic and loose pants with his military boots. It was the first time Talon had ever seen him out of his Academy clothes. It took her by such surprise, she actually paused.

It was strange. How strong he looked in normal clothes. She thought he would have looked ordinary or even weak in his plain pants and shirt. But he looked incredibly formidable, like he could take on Master Li.

267

Talon wished she could capture this moment, wished she could hold on to the image of his lean body resting casually against the wall. Wished she could always remember how gentle he looked with his normally wavy hair curling up from the sweaty heat and sticking to his tan forehead. This was the most relaxed she had ever seen him. She knew it wouldn't last long.

He looked up at her, snapping his gaze from the floor to meet her amber orbs. The moment their eyes met, he tensed, folded arms straining against his chest. To anyone else, he might have appeared impassive, but Talon could see the anxiety in his eyes, the tightness in his jaw, the ever so slight bunching of his shoulders—just a fraction of an inch. And all once, he seemed to compose himself. Exhaling all his nerves as his face hardened and his gaze turned stony, chasing away the brief flicker of emotion.

"I didn't know you were coming," she whispered.

He pushed from the wall and nodded toward the door. "Come."

She didn't ask where. She supposed it didn't matter.

They walked in silence, night birds singing around them, crickets coming out to chirp noisily. When they reached a little shack, Diaz stopped and glanced over at her for the first time since they'd locked eyes in Li's shop.

"Hungry."

It wasn't a question at all, but Talon nodded like he'd asked and reached for the door. "What is this place?"

"They make really good stew."

She smiled, not really knowing what else to say or do. Evelyn guided her inside and found a table. A man came by and served them two bowls of stew with flatbread, even though they hadn't ordered. Apparently, the place only served one item, so no one ever had to order.

"How've you been?" Diaz asked, voice low and raspy.

She dared a glance at him and filled her mouth with stew, so she'd have a second to think. She had been prepared to have his eyes on her, but she hadn't been prepared to find them filled with so much emotion. They brimmed with tears, though none escaped as he blinked and looked down at his bowl.

"I've been fine. Very busy."

He nodded.

"How have you been?" she asked.

Now he filled his mouth with stew. She was fascinated by watching him eat. It was such a human gesture—something everyone did, something everyone *had* to do. But Evelyn was so dead and detached, watching him eat almost felt invasive, like she'd caught him doing something dirty.

"I know you were close with Kotaro—"

"I've been dealing with it," he said sharply.

She winced.

"I'm sorry," he mumbled.

"It's okay."

"I heard Roaring dropped out of the Academy again."

She nodded. "He's returning to Wi to help rebuild it."

"Are you?"

His eyes were on her again and she was glad this time because she got to see the hint of joy that flashed in them when she said, "No. I'm staying here."

"Why?"

"Master Li needs me. And so does Fox."

"Did you ever finish her weapon?"

"I did." She smiled.

"Maybe I'll get to see her use it on her next mission."

Talon tilted her head to the side; Fox had mentioned a new mission,

269

but she hadn't gone into any details except to say she was definitely accepting the request.

"That's why I came." Diaz wiped his mouth. "To let you know about her newest mission at the Academy."

"So soon?" Fox had only just graduated—had only just survived the exams. Talon supported her sister in her endeavors. She understood why she'd enrolled. She was happy KI had someone there for him. But she didn't like how dangerous it was. Kotaro could have easily been Fox or Roaring or KI or even her other friend—Kohlannis.

Diaz leaned closer, catching Talon's attention. "We need her. KI needs her to keep his humanity intact."

She squinted.

"I can't share any more details than that. But I wanted to talk to you about it because I know you're protective of her."

Talon clenched her jaw. "I can't let her go."

Diaz sighed. "She's a student at the Academy now. She doesn't need your permission."

"Excuse me?" He looked at her like she was overreacting which only made her angrier. "She is my little sister—my *youngest* sister."

"I know that—"

"Do you have any younger sisters?" Talon snapped.

Diaz gave her a hard look, a muscle spasming in his jaw. "I have no one."

Talon didn't respond.

"I'm an orphan. But even before my parents were murdered, I was an only child."

"I'm sorry," she said quietly.

He stared at his stew. "Kotaro was like a little sister to me. I had always tried to protect her like one." He swallowed. "I failed."

She was like a sister to him. He truly has no idea how she felt about him.

270

"When is the mission?" Talon asked, just to keep her thoughts from dwelling on Kotaro for too long.

"Less than a week."

"I suppose I have nothing else to say on the matter. Since being her guardian doesn't give me any right to keep Fox from putting herself in danger."

Diaz gazed at her. "There's one more thing."

"Yes?"

"You've been tapped to go on the mission as well."

Her jaw went slack. "I'm not enrolled at the Academy."

"I know. But—"

"What on earth could I do for the mission?"

"It wasn't my decision. My bosses want you there as the active Priestess."

Talon blinked. It wasn't uncommon for Priests or Prophets to travel with armies and kings in the Bible. "But I'm not a Priestess." *Or a Prophetess.*

"No, but you made the crucifix Fox used when she first battled the silver-haired demon. You sensed the Dark energy in Wi when you returned. You've forged imbued weapons for Master Li. And you're personally connected to KI." The lieutenant pushed his bowl away and exhaled slowly. "The order came from the top down. Normally, you would receive a scroll detailing the mission and requesting you to accept or reject within a certain timeframe. But," his eyes flicked up to hers, holding her gaze, "I'm in charge of putting the team together. So I came personally."

"Do I still have the option to accept or reject, even without getting a scroll?"

He nodded, his eyes never leaving hers. "You can say no."

"How long do I have before the Academy expects a response?"

271

"You were supposed to respond days ago. But I delayed."

"Why?" She frowned.

"You're a civilian. You shouldn't be pressured to go." He finally looked away, glancing down at his cold stew. "I tried to fight the Academic Council, but they overruled me. Again."

Talon swallowed. "I see."

"You have two days."

"I'll think about it."

Diaz stood, then he hesitated. "Are you still eating?"

She shook her head. "No."

They walked in silence, working their way through the dark to find Talon's small apartment. She hadn't asked Diaz to walk her home, but she was glad he was beside her anyway. She felt tense and frustrated from everything he'd told her. The Academy wanted her to go on a mission with them. Even though she wasn't a fighter. Even though she had no experience—except getting taken hostage by Mung and her men during her journey back to Wi.

Fox would be going on the mission, too. But she was a sundancer. Even though she was only sixteen, and the youngest of the family, Talon couldn't say she wasn't remarkable. Fox Fire would rival her brother by the time she graduated from Cross Academy.

"Here," Diaz's voice was soft beside her.

Talon glanced up and realized they were standing at her front door. She blinked. "Already."

Lieutenant Diaz nodded. His face was unreadable in the darkness, but that didn't stop the wave of nerves from rushing over her as he stepped into her personal space.

Talon took a step back, bumping into the door. "Uh," she said slowly.

Evelyn caged her in, one hand going on either side of her head. "I don't want you to go on the mission," he said. His voice was strained.

272

His eyes were dark and serious. "I want you to reject the request."

"Why?" She thought he would want her to go, so she could see what Fox did at the Academy. So she'd understand that her sister was safe and could handle herself. But as Talon blinked up at him, she realized he looked angry. "You don't want me there," she whispered sadly.

Perhaps because she was useless. Perhaps because she was a burden.

Talon dropped her gaze. She had realized how useless and burdensome she truly was on her last mission, when Diaz had to turn around and come rescue her—delaying the journey to Wi for days.

"I don't want you in danger," he muttered.

His raw honesty made Talon snap her head up to look him in the eye—and just as she lifted her chin, he kissed her.

It took her a moment to realize what was happening, but, as if her body was in tune with his, Talon reacted without thinking. Her arms wrapped around his neck, and she pulled him closer, gasping when he deepened the exchange. He groaned, hands balling into fists against the door.

Then, abruptly, he pulled away.

Talon stared at him.

He stared back.

"Don't go on the mission," he said.

His hair was disheveled from her hands running through it, his shirt was wrinkled from her body being pressed against it, his lips were puffy from the friction of mashing them against hers. But his voice was direct, like he was giving an order, and his eyes were dead, like he was looking at a soldier—not a woman he'd just kissed.

Talon couldn't get herself to respond, but Diaz didn't seem bothered by her silence. He brushed his hair back, straightened his shirt, and then walked off into the darkness. She watched him go, staring after him in stunned silence.

Only when Talon was sure he was gone did she lift her hand and touch her lips.

26

Fox Fire

"Show me again," KI said with a wild look of excitement dancing in his eyes.

Fox would have sighed and said no if it were anyone else, but she couldn't deny KI—and, she had to admit, this was pretty cool.

"All right," she said, holding up one of the metal rods Talon had given her. To most, they looked like nothing more than short iron poles, but when Fox held them in her hand, she could feel her sister's Light energy flowing through it.

Fox gripped the rod, directing the power as it hummed with life. *Blade*, she told it. And the rod obeyed, shifting into a dagger right before her eyes. KI let out a laugh, grinning ear to ear. Fox couldn't help but smile with him. She'd been shifting her rods into various weapons all afternoon, trying to see if it took more energy to summon certain weapons—or if the rods could be turned into other items, too.

"Talon is a mad genius," KI gushed. He leaned against the giant oak and reached for the other rod still resting in the little wooden box.

"It was God Who gave her the inspiration."

He nodded. "You've got to name them."

"I thought about that last night. I'm going to call them Ammaron

275

Rods."

KI pressed his lips together. Confused.

She sighed. "Aaron. Moses. Miriam. It's a combination of their names."

"Ohh. Like Aaron's staff."

"And Moses being God's chosen leader of the Israelites."

"And Miriam?" KI asked incredulously.

"I'm not going to leave out the woman who stood side by side with two of the most amazing men in the Holy Bible."

KI laughed like he suddenly understood. "She was definitely a cool gal."

"*A cool gal*," Fox repeated.

"Do you feel like Miriam?" he asked, wiggling his eyebrows. "Standing side by side with two legends?"

Fox would have thrown her rod at him, but she didn't want to risk damaging it. "You and Kohl are not legends," she said instead. And then she sighed, holding up one of the rods. "I still can't believe Talon made this for me."

"*I* can't believe you two have been playing with rods instead of training," said a voice behind her.

At first, Fox wasn't going to turn around, but she caught the way KI's face lit up and she didn't want to sour his joy.

"This *is* training," she said, shifting to face Kohlannis.

He smiled at her, but it was shy and uncertain, like he didn't expect her to return it.

She didn't.

He crossed his arms over his broad chest. "Why don't you guys come spar with the rest of us?"

"I don't feel like it," Fox snapped before KI could immediately agree.

Kohl watched her in silence, blue eyes sharp and piercing—cutting

276

out her heart. This was the first time they'd spoken in two days. Classes were awkward. Lunch was painful. And their mission briefings were frustrating to say the least. But Fox refused to give Kohl any more attention or time than he deserved. It wasn't like she missed her anyway, he was too busy with Kressa—sitting with her in class, feeding each other during lunch, Fox had even caught them cuddled up after training yesterday.

It was late and most of the students were packing up to leave, but Fox had run back onto the field to grab her water skin and found Kohl and Kressa by the weaponry barn. She would never forget the way her heart had cramped in her chest, like she'd been stabbed by one of the discarded spears beside Kohl. If she had been thinking straight, Fox would have simply turned and walked away, but then Kohl had opened his eyes, his mouth still covering Kressa's as she stood on her tiptoes and leaned into him.

His vision had immediately snapped to Fox, like he'd somehow known she was there. And he hadn't stopped kissing Kressa. Hadn't stopped his hands from roaming her body. He'd simply gazed at Fox Fire, blue eyes drinking her in like there wasn't another girl right there in his arms. And then he'd looked away like he was bored. Blonde lashes fluttering as he shut his eyes again and pulled Kressa closer.

Then Fox had left.

That's probably why he's over here now, Fox glared at him, *he's just trying to see if I'm angry about it*. She relaxed her glare into the bored expression she'd seen on his face so many times. *I'm not angry. I don't even care.*

"Why don't you want to spar?" Kohl asked.

"Because I'm busy," Fox said as calmly as she could.

"Fox's sister forged her an imbued weapon," KI chimed in. "It's so cool."

"Care to show me?"

277

If it weren't for KI, who was in love with Kohl for whatever reason, Fox would have just gathered her things and walked away. But she didn't want to ruin her best friend's afternoon, so she grabbed the other rod and held them both together. They melted into one long rod and formed a spear.

"Just like what you wanted in Wi," KI murmured, examining the weapon.

Kohl squinted at it. "I almost forgot you two are from the same village."

"Technically, I'm from another village. But I grew up in Wi," KI corrected.

Kohl looked at him. "You never told me that."

He shrugged; his gaze still fixed on Fox's spear. "I don't remember much, to be honest."

Hmm... Fox tried not to let his comment burrow into her worries, but she couldn't help it. The last time she'd spoken to KI about his past, he had remembered almost everything. The details were fuzzy, but he'd been able to recall enough to tell her the name of his village, the names of his parents, and even a description of the man who'd killed them. A tall man with hair like fire and a face calm like still water.

Now ... Now he was telling Kohl he couldn't remember much, or at least he couldn't remember enough worth telling his only other friend at the Academy.

Fox stared at him as he chatted with Kohl about their next mission briefing; they'd been having them every other day, but the three friends hadn't discussed anything about the mission since receiving their scrolls. Probably because KI had already known all about it and Fox wasn't speaking to Kohl now—plus Talon's presence at the meetings made everything so awkward. Fox still couldn't believe her sister had been invited to join the team, let alone the fact that she'd *accepted* the invite.

Things were getting stranger every day.

"Well," Kohl, said, scratching the back of his head. He glanced at Fox and then looked at KI. "I'll see you guys later."

"I can walk with you," KI offered, but Kohl waved him off.

"I'm sleeping at home tonight."

KI nodded. "See you tomorrow, then."

There was a pause which Fox guessed her friends expected her to fill with a goodbye to Kohl, but she kept her gaze locked on her spear and pretended not to notice the blaring silence. Eventually, Kohl walked away.

KI sighed as he watched him go. "When are you two going to get along again?"

She shook her head. "We're fine, KI."

"No, you're not. Not since he started hanging out with Kressa."

"I don't want to talk about Kohl and Kressa," Fox said, taking her rods apart and returning them to the wooden box. She'd have to find a better case to put them in, or maybe keep them strapped to her hip for easier access during battle.

"Neither do I," KI said. "I just want us to get along again. We took a pact, remember?"

She did remember. It was the only thing that made her include Kohl in her prayers at night. No matter who he decided to hug and kiss, she was still his friend. She just hadn't expected it to hurt so much when she realized Kohl was truly serious about Kressa.

"Their relationship came out of nowhere," she mumbled.

KI pulled her into a hug. "So what."

So what... It was easy for him to say that. Kohlannis was like a brother to him. KI was never anything but happy on his behalf. He would never understand why Fox was so upset. *She* could barely understand it. The answer was obvious. That she had feelings for him. But she'd scarcely had time to acknowledge those feelings before they were thrown back into her face.

And now... Fox hugged KI back, inhaling his masculine scent. Now KI was acting strangely toward her. First the kiss in the forest, then the incident in his dorm. And now he was hugging her, his strong hands running down to her waist, gently pulling her ever closer.

She looked up at him and caught her breath. He was staring down at her ... and then he was leaning closer.

He kissed her cheek.

He kissed the line of her jaw.

He kissed her neck.

"You smell so good," he murmured, lips brushing the sensitive skin.

"Thanks," she said quietly.

His tongue glided along her flesh, making her freeze. Fox hadn't been in this position before, but she was sure it wasn't supposed to go like this. Then she felt his teeth graze her skin, the sharpness of his bite was painful enough that she squirmed and pushed him away.

"KI?" She held her neck, sucking in a gasp when she pulled her hand away and found blood on the tips of her fingers. "You bit me."

He stared at her, eyes flicking to her face, then to her neck, and then to the blood on her fingers. They seemed to lock onto the crimson liquid, making every muscle in his body go rigid.

He licked his lips. "You should go."

"I don't understand—"

"Neither do I," he said, voice low and dangerous. There was a darkness in his eyes that Fox thought she was imagining, like a shadow had suddenly been cast over his face. And then she noticed the hardness in his jaw and the thickness of the veins along his neck. Like he could snap at any moment.

"You need to go," he said again. This time, he turned away from her, running a hand through his hair and taking deep breaths.

"If you're not okay—"

"I don't know what I am!" he hollered so loud, students in the distance turned to look at them.

Fox glanced around before taking a slow step toward KI. "You're my best friend."

He calmed at her words, shoulders sagging as the muscles in his back relaxed. "I—I can smell your blood," he whispered. "And ... I don't know why ... but ... I want to taste it."

Fox stared at his back, having *no idea* what to say to that. Then again, there was nothing *to* say. He had never wanted blood before. Had never bitten her before. Had never even made moves on her like that before.

KI was still just a kid. He was tall and strong and handsome, but at fourteen, he hadn't been very interested in Fox or any other girls until recently. Now, he was all dark and flirty and masculine energy. It was so odd.

But it was also charming.

Like watching a boy become a man, the shift in KI's demeaner had been a welcome change. He wasn't the goofy kid from Wi anymore. His behavior finally matched his appearance. Six feet of muscle with raven hair and bright eyes and dangerous smiles.

Except now his behavior wasn't just flirty—it was uncontrollable and paired with bloodlust. For the first time in her life, Fox felt afraid of KI.

"You said you couldn't remember your past earlier."

KI laughed, running his hand through his dark hair again. "It's funny, Foxy. I can't really remember my life before Wi. But I also can't remember things about my life *in* Wi now... Like, the name of the man who raised me."

She swallowed thickly. "Kifu Kato."

"I couldn't remember his name. But there are strange names I do

281

remember. Faces I see in my sleep—of people I've never met, memories I didn't live."

"Because they don't belong to you," Fox whispered, a tear slipping down her cheek. She had known he was changing. Lieutenant Diaz had told her this would happen when she'd first arrived in Wi. But she didn't think it would be so soon. Or so painful.

KI took a long pause. "*Atara*. I don't know who that is. But her name is familiar."

"When did all this start?" Fox asked.

KI turned back around, his eyes misty and sad. "Ever since I heard the howler's cry."

Fox walked quickly, fighting to keep her harried steps from turning into a panicked sprint. She had managed to talk KI into going back to the Academy and seeing Lieutenant Diaz, but now *she* needed to talk to someone. There was no one else who would understand except the one person she was supposed to be avoiding right now. And it didn't help that he had decided to sleep at home tonight.

She stopped in front of the modest, two-story house and stared at it. It hadn't been difficult to find his address. Everyone knew where the Hunger sector was located. It was like a black stain in the city; just follow the shadows and you would eventually find it.

Once she'd gotten into the sector, all she had to do was ask around for Kohlannis. He was kind of famous for a Hunger, being the only one permitted to enter the Academy in the last century. His tribesmen happily pointed her toward his house with shy smiles on their faces.

Some even asked how he was doing with his training.

The kindness had surprised Fox. She'd been expecting to find a sector filled with ghostly pale people who hated everyone and everything—exactly how Kohl had been when he'd first entered the Training Grounds. But the Hungers were shy and uncertain, regarding her with wide, curious eyes and smiling with trembling lips. They were as afraid of her as she was of them.

Fox walked up the pathway to Kohl's front door and knocked. The noise seemed to echo through the house, *tap, tap, tap*.

In the stillness that followed, Fox could just make out a rasping voice that called, "Kohhhhl."

She squinted, listening. But the voice didn't speak again. So she knocked once more.

Tap, tap, tap.

This time, the voice was louder. "KOHHHHHL…"

Fox shivered. That voice didn't belong to Kohl at all. *But then, who?*

The door flew open, revealing Kohlannis. Three different emotions passed over his face before settling on anger—no—*rage*.

"What are you doing here?" he spat, grabbing her roughly by the arm.

She yelped as he dragged her away, slamming the door behind him, but not before she looked back and caught a glimpse of a pale woman with horrible scars. She looked like a ghost, standing in the hallway in a white gown with wispy white hair and dead blue eyes. Fox was happy to get away.

Kohl didn't release his grip on her arm until they were two blocks away, then he turned and shoved her against the brick building. "Why are you here?" he said darkly, stepping into her face.

Fox wasn't intimidated. "We need to talk."

"*Now* you want to talk," he scoffed. "Earlier, you acted like you hated my guts."

"Things have changed."

"So, you *did* hate my guts."

"With good reason."

He sighed. "Did you really come all the way to my house to fight about Kressa?"

No. But she might as well rip the bandage off now. Avoiding the topic would only slow the bleeding, it wouldn't stop it completely.

"You two have gotten very close very fast."

"I know." He looked away. "It's out of control."

She raised her brows. "It isn't hard to keep your tongue in your own mouth, Kohl."

He winced and took a step back. "We're beyond that, Fox."

There was no way he was saying what she thought he was.

"Last night, Kressa came to my room. And didn't leave until morning."

"Kohl…" Fox shook her head. "You could get kicked out of the Academy for that."

"I know—"

"It's not just against the rules, it's a sin against God *and* your own body."

"I *know*," he said again.

"Sex isn't something you're supposed to just have with whoever you want."

"I know!" he yelled.

Silence rang out, smothering whatever else Fox had to say.

Kohl let go of a long breath, chancing a look at her angry face. "I'm not letting it happen again, okay?"

"Maybe you two should take a break."

"That's why I came home tonight. I don't want to be on dorm with her." He rubbed the toe of his shoe into the gravel. "Her room is one

284

floor up from mine. It's in the girls' wing, but she's always able to slip away at night."

"*Always* able?" Fox questioned.

Kohl didn't answer.

"How many times has she *slipped away*?"

For a moment, he didn't speak. Then he closed his eyes and said quietly, "Last night was the fourth time."

"Kohl—"

"I said it's not going to happen again, okay? I mean it."

She folded her arms. "And what will you do if things at home get rough again?" Images of the night he'd come to her room flashed in her mind. It had been such a sweet night. An innocent night. Nothing at all like the nights he'd been having with Kressa.

"Are you going to be able to turn Kressa away then? When comfort is exactly what you want and need?"

He glared at her. "She came to *me*, all right?"

"She didn't sex *herself* down, Kohl." Fox rolled her neck, feeling very snappy like Cat and very prissy like Talon. "A woman cannot seduce an unwilling man."

A very deep, heavy sigh blew from Kohl's lips. "Look, I don't know what I'm going to do, okay? But I'm trying. Can you give me credit for that?"

He was at home instead of at the dorms. And he had confessed to her pretty easily. And he did seem to genuinely regret what he'd been doing.

Fox nodded begrudgingly. Beating him over the head wouldn't do any good. "Do you want me to pray with you?"

He shook his head.

"It wouldn't hurt to pray," she insisted.

"I just don't want to think about it right now."

285

That certainly wouldn't help, but Fox didn't want to push the issue. She hadn't come all this way to talk about his relations with Kressa, anyway.

"Something's going on with KI," she blurted.

Kohl snapped his head up. "What?"

"He's changing faster than before. Losing memories. Seeing people in his dreams. He needs us, Kohl."

"How can we help?"

She hugged herself. "I don't know."

"The mission isn't far off."

"I know. I sent him to talk with Lieutenant Diaz."

"I should go." Kohl glanced toward the massive cross-shaped building in the distance.

"What will you do?"

"I don't know. But I've been there when KI's been sealed; just being by his side will help."

"You think they'll re-seal him?"

"I have no idea, honestly. But it won't hurt to go check on him."

Fox touched his arm. "Kohl, you said you were staying home tonight."

He looked annoyed. "I'm going to help KI. This has nothing to do with Kressa."

"I saw you yesterday," she mumbled. "By the weaponry barn."

His muscles stiffened beneath her hand. "That was a mistake."

"And last night?"

"Was an even bigger mistake." Kohl took a step back, pulling his arm from her gentle grasp. "We took a pact, Fox. I promised to protect him. I'm not going to let Kressa distract me from that."

"Promise," she said firmly. Kohl was the only one who got to stand beside KI with Lieutenant Diaz and Lord Izzy. He was the only one with inside information on her best friend. The only one who could be there when no one else could. KI was possessed and he was cursed. If there was anything good Kohl's dark powers had ever brought him, it was his proximity to KI.

"Promise you won't get distracted," Fox said.

Kohl crammed his hands into his pockets and started down the street toward the Academy. "I promise. Don't worry about it."

27

Roaring

He had done all he could for this place. Blood, sweat, and tears—like they'd come easily for him. Roaring Fire sighed as he stood at the gates of Babel. His sisters didn't come to see him off, he hadn't wanted them to. Cat was there because she was going with him, but Fox and Talon had slept in. It was easier this way.

"This isn't goodbye forever," Cat said, reaching for his hand.

He squeezed her small fingers. "I know. It's just…"

"Our first time apart."

He nodded and his curls fell over his shoulder with the movement. Cat reached up and brushed them back. "I'll braid your hair again when we stop to make camp."

She had done his braids the last time when he'd worn his warrior's garb for Talon's meeting. Now, his hair was loose again and falling all over the place like a wild mane of chocolate tresses. He didn't mind his loose hair, but the braids were neater. And easier to maintain. And Cat seemed to enjoy getting her hands in his hair. She never did much to her own, just piled it up in a neat bun or kept it swept aside in a simple ponytail. But she was obsessed with Roaring's hair.

He rolled his eyes and leaned down to kiss her cheek. "Sure, you can braid it whenever you want, kitten."

"*Kitten*." She laughed and slapped his arm. He hadn't called her 'Kitten' in years, not since she was a little girl and had insisted everyone call her that—because it was cuter than Cat. Roaring had been the only one to feed into her antics, everyone else had told her she was a Chiefana, she wasn't meant to be 'cute.' But Roaring had thought she was adorable, the most charming and spoiled of his three little sisters. He'd called her Kitten until she got older and said it was childish.

"Only my boyfriend should call me something like that," she'd told him.

He didn't make a fuss about it.

But now they were adults and things were different. Cat was all he had now. After nineteen long years of watching over his precious sisters, the family was breaking up. And his new job wasn't to simply look after his family anymore, now he would be looking after the entire village.

Roaring turned around to scan the entourage behind him. The Academy had sent a team of Hunters, Priests, and even students to help with the first phase of reconstruction, not to mention the group of villagers who'd decided to come along. Kifu Kato, Thunder Bolt, Lady Ina Modon, Kifu Ryko. The entire council was there—not to mention loyal Chava who lazily moseyed through the large group, sniffing at equipment and enjoying treats from the Academy students. It would be a long journey, but the Prince of Fire was ready.

No, he thought, shaking his head. *The Grand Chief.*

He wasn't a prince anymore, the veil packed in his belongings was proof of that, but he'd be lying if he said he felt like a king or a chief. It was so weird. To want something for so long, and then finally have it. But not because you earned you. You've got it because it was suddenly, inexplicably, dropped into your lap.

And now, Roaring supposed, *it's time to do something with it.*

There was possibly another Red Face hidden in the city. His little sisters were going on a crazy mission to take KI to the north, and now, of all times, Roaring had decided it was the perfect opportunity to return to Wi.

They can handle themselves, he took a deep breath, watching Captain Payne go through rollcall. *They don't need me anymore*. But he couldn't ignore the niggling feeling that maybe he was wrong. Maybe his timing was off. Maybe going back to Wi could wait a little longer.

"If not now, then when?" Cat had asked him when he'd first shared his concerns with her. She was looking at him now, repeating the same words. A frown on her face, so delicate he'd bet it would vanish if he gave her another sudden kiss.

He smiled down at her. "Why are you asking me that?"

"Because you've got that regretful look on your face again." She placed a hand on each hip, but it just made her look even more fragile, like a doll he could break if he handled her too roughly.

Talon had always been called the weakest of the siblings for her uncertainty and low self-esteem, but Roaring could name a hundred things Talon had done to demonstrate her strength. Returning to Wi alone. Surviving the shadow frogs, getting taken hostage, sensing the Dark energy of the village, training beside Master Li, and now fearlessly deciding to take on a mission despite everyone's urging against it. She had no experience, she had no training, but she was ready to do what needed to be done.

She's a better leader than I'll ever be, Roaring realized.

He had the muscles, but she had the willpower.

But Cat…

It wasn't until now that the Grand Chief realized who the 'weak' sister really was. Which one of them had truly needed his brotherly protection.

Roaring looked down at his sister and took his chances, brushing a kiss to her forehead. Just as he'd suspected, her frown disappeared immediately. It was replaced by a sweet giggle and a shy smile as she pushed him away and complained that he was scaring off the cute Hunters who'd been staring at her.

She's all I have left, he told himself, watching her flounce away to flirt with a soldier from the Academy—a simple looking guy named Hemiah. Roaring had heard his name before but couldn't remember where from.

Captain Payne pushed through the crowd to stand by Roaring's side. She let out a breath, eyes ahead, scanning her men and women one last time. "Are all yours accounted for?" she asked.

He nodded, glancing over at the council who stood by a horse and cart in their traditional Wi clothing. They stuck out like sore thumbs, but so did Roaring in his loincloth and his beaded necklaces with his tribal tattoos on display for all to see. He'd also decided to wear the wolf's cloak Cat had made for him. The cape was hot in the horrible sun, but Roaring had promised to return to Wi the same way he'd left, so he kept the furry garment clipped to his shoulders—the head intact just like before, mouth open in a snarl as it sat on his shoulder.

He caught the captain sneaking a glance at the wolf's head as she looked up and said, "We're ready when you are."

"What's the formation?"

She nodded at a group of teenagers dressed in Academy uniforms. It wasn't the white shirt and slacks from the Training Grounds, these were cargo pants (or leggings for the girls) with white shirts and red accents— uniforms of Gamma Division students. Roaring recognized some of them right away. Wunda Cyruson, Vinny and Montell Lin, Danté Shoren.

"I'm putting the little ones in the front. They'll think they're doing all the work and will complain less during the journey. Plus, we'll be able to keep an eye on them from behind."

Roaring couldn't help but chuckle. It was a good plan. "My team goes next; you can cocoon around and behind us."

"My thoughts exactly."

He turned away. "Are we all set, then?"

"At your command, Grand Chief."

The title made him pause, but only briefly. He looked back at Captain Payne, a slight smile on his face—and then he saw a figure by the gates, a woman watching him, as if she wanted to speak.

"Give me a minute," he said, recognizing the woman. "Tell the others to start the procession. I'll catch up."

Captain Payne nodded and began shouting for the students in front to lead the way.

Roaring Fire walked over to the woman, his eyes staring at the ground as a sudden shyness took over. It was a foreign feeling, one he didn't like at all, but ever since this woman sat in his house and called him her last hope with tears in her eyes, he'd started getting this odd feeling whenever he thought of her.

"Marlo," he said softly.

She smiled. They hadn't seen each other since the exams, except once at the mass funeral, but she had been weeping with Master Moneek over the death of one of her students. He hadn't felt right approaching her. Honestly, he'd felt like he'd failed her. He'd been her last hope and nothing good had come of the exams.

The Red Face had gotten away. A student had been killed. The howler had cried.

Things were a mess. And yet, Roaring was still leaving.

If not now, then when?

He pressed his lips together as the question swam in his head.

"I came to say goodbye," Marlo said, drawing his attention from his

292

thoughts.

He nodded. "This isn't goodbye forever." *Gosh* that'd sounded so much better when Cat had said it. But Marlo seemed touched by his statement as a slow, thoughtful smile spread over her face. She was dark-skinned and beautiful with long dreadlocks that swayed in the gentle breeze. She'd always kept the side of her head shaved, probably a traditional look from the Jo Clan. Roaring liked it anyway. And he liked how strong she was, mentally and physically. She was all muscle, thick arms flexing as she crossed them over her flat chest. But the sound of her voice was womanly and feminine and made his heart swell as she said, "I'll miss you, Roaring."

When he reached out and tugged one of her locks, he was pleased to hear her tiny gasp. "I'll miss you."

"If I asked you to stay and enroll in the Academy, would you say yes?"

He laughed because he knew that she already knew his answer. "My place is in Wi."

She nodded.

"If I asked you to come with me and become the wife of the new Grand Chief, would you say yes?"

Marlo blinked at him. And then, as if his question had just clicked, her eyes widened, and she took a step back.

He shook his head before she could freak out any further. "I would never ask you to abandon the kids at the school." *They need her more than they'll ever need me.*

"My place is in Babel." She stared at the ground, a sudden sadness in her voice.

"That can change."

Marlo's eyes were filled with emotion when she lifted her gaze to meet his. The caravan had begun their exodus—one long line of men

293

and women and Academy students happily leaving Babel. Going home. Roaring ignored them as they passed him by, horses neighing and cattle blowing hot air through large nostrils. Cat waved goodbye to Master Jo and yelled for him to hurry. He didn't respond.

Marlo was studying him, her expression unreadable. But Roaring was not a mysterious man. He stepped forward and made his intentions clear, so she didn't have to wonder. "Your place is in Babel for now. But soon it will be by my side. I'll make sure of it."

Marlo Jo was a Master at Cross Academy. She was from a different bloodline and a different city—even a different Region. She was five years older than him. But Roaring didn't care. He leaned down and brushed her hair from her face so he could kiss her cheek. Then he turned and joined the procession, his long cloak sweeping the ground behind him.

Part IV

28

Yadira

Hosenké was not smiling today. Yadira could have fallen over in a fit of giggles as she watched him glower into the crackling flames of the firepit. It sat in the center of their great lair, spitting heat and sparks as the Births of Carnage stood waiting for the Firstborn. She always arrived last, just as the Thirdborn always arrived first.

Yadira snuck a glance at Seganamé, his punctuality was not surprising. If there was a stickler for the rules among them, it was the Thirdborn—so long as the rules were in alignment with his own agenda.

Yadira had been out scouting when she'd felt the brush of the Firstborn's consciousness in her own mind. Naturally, she had given her access and saw the mental summons for all Nine Births to retreat to the Womb immediately. Yadira was surprised the meeting had been called to discuss Hosenké's failure. But she wasn't surprised when she saw Seganamé already waiting.

He hadn't noticed her when she'd first entered—probably because she had appeared from thin air instead of walking through the front doors. There was no point in learning astral travel if you never took advantage of it. Still, the Sixth Birth of Carnage had been pleased with herself when she'd approached the firepit and found Seganamé staring into the flames, unaware of her presence. His face had been impassive—bored, even. A square jaw, neither clenched nor slack, full lips locked in a painfully stoic expression, noticeable cheekbones that only seemed to add an edge to his blank face.

The only sign of coherence on the Thirdborn's face had been in his eyebrows. Heavy red brows drawn ever so slightly together, like the gentlest pucker of full lips. It was an expression that appeared so bland and simple yet held a thousand different questions knit together between his crimson brows. To anyone else, he would have looked to be merely gazing at the fire, but Yadira had served with the Thirdborn for centuries. She recognized his expression right away.

He was scowling.

But why? she had wondered, and just as the question had formed in her head, Seganamé looked up. Only his eyes had moved, locking onto her like a laser, while the rest of his body remained facing the flames. That was when Yadira felt a familiar shadow of fear curl around her heart, a breath of danger exhaling from Seganamé's very form.

He was the Thirdborn. And he had never let the others forget it. Even the Secondborn cherrypicked her words around him, despite him never reacting to her temper or her venomous tongue. That was probably what made him so scary.

The Secondborn yelled often, and that shook Yadira to her darkened core, but it was when that red-hot anger was met with the chilling calm in Seganamé's deep, velvety voice, that Yadira knew what fear truly was.

That black fear had trapped her where she stood, and Yadira swallowed and hoped that Seganamé wouldn't kill her for sneaking up on him. But he'd only sighed and pulled his carmine hood up to hide his face and his flowing red hair.

"Yadira. Come," he'd ordered.

She obeyed, joining him at the flames. "The Firstborn summoned us

297

all for a meeting."

"Yes," he said calmly. And that was the end of their conversation.

Now, Yadira stood at the firepit with the rest of her Birthed brothers and sisters, still waiting for the Firstborn to arrive. The Fifth Birth was to her right, but Hosenké was not on her left. He'd always thought it was dumb for them to stand in order, so he made it a point to arrive as late as possible and stand in the corner of the room. Seganamé had found his way to the other side of the firepit once the Fourth Birth had arrived. He always had some sort of secret intel to share with him.

Meanwhile, Hosenké seemed to squirm from his stance across the room. Yadira could make out the beads of sweat breaking out on his face, and she doubted they had anything to do with the heat in the room. The Seventh Birth had returned a failure. Just as Yadira had months ago. Unlike Yadira, however, he had no excuse. She smiled to herself, hoping his punishment would be severe.

Just then, darkness covered the room and all the quiet chatter hushed to a still silence. Yadira grounded herself. The Firstborn liked to make a show of her arrival, as if her appearance was some sort of performance. Beside Yadira, the Secondborn crossed her arms and sucked her teeth—the only one in the room bold enough to display her annoyance so openly. Then again, she was the Firstborn's sister, Yadira doubted she would be killed for merely crossing her arms.

The Firstborn rose from the flames in the firepit, erupting from the burning wood and the hissing blaze without the smell of smoke upon her. She was not a sundancer, but her mastery of the dark arts had given her immunity to many of the elements of the earth.

As far as the Sixth Birth knew, the Firstborn was immortal. Or at least very old. Yadira had no idea just how old or how Number One had become the Firstborn. The only thing she knew for certain was that their leader had been handpicked by the fallen angel, Black, and that she was only one of three Births to come face to face with Lucifer himself in her long lifetime.

Yadira shivered at the thought. She was a Birth of Carnage, a woman who had sold her soul to a demon long ago, but even she had never seen Beelzebub in all her time living in the shadows. She wasn't even sure she wanted to meet him. He was her lord. Her master. Her prince. But Yadira would be lying if she said she felt anything but fear towards him. Not loyalty. Not love. Not even respect.

She closed her eyes to clear her head. Such thoughts were blasphemous against the Prince of the Air. "I am in darkness and darkness is in me," she whispered quietly. It was the mantra she had been taught at her Birthing ritual to channel the power of the demon that dwelled within her. Like always, she felt it stir in response to her words. Dark energy pulsed through her veins, claiming whatever vestiges of light had crept through the cracks in her vessel. That's what happened when you allowed doubt to seep in. When you began to open yourself to the other forces of the world. Yadira had read the terrible Scripture that said, *The Word of God is swift and powerful.* The passage sent a ripple of anxiety through her.

Swift. Powerful.

Well, so is Lucifer, she thought smugly.

The Firstborn was facing Yadira now. "Sixthborn, are you listening?" she asked. Only her mouth was visible from beneath the flap of her red hood, the crimson cloak was pinned to the shoulders of her long dress with a clip fashioned in the shape of an IX symbol. The Roman numerical for Nine.

"I am listening," Yadira replied.

The Firstborn nodded and then turned her attention to Hosenké. "You have failed me."

"As we all predicted he would," the Secondborn said quickly.

"I'm sure some of us had confidence in him," the Fourth Birth said in his rumbling voice. He was just a floating puff of black vapors filling the sleeves of a red cloak, but his voice was loud enough to fill the room. Yadira had never seen his face or his true form before. In their meetings, he was almost always a puff of smoke like now, but sometimes his voice was feminine, sometimes it was childlike. He was one of the few Births written in the Academy's records, because of this, he changed his age, gender, and even his form as often as possible to keep the Priests running in circles.

"I did what I could," Hosenké defended himself. "They were waiting for us. They had a plan in place."

"What do we do now?" the Fifth Birth asked. "Obviously, this isn't working."

The Secondborn crossed her arms. Like always, she was levitating over the black stone floors, but as she drifted closer to the flames, Yadira felt her anxiety begin to swell. It wouldn't be long before Number Two was yelling.

"We did what we could," said the Red Face from across the room. He was standing beside Hosenké with a red cloak draped over his shoulders and a new red mask covering his face. Yadira almost smirked. She had heard how he'd almost died to a bunch of Academy students. *How pathetic*, she thought joyously.

Number One turned to the Red Face, and despite her face being hidden, Yadira could *feel* her glaring at him. "You were nearly killed by a bunch of brats. How could you let that happen?"

Though his arms were casually folded over his chest, Yadira didn't miss the way the assassin's hand gripped the material of his sleeve. *He's disappointed in himself*, she realized. *As he should be.* She had failed once, but he had failed twice—even with Hosenké there to help. The two had returned emptyhanded and now the Academy knew the Red Face's true identity. Things were worse now than they'd ever been.

Number Two ghosted over the floor, right up to the Red Face. Her hood flew back as she came to an abrupt stop right before him. Short black hair danced around her shoulders, but as her anger swelled and the Dark energy inside her began to stir, her curls levitated—just as she did over the floor. Yadira watched as they stuck out in every direction, like static shock. A red glow settled over the Secondborn like an internal light had been switched on. She was the face of anger, and the masked assassin was her focus now.

"You have ruined everything!" she yelled, the inverted cross in her forehead seemed to glow as she raged. "I knew you were a terrible investment. You have dishonored Number Nine's name." She leaned down to hiss at him. "I speak death to your soul."

"Darkness come," the other Births chanted in unison.

The Red Face laughed. "I'm *already* cursed. Dying would be a relief." He removed his mask, earning gasps from around the room. "But I can't die."

Yadira looked away. She had only seen the Red Face without his mask once since his Birthing ritual. He was grotesque. Disgusting. Especially when she remembered how handsome and charming he had been before everything went wrong.

The Red Face gestured at himself. "This is what immortality looks like. It ain't pretty. You want to curse me? Death ain't the way to do it. I've been trying to die for years." He chuckled, though there was no humor in his voice. Only sorrow. Only regret. "*Life* is my curse," he said softly. "And every day I breathe is my personal punishment. So you can't hurt me, sweetheart." He glanced around the fire. "None of you can."

Because every second he's alive, he's hurting ... Yadira finished with a shiver.

No one spoke for what seemed like a long time. Even Hosenké held his normally sharp tongue, glowering into the flames again, like he expected to find something there. It wasn't that any of them sympathized with the Red Face; their sudden silence came from the unanimous recognition of their failure as the Nine Births of Carnage.

The Red Face was only suffering because *they* had lost Number Nine. Because *they* had needed a replacement. Because *they* had rushed his Birthing ritual. And because *they* couldn't fix what'd gone wrong. He was cursed because of *them*. And his horrible face and his never-ending pain was living proof of their mistake—it was a horrific reminder that they could make mistakes. And if they'd gotten his ritual wrong, who was to say they weren't wrong about other things?

Like … maybe they were fighting on the wrong side of this Demon War.

Like maybe Lucifer isn't as strong as God, Yadira squinted, and then she quickly smothered those thoughts before the Firstborn sensed them. Instead, she focused on Hosenké who was still sullen and quiet as he waited for his punishment.

It was funny to think that weeks ago, he'd hated the Red Face. Had never trusted him. Had never liked him. But now he was standing right beside him, in silent solidarity as his partner in failure.

"It was not all for naught," the Thirdborn finally said, his deep voice whispering through the consuming silence. The sound of him speaking sent little sparks over Yadira's arms as goosebumps formed on her skin.

Number Two glanced over her shoulder at him. "What do you mean, Number Three?"

Every hood turned to face him as he softly began to explain. "Hosenké failed to capture the vessel, but he was able to summon the howler. The Red Face was unmasked, revealing his true identity, but the Cross has been too distracted by his betrayal to pay much attention to the second spy in their midst."

The Secondborn looked over the flames at Number Eight. "Does your cover remain?"

The womanly figure nodded. "No one has noticed me yet."

"Our plans can still be salvaged," Number Three assured. "Activate the howler and allow Number Eight to take advantage of the chaos that will unfold."

"You will bring us the boy," Number Two ordered, pointing at the Eighthborn.

Number Eight nodded.

"There are some complications," Hosenké said cautiously. "Fox Fire, Roaring Fire, Kohlannis Hunger, and the Priest—Lord Izzy—are all trouble."

The Red Face agreed. "I don't think Number Eight can handle them all alone."

"She won't be alone," Number One said. "We will all attack at once, Number Eight will only be there to grab the boy since she will be the closest to him—you were invited to the upcoming mission, correct?"

Number Eight nodded again. "The mission will begin tomorrow."

"Good," Number One said.

"So, how do we handle the people I mentioned?" Hosenké asked.

Number Eight cleared her throat. "Roaring Fire will not be present. He has decided to return home and will not be part of the escort mission."

"That's one down," Number Four said.

"Kohlannis Hunger has been neutralized," Number Eight continued.

Yadira raised an eyebrow. "How on earth did you neutralize him?"

"Indeed," Number Five added. He was only curious because he was a user of the Void curse, just like his distant relative.

Number Eight shook her head. "I have my methods."

"Are you certain those two won't be a problem?" Number One asked.

"Absolutely."

"Good."

"That still leaves Fox Fire and Lord Izzy," Hosenké pointed out.

"I am confident we can handle them," Number Two said with a wave of her hand. "The vessel's little friend is just a girl. And this Priest—"

"Is nearly unstoppable," the Red Face cut in. "He has a Priestess who aids him. But even without her, I'm not sure Hosenké or I could have beaten him."

Silence charged through the room. There were no worries present—only shivering excitement at the prospect of fighting such a formidable foe.

Members of the Cross were powerful. That much was obvious. But they were easy to distract or disrupt—doubts, worries, sin—it was so simple to get them to slip up or lose faith in their God. But this Priest seemed to have *great* faith, paired with an awesome blessing that even Hosenké could not properly describe.

Users of Light were intriguing, to say the least. Fighting for Someone they hadn't even seen in the flesh. Defending a Voice in their head. A 'Spirit' within. That was why Yadira preferred her Dark energy. It didn't depend on her faith or on how much she trusted some Guy in the sky. She had cold, hard proof of her power. The demon inside her was evidence enough, and he had never failed her. She was powerful, no matter what she believed in. But those who depended on the Spirit within were only as strong as their faith.

What a horrible way to fight, Yadira thought.

But they win in the end…

The words came unbidden, accompanied by a passage that sent tendrils of fear skirting over Yadira's spine. *The light shines in the darkness, and the darkness has not overcome it.*

They win in the end…

She closed her eyes. *They don't win! There is no way the darkness has not overcome the light. Look around.* The Nine had been winning the Great Demon War for centuries. *They* didn't live behind walls. *They* didn't have to train for generations, trying to perfect a 'blessing.' *They* were already perfect. Just biding their time. Waiting for the perfect opportunity to strike.

The opportunity had arrived.

"If this Priest is as skilled as you say," said the Firstborn in a very calm voice. "Then we will kill him before the real fighting begins." She turned to the Thirdborn. "I will send Number Three. Your only job is to kill the one called 'Lord Izzy.' Do it quietly, so the rest of the Cross will be unprepared for our final assault."

Number Three simply nodded.

"The rest of you, stay ready for my summons. The mission begins tomorrow, we must be prepared to attack at any moment."

They nodded.

"Number Eight, you will wait for my cue to take the boy. Understand?"

Number Eight cleared her throat. "Yes, Firstborn."

"Maintaining your cover is your top priority right now," said Number One. "Do not allow anyone to discover your identity."

"Yes, Firstborn."

"Now, go. Be ready to attack. Be prepared to crush the Academy and to destroy their … *hope*."

Number One disappeared in a flourish of sparks and blazing fire from the pit. The rest of the Births took their leave one at a time, until only the Thirdborn and Yadira were left once again.

She timidly looked over at him. "You're being sent out as an assassin."

He lowered his hood. "Yes."

305

"You're not afraid."

"I have no reason to be."

Yadira lowered her own hood. "Seganamé…" She didn't know what else to say, but he had turned to her with such an expectant look on his face, she felt she had to fill the silence. So she blurted without thinking, "Why didn't you take over Carnage?"

The question stunned her so badly, she almost wanted to slap a hand over her big mouth. Any of the Births could challenge a higher Birth whenever they wanted. If they won their duel, they would take that Birth's number and move up however many ranks they deserved. Those were the unspoken rules that kept their power in balance, but it was blasphemous to suggest challenging Number *One*.

Seganamé wasn't bothered by Yadira's question, in fact, the look on his face bordered amusement. Yadira suddenly felt stupid for even asking, as if his reasoning for remaining the Thirdborn should have somehow been obvious to her.

"Do you know why there are nine of us?" Seganamé asked softly.

She shook her head.

"Because of God."

That was not the answer she was expecting.

"God is a Trinity. Three in one."

She knew that—*everyone* knew that. God the Father, God the Son, and God the Holy Spirit. What did that have to do with there being Nine Births of Carnage?

"God is also a Trinity *of* Trinities," Seganamé said. His eyes seemed to fill with admiration as he spoke. "God proved Himself to be all powerful when He demonstrated His mastery of the Trinity of Trinities. Time, Space, and Matter."

Yadira squinted, totally confused now.

"Time," Seganamé explained, "past, present, future. Space: length, width, height. Matter: solid, liquid, gas."

"A Trinity of Trinities," Yadira whispered.

The Thirdborn nodded. There was a strange smile spread over his face, a wild excitement dancing in his burning eyes. He held his hands out at either side and said breathily, "God displayed His power over the Trinity of Trinities in a single verse, thus proving Himself the Divine Authority over all the Earth."

When did He do that? Yadira wondered.

Seganamé whispered, "In the beginning, God created the heavens and the earth."

She gasped.

In the beginning … *Time.*

God created the heavens … *Space.*

And the earth … *Matter.*

"A Trinity of Trinities…"

"That is why there are nine of us," the Thirdborn said. "We are that Trinity of Trinities recreated in darkness. And I," he bowed his head and placed a hand to his chest—right over his blackened heart, "I am the Thirdborn."

"The Trinity of the Births."

When he lifted his head, there was a sinister smile on his face. "I was chosen by Black for this very purpose. Anointed by Lucifer to carry out his will. I am Number Three, and there is no one like me."

Yadira had sold her soul to a demon centuries ago. She was no longer a human being, but something higher. Something elevated. Something enlightened. But at the sound of Seganamé's words, she felt a very human chill skitter through her body.

Now she understood why he had never bothered to challenge Number One or Two. Why he had never seemed interested in ascending or fully giving in to the darkness—becoming less human. He still looked

307

the same as he had before being Reborn, whereas Yadira was seven feet tall with silver hair and pointed ears. She loved her appearance. Loved that she looked more demon than human. People feared her with a mere glance. But Seganamé was so normal looking. So unassuming.

Which is why he's perfect for this assassination. No one would look at the Thirdborn and run. No one would guess he was a demon—so long as he cloaked his spiritual energy to hide his Dark aura and covered the inverted cross in his forehead. That's what Number Eight and the Red Face had been doing to pass as normal humans while in Babel. It had worked for months.

Yadira frowned as she mulled over Seganamé's words. "You sound like you admire God." He had even quoted scriptures from the Bible as he'd talked.

They had all read it, it was important to know thine enemy—and all that. But they had never *quoted* it unless they were blaspheming the Word in rituals or pretending to be Christians like Number Eight and the Red Face had to do at the Academy.

The Thirdborn nodded, his eyes seeming to return to their usual dullness. "I do admire God."

"Why?"

"Because He is powerful."

Yadira took a step back, wondering why Beelzebub or Black hadn't struck him down yet.

Seganamé looked at her. "I enjoy defeating powerful enemies."

She took a breath. *Now I understand...*

Seganamé was not like the other Births. He had not been Born to merely carry out the plans of the organization. He was there because he wanted to be. Because he enjoyed destruction. He wasn't an evil person. He *was* evil. As if Black and Lucifer had birthed an actual child the way Adam and Eve had conceived Cane and Abel. He was the living form

308

of rage, calmed into a pleasant smile. Hatred twisted into dangerously kind eyes. Ash turned to clay, molded into beauty.

An angel of darkness.

He did not need to ascend. He did not need to become something else. Yadira wasn't sure he had ever been human to begin with.

The Thirdborn stepped forward, a black portal opened beside him. "Worry not, young one. All will be well." He stepped through the portal and disappeared.

Yadira hugged herself. She wasn't worried at all. For the first time in a very long time … she was simply afraid. And she wasn't sure what of.

29

Evelyn

It had to be the hottest day of the year. Lieutenant Diaz squinted up at the sun and then lifted his hand to shield his tired eyes from the burning light. He was almost thankful they were headed north, but he knew the trip would be long. At least two months, depending on how long they stayed at the Fortress once they arrived. Summer would be over by the time they got back, which meant the lieutenant was leaving the scorching heat to trek through the punishing cold, only to return to more coldness once the mission was up. The whole thing felt like one very long punishment. But he was sure he deserved it.

Diaz glanced to his left as his new lieutenant sidled up to him. With Captain Payne assigned to the reconstruction of Wi, and Major Marshall holding things down in Babel, Evelyn had been granted full authority over this mission. But he'd had no say in choosing his replacement for Second Lieutenant Kotaro.

He sighed, watching the new soldier approach. She was a gifted young woman, a few years older than Kotaro had been, and clearly built for combat with her muscular arms and sturdy-looking frame. She was just as tall as Diaz and had a look in her eye that betrayed her shy smile as she greeted him.

"Second Lieutenant Raven," she nodded. "Reporting for duty."

"The Raven Tribe," he drawled.

"Clan," she corrected. "We're pretty small."

It didn't matter. Diaz still hadn't heard of them before. "What's your first name?" he asked.

She seemed to blush. "Wonderful."

"Wonderful Raven."

She nodded and scratched the back of her curly head. "Yes, sir."

"What's your blessing?"

"I can cause explosions at will. Even things that aren't flammable."

He quirked an eyebrow. "Useful."

"So I've been told."

"How long have you been a Hunter?"

"I graduated from the Academy at age twenty. That was six years ago."

So she's older than me. Diaz looked her up and down, wondering why she had only just recently been promoted.

Lieutenant Raven seemed to sense his unspoken question. "I am not from Babel. I served at the second Academy."

That explains things. The other Academy rarely offered promotions and most of their decisions came directly from Central. They were sticklers over there, at least that was what Diaz had heard.

He gripped the reins of his horse, gazing out at the crowd before him. They had an impressive caravan of students, Hunters, and Priests. Nearly thirty people travelling altogether. Diaz didn't like their size, but he knew each member's presence was absolutely necessary. They would be travelling across the Four Regions. Going to the most unforgiving of the Four—while escorting a child who exuded so much Dark energy, it made some of the others sick just standing near him. They needed every man available.

"Why don't you start with rollcall?" Evelyn asked his lieutenant.

She nodded and then unrolled a scroll with tiny script written over it. "Fox Fire."

The girl responded by shouting, "Present!"

"Kohl*annis* Hunger."

Diaz smirked as Kohl raised a hand, rolled his eyes, and said, "It's pronounced Kohl-Aww-Niss."

People always seemed to mispronounce his name.

Lieutenant Raven made a note on her scroll that likely didn't matter and kept reading names. "Hope Votoman. Dart Ontello. Sergeant Mung. Kressa Lion. Talon Fire."

A stab of pain went through Evelyn's heart at the sound of Talon's name. She hadn't so much as looked at him since she'd arrived at the Tower that morning. He wasn't surprised. There was no regret for the kiss, just that it hadn't convinced her to stay—and now it was working against him.

Diaz should have known better. Talon was a smart woman, there was no reason to believe she wouldn't have figured out that he'd kissed her just to convince her to stay in Babel where it was safe.

She would never think he'd kissed her because he'd wanted to. Even though he had. It was unprofessional in so many ways, but he hadn't been able to hold back. Self-control had been something Diaz prided himself for having—discipline, dedication, focus. Those were the characteristics he'd first learned when he'd entered the Academy. And he had thrown them all away when he'd found himself face to face with a beautiful woman.

It's always a woman, he groaned internally.

Since the day he'd met her, his resolve had begun to chip away. The death of Kotaro had only amplified the feelings he'd known were already there. Diaz had lost his mother and then the woman he saw as his sister.

He couldn't lose Talon.

But there she was, passing out her hand-carved crucifixes to her little sister and her two friends—KI and Kohl. They were likely imbued with some prayer of protection, which was good, but Diaz wished she didn't have to tag along to pass them out. She should be at home where it was safe, not running out with the danger.

The lieutenant remembered the day he'd interviewed Talon about her village. He had called her a bird in a cage. Had said he'd hoped she would learn to fly while she was there in Babel. Now, she was flying. But he'd realized too late that it wasn't what he wanted. He should have let her stay where she was. Should have encouraged her to remain flightless and caged. It was a selfish wish, he knew that. But he was a selfish man. *That's what loss does to you*, he thought bitterly, *it makes you hold on even when the person you're holding wants to get away.*

Now he was sure Talon hated him. For trying to seduce her into staying. For trying to play with her heart and her emotions, like her feelings didn't matter. They did. Just not enough for him to let her put herself in danger. Diaz didn't care if she hated him for wanting to protect her. Talon was a kind woman. She would forgive him. Eventually.

He glanced over at her as she secured the crucifix around KI's neck. She smiled and kissed his cheek. There was no joy in her acceptance of the mission invitation, but she was here now, and it would be a long mission. Plenty of time for Lieutenant Diaz to earn her forgiveness. And maybe work up the courage to tell her how he really felt.

Lieutenant Raven saluted and then passed him the scroll. "Everyone is accounted for, sir."

"Good." He nodded and mounted his horse. "Tell everyone to get in formation. We're leaving now."

He watched Raven leave to make the announcement. Moments later, the procession began, but Diaz was not in front. They'd decided to rotate the formation every forty-five minutes to throw off enemy scouts. That way KI wouldn't remain in the same part of the procession for too long. The only one who would constantly be by his side was Hope Votoman.

Lieutenant Diaz watched the young student as she casually chatted with the boy, a smile on her youthful face. Hope was their secret weapon. A student with the ability to mask her presence and cloak her spiritual energy. She had gone relatively unnoticed throughout her time on the Training Grounds and had even walked around freely in the Kanen Forest. Her blessing specialized in stealth and analytical tactics—she would make an excellent spy when she was older, but for now her skills would be put to use in disguising KI.

Hidden was the name of Hope's gift, and she would use it to cloak KI's Dark energy, making him untraceable to the enemy. The only problem was that he would also be untraceable to Lieutenant Diaz and anyone else who wasn't looking directly at him. Only Hope would know his exact location at any given time. But that didn't trouble Diaz too much.

She's on our side, he reminded himself. There was nothing to worry about.

The first two days passed with relative ease, even the rotations of the formation were executed with perfect coordination. Lieutenant Diaz exhaled his doubts as he glanced back at his team that afternoon. From his perch atop his horse, he could see KI and Hope riding side by side. The boy hadn't complained a single time since leaving the Academy.

He'd even agreed to being re-sealed the morning before they'd packed up and set off. It had been another painful procedure, but he hadn't so much as winced.

Something's changed with him, Diaz noted. Of course, he'd already known KI was changing. He could sense his Dark energy a mile away—which was why Hope's presence had been necessary—but the lieutenant hadn't realized just how much KI had changed until the kid showed up outside his office, rambling about how he'd bitten Fox Fire in the neck.

Initially, Diaz thought the kids had gotten too frisky and was about to send him off with a reminder to save the fun stuff for marriage. But then he'd caught the look of desperation in KI's eyes, had noticed the intensity of his Dark energy, and realized something was wrong.

The howler. It had to be the creature. The only thing the lieutenant wasn't certain of was whether the dark song had been activated or not. Clearly, just hearing the cry had sped up KI's transformation, but he hadn't tried to run away or venture off on his own in search of the demon. *Maybe there is hope,* Diaz decided. *Maybe there's still time.*

Once they got to the Region of Ice there would be no running off. The Fortress was as inescapable as it was impenetrable. KI would be safe from the darkness and the rest of the world would be safe from him. They just had to get up north.

Lieutenant Diaz felt confident after the team set off on their fourth day. It was his turn to lead the formation, so he made his way to the front and whistled loudly for the others to fall in line.

Lord Izzy moved up beside him. "Things have been going according to plan."

"They have," Diaz agreed.

"Have you seen the kid?"

"How could I not?"

"I meant spiritually."

The lieutenant looked at him. "He's being cloaked by Hope. I haven't seen him spiritually since we first set off."

"I can see him," Izzy said. "He's getting darker by the minute."

"What are you saying?"

A lazy sigh blew from the Priest's lips, like he wasn't at all bothered by the fact that darkness was seeping into the air around them from a fourteen-year-old kid. "I think it's safe to say the song has been activated. We need to keep a close watch on KI from this point forward."

Lieutenant Diaz nodded as he glanced back to where KI should have been. He could just make out his dark hair in the crowd. Hope was right behind him, and Kohl and Fox were on either side. Diaz hadn't wanted the kids to all ride together the entire time, but he wanted them close to help keep KI's humanity intact. *It'll be easier for him to fight the darkness with his friends nearby*, Diaz reminded himself as he gazed at Fox and Kohl.

"You think he'll turn and run off?" Izzy asked.

"I don't know what I think."

"Been too quiet, right?"

He couldn't agree more. There was no question the lieutenant was happy they hadn't been attacked, but he had spent too much time in the Academy to truly appreciate the momentary peace. It was never this quiet for this long.

"Have Dart and Syren scout the area again," Diaz ordered.

Izzy nodded and retreated into the crowd. It wasn't long after he left that the lieutenant heard the cry of an eagle and glanced up to see the majestic bird soaring overhead. Syren was higher up, pushing west to check for enemies. They had eyes in the sky, they had a tight formation rotating at specific intervals, they had a handpicked team of skilled

316

fighters travelling together. No one was getting to the boy.

Lieutenant Diaz returned his gaze to the forward march. *I should welcome this peace. I should be thankful things have gone according to plan*, he scolded himself. *This is good. God is on our side.*

He glanced back at his men—and stopped in his tracks.

No one was behind him.

And when he looked ahead, there was nothing before him.

The trees around him had faded, the grass had disappeared—even the reins of his horse slipped between Diaz's fingers as the animal drifted away. He fell to the ground, his butt hitting the dirt hard. But he was back on his feet in a second, glancing this way and that way as he tried to make sense of what was happening.

He was suddenly standing in an all-white room, surrounded by a stillness that was everything but natural.

"How can everything just disappear?" he muttered, turning in circles.

When he faced forward again, he saw a woman standing before him. His first thought was of the Nine, but this woman wasn't wearing a red cloak, and there wasn't an inverted cross in the center of her head. Instead, there was a crescent moon glowing in her forehead.

"You're a witch," Diaz said. Though the realization should have been worrisome, Evelyn found himself smiling. He'd been wondering when the Moon Coven would make its move. They were the ones responsible for sealing the demon inside KI. They had summoned the monster who'd walked through the Village of Wi with the hopes of retrieving the boy so they could feed on the Dark energy of the demon inside him. But the Academy had shown up and their plans failed.

This was their second attempt to get KI.

The witch smiled, bearing black-stained teeth. They stood out against her pale skin and blonde hair cascading down her back. "Indeed, I am," she agreed.

"And what are you called by the stars?" Diaz asked. He was more than familiar with the customs of witches. He had been cursed by one as a child, after all.

"The stars call me Elsa," she replied. "What do the heavens call you?"

"The heavens call me Evelyn." He walked toward her, unbuttoning his shirt as he moved. Elsa's eyes glimmered with intrigue at the snap of every button. When he was fully shed of his top, she licked her lips, her blue eyes scanning his toned chest and abs. "But the stars named me Nox."

"You have been touched by darkness." Her face lit up; eyes focused on the black lines on his flesh. "It's you..." she whispered.

It's you? Diaz squinted at her, wondering at her words, but before he could question the witch, she was speaking again. "Nox. In my tongue, it is the word for Night."

He hadn't heard his craft name since he'd been cursed. He'd never gone by it. He'd never wanted it. But whenever Diaz found himself in a sticky situation with witches, his cursed name always seemed to help get him out. Or at least distract his enemies long enough for his companions to get him out.

Elsa looked so pleased to find that he'd been touched by dark powers, she was nearly trembling. Then Diaz tossed his shirt aside and held his arms out so she could see him fully. Her eyes roved the patterns of his tattoos, realizing they weren't only the winding lines of a curse but the intricate designs of a seal. Almost immediately, Elsa's seductive demeanor shifted to one of fear. "What have they done to you?"

"They have freed me," Evelyn replied.

Rage burst onto her face. "You think you are *free?*" She waved her hands around to emphasize his location. "You are trapped in my realm, Nox. You cannot get out unless I will it."

He'd thought so. Witches were masters of two things—summoning demons and creating illusions. Their art played with the mind. But Diaz had spent more time than he cared to mention with powerful witches. They hadn't just cursed him, they had taken him in. Trained him. Taught him. Feasted on his spiritual energy. Took pleasure in his body as if they'd owned it. For almost eight years, they *had* owned his body and his mind and everything else in between.

He remembered running away from Major Marshall to answer their beckoning. He remembered slipping out of Babel to surrender himself to their will—begging for more power, hungry for strength. And then he remembered being sealed by Izzy and having the veil torn and the darkness snatched away and the whispers silenced.

Witches were powerful creatures, but only if you feared them.

Lieutenant Diaz didn't fear them at all. He hated them.

And so did Lord Izzy.

There was a moment of stillness before the white walls surrounding Diaz cracked and he saw the illusion around him shatter. Suddenly, the forest returned, the grass reappeared, and Evelyn realized he was standing in front of his horse. Behind him, the rest of his team waited with weapons drawn and blessings activated. They were encircled by a dozen levitating witches, crescent moons glowing in their foreheads.

"Did she touch you?" Lord Izzy asked beside Diaz.

The lieutenant collected his shirt and then very calmly drew his hook swords. "No. We were only talking."

"You suddenly disappeared, and at the same time, all the rest of the witches appeared from thin air."

He nodded. "How long was I gone?"

"Four seconds."

He wasn't surprised. Illusions always messed up your sense of time.

"The boy?"

Izzy let out a chuckle. "You have little faith in me."

319

"Protect him." He pointed his sword at Elsa. "Your magic has no power over me, witch."

She frowned, eyes turning black in her hateful anger, but instead of spewing curses at him, she extended her hand. "Come with me, Nox. I can free you of your seal. I can unlock your full potential. I can give you what Madam Yoncé could not."

That name... He tried not to let his mind wander, but he knew the name was familiar.

Izzy stepped forward. "I will handle this, Evelyn. You protect the boy."

"She trapped me in her realm—"

"Which was her mistake," Izzy said. "She thought you were the strongest here because you were in front." The air suddenly felt electrified with Light energy. The cross in the center of Izzy's head began to glow white. "But she will learn today—the one to fear is me."

30

Izzy, The Executioner

Since the refugees from Wi had arrived in Babel, the young Priest had only used one of his blessings. The Guillotine. Today, he would use another. And, like always, he would enjoy it.

"It has been a long while since I've had to use this particular blessing," Izzy confessed. He could sense Vehenort nearby, undoubtedly cloaking him from injury—but he didn't need her help in this fight.

That witch wouldn't lay a hand on him.

Elsa seemed to finally realize what she was up against. She took a step back. "You are powerful. Imagine what you could do if you joined my coven?" An ugly smile peeled her lips from her blackened teeth. "Beneath all your Light energy is a familiar sense of darkness. You have shadows in your bloodline, Priest. I can sense it."

Izzy exhaled slowly, channeling his Light energy. When he was ready, he bowed his head and whispered a prayer, not at all surprised by the hum of energy around him as if the very air had responded to his power. "Since you think you know so much about my family," Izzy said. "Allow me to introduce you to my brother and sister."

The ground shook with a mighty quake as two coffins erupted from the earth. Elsa screamed, tripping sideways, but she quickly stabled herself and blinked at the scene before her. One coffin lay on the ground, chains wrapped tightly around it, sealing it shut. The other sat perfectly upright—no chains or seals in sight.

"*Yaresh. Mávet.*" Izzy kept his eyes on Elsa, gaging her reaction.

She dropped to her knees. "Life and Death." Frantically, Elsa waved her hands, and the levitating witches surrounding the rest of the team dropped to the ground around her. They were ready for a fight, eyes turned black, crescent moons glowing with Dark energy.

Diaz's team immediately shifted into battle formation behind Lord Izzy. They had anticipated an ambush since they'd left Babel. They weren't afraid, but they were cautious. No one dared step beside the young Priest—except Vehenort who observed just a few feet away, and Hope who had separated from the crowd.

"Do not let him open those coffins!" Elsa screamed.

The witches let out a collective hiss as they moved in, whispering curses and summoning demons to fight by their side.

"Protect Izzy!" Diaz ordered behind him.

Small explosions went off around the battlefield—Izzy knew it was Lieutenant Raven trying to blow the witches to smithereens, but they evaded her targeted attacks and continued their charge. Smaller demons ran past Izzy to fight the team behind him; he heard the clang of swords and blades, even felt the warmth of Fox Fire's flames as she danced with the darklings. But the witches themselves remained solely focused on the young Priest.

One stopped before him and screeched as she swiped at his head, long nails clawing at the air. He sidestepped to dodge, but the ground beneath his feet crumbled at the command of another whispering witch, and he tripped sideways. He was being charged by half a dozen dark maidens—now was as good a time as any to wake his slumbering allies.

322

"Arise!" he called in a loud voice, and everything stilled.

Every witch in the area stopped to stare at the coffins. The one standing upright opened like a closet door, revealing an older woman with white hair and milky white skin. Her eyes were blood-red and seemed to focus on Izzy as she peeled her lids back. There was a long sword grasped in her hand, it dragged the ground behind her as she stepped from her coffin and dropped to one knee.

"Lord Izzy."

"Mávet," he said with a nod.

The other coffin began to shake as the creature locked inside thrashed wildly. The chains cried out in agony as the monster shoved against the box, desperately trying to break free. It bounced on the ground, rocking back and forth, until—finally—the chains gave way with a *snap!* and the top flew off.

The inside was covered in shadows, like a pit of darkness had opened within it. But from the shadows, a small hand reached out and grasped the edge of the coffin.

A child climbed out.

With shackles on his hands and feet and one around his neck, the little boy stood beside the coffin wearing only a loincloth and a smile. He was ghostly pale and had hollow cheeks and wiry limbs like he'd been starved. The look in his eye was certainly hungry, but it was obvious what he desired was not food.

He wanted blood.

"Yaresh," Izzy said.

He crawled toward the Priest, his movements jerky and ticking—more animal than human.

"This is **darkness**," Elsa whispered. "How can you summon the dead?"

"Spirits are neither dead nor living," Izzy corrected.

"How can a good *Priest* control dark spirits?"

He took a step. "It is better that I, a child of God, command them for my King's will than for you, an emissary of darkness, to control them for your own will."

"The spirit of life and death." Elsa laughed, black tears streaking her pale cheeks.

Izzy shook his head. "No. You've got it wrong. Mávet is the spirit of death. She brings it wherever she goes. But Yaresh…" He leaned down to pet the chained boy's head. "He is not the spirit of life. Only God can give life."

Elsa squinted at him. "I don't understand."

"Because your translation of the Old Tongue is slightly off. Yaresh can project part of his soul into a corpse, essentially giving it 'life.' But that isn't exactly what his name means." Izzy smiled at the boy. "Yaresh means 'to possess.'"

Elsa took another step back, her mouth open in a wordless cry. "Retreat," she finally whispered. "We cannot win this fight."

The witches began to back away, dark eyes wild with fear. "I can't open a portal!" one cried.

Elsa's glare landed on Izzy. "What have you done to us?"

"It isn't me," he said.

There was a reason Lieutenant Diaz had insisted on bringing the mysterious Academy student, Hope Votoman. Izzy hadn't questioned his judgment because he trusted his longtime companion, but the council had given him a hard time about bringing the young girl. Izzy was glad Diaz hadn't given in. Hope could cloak KI's presence by smothering his spiritual energy—effectively making him stony. It meant he was plain and ordinary, unable to use any of his supernatural powers or abilities. But that wasn't the only amazing thing about Hope.

She could use her blessing on more than one person at a time.

"Your Dark energy is being suppressed," Izzy informed the witches. He ignored the urge to cast a glance at Hope for fear of bringing attention to her as she fought darklings beside Vehenort. "That means you can't cast any spells or do anything with your Dark energy."

Elsa choked out a sob. "Run!" she told her coven maidens. "Run away!"

Lord Izzy watched them sprint across the open field.

"My lord?" Mávet said.

He nodded. "Kill them all."

The screams only lasted a few moments. Izzy didn't even bother following Mávet or Yaresh. With the witches being smothered by Hope's blessing, they were virtually defenseless. He watched from a safe distance as Mávet chased them down, her white robes flowing around her as she slashed at them with her sword. Their blood stained her clothes red.

Yaresh, joined the fray, unbothered by his shackles as he ran on all fours and leapt onto the back of a retreating witch. She screamed as he ripped at her hair, yanking her head back so he could eat her face. When her screaming stopped, he kissed her dead lips and her corpse awakened—manipulated by the invasive presence of his dark soul. He sent the dead witch into battle, guiding her toward her own companions like a puppet on a string. One of the most devastating things about Yaresh's power was that he gained full control of the corpse he possessed ... including their blessings or curses.

Izzy was thankful Hope's gift was still working, smothering the powers of the witches. That meant Yaresh couldn't do much with his new toys. But he didn't need their dark abilities to massacre twelve women. He was dangerous all by himself.

Hope dropped to one knee behind Izzy, exhausted from fighting darklings and simultaneously suppressing a dozen powerful witches. Izzy called his summoned spirits back, not wanting to risk them getting overwhelmed since the dark maidens had regained their powers.

Mávet returned without trouble. "Elsa, the leader, escaped. She opened a portal and fled with two other witches."

Izzy nodded. "Good. Let them share what happened here." He peered into the distance. "Yaresh has not returned."

"He possessed three of the witches," Mávet said. "He is likely still controlling them."

This wasn't the first time Yaresh had disobeyed Izzy's command to have fun with his captives. Which was exactly why he had imbued chains and shackles hanging from his arms and legs.

With a sigh, Izzy walked over and touched Yaresh's coffin. It responded with a loud creak as the chains stretching out across the field began the retract.

Mávet returned to her coffin without a fuss, quietly climbing inside and closing her eyes. She whispered goodbye just before the door shut. "Until next time, Lord Izzy."

Izzy nodded, watching as Yaresh was dragged back to his coffin, kicking and screaming. He appeared as a starved child to gain sympathy from those who did not know him, but Izzy had mastered his Executioner blessing long ago. He'd spent too much time with the deadly spirit to be fooled by his looks. Yaresh was evil.

The childlike spirit spewed curses at Izzy as his chains cranked, pulling him closer to the coffin. "No, no, NO!" he screamed, banging his head on the ground. The coffin shook when he was dragged back inside, his small hands clutched the edge of his deathbed, neck straining as he peered over the side. "Please let me stay," he whispered. His eyes were large and filled with as much fear as there was hatred and evil.

Izzy shook his head. "The Lord rebuke you," he said very calmly.

Yaresh clamped his small hands over his ears and shrieked. As soon as he let go of his coffin, his chains yanked him into the black depths below and the top of the casket sealed itself shut.

A sigh filled the air as Lord Izzy released both coffins, sending them back where they'd come from. The cross in the center of his head reverted from white to black as he dialed back his energy.

"You did well, Master," Vehenort said.

"And the others?" Izzy glanced back at the rest of the team. Elsa and her witches had summoned a horde of demons to attack them while they remained focused on Izzy. Even Vehenort had been forced to momentarily forget about her master and fight beside Hope.

She shook her head. "No deaths. But a few are injured."

"The boy."

"Still safe," she said proudly. Then she stooped to pick up Hope who had passed out from overexertion. "We need to find a place to rest and recoup."

Izzy couldn't agree more.

31

Roaring

The first week of travel was so easy, Roaring dared to call it fun. His team enjoyed frequent breaks where they would gather for meals or tea and enjoy stories of past missions. One night, Wunda Cyruson told a ghost story of the founder of her tribe—how a man named Cyrus the Unmarked became the first ever earth-dancer and used his gift to help build the walls surrounding Babel.

"He was one of the first leaders of Babel and even helped lay the foundation for Cross Academy," Wunda had said proudly. "But he died young, betrayed by some of his closest allies."

Roaring had felt bad until Wunda leaned forward and whispered, "Legend says, he didn't really *die*. When he was stabbed in the back, he activated one of the most elite abilities of the Cyruson Tribe." Her eyes swelled with wonder. "He petrified himself."

Roaring frowned. "Petrified?"

"Yep," Wunda said, tapping her chin. "He turned his body to stone and then sealed himself away in an earthen tomb. The Cyruson elders say his fossilized body is still buried somewhere in the catacombs beneath the Academy."

"I didn't know there were catacombs beneath the Academy," the

Grand Chief said quietly.

"They were built by Cyrus the Unmarked. Originally designed as tunnels for escape in case Babel was ever overwhelmed by enemies. Over time, they became underground burials for the great warriors of the Cross." Wunda made an unreadable face. "But today, the tunnels have been expanded. They stretch throughout all of Babel, with hundreds of winding routes—like another city right beneath our feet."

Roaring had only nodded, intrigued, but still doubtful. Wunda's story was just a myth, and even if there was truth behind it, the Prince of Fire was going back to Wi now. He had no interest in catacombs or buried tribal leaders. His goal was to get home and rebuild what was lost. Rise again.

The only signs of trouble the team bumped into was a trail through the woods that led them to a nest of smog worms. Gigantic, limbless creatures covered in mucus and slimy to the touch. Smog worms lived in swamp areas and enjoyed eating live animals, or even unsuspecting humans. Their teeth were razor sharp, lining their cylindrical mouths like a tunnel of knives, and their mouths opened wide enough to fit a small child without issue.

When Roaring's caravan stumbled upon the smog worms, Wunda and four other members of the Cyruson Tribe used their earth-dancing to harden the mud of the swamp into solid ground, sealing a concrete grave over the worms.

Roaring didn't feel bad. The worms were fortunate to be trapped underground—they could burrow through the swamp and possibly find their way out. He would have burned them all alive if it weren't for the Cyrusons.

After the smog worms, the group found their way to Koh Village where Roaring met Chief Ramah. They stayed for two nights, and Roaring enjoyed himself in the new village, touring the quaint settlement and training with their Regiment Hunters for an afternoon. When it was time to leave, Chief Ramah pulled him aside for a word. From one chief to another.

"You are young. That will affect the way people see you and your leadership. But it doesn't have to affect the way you see yourself."

Roaring had nodded, feeling pride and confidence storm in to replace the anxiety he'd been trying to hide.

Chief Ramah slapped a heavy hand to his strong shoulder, exhaled a puff of smoke from his pipe. "Don't let anyone think less of you because you are young. Be an example to all Believers in what you say, in the way you live, in your love, your faith, and your purity."

Roaring recognized the scripture right away. *I Timothy 4:12*. He stored the passage in his heart, repeating it to himself as he set off toward Wi once again.

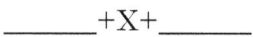
_____+X+_____

"We're making great time," Captain Payne said, gently urging her horse forward to walk beside Roaring. "If we maintain this pace, we'll reach Wi a day early."

Roaring nodded. "We haven't bumped into any darklings other than the smog worms."

"I'm thankful."

He didn't respond.

Captain Payne sighed beside him. "You should be thankful for this relative peace. We'll be working day and night once we get to your village."

"If the darklings aren't attacking us, that means they're busy bothering someone else." Roaring gripped the reins of his horse. "I am grateful for this momentary peace. But I can't help but wonder what it cost."

Captain Payne didn't bother him again.

When the caravan reached Wi, the Prince of Fire pulled his horse to a stop. It had been too long since he'd last seen Wall Yamina. It stood over 40 meters high, packed 5 meters thick of solid stone. The great Guardian of Wi had stood the test of time and war for hundreds of years. Legions of demons had not been able to penetrate the barrier, but one giant demon on one dark night had ruined centuries of rich culture and hope.

Why now? Roaring wondered, staring at the crater-sized hole in Yamina where the giant demon had first stomped through. He had wondered many times why that attack on Wi had been successful. Why hadn't God protected them? Why had the demons finally won? The questions haunted the young prince, threatening to break him just as the demon had broken Yamina.

Someone punched his shoulder and he turned, suddenly, to find Wunda standing beside him. Dark skin, thick muscles, and a heavyset frame, Wunda's friendly punch was strong enough to send Roaring stumbling forward a few steps.

He glanced back at her with a crooked grin on his face. "What was that for?"

"You were staring at the hole in the wall with a depressing look on your face. That was my way of saving you from your own thoughts."

"Thanks."

She smiled. "No problem."

Roaring watched her rejoin the others—all the gifted students from Babel, Captain Payne's team, and the few volunteers from the Cyruson Tribe. *That's why the Walls came down*, Roaring realized.

If it weren't for that dark night, the Village of Wi would still be lost in time. Hiding behind their Walls. But now they were allied with Cross Academy, their new Grand Chief had been trained by one of the best Masters of the institution, and their eyes had been opened to the world around them. It had taken a terrible night of violence and had cost the sacrifice of thousands of lives. But it had also given the survivors the means to protect the lives of thousands more. To learn more about themselves and their neighboring Regions. And to rebuild what was lost—better than it was before.

To rise again.

The demons didn't win that night, Roaring told himself. *Not at all.*

As the team made their way into Wi, Roaring forced himself to look around and take in everything. The destruction, the devastation, the evidence of loss right before him. Men and women from the Academy had been in Wi for the last few months, studying the scene and collecting data to put together a theory on exactly what'd happened and why.

They had cleared out the demons and all the debris, but the village was still in shambles. Crumbling houses, smashed trees and huts, scorch marks found on the roads. It took everything Roaring had not to lash out in anger, to release his flames with a warrior's cry of vengeance. But Cat was beside him, her mere presence keeping his temper in check. She clutched his arm as she walked in step with him, trying hard to hide her tears.

He saw them. Every single one. And he would make the darklings—the Nine—pay for each one.

Roaring stopped by a charred tree and pulled Cat into his strong arms, brushed a kiss against her forehead. "It's okay, Kitten. We're here to rebuild. The village won't look like this for much longer."

332

"This was our home," she whispered.

"It's still our home. The destruction hasn't changed that."

"I want everyone here to pray together tonight. I want us to welcome God into Wi again so that *He* can protect us—not the Walls."

He nodded which made her smile weakly. "I'm sorry I'm not strong like you."

Roaring looked away. "You walked through the village and couldn't control your tears. I walked through and could barely control my anger. The devastation made you sad, but it made me enraged. It made me wish for vengeance. For bloody violence. But you decided to pray and ask for God's intervention. Tell me, sister," he lifted her chin, "who is truly the weakling here?"

"You're not weak."

"Not physically. But emotionally…"

Cat smirked. "Roaring Fire has a weakness."

He smirked, too. "He does."

"That's exactly why I decided to return. Someone has to keep you in check." She punched his toned arm. He didn't feel it. "I've got to make sure you don't go shooting fireballs at anyone who ticks you off."

Roaring laughed, broad shoulders bouncing, but whatever reply he had was cut off by Captain Payne who called behind him, "Grand Chief?"

He turned. "Yes, captain?"

"My analytics team has a camp already set up in the innermost ring. We can stay there tonight."

They followed Payne to the camp, though they didn't need her guidance, but they were thankful for her help—and especially thankful for the tents that'd been set up and the fire that was burning when they arrived.

A small team of Academy Hunters and Priests sat around the flames, serving plates of food. A large Priest looked up when Roaring, Cat, and Captain Payne approached. He had an average look, smooth olive-toned skin and dark hair with welcoming brown eyes. And then he stood, and Roaring realized he was at least ten feet tall.

"Lord Razzle," Payne said, greeting him with a handshake. "Nice to see you've held down the fort all this time."

He let go of a ground-shaking laugh that seemed to rumble through Roaring's bones. Even Cat fidgeted beside him. "Captain Payne! How were the travels? How is my pretty wife?"

"Lady Shakira is well. And the travels were peaceful."

He pressed his lips together. "I am glad to hear that."

"This is the Grand Chief of Wi and his younger sister. Roaring and Cat Fire." Captain Payne said.

"I thought the Grand Chief of Wi was a woman?"

"The leadership has changed." Roaring offered his hand. "I hope you don't mind."

Razzle bellowed another earthquake laugh. "Of course not! Though, I have to say, you're not as pretty as the last Grand Chief."

"I second that," Cat said.

"Here, here," Captain Payne agreed.

Roaring eyed them all, feeling betrayed.

"There are tents set up," Razzle explained before he could scold them. "More than enough space for your crew. And we also prepared enough food for everyone."

Roaring glanced over his shoulder at the fire burning in the center of the camp. His stomach growled as his amber eyes landed on the roasting boar. A Hunter cut a thick slab of meat from the thigh, his fingers glistening from the salty fat, and placed it on a plate with a heaping pile of rice and black-eyed peas.

"I could show you around the camp," Razzle said. "The giant's hand was removed last week. That was an adventure." He chuckled. "But there are many other things I'd like to report about this village. It is so rich in culture—in *tradition*! I could see how beautiful it once was in the rubble we cleared. The paintings, the clothing, the dried foods stashed in barns. You managed to maintain such a powerful connection to the land and—"

"Lord Razzle, can we discuss this over dinner?" Captain Payne interrupted.

The massive Priest laughed sheepishly, an embarrassed smile spreading over his face as he realized he'd been rambling. "Of course. You all must be so tired and hungry."

Captain Payne grunted something about boar and marched away. Cat waved at Hemiah and flounced off to flirt.

Roaring looked up at Lord Razzle. "I appreciate your enthusiasm for the village."

"I have a love for culture. When the Cross requested I join the reconstruction unit, I agreed without hesitation."

"I'm glad you're here."

"So am I!" He slapped Roaring's back so hard, the Grand Chief bit his tongue to keep from yelping. "Normally, they put me on the frontlines."

"I wonder why," he said drolly.

Razzle laughed and slapped him again. Roaring cringed. He couldn't remember the last time someone had made him feel so small. So fragile.

"You're funny."

"You're strong," he grated.

"It's the Shoren in me! But, aye, you look mighty strong yourself. And tall!"

Roaring nodded, walking toward the fire and the roasted boar.

"How tall?" Razzle asked.

"Six-foot-six."

"Ahh, another foot and you'll be as tall as my cute little wife!"

32

Evelyn

Lieutenant Diaz groaned as Izzy pressed his fingers into his torso, prodding at his ribs. He was sure they were broken, a kind gift left behind from the horde of demons the Moon witches had summoned. Diaz was used to injuries, he was a Hunter of the Academy, but now was not the time for pain. He had to stay focused. Alert.

"At least two are broken," Izzy murmured. His bright eyes seemed to dim as he trailed his gaze down Evelyn's beaten body. "Your seal…"

For a heartbeat, the lieutenant worried the Priest would hold him down and re-seal him right there, but Izzy clicked his tongue and stood. "It looks good."

Diaz let go of a painful sigh. "I need a healer."

"I'll get Syren."

After Izzy chased away the Moon Coven, the team took up shelter in the woods with scouts on patrol 24-hours. Lieutenant Raven made all the arrangements while Diaz rested—Izzy's orders—but it'd been five days now, he needed to get back on his feet.

The lieutenant calmly watched his childhood friend leave his tent and then threw his head back in agony. Everything hurt. The fight had been exhausting, and then he'd ignored his injuries and trucked through the woods for two days before passing out right there in the saddle of his horse. He'd awakened in a tent, blinking up at Izzy and, to his surprise, Lady Talon. The two forced him to remain in his makeshift bed, a palette piled with blankets and an overstuffed pillow.

The flap to Izzy's tent opened to reveal Talon and Syren. Diaz kept his gaze on the Gamma Division student, unable to look Talon in the eye. They still hadn't spoken much since he'd kissed her. He got the feeling they probably wouldn't speak much ever again.

It didn't matter to him.

As long as Talon was safe, she could ignore him for the rest of his life.

Syren was beside him, her golden eyes scanning him from head to toe, sucking in a little gasp as she traced the winding lines of his black seal.

He looked away. Diaz had always been able to hide the markings under his shirt but after Izzy had re-sealed him in the hospital, the seal had grown. Now it trailed down the length of his arm, wrapped around his wrists and covered part of his hands and fingers.

He hated his seal.

It marked him. Let everyone know there was darkness inside of him. People looked at him queerly now, as if they were afraid of him. He couldn't imagine how KI dealt with the treatment at such a young age.

Syren knelt beside him. "Lieutenant Diaz, I'm here to heal you. I'm sorry I couldn't come sooner."

He only nodded. Against Talon's wishes, Izzy had decided to hold off on a physical examination until Diaz was steady enough to remain conscious for more than an hour. Lady Talon hadn't understood why, Diaz could tell just from looking at the pinched expression on her normally pretty face.

Evelyn was his most dangerous when unconscious—when the

338

darkness inside had the opportunity to invade his mind and take control of his body again. Healing him would have been like healing up one of the Nine and setting him loose. It was best to just let him suffer his injuries until he regained consciousness and control over himself again.

But the lieutenant couldn't explain that to Talon. At least not in front of the teenager. So he kept his mouth shut as Syren clasped her hands together and whispered a prayer. When she finished, she extended a hand and offered him a shining gem.

"It's the physical form of my spiritual energy. If you eat it, you'll be healed," she explained with a sweet smile.

Diaz reached for the crystal, gritting his teeth at the pain. "Thanks," he grunted.

The gem crunched between his teeth, bursting in his mouth in a sweet, honeylike explosion. He felt energy flood through his body, felt his sore muscles relax, his broken bones realign and repair. A sudden coolness invaded his frame, running through his veins and spreading through his entire body. He felt it in his toes, a buzzing in the soles of his feet—like he could get up right now and run a hundred miles without stopping.

Diaz's breath hitched and he pitched forward with a gasp, eyes shooting open. "Wow," he whispered.

Syren was smiling at him when he looked up. "Welcome back, lieutenant."

"Thank you."

She inclined her head and then discreetly glanced at Lady Talon who sat beside the lieutenant, her eyes still filled with sadness and concern. "I'll go get Lord Izzy," the young student said quietly. Then she stood and retreated from the tent.

"You're upset," Diaz said. He stood and almost went to his water basin, but then he changed his mind and just stood there awkwardly. He desperately wanted to wash himself but not with Talon in the room. He doubted she would appreciate his nudity.

Talon turned to look at him, tears glistening in her amber eyes. "I don't know how I feel."

There was obviously a lot more to that statement than Diaz could put into words. The only response he could give was an inaudible grunt as he folded his arms across his sweaty chest.

"I was angry with you for what you did in Babel. On my own front steps. But when I saw you fall from your horse," she hugged herself and closed her eyes for a moment, "all the anger vanished. In that moment, all I felt was fear."

"You don't have to be afraid for me," he said softly.

"But I do. Because you're clearly not afraid for yourself. You don't care what happens to you, do you?"

He wanted to nod and pretend that he did, but the truth was that he didn't. His mother, father, and his closest friend were all dead. He was running out of people to live for. Wondering if the fight was even worth it anymore.

Talon stood and marched right up to him. "You kissed me because you thought you could use my emotions against me. You thought that little gesture would be enough to sway me to do whatever you asked." She clutched the crucifix around her neck. "It would have worked if it hadn't been so obvious."

Diaz pressed his lips together, almost embarrassed. He couldn't remember the last time he'd thrown himself at a woman like that. Couldn't remember the last time he'd cared about a woman so much.

"The saddest part," Talon sniffled, "is that I would have stayed if you had simply asked me to. If you had told me the truth."

He stepped forward and brushed his thumb along her cheek. "And what is the truth, little bird?"

340

Amber eyes met his hazel orbs. "That you care about me."

He would never say it aloud. But he wouldn't deny that she was right.

"I understand why you did it," Talon said, leaning into his touch. "I just wish…"

"Wish what?"

"I wish you would let me care about you, too." She pulled away and swiped at her leaking eyes. "I had to sit in this tent and watch you fade in and out of consciousness because you hid your injuries from the team. I had to pray and ask God to keep you safe because you don't value your life enough to keep yourself safe. Do you know how much that hurts?"

He did. In his own way.

Diaz had lost nearly everyone he cared about. He knew the pain of watching someone suffer, knew the stabbing ache of walking in limbo—not knowing whether your loved one would live or die. Everyone said you got used to death when it happened so often. That Hunters were the most hardened soldiers of the Four Regions. But that was a lie.

Each death hurt. Each death meant something.

When it became clear the pain would never dull, Evelyn had finally decided to follow his mother's advice.

Don't let it in…

Not the pain or the passion, either. If he couldn't feel his hatred, then he certainly wouldn't feel any kindness. Any concern. Any *love*.

He looked at Talon, watched her shoulders bunch as she tried to stifle her sobs. She was crying for him. It made something twist in his heart. In all these years, Evelyn had placed a cage around his emotions because it hurt too much to care for others. But he'd never once considered how it might have felt to have someone else care for him.

He opened his mouth with no clear plan on what he wanted to say, so he surprised himself when the words slipped out. "I'm sorry."

Talon stopped her crying and blinked at him, eyes red and watery and her lips quivering with emotion. She was preciously cute, her puffy lips perfectly shaped and kissable. The lieutenant had to force himself to look into her eyes for fear of claiming her mouth for himself.

"I'm sorry," he said again. "I'll … I'll let you care." He swallowed. "About me."

Though tears ran down her cheeks, Talon smiled. "You try so hard to keep it all out. But it's okay to let it in, Eve."

The words sent a jolt of both pain and pleasure through his heart and soul. They went against everything he'd lived by since he'd lost his mother.

Don't let it in…

Now he was being told to do the exact opposite. He wasn't sure he could, but he was certain he wanted to try.

Lord Izzy pushed the tent flap aside and ducked his head in. He glanced at Talon and paused. "I didn't mean to interrupt—"

"I was just leaving," she said quickly.

Izzy nodded and stepped aside so he could hold the tent open for her. He pretended to mind his business as Talon gave Diaz one last lingering look before she turned and left.

The lieutenant glowered at his old friend. "What do you want?"

Izzy smiled. It was boyish and pleasant to anyone who didn't know him well. Blonde hair, bright, charming eyes, a heartbreaking smile, and suntanned skin. Izzy was quite possibly the *cutest* Priest of the Cross, but the way his bright eyes narrowed on Diaz, and the shiver of fear that skirted up the lieutenant's spine betrayed all the kindness he exuded.

Evelyn stared at the cross in the center of Izzy's head to keep from looking directly into his gaze. Sometimes it was hard to pretend they were merely friends looking out for each other. Izzy was his spiritual guardian. He was responsible for his seal and its maintenance. And he took it personally whenever Diaz allowed his seal to break. He wasn't in his tent out of the kindness in his heart, he was there to make sure the lieutenant didn't screw up and disappoint him yet again.

"I came to make sure you got healed up," Izzy said.

Diaz finally went to his water basin and stripped himself bare. "I'm much better. Thanks."

"There's something else."

"Shoot."

"The Moon Coven."

"Elsa Attra got away."

Elsa was the witch who'd summoned the giant beast to Wi in the first place. Killing her would have been a huge success, capturing her would have been even better. But she'd slipped away.

Izzy nodded, folding his hands into the pockets of his black robe. "But she mentioned something interesting before everything went down."

"Madam Yoncé." The name of a Dame Witch—the one in charge of the coven. Since her name had been uttered by Elsa Attra, it was natural to assume Madam Yoncé was the Dame of the Moon Coven. That was excellent intel—which Diaz would send back to the Academy with a messenger hawk—but he wouldn't be able to send any more info than that. Like why Elsa had mentioned her. And what Madam Yoncé had to do with him.

"She said she could give me what Madam Yoncé could not." Diaz closed his eyes as soap bubbles ran from his sudsy hair and into his face.

He heard Izzy sigh across the room. "I think she was talking about your seal."

Diaz paused. "You think Madam Yoncé has something to do with my curse?"

"I think she might be the witch who placed it on you."

"Big gamble," he mumbled.

Diaz would have loved to allow hope to fill his heart at the thought of finding and defeating the Dame, but the truth was that him and Izzy had gained many leads about his curse over the years and none of them had turned out to be anything more than a rumor. Diaz was almost convinced they would never find the witch who'd cursed him. But he had to admit her name sounded awfully familiar. He just wasn't sure why.

"I could go after Elsa and chase down this lead while it's still fresh. But…"

"But," Diaz sighed. "I need you here."

"Not just for the boy." Izzy planted his bright eyes on the lieutenant. They glimmered with controlled excitement as he spoke. "There is trouble in the camp."

"I know," Diaz exhaled. "I wasn't sure until the witches showed up. But now I'm certain."

"We've brought the second Red Face with us." Izzy smiled like he was happy about this. Diaz supposed, in a way, that *was* something to be happy about. That meant the masked assassin was with them, not hiding out in Babel or reunited with the Nine. But it also meant…

"There is a spy in our ranks. Giving away our position to the enemy," Diaz said slowly.

Izzy nodded, looking away as he stepped back to rinse the suds from his body. "KI was being cloaked by Hope the entire time. There was no way we should have been discovered by the Moon Coven."

There was one way.

"We're a troop of thirty Christian soldiers travelling together as one," Diaz explained. "We're giving off a massive storm of Light energy. The immense amount of spiritual energy around us should have warded off enemies—the same way explosions make people flee the area. But the Moon witches are powerful. They could have picked up our energy

344

signature and easily found us, convinced they were strong enough to take us on."

"They were wrong," Izzy said, a dark look on his face. Diaz caught the way his eyes narrowed to slits as he glared at the floor, undoubtedly thinking of how Elsa slipped away.

"There's still a chance the witches didn't trace our signature." Diaz reached for a towel. "Darklings don't go around searching for Light energy signatures."

"Which means they were likely tipped off by a spy in our ranks." Izzy ran a hand over his blonde hair and then stopped abruptly to fix the white zucchetto on his head. It should have been black in color, but Izzy's attire was not determined by his rank in the Cross. It was defined by his power and ability. He had earned the white cap.

"I'm guessing you have a plan in place to root out the spy?" Diaz said lazily. He found a clean uniform that'd been left out for him and began dressing himself.

"I have something in mind. But it'll involve breaking up the team."

Evelyn focused on the buttons of his shirt. He didn't want to split up. Travelling in smaller groups would break up their giant Light energy signature, which would make it easier for them to hide their presence from powerful enemies. But it also meant they wouldn't be able to communicate easily or back each other up if more enemies appeared. And it was a guarantee that enemies would appear if they didn't get rid of the spy. The second Red Face.

That meant the lieutenant had little choice.

He looked up at Izzy and wasn't surprised to find him smiling. He could feel his potent spiritual energy coming off him in waves, like the very thought of finding the spy was getting him hyped up. Diaz smiled too. It would be nice to finally come out on top. Catching this spy would make their travels that much easier.

345

"Tell me your plan."

33

Roaring

Ryko's voice drifted into Roaring's tent. "Grand Chief? Are you awake?"

Roaring adjusted the cloak pinned to his shoulders and pulled the tent flap back. He smiled. "Awake and ready to go."

Ryko smiled back and then nodded at Cat who stood grinning beside him. "Today's gonna be a busy day," she said cheerily.

Chava agreed with a lazy bark that sounded more like a roar. Roaring bent to scratch her between the ears and then followed his councilmembers to the center of their camp. A Hunter he didn't recognize stood over a giant cauldron stirring porridge. He was joined by Lady Ina who ladled out bowls to anyone who wanted a serving. Roaring heard her girlish laughter across the clearing.

"Good morning, Grand Chief!" Ina said excitedly. She passed him a bowl. "It's porridge made from boiled cassava and ground nuts."

Roaring drank the porridge down. It burned but once the searing heat passed, he licked his lips and grinned. "It's good."

Ina clapped her hands together. "Delightful!"

Roaring thanked the Hunter and Lady Ina before he turned to leave. The three of them walked all the way to Yamina. It took them a long while, but Roaring wanted to see every part of the village. Captain Payne had arranged a team to tear down buildings that were beyond repair; Kifu Kato and Kifa Thunder volunteered to help. The sound of their destruction rang throughout Wall Wi and Wall Nunpi.

In the outermost ring, the kids had been put to work. Wunda and her relatives worked to restore Yamina by using their earth-dancing to pack the hole with stone and hardened mud. Hemiah used his blessing to rapidly produce trees which were chopped down by a small squad of Hunters. Vinny and Montell used their blessing to make the logs light as a feather so they could carry them into the village as easily as Roaring could carry an armful of sticks.

When the lumber made it into the village, Danté Shoren arranged it into log houses. Normally, the Regiment would have required a team of at least ten men working all day for a week to build one nice cabin. But with Danté's gift, she could easily stand thrice the size as Lord Razzle. It took her three hours of labor to build her first cabin, carrying and piling logs like she was piling bricks.

Roaring stood at the edge of the worksite, watching in silent awe as the students worked tirelessly. Not long ago, those kids had been his classmates. Now they were helping him rebuild his own home. The Academy's report had said it would be a long project—months or even years—but as he took in all the hard work around him, the Grand Chief wasn't so sure anymore. If he were a betting man, he'd say the village had a chance at completion before winter arrived. Less than six months from now. It was a longshot, but he liked to think of himself as a man of faith.

"They're working hard," Ryko said, standing beside Roaring.

He nodded, hands on his hips. "I can't believe this."

"Neither can I. Think of how long this would have taken without Cross Academy's help."

"I don't want to think about it." Roaring chuckled.

"We could never repay them for this," Cat said.

"We're not asking for repayment."

Roaring turned to find Lord Razzle standing with a smile on his face. "I'm happy you found your way out here. The work is tough, but it will be worth it."

Roaring nodded. "How many log houses will Danté make?"

Ryko stepped forward. "That's what I wanted to discuss with you, Grand Chief. The outermost ring didn't have many buildings in this area—it was mostly shrubbery since the poorer villagers didn't have as many resources to build homes."

Roaring frowned and turned around, peering into the village. All his life, there had been three Walls in Wi, dividing the citizens as much as protecting them. The outer rings didn't have as much coin or as many resources as those in the inner rings. Roaring hadn't ever thought anything of it because he'd never known any other way of life. But after spending months in Babel, he realized things could be different. They *should* be different.

"We're not rebuilding the village exactly as it was before," he announced.

Ryko sounded confused. "Grand Chief?"

"Wall Yamina will be the only Wall in Wi from now on. We aren't repairing the other Walls—in fact, we're tearing them down."

Even Cat raised her brows in shock.

"Lord Chief," Ryko started, but Roaring raised a hand.

"That's my decision, Ryko. I'm not changing my mind on this."

"How will we separate the poorer classes from the inner ring villagers?"

A deep crease formed on Roaring's forehead as he scowled. He hated explaining himself. "We aren't separating the classes anymore. Anyone can have a home in any area of the village. So long as they can afford it."

"But… that would mean the outer ring villagers could save up and buy an inner ring home—they could buy up all the homes from the rightful inner ring families!" For some reason, he sounded panicked by this.

Roaring only smiled. "Good. That way I won't be holed up in the center of the village anymore." He jerked his chin at Danté who was setting the roof to a small cabin. "I could live out here, right beside the Walls I've sworn to protect."

"You would be *right there* if anything breached Yamina."

"Exactly." Roaring looked at Ryko seriously. "I can't lead the people into battle if I'm hiding behind them. I belong out here, Ryko. If you want to remain in the inner ring, then save up and buy a house there. But I'll be living out here. As close to Yamina as possible." He titled his head back to look up at the massive wall. "I want my home to be the first thing the villagers see when they return. I want them to know I'm here. I'm standing watch over them."

"How noble," Cat said sarcastically. "You're an amazing king."

King? Well, he supposed he wasn't a *Prince* of Fire anymore—not as the Grand Chief. It was time he stopped calling himself that already. *And* it was time he stopped dicing up the village into rings since the Walls wouldn't exist anymore.

"From now on, Wi will be broken into sectors. We'll name them after some of our fallen brethren," Roaring said with a nod. "I want the area around my cabin to be called the Wolf's Den. After my late father, Wolf Fire."

Although he clearly didn't like the Grand Chief's new plans for the village, Ryko couldn't stop himself from nodding reverently at the mention of Kifu Wolf's name. He had loved the Regiment leader as much as he'd loved his own father.

"That is a great name, Grand Chief," Ryko said softly. "He would be

350

proud of you."

Roaring laughed. "There is no doubt in that. My wonders lie in whether the former Grand Chief, Reign of Fire, would be proud."

"Our mother was a tough woman," Cat said.

"That she was."

"Grand Chief, if I may interrupt..." Lord Razzle stepped forward almost shyly, which was awkward to see—like watching a bear twiddle its fingers.

Roaring nodded. "Yes?"

"I wanted to have a word with you regarding my findings of the village."

"You said there was much to report last night," Roaring recalled.

"There is, but it'll be much easier to show you instead of telling you." He motioned behind him. "If you'll follow me, Captain Payne is waiting in the second ring."

"Of course," Roaring said.

The King of Fire left Ryko and Cat with a few ideas on the layout of the Wolf's Den. They weren't perfect, just a few cabins and a shack for the Regiment to meet, plus a training area and a check in/checkout station for coming and going villagers. He would need to sit down and sketch up a blueprint later, but his sister and his best friend seemed to have an idea of what he wanted. They both promised to direct Danté as best they could while Roaring was away.

It took thirty minutes for Razzle and Roaring to reach Captain Payne. She greeted both men with a nod.

"About that report," Roaring said carefully.

Razzle swallowed. "Yes. You can get the scope of the damage to the village just from looking around. What I have to report is something you must see with your own eyes."

Roaring looked puzzled but didn't raise any questions as Razzle turned to walk away. He followed the massive Priest in silence, heading into the dense shrubbery near a destroyed part of Wall Nunpi. The ground had been cracked and caved in near a toppling shack that'd once been a chop bar selling light soup and pounded yams. When Roaring was close enough, he realized there was a massive hole beside the shack—deep enough for him to fall into and die.

He frowned and stepped back. "Was this done during the attack?"

"Initially," Razzle answered, then he motioned to the side of the hole where Roaring noticed steps carved into the earth. "We did some excavating when we noticed the charged energy seeping out of the hole."

"Charged energy," he repeated.

Now Captain Payne stepped forward. "There's a storm of spiritual energy swirling inside that hole."

"What's it coming from?"

She shrugged. "That's what we've been trying to find out."

"Why haven't you gone down and looked?"

Captain Payne and Lord Razzle exchanged looks. "We tried," Razzle finally said. "But after about two miles of digging, we bumped into a big problem."

"What sort of problem?"

Instead of answering, Razzle turned and marched down the stairs and into the hole. Roaring followed.

They walked in a stiff silence; each step the Grand Chief took carried him deeper underground in the winding tunnel dug by the Academy soldiers. When the light began to fade, Roaring opened his palm and breathed a flame into his hand. He caught Captain Payne glancing over her shoulder at him as the fire crackled against his skin.

"Here," Razzle said, stopping.

Roaring walked up beside him. They were at the top of what looked like a cliff that dipped into the bowels of the cave. Nothing but darkness waited over the edge, summoning a storm of questions in the Grand Chief's head.

"I don't understand," he said quietly. His words echoed around the hollow chamber.

Razzle pointed below. "Look closer."

Roaring followed his finger, blinking into the inky shadows until he spotted something deeper below. A small splotch of orange glowing in the distance.

"What..." Roaring whispered, but as the word left his mouth, understanding burned through him. "Lava."

Captain Payne nodded. "The Village of Wi is sitting on a volcano."

He knew that. Almost everyone in Wi knew that.

As children, Roaring and his siblings had listened to their parents recount the legend of their tribe, how the First Flames had been sundancers so fierce, they had deliberately built their homes over a volcano just to demonstrate their power over it. It was said a mighty sunrider was born each time the volcano erupted—giant, winged beasts bursting from the lava and flames like fire formed into flesh. The greatest of the Flames had been strong enough to tame and ride the sunriders, sitting atop the creatures as one would sit on the very rays of the sun.

But that had only been a legend. A myth. A bedtime story at best.

At least that was what Roaring had always believed. But now that he was standing inside a volcano, staring at a splotch of molten lava, he had no idea what to believe.

"It seems the volcano has been inactive for hundreds of years," Lord Razzle said calmly. "But raging lava isn't what scares me. It's all the spiritual energy we can sense inside this place."

353

"It's concentrated deep inside the volcano, beneath the lava," Payne said, staring into the depths of darkness. "Something is alive down there. Something big."

"It might have been asleep for as long as the volcano has been inactive." Lord Razzle turned to Roaring. "But all the activity and rumbling from the attack on Wi seems to have woken it."

"*It...*" Roaring let the word hang in the air, echoing throughout the dark cavern.

"*It* could be anything. A horde of demons lurking underground. A buried Priest—"

"Still alive?" Roaring asked. "I learned about spiritual energy while training at the Academy. From my understanding, it is only present in living things."

"Your understanding is correct," Payne told him. "In most cases."

He tilted his head, and she explained, "There are some Priests so powerful, even their corpses give off spiritual energy."

"Like the Prophet Elisha," Lord Razzle said. "In the Book of Second Kings, a dead man was thrown into his tomb. As soon as his body touched Lord Elisha's bones, the dead man came back to life and stood on his feet."

Roaring chewed his lip, remembering the story from the Bible. Elisha had been one of his favorite Prophets. He had chosen to follow Elijah at a young age, leaving behind his family and friends to live a life that would require sacrifice. And when the time came for him to receive a blessing from his teacher, he hadn't asked for riches or honor. He had asked for a double portion—a large measure of the Holy Spirit to be poured over him. Instead of glory, Elisha had only wanted God to equip him for his journey ahead.

Roaring wanted the same. He had always felt haunted by the fact that the gift of fire had disappeared from his bloodline—or that *all* blessings had vanished from Wi for two-hundred years—but after living in Babel, he was certain they would return if the village dedicated itself to God once again, just as Cat had suggested the night before. The King of Fire wasn't sure what lay ahead on his new journey and his new responsibilities, but he knew he wanted God to be part of it.

That is my goal for as long as I wear the Veil, Roaring promised. *To put You first, God. And to inspire my people to do the same.*

"So, what happens now?" the Grand Chief asked.

The Priest took a deep breath. "Now you decide if you want to rebuild your village over this volcano and the creature living inside."

The First Flames had conquered the volcano and had managed to tame it whenever it erupted. But Roaring was only one sundancer. He was strong. But not strong enough to control a raging volcano.

"Is the volcano active?" he asked.

Lord Razzle pressed his lips together. "I don't think so. But every time the spiritual energy stirs, the lava rises. My guess is that the volcano will erupt when whatever's inside is ready to leave."

He nodded. "I came back to rebuild what was lost. But now I'm not sure if that's possible."

What was he supposed to do? Build his home on top of an unpredictable volcano with a monster living inside? But returning to Babel wasn't an option. He had come all this way. He wouldn't turn back now—not after defying tradition and becoming the first male Grand Chief of Wi. His first order could not be a failure, or the rest of his reign would be ruined.

"How big is the volcano?" Roaring asked. The First Flames had built their homes over it, but the Village of Wi was three times the size it'd been when they'd first settled down centuries ago. Maybe they could rebuild around the volcano—their numbers had dwindled since the attack; they didn't need all the space they had.

355

Razzle gave him a thoughtful look. "It's about half the size of the second ring."

That wasn't so bad. Maybe he could work around this.

Lord Razzle patted him on the back. "You have a lot of thinking to do, Grand Chief. I wouldn't make any quick decisions."

But he had to make a decision soon. There were people rebuilding and constructing throughout the village that very moment.

Roaring sucked in a lungful of air. "I'll talk with the Council about it."

The Council was not pleased with the news. Even Ryko looked disheartened as he stared into his bowl of rice and charred boar. Beside him, Kifa Thunder rubbed her chin.

"We cannot stay in Babel, but we cannot live over an active volcano, either."

Kifu Kato leaned forward, placing a hand on each knee as he sat cross-legged on the floor. "The volcano *isn't* active."

"But something is alive inside of it," Lady Ina said. "It could cause an eruption at any given moment."

"Or it could remain dormant for the next five-hundred years," he snapped.

"Is that a chance you're willing to take, Roaring?" Cat reached up and touched his shoulder.

He flinched at the coolness of her small hand. "It is. But this isn't about what I'm willing to do. It's about the village. Can we really rebuild and allow our brethren to move back into Wi knowing there is an unpredictable volcano beneath their feet? Could we live with ourselves if we kept that a secret and then it erupted?"

"We don't have to keep it a secret," Thunder suggested.

The room fell quiet. They had gathered in Roaring's personal tent since it was the only one large enough to hold them all.

Roaring nodded slowly. "I agree with Kifa Thunder. We could tell the villagers—"

"You want to let the villagers know they'll be living over a volcano?" Kato said hotly. "Nephew, I thought you were smarter than that."

"Careful, Nuncle, I might be your kin, but I am still your Grand Chief, and you will treat me as such."

Kato leaned back on his cushion, his eyes filling with resentment as he worked his jaw. "My apologies, *Grand Chief.*"

"I don't want to cause panic amongst the villagers," Roaring went on, "but I will not keep a secret like this from them. I want to be upfront."

Cat nodded beside him. "We can tell the villagers the truth. That way, anyone who decides to move back to Wi will know exactly what they're getting into and will be prepared. Anyone who doesn't feel safe can stay in Babel until we've solved this problem or until they feel comfortable coming home."

"That sounds agreeable." Ryko nodded along with Lady Ina.

"Shall we vote?" Roaring asked.

"That's hardly necessary, Grand Chief," said Thunder. "Kifu Kato is obviously the only one who disagrees. And he is outnumbered."

Roaring couldn't argue with that, so he dismissed the councilmembers with a flick of his wrist. They filed out one by one, even Cat left with Chava following behind, but Kifu Kato stuck around.

The Grand Chief wanted to sigh when he noticed his uncle lingering by the tent entrance. He was scowling, like usual, but there was a hint of concern etched between his drawn brows.

"Nephew," he said when Roaring approached. "I have something else to discuss with you."

"Should I call the Council back?"

He shook his head. "This is a personal matter."

He frowned.

Kato stepped closer. "Rebuilding the village is our top priority, but there is another important issue that must be solved quickly."

Roaring blinked at him.

"As the Grand Chief and the only sundancer in the village, you need to produce an heir to the Flaming Veil."

Roaring took a deep breath. "I'm not ready to produce an heir." He couldn't stop himself from thinking of Marlo Jo. He certainly had feelings for her, but neither of them had the time for love. Neither of them knew when they ever would.

Kato rolled his eyes. "You need to have an heir on the way before the reconstruction is complete. I thought you would be happy about this."

"I'm too busy for a wife."

"Who said you'd have to make time for one? You just have to put a child in her." His uncle nudged him with his elbow, a lecherous smile slithering across his face now. "That's the fun part."

Roaring didn't laugh at his terrible joke, which made Kato's stupid smile wither on his face. "You've never had a woman, have you?"

He let out a longsuffering sigh. "Not that it's any of your business, but I've had plenty of women, Nuncle."

He wasn't proud of it. There had been a time when Roaring would join Ryko and other Regiment Hunters on trips to outer ring taverns to find pretty young girls who would trade their bodies for a few coins. Roaring remembered rolling around in a maintenance shed with a girl whose name he couldn't recall now. She had been his favorite until she'd asked him if he would marry her since he had broken her virtue.

"I've never laid with anyone else but you, my prince," she had said with an innocent look in her eyes. "I can't have any other man now. No one will marry me if they find out about … this." Her eyes had flickered through the shed, landing on each piece of their discarded clothing.

Roaring had stared at her in horror. He'd had no idea she'd been a virgin when he'd met her, or that she hadn't enjoyed other men since he'd picked her up. They had been meeting a few times a week for months but marrying her had been out of the question—his mother would have had him ousted from the village before she let him marry an outer ring girl. Let alone a prostitute. But the weight of what Roaring had done—of what he had been doing for months—had hit him hard that day.

He never touched that girl again. Or any other woman since.

Not until marriage, he reminded himself. *Like I should have done in the first place.* He remembered the scripture Chief Ramah had given him days before, *Don't let anyone think less of you because you are young. Be an example to all Believers in what you say, in the way you live, in your love, your faith, and your* **purity**, I Timothy 4:12. Roaring sighed internally. He had always demonstrated love toward his precious little sisters. He had learned the importance of faith at Cross Academy. But he hadn't been a great example of purity. *Not at all*, Roaring frowned. But he had done his due diligence once he'd realized his mistake. He'd repented and asked God for forgiveness and had promised he would never take his purity for granted again.

Two years later, he still hadn't broken that promise, patiently waiting until he could enjoy a woman's warmth yet again. But now that the chance for such enjoyment was right there in front of him, he couldn't get himself to grab it.

It didn't feel right. Marrying just for the sake of producing an heir.

Roaring shook his head. "I don't want to get married right now, Kifu Kato."

"Don't be stubborn—"

"I'm not being stubborn," he said angrily. "We are rebuilding our village, trying to figure out what to do about the volcano beneath it, and praying we don't start a panic—or accidentally cause an eruption. And in the middle of all this, you want me to find a woman?" Roaring opened the flap to his tent. "I have bigger things to worry about."

Kifu Kato followed him out. "But what about the heir?"

"I name Cat Fire as my heir," he said without hesitation. "Until I have a child of my own, Cat will be considered my successor. If something should happen to me before fathering children, she will wear the Veil in my stead." Roaring looked back at his uncle. "How's that?"

He fumbled for words. "I—well—I suppose that is fine."

It would have to be.

"Good."

34

Fox Fire

This isn't fair. Fox Fire huffed as she packed the last of her things and slung her sack over her shoulder. After Lieutenant Diaz got back on his feet, he announced he would be breaking up the caravan into smaller groups to draw less attention. Fox thought for sure she would be assigned to KI's group, but Diaz had told her that wasn't the plan.

I'm his best friend, she ground her teeth together, anger rising as she mulled over the lieutenant's words.

"That's the very reason why you shouldn't be on his squad," Diaz had said. "Because the enemy will be expecting you two to be together."

So she had been assigned to a separate squad—the decoy squad—to purposely draw the enemy's attention while KI slipped away with another team.

It was a solid plan, Fox had to admit, but she hated being so far away from the action. She hated being so far away from KI. Diaz didn't know how much of him had changed in the last few weeks. He didn't know how close he was to slipping.

Fox left her tent and began breaking it down, ignoring the squawking of the giant birds overhead. They were further north than she had ever been, beyond the Kanen Forest and outside the protection of Babel.

This was uncharted territory for the sundancer, and while that sent excitement zinging through her body, it also filled her with anxiety. The Region of the Lion was big, but the Region of Ice was enormous—as large as the other three Regions combined. And totally frozen.

They hadn't reached the Region of Ice just yet, but it was obvious they were getting close. Fox could feel the chill of the breeze brushing against her skin, making the flesh of her arms pebble with goosebumps. She could feel the subtle cold wrapping its arms around her, cooling her down to her bones. Her body shivered during the day and her teeth chattered at night, but she refused to complain. This was for KI, for her best friend. There was no backing out now.

When her tent was finished, Fox knelt and stuffed it into her rucksack, then she checked to make sure her Ammaron rods were secured at her hip. She held them up, one in each hand, and issued a mental command. *Bracelets.* Her Light energy stirred as it responded, pouring into the rods, and shifting them into the jewelry she wanted.

The bracelets weren't normal ones meant for decoration. The one on her right wrist was made of flint while the one on her left was made of steel. When she struck them together, they created a spark for her to ignite and make flames for her sundancing. She'd used that tactic when the Moon witches had summoned the horde of demons. Kohl, KI, and Kressa had fought fearlessly by her side. Even Talon had joined in, using twin daggers to stab and hack at her enemies. She didn't take down as many darklings as the rest of the group, but she had held her own without question.

Fox smiled, feeling proud of her older sister. Shock and worry had plagued her when she'd found out Talon had been tapped to join the mission. Fox had thought she would be stuck trying to protect KI *and* Talon while travelling. But her sister had proved to be everything but a burden. She'd made crucifixes for Fox and her classmates, to offer extra

362

protection since they were just students and not hardened soldiers like Diaz or Izzy or Lieutenant Raven. And she had offered prayers on Hope's behalf when the young girl grew tired from cloaking KI for hours on end. That was the very reason she'd been assigned to KI's squad for this phase of the mission.

Talon, Hope, Kohl, and Kressa were all together with KI. Hope kept him cloaked while Talon prayed to keep the girl's strength at its peak. Meanwhile, Kohl and Kressa were his guards; both students had battled the Red Face one-on-one and had witnessed Hosenké's power when he'd attacked. They weren't as experienced as some of the Hunters or Priests, but Diaz had feared placing someone powerful like Izzy on KI's squad would be a dead giveaway that the boy was there being protected by a strong guardian.

Travelling with lower ranked fighters would allow their squad to move undetected for longer periods. The plan was to travel separately for three days and then meet at designated locations to regroup or swap members on certain squads. Fox had spent her first two days travelling with Lieutenant Diaz, Dart, Lady Vehenort, and two Priests she didn't know. On the third day, she was swapped with Syren to travel with Lord Izzy.

She glanced over at the young Priest now, watching him slide a pair of white gloves onto his hands. They were pale compared to the suntanned skin of his face and neck. She wondered how ghostly he looked beneath his floor-sweeping cassock—*even more amazing is how he manages to fight in that thing*, Fox pondered.

A shiver crawled down her neck as she remembered the two spirits he'd summoned to fight the Moon witches. The sight of the coffins had been enough to scare her hair white, and then the coffins had *opened*, and two mystic beings had stepped out. It was incredible. It was terrifying. It had taken Fox's breath away. To think a single person could be so strong.

Thank God Izzy's on our side.

He looked over at her, the cross in his forehead reflecting the sunlight for a moment. "Ready to go?" he asked.

She smiled and nodded. It was awkward travelling alone with Lord Izzy, but at least he was nice. He didn't speak much, but he didn't have to. He was an excellent guide and whenever he asked for her opinion on which direction they should go, he made it seem like he genuinely appreciated her input. She had led them in a circle twice yesterday, but he'd only laughed and patted her shoulder.

"It's a learning experience," he'd said. And then he'd pulled out a map of the area and pointed out all the different landmarks. When it was time for dinner, he'd let Fox have the map.

"I've got it memorized."

She spent the night huddled beside a candle with it clutched in her hands, trying to memorize it too.

Izzy walked over and passed her a strip of jerky. "We've got a lot of ground to cover but if we make it to the next village before sundown, we might be able to find a room for the night."

Fox's face lit up as she gnawed on her dried meat. Lieutenant Diaz had instructed them to keep a low profile, but she wasn't about to stop Izzy from booking them a room to sleep in. She was tired of rolling out a blanket on the hard ground.

The boyish Priest grinned. "Avanté Village is the closest one to us. I've been there twice before—there's a little hub with amazing banana bread and sweet milk." His eyes filled with awe. "And berry pie and chocolate cakes—the kind you cook in a pan and smother with maple syrup."

Fox's smirk went from excited to goofy. *I never knew Lord Izzy had a sweet tooth.* She was glad he did, otherwise they'd be eating jerky and nuts

364

for dinner again.

They walked together until late afternoon. Izzy kept a tough pace, but Fox didn't mind. Thoughts of sweet milk and chocolate pancakes kept her fueled and ready to go. Sometimes Izzy spoke just to fill the silence and sometimes he sang hymns to Jesus so beautifully, even the birds overhead sang back in cheerful, melodic whistles. By the time the evening rolled around, sweat had soaked through Fox's shirt and had even matted Izzy's hair, despite the chill in the air. Blonde strands stuck to his forehead and his neck, she watched with a smirk every time he stopped to adjust the collar of his thick robes.

"Almost there," he'd told her when they'd stopped to fill their waterskins in a pond. Fox had only nodded but she couldn't stop herself from glancing westward, her amber eyes tracing the sky as she anticipated the sunset.

She didn't have to worry for long. Izzy had surprised even himself when he'd pushed through a thicket and came face to face with the front gates of Avanté Village. Rejuvenated by the sight of the village, Fox and Izzy made their way through the settlement toward the little inn the young Priest had mentioned before. He bought them both a plate of chocolate chip pancakes and a mug of sweet milk to wash it down.

Fox couldn't believe what she was eating. She had never tasted chocolate before, had never even heard of a pancake—not even in Babel. Her plate was piled high with flat little discs of sweet bread dotted with chunks of chocolate. At first, Fox thought the pancakes looked crude and unappetizing. The chocolate was goopy and melting into the bread, the pancakes themselves were warm but seemed so odd to her. What was the point in flat bread if you couldn't use it to wrap up meat?

Then she'd tasted it and her heart sang. She had almost stood on top

365

of the splintered wooden table and shouted praises to the Lord, but she controlled herself and remained seated. Besides, how could she stuff herself full of chocolate pancakes if she stopped to sing at the top of her lungs?

Izzy had laughed when her eyes had grown wide on her first bite. He'd ended up buying her two more plates and another mug of sweet milk. The milk had been iced so it was freezing cold and had the twang of honey in its aftertaste. That was, perhaps, the most delicious meal Fox Fire had ever eaten. She reminded herself to ask Cat to make pancakes for her when she returned to Babel. Then her mood grew sour when she remembered Cat wouldn't be in Babel when she made it back. *And*, Fox glowered as she set her rucksack down by her bed now, *I may not even make it back to Babel.*

She pushed her negative thoughts aside and knelt before her bed to say her prayers. It had been a long day and all the food was making her eyelids heavy. Lord Izzy had gotten them one room with two beds so they wouldn't be far apart. They stayed in the back of the inn, sharing a dingey room with smelly candles and creaky beds but Fox wouldn't complain. She wouldn't have even cared if the beds were infested with fleas—she was so tired and so sick of sleeping on the ground.

"Thank You, Lord Jesus, for the great meal," she prayed aloud. "Thank You for keeping me safe—and Lord Izzy, too. Bless us to meet up with the other squads tomorrow. And bless KI to be okay. In Jesus' Name, amen."

Lord Izzy was smiling at her when she stood and threw her covers back. "That was a sweet prayer, child."

She wrinkled her nose. "Child? You're not much older than me, Lord Izzy. Just much more powerful."

He laughed with his head tilted back. "I'm older than you think."

She didn't care. Today had been a day full of travel and tomorrow

366

they would meet up with another squad and swap members again. For now, Fox just wanted to sleep and dream and snore until morning.

She climbed into her rickety bed and sighed as her head sank into the old pillow. She hadn't even bothered to change into her sleeping clothes. There was no need when she was this tired and this full. Before she could count to five, she had drifted into a deep sleep.

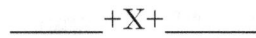

The sun was harshly bright despite the chill outside. Fox frowned at the light as it shined right onto her face. When she peeled her lids back, a painful groan slipped from her lips.

She heard Izzy laugh across the room. "Wake up, Fox. We've got to be on the other side of the village in less than an hour."

She wanted to roll over and sleep until the afternoon, but thoughts of seeing KI in an hour sent a surge of energy through her body. Fox sat up and threw her holey blanket back, stretched her limbs until her back popped, and then trudged to the basin on the desk in the corner. The water inside was warm and clear—either Lord Izzy hadn't used it, or he'd had it refilled for her.

Fox glanced over her shoulder at the young Priest. He was studying a book from the slanted shelf at the window. When he looked up and noticed her gaze, he blushed and turned his back to her.

Fox hesitated. She could ask him to leave, but she didn't want him to be too far. She had never been away from Wi or Babel, the thought of being alone in another village—even for just a few moments—sent a stab of fear through her chest. *I'll just wash my face*, she told herself.

She scrubbed her face with the soap from her own supplies and then chewed a mint leaf. When she finished, she cleared her throat, but Lord Izzy still didn't turn around. He leaned forward and opened the window to poke his head out.

"What a village. It's so nice here, I wish I could stay for a few weeks."

Fox hadn't looked around much when they'd walked through, she'd been too tired yesterday to do anything except eat and sleep. But she nodded anyway and moved to the polished mirror to pull her hair back into a curly ponytail.

Izzy turned around finally. "It's a beautiful day, isn't it?"

"Yes, it is," said a deep voice across the room.

Fox's heart stopped and she turned, very slowly, to find Izzy standing in front of the open window. Her breath caught in her throat, but not because there was a man at the window—she couldn't breathe because of the look on Izzy's face.

Utter shock.

Lord Izzy, the man who had summoned the spirit of death to fight at his command, had been caught off guard. There was a man standing right outside his window, and he hadn't seen or heard or sensed him coming.

Fox's wide eyes moved from Izzy to the man at the window. She had not seen him before, but a sense of recognition bloomed somewhere in the back of her head. *A striking man with hair like fire and a face calm like still water...* She had heard that description, but she couldn't remember where. Not that it mattered much right now.

As remarkable as the man's hair and face were, the inverted cross in the center of his forehead stole most of Fox's attention. He smiled at her as he leaned into the window, then his eyes slid over to Izzy.

"Good morning," he said, and his voice was smooth and silky and deeper than she would have expected from such a charming face.

Izzy turned around stiffly, but he didn't speak. Fox could feel the

368

shift in the air, could feel the sudden charge of spiritual energy growing around her. And like watching the hairs on a cat's back rise in aggression, Izzy's shoulders seemed to tense as he stood a little taller and faced the demon man head-on.

"How did you find me?" he asked in a voice that walked the very edge of calm, teetering the line of rage.

The man sighed. "I will always be able to find you, Israel."

Fox's ears perked. *Israel?* She had never heard anyone call him that—it'd only ever been Lord Izzy. She looked back at the two men, staring each other down. Their demeanor toward each other was charged with animosity, but there was no mistaking they were familiar with one another. *How* familiar was the question—but before Fox could guess at an answer, the smiling man was talking again.

"The Nine sent me to kill you," he said to Izzy. "I'm supposed to do it quietly."

He had walked right up to Izzy's bedroom window and announced he was there to assassinate him—there was nothing quiet about that at all.

Movement drew Fox's gaze. The man reached into his red cloak and pulled out a scroll. At the same time, Izzy shifted to run, but the man was faster than he looked. His armed whipped out and caught the young Priest by his collar, yanking him out the window and into his arms.

Fox screamed and ran forward, but she didn't get more than two steps before the man tossed the scroll through the window. The moment it hit the wooden floor; darkness exploded into the room.

Fox could not see. She could not hear. She could barely breathe—but that was mostly because of her mounting fear. Everything around her was black, she wasn't even sure if her eyes were open or closed.

I've got to get out of here! she told herself. She struck her bracelets together and felt a flame come alive in her palm, but it brought her no light. *This darkness isn't normal...* Fox got on her hands and knees and began to crawl toward the direction of the window. The red-haired man had tossed a scroll inside, that had to be what'd summoned the shadows.

Her hand brushed against something cylindrical and papery—Fox clutched it and used her bracelets to summon a flame again, hoping to burn up the scroll, but nothing happened. She could feel the heat of the fire in her hand, but she could also tell it wasn't burning up the parchment. Frustrated, Fox closed her hand to snuff out the flame and resorted to just tearing up the scroll.

The room immediately brightened.

She blinked at the scroll. "He used this to summon the darkness."

Fox turned the little roll of paper over in her hands, examining it closely. There were words written on the inside when she unrolled it, all of them were in the Old Tongue. Fox hadn't paid much attention to her classes when she'd lived in Wi, but she could recognize enough words to understand the writing was a curse. One that summoned darkness. She remembered a woman on her first day of training, she had taken down Fox's information by whispering into parchment—Fox's name and height and weight had appeared on the paper as if the woman had written it with ink and quill.

Questions swirled in Fox's mind. *What if that blessing could be used to whisper curses onto scrolls?* The roll of paper would become its own weapon. The curse would be activated when the scroll was opened, but easily destroyed when the scroll was torn. It was a very tactical, inconspicuous way of fighting.

But Fox didn't have time to be impressed. Lord Izzy was missing— snatched out of the window by the red-haired man. She had no idea where he'd been taken, but she didn't have to wonder for long. As Fox unrolled the scroll further, she saw what looked like a map marked with a red IX.

Of course Fox had to wonder why the red-haired man had left her a way to find his location, but she decided the reason didn't matter. He'd kidnapped Lord Izzy after announcing he was there to kill him. Fox had to go after him.

Thankfully, she had memorized the map Izzy had given her in the woods. She knew the marked spot on the scroll was outside the village and that it was far—in the opposite direction of where she was supposed to meet up with the other squads to swap members.

The others might have been attacked as well, Fox realized. She hissed through her teeth as she grabbed her rucksack and climbed out her window. There was no time to think this over. Even if they had been attacked, KI was with Kohl and Kressa and Talon—he was on a formidable team that would keep him safe. But Lord Izzy wasn't.

Jesus, Fox prayed, taking off toward the village gates, *please give my friends the strength to protect KI. And give me the strength to protect Lord Izzy.*

35

Israel

Izzy blew his golden blonde bangs from his eyes and tried to sit up. It was a struggle with his hands tied behind his back and his feet knotted together with a thick rope. Every little movement made the ropes brush against his skin, almost burning with the friction.

The last thing he remembered was seeing a Birth of Carnage at his window. He silently scolded himself. *I should have sensed his presence long before I saw him.* But he hadn't. He hadn't even been able to react when he did finally turn and find the red-haired man smiling down at him. There was no shame in his mistake, he'd been face to face with the Thirdborn, after all.

But still…

Izzy grunted and rolled onto his side, flopping like an inchworm as he tried to sit up without using his hands or feet. The room was dark, and the floor was hard and cold, it didn't take much investigation to realize he was in a cave of some sort. The smell of dirt and moss and sweaty vines filled his nose as he took a deep breath and finally sat upright. The room tilted as he shifted his position and he blinked into the darkness around him. A tall figure came into focus, hidden in the shadows on the other side of the cave. Izzy didn't have to wonder who it was.

"You're awake," said a smooth voice from the darkness. It seemed to echo longer than it should have, bouncing off the cave walls and filling the small area.

Izzy glared ahead. "These ropes won't hold me—"

"Yes, they will. They are woven by cursed thread, binding you with a spell that disrupts the flow of your spiritual energy." He paused, as if to let that sink in. "You are spellbound."

Izzy gulped. If he couldn't use his spiritual energy, then he was nothing more than a stony nobody sitting before a demon king. He squeezed his eyes shut and tried to pray, *Dear God*—a searing ache flared at his temples, and he cried out in pain.

The figure across the room chuckled. "The ropes block your prayers, too." His red hair glowed as he stepped into the light. It cast a spotlight on his face, pearly smooth skin and calm eyes that danced with flecks of gold. His nose was angular, fitting for his strong jaw and full lips which curved into a smile as his gaze landed on the young Priest. "Did you think I wouldn't come prepared to deal with you, little brother?"

Izzy's glare darkened. Seganamé had never let him forget exactly who his enemy truly was. A hateful reminder that the anchor of the Nine was his very own kin.

Elsa Attra had said there was darkness in his bloodline. Seganamé's sin was so potent, she'd been able to sense it merely through Izzy's raw hatred toward him.

"I thought you came to kill me, not tie me up and talk," Izzy said.

"It's not time to kill you." He turned and stared at the wall, like he was looking *through* it. "Soon, Israel. Very soon."

Izzy wanted to scream. No one except Seganamé ever used his real name—there wasn't anyone alive who remembered it. He should have been happy to have someone old enough to know it—and cared enough

373

to use. But every time the Thirdborn said it, Izzy felt like he was whispering a curse.

"What about the girl?" Izzy asked, wincing as the ropes rubbed against his wrists and chafed his skin.

"I left her."

"That was a mistake," Izzy said with a smile. "She'll come after me no matter what. She's a tough girl."

"I know that," Seganamé said plainly. He finally peeled his gaze from the wall to look at his brother. "I made sure she would be able to find you."

"I don't understand."

Seganamé sighed. "The ropes aren't just binding you; they are draining your spiritual energy. You will need someone to help you when I leave." Seganamé stepped closer and stared down at him as he explained, "My task is to assassinate you, but not because you're on the Nine's hitlist—they want you dead because you intervened last time. We cannot have that again."

Izzy squinted in thought, forehead wrinkling. *He's talking about Hosenké and the Kanen Forest.*

"But I'm not ready to kill you yet, so I'm holding you here until my brothers and sisters accomplish their goal."

Brothers and sisters, Izzy had to stop himself from rolling his eyes. The only brother Seganamé had was tied up in front of him, and he'd come to kill him.

"Taking me out of the fight will not be enough," Izzy said. "My comrades are all just as strong as I am."

"No, they're not."

Seganamé turned and walked back to the other side of the cave. He sank into the comfy-looking folds of his large red cloak. With the thick cowl of his robes covering his face from the nose down, all Izzy could see was his bored eyes. He closed them and his head sagged to the side. A deep breath filled the air, and Seganamé tucked his hands into his long sleeves.

Izzy couldn't believe what he was seeing. *Is he ... sleeping?* he wondered, but his brother quickly corrected him like he'd just read his thoughts.

"I'm meditating."

Of course, he grumbled inside.

"If you're not going to kill me, then answer my question," Izzy demanded.

Seganamé didn't open his eyes as he said calmly, "Ask."

"Is there a second Red Face?"

A slight smirk tugged at his brother's lips. "Yes and no."

"That isn't an answer—"

"I'm not going to feed you information on the Nine. You should know that, Israel."

He huffed and blew fruitlessly at his sticky bangs. "It doesn't matter anyway. The Nine will not beat the Cross. God is on our side."

Seganamé's eyes flew open—and for the first time, they weren't calm and bored-looking. They were filled with rage. The wall beside him splintered with cracks as he released a sudden charge of Dark energy. It was the closest Izzy had ever seen him to losing his temper.

"Your God doesn't scare me."

"*Your God,*" Izzy mocked. "He is *everyone's* God. And you will bow to Him one day, whether you want to or not."

Seganamé sighed deeply. "When the time comes, I will do what needs to be done."

Izzy looked away and tried to pray again. *God*—another sharp pain bolted through his head, burning at his temples until he gasped and fell over. He squeezed his eyes shut against the sudden ache; when it finally

375

subsided, he looked up to find Seganamé staring down at him.

He shook his head like he was disappointed. "I warned you about praying."

Izzy wasn't surprised his brother had taken precautions. *The prayer of a righteous person is powerful and effective,* he remembered his Bible well—even though the very thought of it sent a ripple of dizzying pain through his body and into his head again. But Izzy knew the Word was right. Seganamé's cursed ropes were proof of that. Otherwise, he wouldn't have bothered binding Izzy at all. Prayers had the power to weaken darklings, it was every Christian's first line of offense and defense—even Christians without blessings could defend themselves using prayer. But as long as Izzy was spellbound, he couldn't even begin to pray without getting punished for it.

Seganamé said, "I cursed those ropes myself. Dark energy is activated whenever you attempt to pray. Each time you try, the pain will intensify … until it kills you." He shrugged. "Or until you stop trying to pray."

Izzy desperately wished he could free himself and kill his brother. It wasn't a very Christian thought, but his brother was not a very reasonable man—he was barely a man at all anymore. The inverted cross on his forehead marked him as more than just a 'sinner,' he was an ally of Satan. Someone who had willingly accepted the devil's power in exchange for a great sacrifice.

Izzy ground his teeth together. He had witnessed that sacrifice with his own eyes, had heard the screams of his own mother, and had watched as Seganamé had smiled down at her writhing form. Proud to offer her to Satan. He would never forget the moment the dark sign appeared on his brother's flesh, making it known to the world which side he had chosen in this spiritual war.

They had been enemies ever since.

"Here is something I can tell you, Israel." Izzy looked up to see his brother looking right at him. He gave a slow blink as he murmured, "The witches who attacked you—"

"The Moon Coven."

"Yes. Their lair is near a small village called Autumn, in the Region of Smoke and Ash."

Izzy's bright eyes widened. "Why are you telling me this?"

"Because I know you will find them and kill them."

"You could just go kill them yourself."

"We have shed enough of their blood." Seganamé looked away. "The dark spirits are displeased with the Nine's carelessness."

Izzy quirked an eyebrow.

"The Moon Coven might have betrayed us, but they are still emissaries of Satan. We are not allowed to mistreat them unnecessarily."

Izzy could have asked about the betrayal of the witches and how they'd tried to capture KI for themselves, but he truly wasn't interested in the fine details. He had a location of the coven's hideout. He wouldn't question it at all.

Seganamé suddenly snapped his head toward the back wall of the cave. His eyes glazed over, and he muttered to himself, then the stone walls and the concrete floor began to shimmy and dissipate.

Izzy blinked and when he looked around again, the cave was gone, and he realized he was sitting in the forest outside the Village of Avanté. *The cave was an illusion*, he exhaled slowly. If he weren't spellbound, he would have realized that the moment he'd first awakened, but he refused to dwell on his captivity.

"It's time for me to go," his brother announced, then he smiled as the bushes nearby rustled, and Fox Fire stepped through.

She was out of breath and there were dried leaves tangled in her curly hair, fallen loose from her ponytail as she'd dashed through the trees. Amber eyes were filled with rage as they locked on the Thirdborn. Fox

377

raised her fists without hesitation; there was a *clink* as she struck them together, and then her hands went up in flames.

"Let him go!" she shouted angrily.

Seganamé very calmly waved a hand at her. "Worry not, child. I didn't hurt your precious Priest." He returned his gaze to Izzy. "Remember that I chose not to kill you. Remember the information I gave you. Remember my mercy."

Izzy shifted uncomfortably.

"Nothing is free in this world, little brother." Seganamé held up a palm and a black portal opened beside him. "I will come for payment one day."

Fox Fire didn't move as the red-haired man stepped through the dark hole and disappeared, but Izzy knew she was not frozen out of fear. The open-mouthed look on her face—the way her eyes wildly danced around, glancing between the dissipating portal and the young Priest—he realized she was frozen out of shock.

Izzy didn't blame her. She had heard a lot in very few words. Seganamé had appeared outside his window, announced he was there to kill him, yet had returned him unscathed. He had called him by his real name and had referred to him as 'little brother.' He'd even mentioned his mercy and the information he'd voluntarily surrendered.

Fox knew a lot more than she needed to know, but she wisely chose to ignore her shock and instead focused on freeing him. Using her rods, she created a blade to hack at the ropes that bound him. When the cursed ties fell from Izzy's hands and feet, Izzy felt a wave of exhaustion wash over him from head to toe. He gasped as he tried to stand and realized he was too weak. He had lost far too much spiritual energy, more than he'd realized.

Fox was there to assist, bracing him against her and placing one of his arms over her shoulders. She grunted as she began a slow march

378

toward Avanté Village.

"We're going back," Izzy said groggily.

He felt her nod beside him. "I heard explosions as I made my way through the woods. Something is happening."

"They've been attacked," Izzy mumbled. Seganamé had told him as much when he'd confessed he was only holding him until his brothers and sisters accomplished their goal. There was no guess as to what that goal was—the same goal it'd always been since the Village of Wi had been destroyed.

"We're going to help," Fox said firmly.

"It's a long walk."

She nodded and took a few heavy breaths. "That gives us time to talk."

"You've got questions."

"Do you have answers?" she asked.

He was exhausted—drained of almost all his spiritual energy, fighting just to stay conscious. But he wouldn't rob his rescuer of the truth. *Besides*, he decided tiredly, *it'll be nice to finally talk. To finally share the secrets that haunt me.*

36

Fox Fire

Fox Fire tried to keep her breathing steady as she held onto Izzy and marched down the hillside toward Avanté Village. He hadn't spoken much since the red-haired man had left, but he had promised Fox he would answer any question she asked. She just couldn't think of what to say, or how to say it.

So much had happened in such a short time, after such little interaction. Fox hadn't known Lord Izzy very well, hadn't even been in the same room as him more than a handful of occasions. But she suddenly felt like she knew more about him than even the likes of Lieutenant Diaz.

"The red-haired man," she said slowly.

Izzy grunted as he limped beside her.

"He was one of the Nine, right?"

He nodded. "They always wear the inverted cross and the IX symbol somewhere on their attire. Once you're strong enough, you'll be able to discern their Dark energy signatures. Then you can sense them even in a crowd of people."

"But you hadn't sensed him," she said quietly.

Izzy panted, grimacing as she adjusted her grip on him. "I hadn't."

"Was he cloaking himself?"

"Likely. Seganamé is certainly powerful enough to cast a spell that would hide his presence. Even from me."

"*Seh-guh-nah-may*," she repeated slowly.

Izzy smiled despite his pain and exhaustion. Fox could see the red bruises on his wrists as she shifted her shoulder to carry more of his weight. The wide sleeves of his cassock slipped up further to reveal burns and scars—*those aren't from the red-haired man*, she noted.

"That's his name. Seganamé."

"I didn't know the Nine had names," Fox confessed. Then again, until joining the Academy, Fox didn't even know demons could take on human form. Unless Seganamé and the rest of the Nine *were* humans, instead of merely 'human-shaped.' The red-haired man had seemed to know Izzy. He'd called him a different name and had even referred to him as 'little brother.'

She looked at the worn Priest. "You two know each other." It wasn't a question.

Izzy nodded slowly. "He's my older brother."

"But how? He's got to be *old*." If she remembered correctly, Lord Izzy had grown up in Babel—side by side with Lieutenant Diaz. They had met in the city orphanage and kept in touch even after Diaz was adopted by Major Marshall. They'd even entered the Academy together, along with Second Lieutenant Kotaro.

Izzy let out a long sigh, like he was trying not to fall asleep. *Those cursed ropes must have drained him dry*, Fox remarked.

Izzy took another deep breath. "I'm just as old as my brother."

"I don't understand."

"It's our blessing. Longevity."

"You age slowly," she guessed, but he shook his head.

"I age the same as everyone else."

381

"Then how?"

Izzy smiled. "When I turn fifty, my internal clock is switched, and I begin to age backwards. When I reach infancy, the clock is switched again, and I'll age back up to fifty. Over and over until I die."

Fox stared at the side of Izzy's face; she hadn't even realized she'd stopped walking until he gently tugged her forward. "Don't stop now, we're not far."

She looked ahead. The Priest was right, they were less than a mile from the village—Fox just hoped they would get there in time to help out her friends. She'd heard the explosions as she'd made her way through the woods to find Lord Izzy but had made the difficult decision to keep going. Now she was heading back into Avanté, right toward the danger.

"So, longevity…" Fox said slowly.

"It's an interesting blessing."

"When will you die?"

He thought a moment. "I guess when someone kills me."

"And Seganamé?"

His voice grew dark. "When I kill him."

"You want to kill your own brother."

"I do. It's the only thing I have ever wanted in this life."

"How long has your life been?"

Silence.

"I don't know. I was born before the Great Demon War began; I stopped counting the years after six-hundred or so."

She gaped at him. he'd stopped counting after *six-hundred*. And he was born *before* the War. *It's been raging for over seven-hundred fifty years*, Fox thought in awe, then she gasped and dared a look at her companion. "Seganamé called you Israel…"

He nodded.

"And you've been alive for almost a thousand years."

He nodded again.

"Are you ... *that* Israel?"

Izzy laughed and shook his head like he'd gotten that question before. "No. Israel is just the name I chose when I became a Priest." He glowered and mumbled, "For the third time."

Fox raised an eyebrow. "The *third* time?"

"I can't stay in one place for too long, people start to notice me getting younger after a while. So I've bounced between the Academies, going through training like it's all new to me every few hundred years." He shrugged. "The first time I took the exam, I actually failed. Went back and tried again after a hundred years and passed with flying colors."

Fox exhaled dreamily. "That's amazing."

"When you've got nothing but time and determination, it's really just another task on your to-do list."

"You were determined to become a Priest."

"Joining the Academy—and becoming a high-ranking Priest—gave me access to resources I needed to hunt my brother down. And it gave me a place to train and safely use my blessings."

"*Blessings?*"

Plural...

He hesitated. "I have more than one."

"The Guillotine," she said, thinking of his battle with Slaine in the Kanen Forest.

"And Longevity, and eleven others. Thirteen total."

Fox closed her eyes a moment. She had been shocked when Montell had revealed you could be born with two blessings—but *thirteen?* If it had been anyone else making such a claim, she wouldn't have believed it, but the black cross in the center of Izzy's head was clear evidence that he was in a league of his own.

"How did you get so many blessings?"

Izzy laughed. "How did anyone get blessings in the first place?"

She wasn't sure.

"Blessings are living prayers. Physical manifestations of the prayers of power and protection our ancestors whispered at the start of the Great Demon War."

"They just asked God." Fox blinked at how simple it was.

"Some blessings have died out; others are generational and have lasted through the centuries. But it all began with a prayer."

"So, you prayed and asked God for thirteen Gifts and He just gave them to you?"

"The Bible says, *ask and it shall be given...*" Izzy chuckled. "But it also says patience is a Fruit of the Spirit. I didn't even ask for thirteen blessings. I asked for strength. I asked for His favor. Sometimes He answered by literally giving me a surge of power in battle, other times He awakened a new ability within me." He glanced over at her. "The truth is that I didn't get a new blessing the instant I asked. Some didn't manifest for decades. And it took me even longer to master them. But they did come from God—without need of a special bloodline or a sacrifice. They were, quite literally, *Gifts.*"

Fox thought for a long moment, wondering if she could do the same. If God would answer her, too. *Izzy is so old*, she reminded herself. He had the time to nurture his faith and his patience to wait on God. Only someone with Longevity could accomplish what he'd done.

"Where do you go when you aren't a Priest?" she asked, her mind drifting back to the blessing he'd been born with. The only one he hadn't asked for. "Where do you go when you're a child again—where does Seganamé go?"

"Seganamé has looked the exact same since he joined the Nine. I think he has acquired some sort of curse that stops him from aging

384

altogether." Izzy chewed his thoughts for a moment. "Personally, I have an old friend I stay with when I get too young to fend for myself."

"Someone else with your blessing?"

He shook his head. "My brother and I were born before the Great Demon War began—"

"The gift started with the two of you," she said quickly.

He nodded, impressed. "Both our parents are dead and neither of us ever married or had children. So we're the only ones alive with the blessing of Longevity."

"If that's the case, why do you want to kill him so badly?" she asked. "That would leave you as the only living person with Longevity."

Seganamé being one of the Nine was good enough reason to want him dead, but the way Izzy spoke seemed so personal. Almost like killing him had nothing to do with his sinful ways.

The Priest let out a long sigh. "I have no choice. It's my fate."

"I don't understand."

"Israel is the name I chose when I graduated from the Academy. But Seganamé changed his name, too. When he joined the Nine."

Fox nodded, urging him to go on.

"The name I was born with is Jacob. And Seganamé's real name is Esau."

She took in a sharp breath. "I thought you weren't the biblical brothers?"

"We aren't. Esau and I aren't twins. He's actually seven years older than me. When he was born with all that red hair, my father couldn't help himself and named him Esau."

"But I thought Esau wasn't the best guy in the Bible," Fox mumbled. There were plenty of other names to choose from. Names of people that God *didn't* hate.

Izzy seemed to know what she was thinking and laughed weakly. "My parents were in the occult, Fox Fire. They chose Esau's name *because* he was hated by God."

She froze, halting right there on top of the hill they'd just crested. "What?" she whispered.

He nodded, staring straight ahead as he spoke. "My mother and father were part of a cult that worshipped the Night God, Sorcer. Meaning, they were *sorcerers.*" He squinted. "But 'Sorcer' is just another name for Satan."

"So, they were actually Satanists," Fox said.

"There is no difference between Satanism and sorcery. If you aren't worshipping Christ Jesus, the One True God, then you are—by default—worshipping the devil. Plain and simple."

"There is no other God but the Almighty." Fox inclined her head and began walking again after a few moments of silence.

Izzy continued his story. "My parents were sorcerers who were raised to hate God and love Satan. They named my brother Esau as a way to thumb their nose at the Bible—embracing the one who had been hated by God." He swallowed. "But my mom eventually gave her life to Christ. When she gave birth to me and told my father she wanted to name me Jacob, he realized she'd converted and tried to kill her. My mother escaped and we lived on the run for ten years."

"That's incredible," Fox whispered.

"It was. We never had much, but we were happy. My mother was finally out of the occult, and she had managed to take me with her. We were free." Izzy frowned. "Until Seganamé showed up outside our home one day. He'd remained by our father's side all that time, growing deeper in sorcery. At age seventeen, he was strong enough to overpower and kidnap both me and our mother."

Fox remained silent as Izzy paused, mulling over his next words. His story was centuries old, but the look on his face made it obvious his pain

386

was still fresh. As if all of this had occurred just a few years ago.

"He brought us back to our father and then killed our mother right in front of me," Izzy said softly. "She had been a sacrifice to Satan— Seganamé's official graduation into the highest rank of sorcery."

"Wow," Fox said, almost to herself.

Izzy didn't speak for a long moment. "Unlike God, the devil never gives anything for free. In order to obtain his power, you must offer a sacrifice—something living and something of value. You can kill animals, but that's small game. You can kill humans, but even that will only take you so far unless the person is close to you."

"That's why he sacrificed his mother."

"And its why he sacrificed his father years later, after I escaped."

Fox blinked at him. "You escaped?"

"Yes. Neither Seganamé nor my father wanted to sacrifice me after they'd gotten me back. They wanted me to join the occult, but I had been raised Christian by my mother. I refused and rebelled and when I got the chance, I ran away. I was fifteen at the time."

Fox stared at him, trying to imagine a fifteen-year-old boy on the run from his own father and brother.

"When I was in my twenties, Seganamé came after me again. It was then that I realized he'd joined the Nine and had changed his name. He told me he'd sacrificed our father as his initiation into the Births of Carnage, and he intended to sacrifice me so he could gain the power to kill God. But I managed to escape yet again."

Fox's nose wrinkled. "You cannot kill God. He is Almighty."

"I know," Izzy agreed. "But the devil has convinced him it is possible."

"If he wants to sacrifice you, why'd he let you go?"

"Because I'm not as strong as him yet. The more powerful your sacrifice, the more it will be worth to Satan. Seganamé will be blessed with all the power I possess if he succeeds in killing me. So he wants me to get as strong as possible. After almost a thousand years of fighting each other, he still doesn't think I'm worth it."

Fox didn't know what to say. Izzy was the most powerful Priest she had ever seen. "How much stronger do you need to be?"

He seemed angered by the questioned, grinding out the words, "I don't know."

"But you want to kill him just as badly as he wants to kill you."

He nodded solemnly. "It's my fate."

"No, it isn't. God created us for great and wonderful things, not to murder our own kin."

"It wouldn't be murder," he said hotly. "It would be an offering to God."

"A sacrifice," she whispered.

"Not like what you're thinking." Izzy grunted, though in pain or anger—Fox wasn't sure. "Seganamé *must* die. He is evil. He worships the devil. He kills people just to gain power. His very existence is an insult to God." He exhaled hard. "God *hates* Esau."

"Not this Esau," Fox said without thinking.

Izzy stopped walking to stare at her.

"God still loves your brother, and if he repents, He'll forgive him for his sins. Just like He forgives you and I every day."

Izzy shook his head. "Then why did God give me thirteen different blessings? Why has He let me live for over seven-hundred-fifty years?" He leaned closer to her. "Because He wants me to kill Seganamé."

Fox opened her mouth to protest, but Izzy cut her off.

"Even his name is evil. Do you know what it means?"

She shook her head.

"*Seganamé.* It's the tongue of our clan, a language that died out a few hundred years ago, but I will never forget the meaning of that word."

Izzy looked at her again, bright eyes blazing with rage and hate. "It means, *say his name.* A plea to God—not to accept and love the one He hates, but to acknowledge him. To look down and see him as His equal. The one who would dare rise up in challenge to the King of Kings."

Fox shivered, watching Lord Izzy frown at the ground as thoughts of his brother raged in his head. She had no idea what to say, had no idea if she *could* say anything. Izzy was right about so much; Seganamé was evil. Seganamé was an enemy of God so long as he stood as an ally to Satan. Seganamé didn't deserve to live.

But taking his life was not Izzy's job. Fox refused to believe it.

Both of them had been named after brothers of the Bible who'd fought with each other even in the womb. Their fate had been determined before birth—for the older to serve the younger. For God to love Jacob and hate Esau.

But Lord Izzy was not that Jacob and Seganamé was not that Esau.

And, Fox added, *Esau forgave Jacob.*

She glanced at the Priest beside her, still fuming in his anger and his poisonous memories. *But maybe this story isn't about Esau's forgiveness, maybe it's about Jacob's.*

"You asked why God has allowed you to live this long," Fox began.

Izzy looked up at her and nodded.

"Maybe it isn't because He wants you to hunt down your brother to kill him. Maybe it's because He wants you to hunt him down and forgive him. To love him again."

Izzy looked puzzled, like Fox had just spoken in another language.

"Why would I ever love him? God doesn't even love him."

"That isn't true!" she said loudly. "Your brother is *not* hated by God. His name was just something his horrible father gave him to mock God. He *isn't* Esau and you *aren't* Jacob. You're not fated to fight each other for eternity. You should be working together. Helping the Cross.

389

Fighting for God as one."

Izzy was silent, like the thought had never occurred to him before. Not in all his seven-hundred years.

"Or maybe you've been allowed to live this long because God doesn't want you to die with unforgiveness in your heart," Fox said quietly. And then she took Izzy's hand and started walking again.

37

Kohlannis

Everything had been going according to plan for days. Travelling swiftly, quietly, and trying altogether to keep KI safe. Kohl's team had finally made it to their next rendezvous point, Avanté Village. KI smiled up at the gates, Kressa laughed and bumped her shoulder against Kohl's, he took her hand and squeezed it. Even Hope and Talon exchanged joyful looks, despite the weariness of their long travels.

Everything was fine. They had already decided they would stop at an inn for some iced milk and chocolate pancakes that Kressa was quite fond of—she had apparently grown up somewhere near Avanté and had eaten at the inn on more than one occasion. Talon and KI were the most excited for the food, and when Kohl realized they'd never heard of chocolate *or* pancakes before, he had gotten excited too. It was hard not to think of the first time he'd made chocolate chip pancakes for his little brother. Being able to see KI try it would be like reliving the entire experience.

Kohl was happy.

And just like that, everything fell apart.

The group had *just* crossed the gates into the village when they heard the first explosion—somewhere in the distance, but close enough to shake the ground beneath their feet.

"Hold on," Kohl said.

Talon grabbed her crucifix and immediately began to pray.

"What's going on?" KI asked.

Kohl shook his head. "I don't know."

"Someone's attacking the village." Kressa stared into the distance. "You know what that means."

Kohl knew exactly what it meant, but he didn't want to admit it, like saying it aloud would somehow summon the Nine right to their location.

"They've found us," Hope whispered when he didn't speak.

"Not yet." KI's voice was firm for once, like he had suddenly forgotten he was only fourteen. "As long as you're keeping me cloaked, they haven't found us at all. Only part of the team."

"The decoy teams," Kressa said.

A pang of guilt and worry shot through Kohl's heart. Fox had been on one of the decoy teams. He couldn't stop himself from wondering if she'd been caught up in the explosion.

"What do we do?" Hope asked.

Talon had been placed in charge of the squad, so all the kids looked up at her with expectant eyes.

She pressed her lips together as she rubbed her cross-shaped pendant between her fingers. Kohl was wearing one, along with Hope, KI, and Kressa. She had made them and blessed them herself before passing them out. Kohl couldn't stop himself from reaching up and touching his own. He wasn't sure if he was imagining things, but he'd swear he felt a hum of energy tickle his fingers the moment he grasped it.

"We could go into the village and try to investigate," Talon suggested. "The others may need our help."

"But that would mean taking KI right to the enemy," Hope said.

Talon nodded. "Or we could head back into the woods and try to rendezvous at Point B." That was their second meeting spot, chosen in case the groups faced trouble. As leader of her squad, Talon was the only one who knew the location of Point B. Operating on a need-to-know basis had kept them safe so far, but the explosion was more proof that someone inside was feeding intel to the enemy.

"I'm making the executive decision to leave," Talon said confidently.

"I think we should go fight," Kressa insisted. She stood her ground and looked Talon right in the eye. "If our comrades are in trouble, we should do everything we can to help. Not run away."

"Keeping KI safe is our priority—"

"More than saving our own friends?"

"Kressa." Kohl touched her shoulder.

She flinched away. "How could you abandon them?" Then her eyes grew dark, and her jaw ticked before she unscrewed it and said, "How could you abandon dear little *Fox*?"

She spoke the words like they were bitter in her mouth, spitting out Fox's name as if the sound of it was blasphemous. The question made Kohl subconsciously retract his hand from her arm, and he stared at her like he didn't know his own girlfriend.

Maybe he didn't.

Or maybe she was right.

Kohl couldn't pretend he'd never had feelings for his *dear little* Fox, but all too quickly, things had heated up between him and Kressa and before he had time to think about what was happening, she was sneaking into his dorm and staying all night. But all along, she had known who was in his heart—and who'd been on his mind when he'd been with her.

He hated himself.

He had used her as a distraction from the horrors he faced at home and the complications he faced at school. Had even used her to distract him from his confusing feelings for Fox. But Kressa's knowledge of exactly what was going on made it so much worse.

She had known everything. She had known how much he'd cared about another girl but had never raised a question or issue about it.

Why not? Kohlannis wondered for the first time, his sharp eyes narrowing on the girl he thought he might have loved.

He pushed the thoughts away. Kressa had a point, whether he wanted to admit it or not. He didn't want to turn and run when Fox and the others could be fighting for their lives inside.

Kohlannis snuck a glance at KI as the boy tried to reason with Kressa. He was still in favor of leaving, but that was no surprise. KI had never liked fighting, and right now his presence would hinder more than it would help. He was the reason all this was happening; Fox would lose it if he walked right into the village and made it easy for the enemy to get to him. And she would never let Kohl forget how he had failed him. How he had failed *her*.

Besides, Kohl thought, glancing between his friends, *I can't fight right now anyway*. He hadn't shared it with anyone, but ever since he'd left Babel, he'd felt … weak. Not physically. Just spiritually. Like he couldn't access his powers.

Kohl had made it clear since first stepping onto the Training Grounds that he wouldn't use his blessing to get himself through the Academy. He was used to not using his Gift. He was used to fighting like a normal, stony student. The seal on his body had always made it difficult for him to use his gift anyway; it limited his power, stifling his spiritual energy so he could never reach his full potential. And when he'd broken his vow and had used his blessing during the entrance exams, Izzy had stepped in immediately afterward and placed a new seal to dampen his powers even further.

"You're stronger than we realized," had been his only explanation.

Maybe that's why I've felt so weak, Kohl pondered, listening to Hope and

Kressa snap through an argument about standing by their friends or following orders. The argument got so bad, Talon had to step between them and physically push the girls apart.

She glared at them both with her arms crossed like an angry mother. "That's enough!" she clipped. "It doesn't matter how anyone feels about it, I've made my decision and that is final." She turned to leave. "We're going to Point B. Now follow me."

KI and Hope immediately followed. Kohl went to move but stopped when he noticed Kressa was still standing there. He turned back and offered his hand, hoping his sheepish smile would be enough of an apology. They had a lot to talk about once they reached Point B, but they didn't have to fight *right now*.

Kressa looked at his hand and then shook her head.

"Don't be stubborn, babe," he said.

She lifted her head so he could see her face and her expression shocked him. She wasn't angry she had lost her argument or sad that they were abandoning the others. The way her shoulders straightened and how her mouth seemed to flatten as she pressed her lips into a thin line—she looked determined.

"I can't let you guys leave," she said firmly.

Talon stopped walking and turned back around. "What?"

"You lost, Kressa," Hope said. "Get over yourself."

Kressa ignored her. "We are going into Avanté Village."

"No, we aren't," Talon said.

Kressa shrugged. "I don't care if *you* go. I only need the boy."

Silence stretched over them until Kohl couldn't take it anymore. "What are you talking about?"

She looked at him dead-on. "I'm the second Red Face. And it's my duty to bring KI to the Nine. They're waiting inside for us now."

Before Kohl could react, Hope dashed forward with a blade drawn.

395

"You traitor!" she yelled, lunging at the girl.

Kressa disarmed her faster than Kohl thought was possible. She twisted Hope's arm behind her back and then hit her so hard, she immediately went limp and fell to the ground. "I'm only going to say this once," she announced, "give me KI and then walk away."

When no one made a move, she sighed. "None of you can beat me, so just give up peacefully."

"What makes you so sure we can't beat you?" Talon said.

Kressa laughed. "You're stony. KI is frozen stiff. Hope's unconscious. And Kohl is spiritually fractured."

Spiritually fractured?

Kressa sensed his confusion and spared him a glance. "It was my job to gather intel on the people who would cause us the most trouble when we made our move. You never used your gift during training, so I had to charm it out of you. After what you did in the entrance exams, I realized you'd be a real issue if we ended up fighting. So I did what I had to do to weaken you."

Kohl's nostrils flared as he glared at her, already knowing the answer to his question before he even asked. "And what exactly did you have to do?"

A simpering look took over her pretty features. "I slept with you."

Talon and KI gasped.

Kohl ignored them; it wasn't the time to be embarrassed about his privacy. "You used me."

Just like he'd used her.

"You were a problem—a powerful problem—and I had to deal with you. The easiest way to fracture a Christian's relationship with God is to sleep with them," Kressa explained proudly. "Sex creates a soul tie between acting parties which opens a spiritual doorway. That doorway allows each participant to share whatever spirits they've got with their

396

partner." She tossed her head back and laughed, strawberry blonde hair falling over her shoulders. "You allowed my dark spirits to enter your soul. You gave them permission to wreak havoc in your life. Each time we were together, their influence grew stronger."

"And now I am broken," he whispered.

The bitter part of him wanted to blame Kressa. She had lied to him and had used him and had only been interested in him because it was the easiest way to disrupt his powers. The easiest way to make sure he wouldn't be a problem when the enemy made their move. But Kohl knew he'd played a role in this too.

Kressa hadn't forced herself on him. Just like Fox had angrily told him in the alleyway—*a woman cannot seduce an unwilling man.* And he had been more than willing. Had even been eager.

Despite repenting and asking God for forgiveness, despite promising Fox that he would stay away from Kressa and get himself under control, Kohl had failed again. He'd returned to the dorms and had knocked on *her* door.

Now he saw just how big his mistakes had been.

And KI was about to pay for it.

"Come with me, KI," Kressa said, hand extended. "And I won't hurt your friends."

"They were your friends, too. Just ten minutes ago," KI told her.

"And now they're my enemies."

Talon stepped forward. "You don't have to do this, Kressa."

She rolled her eyes as she retracted her hand. "I guess we're doing this the hard way."

Kohl watched as Kressa's skin turned from its normal pale complexion to the steely color of metal. Then it clicked. The metal limbs made her so much stronger than normal—strong enough to pose as the Red Face when Slaine was busy, and sturdy enough not to rot away when she had to battle him one-on-one.

She had pretended to fight him. Pretended she was trying her hardest to take him down during the entrance exams when she had worn the mask herself not long before. Kohl remembered the way the Red Face hadn't used any fire, how his voice had sounded strange yet familiar—altered by metallic vocal chords. And how he'd walked through Fox's flames without getting burned ... *protected by metal skin*, Kohl realized.

Kressa was a traitor. She had never been their friend. Had never been his lover.

"Kressa..." he whispered, somehow heartbroken.

She looked at him, a flat expression on her iron face. "That's not my name," she said calmly. "You may call me Atara: The Eighth Birth of Carnage."

She pulled out a small item from the pack strapped to her hip. Kohl didn't realize what it was until it was too late. As he turned to run, an explosion went off right behind him.

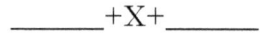

Kohlannis drifted back to consciousness, suddenly aware of every ache and pain in his entire body. There was someone screaming beside him—*a girl's voice.* He sat up and found Hope crying and shaking his shoulder.

"You're awake!" she wept, hugging him tightly.

He blinked. "What..."

"Kressa—Atara! I don't know what to call her, but she set off a bomb."

He gasped and it hurt his lungs. "Did she kill everyone else?"

Hope shook her head, but that didn't stop him from glancing around

398

in search of bodies.

"Where's Talon and KI?" He didn't see them at all. Dead or alive.

Hope said, "Kressa took KI's body."

"His body?"

"He was knocked out from the explosion. It wasn't strong enough to kill us—she needed him alive."

"And Talon?"

She looked worried. "Talon went after them when she woke up."

"How long ago was that?"

Kohl struggled to his feet as she answered, "Ten minutes."

"I'm going after them."

"How?" Hope asked. "You're weak from the explosion and Kressa said you were spiritually fractured. You can't fight."

"I can't just sit here, either!" he barked.

Hope jerked away in fear, and he cursed himself for his foul temper. He'd been made a fool of, had even sinned against God for a girl he thought he was in love with, and he'd felt bad for using her as his emotional pillow. Only to find out he'd been the one getting used all along.

He was more than angry. He was filled with hate. And he needed to release it.

"I'm going after them," Kohl said again because who better to release his hatred on than the woman who'd betrayed him? It also wouldn't hurt that killing her would help save KI.

Kohl took off toward the village.

38

Fox Fire

They heard the explosions. It wasn't like you could ignore them. But there was nothing Fox nor Lord Izzy could do with him in his weakened state, so they trudged along until they finally made it to the western gates of Avanté Village. Smoke rose into the sky; they could see it even from a distance. Screams followed, a combination of voices from the villagers and voices of Hunters and Priests locked in battle.

Fox looked over at Izzy. They had finished their walk in silence, allowing him some time to rest, but he was still in no condition to fight. Not against any of the Nine, at least.

"Go," he told her in a raspy voice. "I can't do anything right now. I'm just slowing you down."

"Lord Izzy..." She didn't want to leave him behind, but it was hard to ignore how right he was.

He shook his head and weakly pulled away, grasping the wooden beam of a tavern to stay upright. "You got me out of the woods and back to safety. I'll be fine for now. Just go."

She looked at him once more, willing herself not to cry. Not to break down and regret the fact that she was about to abandon him. *God, please protect him,* she prayed inside. And then she turned and jogged into the village.

Running past destroyed homes and buildings, jumping over broken pottery, piles of debris, and unidentified bodies. Avanté hardly looked any different from Wi. *Not again*, Fox thought, pumping her arms as she ran. *Another village will not be destroyed because of us ... Because of KI.*

Fox didn't get more than half a mile before she saw a familiar figure running across a clearing near the market.

Recognition hit her with a gasp. "Kressa!"

The figure stopped and whipped its head at her; it shined in the sunlight, glinting off her metallic skin. *That's definitely Kressa*, Fox thought, then she noticed the crumpled figure in her arms and took off running toward them.

"KI! Hold on!" Fox cried. She was out of breath when she reached her friends, but that didn't stop her from crushing them both in a hug— even though KI was unconscious. "What happened?"

Kressa swallowed. "We got caught up in an explosion. I'm taking him to safety."

Fox frowned. "Then why are you heading toward the fighting? You should go to the western gate." She motioned in its direction. "I just left Lord Izzy there, he'll keep KI safe while we help the others."

"Lord Izzy's alive?"

Fox blinked at her. "Why wouldn't he be?"

She licked her lips and said quickly, "Because you're here alone. I figured he must be dead if you're by yourself."

"You're alone too."

"The others are—"

"Fox!" Talon's voice rang out, immediately catching the sundancer's attention.

Fox turned to find her sister, but stars burst into her vision as she was suddenly struck from behind. She let out a cry of pain and dropped

401

to her knees, instinctively rolling to the side to dodge Kressa's foot as it came down beside her. Her boot crushed the earth where Fox had just been, drawing a gasp from the girl. *She tried to stomp on me.*

Just then, Talon ran into the clearing, panting and frantically waving her hands over her head. "Fox! Don't trust her!"

She didn't need to tell her twice. Fox struck her bracelets and ignited a ball of fire around her fist, but she didn't attack. Kressa was still holding KI in her arms. In an instant, she'd gone from rescuing him to holding him hostage.

"What's going on?" Fox asked.

"I'm taking KI to the Nine."

She would have asked why, but she really didn't care about the reason. Kressa was not taking her friend. Fox would die before she let that happen.

Talon finally caught up, placing her hands on her knees to stable her breathing as she explained, "She's a traitor. She tried to kill us—"

"The blast was only strong enough to knock you out," Kressa snapped. "I didn't want to risk hurting KI too much."

Fox looked down at him, noticing the burns on his arms and legs for the first time. They were healing right before her eyes—*hopefully, he'll regain consciousness soon. Please, God*, Fox prayed.

As if on cue, KI's eyebrows twitched, and his eyes fluttered open. The only thing Fox registered on his face was anger. Before Kressa had time to react to his sudden revival, KI raised his fist and cracked her in the jaw.

Her head whipped back with a *snap!* and KI fell to the ground as she lost her grip on him. He got to his feet faster than Fox had ever seen him move, but Kressa was just as swift. In the time it took Fox to blink, the two were locked in battle, exchanging brutal blows like they wanted to kill each other.

Fox had no idea what to do. She wanted to help, but there was no room for her to intervene. If she threw any flames, KI would be hit too. *I'm not even sure it would affect him*, she told herself, watching as he took a punch from Kressa and barely reacted—except to counter with his own jab. The force of his blow sent her reeling back, but the metal girl pivoted and caught his fist as he tried to attack again. They froze in a standoff while Fox and Talon watched helplessly from the sidelines.

I've never seen him fight so fiercely. Not at the Academy, and especially not in Wi. Fox hardly recognized her friend.

"KI!" cried a voice from the other side of the market.

Fox snapped her head up to see Kohl sprinting through the stalls with Hope right behind him.

"Kohl!" She immediately took off running toward him.

They met with a crushing hug before she pulled away and said frantically, "KI and Kressa are fighting! We've got to do something!"

Kohl stared at the two students, his mouth open and his eyes filled with shock and … *hurt?* Fox had no time to figure out his emotions. She shook his shoulders and said again, "We've got to do something!"

Kohl took a step back, breaking Fox's heart. *He doesn't want to fight against Kressa*, she realized. The revelation was numbing, but there were more important things to worry about.

Fox turned to Hope. "Cancel her spiritual energy!"

Hope nodded and began to whisper a prayer. Almost immediately, Kressa's movements became slower; KI took advantage of her sudden weakness and landed a terrible punch to her jaw that knocked her off her feet. He loomed over her, wearing a dark smile, and grabbed her by the hair.

In a voice Fox did not recognize, KI said, *"Epistrofi."*

"That word…" She had heard it in her studies at the Academy.

"It's Greek," Hope explained. "One of the Old Tongues of the Bible.

It means, '*return*.'"

Suddenly, the metal peeled away from Kressa's body, *returning* her skin to normal flesh. She gasped as KI held a fistful of her pretty hair, silky strands that were such a deep shade of strawberry-blonde, it almost looked pink. The hairs along the line of her forehead turned red at the root, tiny dots of blood pooling on her scalp from KI's cruel grip.

He yanked her head backwards, exposing her neck, and then he bit her.

Kressa screamed like she'd been stabbed with a foot-long blade. Her body jerked at the pain, and she clawed at KI's hands, trying to free herself. Her fingernails left ribbons of blood streaking down his wrist and arm, but the cuts disappeared as KI's flesh began to turn to metal...

Fox gasped.

"He's sucking her blood," Hope whispered.

Fox had heard horror stories around the campfire and even on the Academy campus—tales of cursed creatures who thirsted for blood. She couldn't remember what they were called, but she was sure she was looking at one.

Memories of the day KI had almost kissed her formed in her head. How he'd gone from brushing his lips against her skin, to biting her neck so hard he'd drawn blood. Blood he had confessed he'd wanted to taste.

Maybe he is one of those bloodsucking darklings, Fox admitted. *Or maybe he's something more.*

She stepped forward. "He isn't just sucking her blood ... He's sucking out her spiritual energy."

Kressa slapped at his hands, but he paid her no mind. The look on his face was different, bearing an expression Fox had never seen him wear. He didn't look like KI, not the charming boy with the goofy smile she had loved so much. He looked angry. Hateful. Bloodthirsty.

"You'll kill her," she whispered.

Talon moved closer. "KI…"

"We've got to stop him." Hope could barely stand as she clamped a hand over her mouth and swayed on her feet.

Fox took a deep breath and struck her bracelets together. She didn't want to hurt KI, but she also didn't want him to kill Kressa and steal her power. *If he does this, he will be consumed by the darkness inside.*

Fox raised her blazing fist—and a black portal opened behind KI and Kressa. Eight figures emerged in red cloaks. Fox did not have to wonder who they were.

"The Nine Births of Carnage," Kohl whispered beside her.

Fox looked at each one of the Births, shocked by how many she recognized. The silver-haired demon, tall and powerful, just like she'd been in Wi. She even donned her four swords. Hosenké who stood smirking like something was funny. And Seganamé with his flowing red hair and unnaturally calm face.

He stepped forward, gaze narrowing on KI. "That's enough, Zuriel," he said.

Fox frowned—so did everyone else, except the Nine.

KI released Kressa and turned to face the crowd of darklings. He took a slow step back. "I'm not going with you."

"You don't have a choice," Seganamé told him plainly. "We have come all this way for you. We will not fail."

As if to prove Seganamé's point, Hosenké summoned a horde of demons to surround them. The message was clear. If Fox and her friends resisted, they would be devoured by a throng of darklings.

"Where's the rest of the decoy teams?" Fox whispered to Kohl, hoping reinforcements would come to save them.

Kohl subtly shrugged. "We never made it into the village. By the looks of things, they were likely ambushed by the Nine."

And now the Nine stood before them.

405

"Do you think they're alive?"

"There's no way to tell."

Seganamé took a step toward KI, drawing Fox's attention. She gasped and shouted without thinking, "Don't touch him!" Fire raged in her hands, begging for her to unleash it on the demons before her, but she controlled herself. Lashing out against all of the Births of Carnage would likely end in her untimely death—and KI's kidnapping.

The Thirdborn merely smiled at her. "It's been fun, children. But it is time for us to go." He turned to KI and extended a hand. When the boy didn't take it, he said, "You are surrounded by the most powerful demons in the Four Regions. Four Gamma Division students do not stand a chance against us."

"I am not a student," said Talon behind him. She stood with her shoulders back and her eyes glaring, as bold as Fox had ever seen her.

Seganamé turned very slowly. His eyes traced her frame from head to toe before he replied, "I know. In fact, you'll be coming with us, too."

Kressa, who had limped over to the rest of the Nine, made a face. "That wasn't part of the plan."

"Can't you sense her spiritual energy?" he questioned. "She will make a wonderful sacrifice to give us strength during the transitioning ritual."

Fox choked on a sob as Seganamé made a motion to the other Births and two cloaked figures stepped toward her older sister. "Wait!" she cried, but they didn't listen.

Without thinking, Fox launched a fireball at them but the one closest to her lifted his hand in defense. A black hole appeared in his palm and sucked the flames into it. He kept walking without missing a beat.

"How…" Fox dropped to her knees.

"Void can be quite useful in the hands of a master," Seganamé murmured. His eyes found Kohl's. "Imagine what you could become if you rid yourself of the shackles of the Cross."

406

Kohlannis did not respond.

Kressa suddenly fell to the ground. One of the Nine swayed on his feet. Seganamé winced. He turned with a frown to look at Talon who was being held by the two Births. Her eyes were closed, and her mouth was moving, muttering something only she could hear.

"She's praying," Seganamé said angrily. He glared over at one of the Births who seemed unaffected by the sudden charge of Light energy around them. "Cloak us!" Then he planted his angry gaze on Hope.

With a gasp, the young girl clutched the sides of her head and let out a horrific scream.

"Stop!" Fox cried, scrambling to her feet in time to catch Hope as her knees gave out. She writhed in Fox's arms, gasping for breath as her eyes rolled to the back of her head. Blood trickled from her ears. Her muscles seized so tightly, she gripped Fox's arm with the strength of a bear.

"What are you doing to her?" Fox screamed.

Seganamé seemed undisturbed by the situation. "I'm killing her." When Hope's shrieking ceased and she went limp in Fox's arms, he looked over at Kohl and the boy immediately grabbed his head and cried out in pain.

"Stop!" Fox hollered to no avail. Tears ran down her cheeks. "Please…"

Seganamé glanced at Talon and then at KI. "You are running out of friends. Come with us peacefully or I will kill them all and then find random villagers to execute."

KI looked at Hope, dead in Fox's lap. He looked at Kohl who was bleeding from one of his ears now, still clutching his head in pain. Then he looked at Fox Fire, and his skin shifted from metal back to its normal flesh.

His eyes never left hers as he said, "Okay. I'll go with you."

Fox shoved Hope's body away and ran to him. "No! We can still try to—"

His hand lashed out and grabbed her before she could even register the movement. She was suddenly in his arms, sucking in a lungful of his husky scent. He smelled like smoke and grass and salty tears, but she was vaguely aware of the scent of blood on him, too.

She took another breath. KI's smile filled her mind's eye, stretched wide against his olive skin. His bright eyes and his light hair. Back when he'd been a blonde and they'd been happy and the world hadn't fallen apart.

They were innocent then. Two teenagers with wide eyes and big dreams. A secret crush Fox wouldn't admit to. A friendship neither of them would ever let go.

Now he was saying goodbye as he pulled away and looked at her through eyes she did not recognize, with a face she could barely call his. He was handsome. Very handsome. With his strong jaw and his hazel orbs and his dazzling smile. But he was not himself. This person before her was not the goofy kid from Wi, he was a man. And before him, Fox felt very much like a little girl.

"KI," she whispered, tears streaking her face. "We can still fight them."

"No, we can't. Not now."

Not now. The words ignited a fire within her. They could fight them later. When they had better numbers. When the time was right. When the Nine least expected it.

But... She looked at her friend. "You won't be the same. They'll change you soon."

Would he still fight on her side, then? Would he even remember her?

He smiled, brushing away her tears with his thumbs. "Then remember for me. Fight for me, Foxy. And never give up." He leaned toward her, his lips brushing against hers with each word he whispered. "We made a pact. Remember, beautiful?"

She sobbed. How could she ever forget?

"We'll come after you. Kohl and I together. We won't let them have you for long."

He kissed her, pulling her close, until it felt like they were one. "Good. Because I belong to you."

Seganamé stepped forward and opened another portal. "It's time."

KI's lips lingered, holding Fox for just one more moment. When he pulled away, she felt like part of her had been ripped out. She clutched at her chest, heaving for air as she watched him move toward the black shimmering hole. Her knees buckled. But Kohl was there to catch her, leaning her against his body for support.

KI looked back at them both, nodding at Kohlannis. "Take care of her," he said.

Kohl nodded.

"I'll take care of Talon," KI told them.

Fox's teary eyes went to her sister, still held by two members of the Nine and bound by rope that looked similar to what'd been tied around Izzy's hands and feet. She looked like she was crying, but she found the strength to mouth goodbye to her baby sister. Fox could only nod in response, too overwhelmed to even form words anymore.

With one final glance back, KI stepped into the portal and disappeared. The Nine followed, dragging Talon along. In a moment, Fox was left standing beside Kohl. Hope's dead body lay at their feet, Izzy was still hiding at the other end of the village, and the rest of their once 30-man-squad was nowhere to be found.

"What are we going to do?" Kohl asked.

Fox let go of a long sigh. "I don't know."

409

Continue the series...

The Nine Births of Carnage (2022)

The Testament Relics (2023)

More books by Valicity Elaine and TRC Publishing!

Christian Fantasy

The Scribe

The End of the World series

Christian Romance

Withered Rose series

The Living Water

The Woof Pack

Christian Science Fiction

I AM MAN series

Christian Children's Fiction

Too Young

Tap here to join our monthly newsletter and stay updated with new releases, sales, and giveaways!

ACKNOWLEDGEMENTS

You made it through Book II! You're AWESOME! Thank you so much for sticking with this story. I worried that some of the content would be too dark for some readers, but I refused to shy away from portraying our enemies because I realized their darkness was just another chance to showcase the wonderful Light of Christ.

I hope you enjoyed this book and I look forward to seeing you in Book Three, The Nine Births of Carnage. Until then, check out my other Christian works!

I AM MAN (science fiction series)

Withered Rose (Romantic Suspense)

To stay updated on releases and other books published at TRC, visit our website; therebelchristian.com and join our monthly newsletter! Don't forget to follow us on Instagram @TRC_Publishing

The Rebel Christian Publishing

We are an independent Christian publishing company focused on spreading the Gospel through good books. Visit therebelchristian.com to check out our books!

www.ingramcontent.com/pod-product-compliance
Lightning Source LLC
Chambersburg PA
CBHW072020020726
47501CB00006B/1884